Eternally Wild

Love and Lush, Book 1

Cherié Summers

Cover designed by Cherié Summers
Editing by Laura McNellis EIC AlternativEdits

This book is a work of fiction. Names, characters, places, and incidents either are products of the author's imagination or are used fictitiously. Any resemblance to actual persons, living or dead, events, or locales is entirely coincidental.

Cherié Summers
Visit my website at www. cheriesummers.com

Printed in the United States of America

First Printing: August 2018

ISBN: 978-1-7181-9524-0

Dedication

For Michael
You left us too soon.
But left us so much.
Forever loved.
Eternally wild.

Chapter One

Caesar Blue

Melanie Davis stood in an aisle of her local wholesale club comparing boxes of toothpaste when her nose was suddenly assaulted by the sweet scent of vanilla. Then came an almost electrifying sensation as a warm body brushed against her from behind, propelling her forward. She bumped into the stack of toothpaste, causing a few boxes to fall to the ground. She bent to retrieve them, and when she straightened back up, a gorgeous man was standing directly in front of her. Shocked, she gasped audibly. The resemblance was uncanny.

"Pardon me." He flashed her a brilliant white smile as his gaze traveled sensually over her body.

Her face warmed as she nervously smiled back. He was stunning!

"Excuse me," she squeaked. Flustered, she quickly moved to the next aisle, where she took a deep breath and let it out slowly, trying to regain her composure and calm her pounding heart.

Wow! Talk about a lookalike. She hadn't given much thought to Caesar Blue in years, even though he'd been the lead singer of her favorite band, Lush. She'd been a sophomore in high school when Lush skyrocketed to the top of the charts with their first album. The band's members were barely out of their teens themselves. Caesar Blue, Johnnie Vega, Kurt Rain, and Rhett Star. Three Americans and an Irishman who'd met in high school in Philadelphia and formed a band. A band that defied genres by playing rock music infused with a healthy dose of funk and soul. The resulting sound was danceable and incredibly sexy.

Unfortunately, with rock and roll fame came the standard practice of excessive alcohol and drug use. It spiraled out of control and had eventually caused Caesar to lose his life. A freak accident the authorities had called it. Devastated is how she'd felt upon hearing the news.

I should snap a photo of him. Though with looks like that, he was most likely already a social media sensation. Pulling out her phone, she walked back to the toothpaste aisle. Damn! Too late. He was gone. She closed her eyes and inhaled. The heavenly scent of vanilla lingered.

Slipping her phone back into her purse, she headed to the feminine hygiene products and grabbed a box of tampons that would last a few months.

"I've never seen so many different types of condoms," a masculine voice noted. "Any idea which are the best?"

It's him! He was holding several boxes of condoms and looking her way. Her face burned again. Especially when she remembered the supersized box of tampons in her hand. Quickly, she shoved the box back on the shelf.

He shook the condom boxes, flashing her another smile. "Any ideas?"

"No...sorry," she stammered.

"Maybe I should get them all. Do some product testing. Care to help me out?"

Her pulse raced wildly. What's he suggesting? He had to be in his twenties while she was soon turning forty. Caesar Blue lookalike or not, it was a ridiculous suggestion.

"How about it?" He eased closer to her. "Want to take me home and get naked? I'd love to gaze into those beautiful blue eyes all night long."

His voice was like liquid chocolate—smooth and silky. The sound of it tempted her to taste him. *So much like Caesar.* Melanie glanced at the customers nearby. She was being propositioned for sex in a public place, and no one seemed to notice. How could they ignore this beautiful man dressed in tight black jeans and a sheer black, button-down shirt?

Ignoring his proposal, she grabbed the box of tampons from the shelf, dropped them in the cart, and moved past him. *Damn! He smells amazing. Like sugar cookies.* Everything about him was delicious.

"I knew it," he taunted. "Uptight...and scared to have a little fun."

Never one to back down from a challenge, she stopped in her tracks and turned to him. "You don't know me. I could be married...or in a relationship. Not to mention the fact that I'm much older than you. It has nothing to do with being uptight and everything to do with the fact that you're rude."

His boots didn't make a sound as he swaggered over, moving like a lynx stalking its prey. His gaze never left hers. Those dark eyes were hypnotic, as if trying to cast a spell on her. A thick tangle of gold-tinged curls bounced around his face with every step. His lips were pursed, as if at any moment, he might kiss her. Every move he made was sensual. *Just like Caesar.* Maybe he performed in a tribute band.

Ever so slightly, he touched the ring finger of her left hand where there was no wedding band. "Are you saying if I'm polite, you'll say yes?"

"You're unbelievable." She forced her gaze from his. He was so attractive, so sexual. It unnerved her.

"So I've been told." He took the box of tampons from her cart, nodded, and gave a light laugh. Then he moved in closer, his lips lingering near her ear. "I get it now. But just so you know. This has never stopped me."

Completely mortified, she shook a finger in his face. But for the life of her, she couldn't find the right words to tell him off. He grabbed her finger, pressed kisses along the side of it, then slowly sucked it into his mouth. Her eyes widened. *What's wrong with this guy?* She'd never met anyone so sexually aggressive. And she hated to admit...he was turning her on. He slid his mouth back up her finger, then kissed the tip of it. His smile returned. Her mind raced with thoughts of Caesar. Hadn't he been just like this? A womanizer who'd bedded countless women? This guy was taking the lookalike thing too far.

He moved in even closer. His chest rubbed against hers, causing her nipples to harden. "Come on, you know you want me. You haven't been able to stop thinking about me since I bumped into you."

And suddenly, she had the best response. "You know, Johnnie was always my favorite."

His face wrinkled in disgust. Before he could utter another word, Melanie turned heel and walked away, leaving her shopping cart behind.

Just before she got out of hearing range, he slipped in one final remark. "Even though he killed me?"

The mysterious doppelganger's words were stuck in her head as she drove home. Johnnie Vega hadn't killed Caesar. At least that was the official word from investigators. Truthfully, no one really knew what had happened during the band's summer vacation in the Sedona Mountains. The retreat, meant to clear their heads so they could begin writing songs for a new album, had instead turned into a tragedy.

One evening, Johnnie and Caesar had gone hiking, climbing as high as they could to get closer to the stars. Closer to heaven. When they'd reached a scenic spot, they'd apparently taken some hallucinogenics. Johnnie woke the next morning, his head half hanging over the edge of a cliff. Sitting up, he'd spotted his best friend lying lifeless among the rocks in the ravine below.

As she entered her apartment, Melanie remembered how devastated all the band members had been, but none more than Johnnie. He blamed himself, even though he testified that he couldn't remember what happened. Investigators concluded it had been an accident, and that Caesar being intoxicated had most likely slipped and fallen to his death. Still, many fans had blamed Johnnie. Blamed him for the drugs and alcohol and for being on that mountainside. While Rhett and Kurt had gone on to other bands and more musical success, Johnnie had never been able to get past losing his best friend.

She set her purse down in a chair by the front door, then went to change into something comfortable. Once in her joggers and tank top, she padded into the kitchen and opened the fridge. She pulled out leftovers and popped them into the microwave. Next, she grabbed a bottle of water. When she closed the refrigerator, her eyes were drawn to the calendar attached to the door. *July 22.* The same day Caesar died. Goosebumps raced up both arms. *What a coincidence.* And how many years ago? She counted in her head. *Sixteen. It's the sixteenth anniversary of his death.* She wondered about Johnnie. *What's he doing? Is he still alive?*

She grabbed her laptop from its bag. While eating dinner, she poured over the internet, looking for information. Normally, she was too busy with work to get involved with frivolous internet searches, but tonight she took her time, pausing to read the many articles about Lush. Then she moved on to the fan pages. She found a great photo of Caesar and enlarged it on her screen.

"Damn." She took a sip of water. The lookalike could be his twin. *Does he have a younger brother?* She did another search to find out. *No siblings.*

She googled tribute bands, and there were a couple. But while there were slight resemblances between Caesar and the lead singers, none of them could hold a candle to him. Caesar had been achingly beautiful. The way he walked, talked, and moved on stage was sensual magic. It was very feline...soft...slinky...stealth. His deep brown gaze could penetrate your soul, and every female fan had sworn he was singing or talking directly to her alone.

Then there was Johnnie. She found a nice photo of him and enlarged it as well. While Melanie had always given Caesar his props, Johnnie *really* was her favorite. He was the bad boy, wild and crazy, but also impossibly charming, with his big, brilliant smile that lit up any room he entered. His face was chiseled to perfection with cheekbones that would make any supermodel envious. His blue-grey eyes always seemed filled with mischief. While Caesar's thick curly hair flowed around him, Johnnie kept his wavy dark brown hair close-cropped. She smiled remembering the bedroom of her teenage years. She'd covered one wall with posters of the band, but the headboard of her bed had belonged to Johnnie. Every morning, she woke up to his dazzling smile.

She typed in Johnnie Vega, hoping to find out what he was up to now. The most current article was several years old. He'd apparently done another stint in rehab because a tabloid photographer had caught a glimpse of him leaving one in San Diego. Did leaving mean he'd completed the program? Or had he walked out? As much as he'd been a charmer, he'd also had a short fuse. Full of fire and passion, Caesar had always said. *Where is he now?*

She started to look up the rehab center but instead got distracted by a search of San Diego. She'd lived in the coastal city as a child when her father was stationed there. He was then sent to Jacksonville, Florida, where the family resided even after her father retired from the Navy. She'd eventually moved to Atlanta to work, but she'd always wanted to go back to California where there were more opportunities for writers in television and the movies. A quick look at properties for sale in San Diego reminded her of the main reason she'd not returned to the west coast.

"Ouch!" she muttered when she saw a condo smaller than hers that was double the price she'd paid.

Noting the time, she groaned. That was why she avoided getting online. It was a time drainer. She turned off her laptop, put it away, and headed for her room. She'd take a shower and get some sleep. Tomorrow was Friday, and she was looking forward to the weekend. It would be one of the few she was taking time off to enjoy. There was a music festival in town, and she'd been invited by some coworkers. They were younger, but it had sounded like fun, so she'd agreed to go, even though most of the bands playing were unfamiliar to her. It would be nice to get out. Since moving to Atlanta eight years ago, she hadn't spent a lot of time socializing. Instead, she'd focused on building her career.

Standing under the hot water, she thought about her birthday next month. *Forty.* It was supposed to be a milestone, and her parents had asked that she come to visit. She was still contemplating. It would mean taking another weekend off. She was a senior news writer, and even though the team could manage without her, she always felt compelled to be nearby. *Then again, I'll only turn forty once.*

Chapter Two

"We're going to get closer to the stage!" Lori yelled over the music. "Want to come with?"

"Actually, I'm thirsty. I'm going to find something to drink," Melanie yelled back, wiping the sweat from her face. "Want anything?"

"You probably won't be able to find us again," Kristy told her. "We'll text you when this band's finished and tell you where to meet us."

She nodded. "Sounds like a plan."

Holding one another's hand, the two younger women snaked through the crowd toward the stage. Melanie made her way through the back half of the crowd. They were tightly packed, and she couldn't wait to be away from the throngs of people gathered for the show.

As soon as she made it out of the crowd, she headed for the row of food trucks nearby. One immediately caught her attention. *Smoothies.* That would hit the spot perfectly.

"What's your flavor?" The vendor was an older man with long grey hair pulled back into a ponytail.

"Strawberry banana." It would cool her down and provide some nutrients as well.

"Enjoying the show?" the man asked while blending the ingredients together. He was wearing a tie-dyed shirt and a necklace made of puka shells.

"Except for the heat," she replied. "Whose idea was it to hold an outdoor festival in the middle of July?"

The man chuckled. "Not sure. But the kids don't seem to mind. And I make a pretty penny myself. So, I can't complain."

She nodded in the direction of the first aid tents. "I wonder how many cases of heat exhaustion they'll be treating today."

"All in good fun." He handed her the smoothie. "If the heat's too much, head back up the sidewalk to that line of trees. Some nice shade in there."

"Thanks. I'll do that." She took a sip and smiled. "Mmm . . . delicious."

The noise from the concert grew quiet as she walked toward the large live oaks. There was only a handful of people resting in the area. *Privacy, quiet, and shade!* She soon found the perfect spot and slowly sank to the ground. Leaning against the tree's trunk, she sipped her smoothie. She grabbed her phone and texted Lori and Kristy, telling them where she was. She'd stay there until they found her later.

When a cool breeze whipped through the trees, she tilted her head back and closed her eyes. *Maybe I need a nap.* The sun seemed to have zapped all her energy.

A drop of water hit her face. *Rain?* It hadn't been in the forecast. Another plopped on her face, and she wiped it against her hot skin. It felt divine.

"You didn't bring sunscreen?" a familiar voice asked.

Melanie's eyes flew open. *What's he doing here?*

The Caesar lookalike stood above her, holding a bottle of water. There was no rain. He'd been dropping water on her face.

He squatted and placed a hand against her cheek. "That's going to be a helluva sunburn."

She was too exhausted to pull away. Besides, he seemed different this time. Gentle. Not aggressive.

"Here." He held out the bottle of water. "Drink this."

"I just had a smoothie."

"You look like you're about to pass out." He sat down beside her.

"Just tired."

He tenderly stroked her cheek again. "That's what people usually say right before they pass out."

"I'm okay." But the concern in his eyes caused her to take the bottle and drink.

His soft touch went to her shoulders. He frowned. "You're burned here as well."

She nodded and sat up straight. He was wearing all black again, only now with a leather jacket. *And he's worried about me passing out?* "What are you doing here?"

"It's a music festival. I'm all about music. Where else would I be?"

"Are you in a band?"

"Used to be." His hand was on her knee now. His thumb moved back and forth, lightly touching her. It was surprisingly soothing. And sensual.

"Thought so."

"Oh?" He raised an eyebrow and smiled sweetly. "You've been thinking about me?"

"It's hard not to. I mean you look so much like him."

"Who?"

"Caesar Blue." She shook her head. "Do you even know who that is? I mean...he's older than me or would be."

He smoothed her hair back, staring into her eyes. "Yes, I know who he is."

"Was it a tribute band you were in? For Lush?"

He dropped back onto the grass, laughing.

She couldn't help smiling. He looked adorable lying in the grass, grinning up at her. "Did I say something funny?"

"I guess this is the part where things get difficult." He sighed. "I knew it might be hard to explain."

"Excuse me?"

Quickly, he sat back up. "How big of a Lush fan were you?"

"They were my favorite band during high school and college."

"Was Johnnie really your favorite?" He narrowed his eyes. "Or did you just say that to rattle me?"

"Yes..." She laughed lightly. "And yes."

Looking away, he picked a dandelion and twirled it between his fingers. "We were always so competitive with one another. Seems so stupid now."

"Who?"

"Johnnie and me."

"You know him? Is he okay? I tried to search for information about him after I met you, but I found nothing recent."

His gaze went skyward. "Yes, I know Johnnie. We're like brothers. Went to school together...created together..."

"Come on, you're taking this lookalike thing way too seriously." She nudged his leg gently. "Wait. I've got it. They're making a movie about the band, and you're playing Caesar. That's it, right?"

"You think I'm an actor?"

She scooted closer, examining his face. Reaching out, she brushed back the curls from his eyes. "Have you always looked like him? Or did they perm and color your hair to look like his?"

Roughly, he grabbed her wrist. "Look at me, Melanie. *Really* look at me."

"How do you know my name?"

"I know things." He loosened his grip on her hand and rubbed her wrist gently.

She gazed into his eyes. Deep, dark brown eyes that seemed to penetrate her soul. Over his left eye, a small scar. In the band's early days, they'd played the bar circuit, and one night a drunk patron had thrown a bottle at...*Caesar.*

Her hands flew to her mouth as she gasped. Timidly, she reached out again, her index finger softly stroking the scar.

"A drunk idiot. Thank God all I got was a scar. He could have put my eye out. Rhett and Johnnie beat the shit out of him while Kurt took me to the hospital for stitches."

Grabbing his wrist, she slid his jacket and shirt sleeve up his arm. On his underarm, just above his wrist, a tattoo of an angel resided there, with Caesar's mother's name. Naomi. She died of cancer when he was twelve.

"Want to see this one?" He unbuttoned his shirt, exposing his toned chest. Musical notes with a verse from Lush's biggest hit were inked over his heart.

This is crazy! He's not Caesar. Why would I even consider that an option? Caesar is dead.

As she touched the tattoo, she took a deep breath, then slowly exhaled. "Well, you've certainly taken fanboy to a whole new level."

He stroked the top of her hand. "How do I make you believe?"

"What is there to believe? Caesar Blue is dead."

"True."

"At least we agree on something."

"Is it so hard to believe that I'm Caesar Blue?"

"We just agreed Caesar is dead."

"Yes. I'm dead."

Melanie yanked her hand away and scrambled to her feet. "Now you're talking crazy. I have to go."

"No, you don't." He stood as well.

"I have to meet my friends."

"They're not your friends. Just women you work with."

This is getting weird. "Have you been stalking me? Is that how you know my name?"

He rubbed his head. "I *have* been following you. But I knew your name before then. Just like I know those girls met some guys and left with them. They want you to take an *Uber* home. Is that like a taxi?"

"It hasn't even been an hour since I left them in the crowd."

"Check your phone."

"What?" She pulled out her phone. "There's no message here."

"It's coming."

Just then, she received notification. She was almost afraid to look. "Go ahead. Check it."

It was from Kristy. A message accompanied by a photo of two smiling guys.

"Do you believe me now?"

"Is this some crazy joke the three of you are pulling on me?"

He shook his head. "I don't know them."

"Then how did you know?"

"I have some powers."

"Oh my God!" She huffed and began walking away. "Now you're a superhero!"

He followed and grabbed her arm. "I'm a ghost I think. Maybe an angel? A spirit of some sort. I'm not entirely sure myself."

She burst out laughing. "Now I've heard it all."

"My powers are limited, but I can sometimes see things...actually it's more like feel things that are going to happen."

"Then you can see that I don't believe you. Oh, and I'm leaving. Did you see that?"

He pouted and let her arm go. "I only see things when I try."

"Goodbye." She started walking again.

He stayed put and closed his eyes. "You're going to ride home with a young man from Kenya. A college student studying medicine. He'll tell you about your sunburn."

She stopped and looked at her pink shoulders. "It's sort of obvious."

"Tell him not to take you on the highway. Keep to the backroads."

She shook her head. *This guy is certifiably insane.*

"Please. I don't want you to get hurt."

She began walking again.

"I'll see you again soon, Melanie."

Is he a stalker? Maybe she needed to call the police. He seemed tame. Pretending to be a dead rock star wasn't exactly violent behavior, but who knew what he was capable of.

As she passed the smoothie truck, the owner called out to her. "Enjoy the smoothie?"

She gave a thumb's up.

"He's telling the truth," he yelled after her.

Without responding, she sped up. She grabbed her phone and requested an Uber. There was a designated pick up area at the festival, and when she arrived, she was glad to find about forty other people waiting. *Safety in numbers.* She took a quick look around and didn't see the lookalike. What a relief! Strangely though, she felt a bit let down. It had been a while since a man had pursued her...and even longer that one had intrigued her as much as this one did. She wasn't sure if it was because he was so attractive or because she'd minored in psychology in college. *What mental illness is he suffering from?*

She saw her Uber driver, a young black man, driving a *Nissan Juke*, and waved at him.

The car pulled up to the curb, and the window came down. "Melanie?"

"Yes," she replied, getting into the front seat next to him.

"Hello, I'm Akeyo," he said politely. "Your address is near Grant Park?"

"Yes." She smiled.

"I love that area of Atlanta. Once I get out of medical school and become a doctor, that's where I'd like to buy a house. Near the zoo. My son loves going there."

Medical school? "You have it all planned. That's great. Always good to have goals."

The young man nodded and smiled. His teeth were gleaming white against his dark skin. *He has an accent. Is he from Africa?*

"Ever since I was a little boy growing up in Mombasa, I have wanted to come to America to study."

She felt a bit of relief. "Mombasa?"

"Yes. It's the second largest city in Kenya, after Nairobi."

Sweat broke out on her forehead. She looked out the window and bit her lip. Her heart kicked into overdrive as she realized they were nearing the exit to the highway. *What if?*

"Do you mind not taking the highway? I'll pay extra if you take the back roads instead."

"No problem. You're my last rider. I have to get home and study for an exam."

"Thank you."

The young man continued to talk. She nodded, pretending to listen as he told stories about life in Kenya and about how difficult the transition to America had been. He laughed loudly as he talked about baboons raiding his grandmother's garden, while she sat quietly, deep in her thoughts about Caesar Blue. *Is he really a ghost? Is it possible?* She'd never given much thought to the paranormal or to what happened to people after they died.

"Do you believe in ghosts?" she blurted out.

He looked at her strangely. "Why are you asking?"

"You're studying to be a doctor. You've probably seen a few dead bodies. Do you think it's possible that they become ghosts and can walk around with us?"

"Did you see a spirit, Ms. Melanie?"

"I think...maybe I did."

"People believe different things. Religion comes into play. Culture, too. My ancestors believed you could be visited by spirits of dead loved ones."

"This one told me all about you before I met you. That you'd be a medical student from Kenya."

Akeyo rubbed his chin. "Interesting. Now my curiosity is piqued. Did he say anything else?"

"Yes. He said not to take the highway."

Akeyo began pressing buttons on his radio until he found a news station. He let out a low whistle as they listened to a report about a major pile-up on the highway.

"There's possibly thirty cars involved. Ambulances are on the scene," the reporter went on.

"If you see your ghost again, please give him my thanks."

Nervously, Melanie brushed back the hair from her face. "I will."

They drove in silence the rest of the way to her condo.

"Take care of that sunburn," Akeyo told her when she got out of his car. "Aloe works best."

Trembling, she waved goodbye and walked to her front door. And there he was. Sitting on her steps. When he saw her, he leaped up and hugged her tight.

"Thank God you listened to me."

Right then it didn't matter if he were some crazed stalker. She felt safe in his arms. She clung to him as tears slid down her face. Her body heaved.

"You're safe," he cooed, softly. "I won't let anything happen to you."

She pulled away, wiping at her tears. "What are you doing here?"

He wiped a few away, too. "We can talk inside. I'll try my best to explain things."

"You want me to let you into my house? I don't know you."

He held her face, and that penetrating gaze was locking onto hers again. "You do know me."

"Even if what you say is true...that you're Caesar Blue...I...I don't know you."

"Did I seem like a bad person? Aside from being an idiot with drugs and alcohol?"

No. The only person Caesar ever hurt was himself. His fans and bandmates had been hurt by his death, but in life, Caesar had been a gentle soul. Even the many women he'd loved and left never said an unkind word against him. Instead, they heaped praise on him, fawning over him long after their breakups. He'd made every fan he met feel special, and during tour stops, he'd visit children's hospitals to bring gifts.

But is this Caesar? She found it hard to believe he was a ghost. Maybe he could explain it better if she allowed him inside.

She opened her purse, took out her keys, and conceded, "Come on then."

"This is a beautiful place," he said, stepping into her foyer. Immediately, he bent over and removed his boots. "Don't want to scuff your floors."

She kicked off her flip-flops and saw that the blazing sun had even reached her feet.

He reached into the inside pocket of his leather jacket, pulled out a bottle of aloe, and handed it to her. "I picked this up on the way over. I was worried you didn't have any."

"On the way over?" she asked, taking the bottle from him. "How did you get here? Did you fly? Or like, materialize out of thin air? How does it work?"

"First things first. Let's get this sunburn taken care of."

Is he stalling? Is it all just bullshit?

"I need a shower first. I must smell awful."

He leaned in, placed his nose against her neck and inhaled. "You smell very...primitive."

His vanilla scent...his closeness...the slight touch of his curls brushing up against her skin unnerved her. Her heart thudded in her chest, and her nipples hardened. It had been a long time since she'd been alone with a man. Much less one this beautiful.

She ducked away from him. "Is that a polite way of saying I smell like sweat and dirt."

"Nothing wrong with a little sweat and dirt." He winked.

She grabbed the remote from the end table and turned on the television. "Watch some television while I get cleaned up."

"Hurry back, please."

She nodded and rushed into her bedroom where she grabbed a pair of lounge pants and a tank top to put on after her shower.

"Yikes." She cringed when she saw her bright pink reflection in the mirror. She was surprised she wasn't hurting yet. Then again, her mind had been elsewhere until now.

Thinking a hot shower might be too much, she ran the water until it got slightly warm, then stripped off her clothes and stepped inside. She turned the water temperature down until it was more on the cold side. It felt amazing against her hot skin, and she lathered up quickly. She didn't want to leave Caesar alone for too long. Who knew what a ghost could get up to? *Or a crazed fanboy stalker.* After rinsing the soap from her body, she soaked her hair so that she could shampoo.

Closing her eyes, she faced the water and lathered up her hair. Suddenly there were two more hands massaging the soap into her hair. How in the hell had he snuck in here? She'd not heard a thing.

"What are you doing?" Instinctively, she dropped her hands to cover her breasts. *As if that's going to help.*

"Assisting." He continued to massage her head.

"I don't need help." But she had to admit it felt delightful.

He whispered in her ear, "Humor me, please."

His hot breath on her neck excited her. She'd not had sex in years. *Wait! Why am I thinking about sex? Can ghosts even have sex?* She wanted to turn around and look at him, but part of her was frightened. Not by what she would see, but because she wanted to see it so badly. *He's too young. Too dead. This is crazy!*

"Time to rinse."

Now she *had* to turn around. She closed her eyes again then ducked her head directly under the water to rinse the soap from her hair.

"Open your eyes, Melanie."

She did and kept her gaze on his, willing herself not to look down. "I didn't hear you come in."

"Guess I don't make a lot of noise."

She smiled. "Did you come through the wall?"

He laughed. "Now that I know I did not do. And I can't do."

She loved the way the lines around his eyes crinkled when he smiled. And his hair. She couldn't resist and reached up to run her hands through the mass of curls.

"You want to wash my hair?"

"You smell so good. I hate to wash that out."

"I always smell like this." He switched places, ducking under the water. "It won't go away. I promise."

When she put the shampoo in his hair, she allowed herself to look down. He was lean and lithe as he'd always been. His butt was small, taut, and muscular. She remembered what he'd said about being able to see into the future and wondered if he knew what she was thinking. *Does he know how much he's turning me on?*

"I love your hair."

He chuckled. "If I had a dime for every time someone told me that."

"You'd still be a millionaire." She inhaled sharply, then sighed. "I mean you were..."

"Your hair is amazing, too." He turned around and his gaze traveled down her body. He smiled. "A natural blonde, I see."

She turned her gaze from his body, embarrassed by his scrutiny, yet aroused as well. He'd been with so many women and to have him impressed with her body was a turn on. It wasn't perfect by any means. She didn't belong to a gym, but she did enjoy walking through the trails of the park.

He cupped her chin and brought her gaze back to his. "Why won't you look at me?"

"You scare me."

"I'm not here to hurt you." He ducked his head back into the water to rinse.

"I'm scared of how I'm feeling."

"Why is that?"

"I haven't felt this way in a long time."

He turned the water off, opened the shower door, and stepped out. He dried off, then dropped the towel to the floor. "I want you to look at me."

She blushed and turned away. "I can't."

"Now you're being silly. Like a school girl." He handed her a dry towel. "Not a woman who's about to be forty."

How does he know that? She began to dry herself. "I can't help it. This is embarrassing. We hardly know one another."

Suddenly, she was grabbed, then lifted over his shoulder. She squealed as he carried her into the bedroom and deposited her onto the bed. He grabbed the bottle of aloe off the nightstand, then crawled in next to her.

"Let's take care of this now."

She sat up beside him, feeling self-conscious again. She pulled a blanket around her.

He yanked it away. "You're beautiful. Stop hiding it."

Her lips went to his. She couldn't help herself as she planted a hard, demanding kiss on his mouth. It was fast, quick, and unexpected. She pulled away equally as fast, and her cheeks felt hot.

He seemed surprised. "Guess you're not feeling scared anymore."

She hung her head. "Sorry."

"For what?"

"That was a horrible first kiss."

"I didn't kiss you back. So, it doesn't count."

He *hadn't* kissed back. *Why not?* They were naked on a bed. *Isn't that his intention?* She bit her lip, turning her back to him to hide her disappointment. Maybe ghosts *couldn't* have sex.

A cool drop of aloe plopped onto her shoulder, and he massaged it in. His touch was gentle. Even more arousing. He swept her hair aside and put some on her shoulder blades.

"Tell me again what you are. A ghost? An angel?"

"A bit of both maybe."

She thought about the incident at the store. How people had ignored their conversation. "Am I the only one who can see you?"

He was quiet, and she turned slightly to look at him.

"I'm not sure," he finally said. "I'm new at this."

"But it's been sixteen years since you died."

His eyes widened as he slid from the bed. She saw everything now. But seeing his cock was not the thrill she'd thought it would be. Not when she was distracted by his panic-stricken face.

"I'm sorry." She flew to him and pushed the damp curls from his face. "I thought you knew."

Tears slid down his face. "Where I was, there was no sense of time."

"Come back to bed." She propped up pillows, and they both relaxed against them. "The day we first met...that day was the sixteenth anniversary of your death."

She felt awful as he began to sob. Wrapping her arms around him, she held his head to her chest, trying to comfort him. After a while, he fell asleep with his head in her lap. Deep in thought, she caressed his face and ran her fingers gently through his hair. She was at a loss. He'd been so confident when she met him—like he had himself together. That obviously hadn't been the case. *How can I help him?*

Gently, she lifted his head and scooted out from underneath.

He grabbed her arm and groggily pleaded, "Don't leave me."

"I'll be right back."

"Promise?"

She kissed his forehead. "Promise."

When she returned, carrying her laptop, she saw he'd snuggled into a pillow and fallen asleep again. She lay down beside him and began a new online mission. Researching ghosts and angels.

It was nearing six when he awoke again. By then she'd ordered pizza and was deep into an article about spirits of the dead.

"Why are your clothes on?" Was the first thing he muttered.

"I'm not used to running around naked...like you obviously are."

He laughed and rolled back onto his pillow. "Only when I'm not on stage."

"I got hungry and ordered food." She paused for a moment. "Can you even eat?"

He shot up and grabbed a slice from the box near the foot of the bed. "Let's find out."

"It's veggie. I'm a vegetarian...like you."

He took a bite and smiled. "Damn."

"That good?"

He didn't answer, but kept eating and eating, until the box was empty. Then he let out a loud burp. "Sorry. I ate all your food."

"We can order another if you're still hungry."

"Can we? I swear it's like I haven't eaten in..." His voice faded, and he appeared sad once again.

"I've been doing some research." She showed him her laptop screen, and he scooted closer. True to his word, he still smelled of vanilla. And although he'd gone to sleep with damp hair, his curls were perfect, as if he'd just walked out of the hair salon.

"What is this?" He ran his hand over the keys. "A typewriter of some sort?"

"A laptop computer. We have the entire world at our fingertips now."

"Show me how it works."

"I'll show you how to order a pizza." After a few clicks, they had another veggie pizza on the way.

"Look at this." She showed him a webpage she'd been reading. "It's the history of ghost lore and what different cultures believe. You mentioned being an angel. Did someone actually tell you that?"

He seemed to drift away, as if he were trying to remember something. "I don't remember anyone talking to me. It was more like a feeling. That I had to go back."

"Do you know why?"

"Something or someone was giving me this feeling. Someone needed my help. And I had a purpose...to help this person."

"Why me? I mean...I don't need help."

"You're alone most of the time. Except for at work."

"So you *have* been following me around."

"A few days." He seemed to get lost in thought again. "But it's like I just knew it's you I'm supposed to help. You told me you hadn't been with a man in a while."

Did I say that? Or did he read my thoughts? "I'm not religious, but I have a hard time believing any god would send you for sexual purposes."

"Maybe you need friendship."

Is that it? True. She hadn't made many friends since coming to Atlanta. But that was by choice. She'd been too busy with work. Her career came before everything else. And having a gorgeous, dead rock star as a friend? How was that better?

"We're going to be friends then?"

He touched her cheek. "I think it's already more than that, don't you?"

"Let's get back to research." Her cheeks were hot while she typed *angels* into the search engine, and pages of articles were found.

"All these?" He moved his finger over the list on the screen.

"Looks like we have a lot of reading to do." She scrolled down the list.

"This one." He pointed to one that read, *Angels Among Us.*

As she opened the page the doorbell rang. "Pizza's here."

"Great!" He leaped out of the bed. "I'm starving."

She laughed. "You're also very naked. I'll get it."

"But then we'd know if others can see me."

"We'll experiment when you have clothes on."

"Didn't I deliver here earlier?" The young woman asked her. "Did you drop your pizza or something?"

Melanie took the pizza box from her. "No. I have a hungry man in the house."

Suddenly, Caesar was at the door, naked and grinning. "That would be me."

The young woman looked him up and down. "I see. Guess you two have been working up an appetite."

She sees him.

"I told you not to come out here," Melanie scolded, handing him the box. He disappeared back inside.

"Sorry about that." Melanie handed the woman a tip. "He's not from around here."

"I ain't mad. Get it while you can, girl. That's one fine piece of ass if you don't mind me saying so."

Melanie couldn't help smiling. "Thank you."

The woman walked to her car. "If you need any more pizzas delivered...ask for Tanya. I'll be happy to come back."

"We'll do that." Melanie closed the door.

She found Caesar on his second slice when she entered the bedroom.

He flipped over onto his stomach. "Do you think my ass is fine, too?"

Ignoring him, she grabbed her computer and sat down. "Back to work."

He slithered closer and set his chin on her shoulder. "Come on, tell me."

"Stop. I'm reading this."

His mouth went to her ear, and his whisper was hot. "I know you like when I do this."

She did, but she was trying to focus on the information she was reading. About how there were spirits among us, here to do unfinished business and to help those in need. It became more difficult to ignore his soft lips when they pressed against her neck. She shuddered, and her nipples hardened.

"Oh my God, Caesar. Look."

"Later." His mouth traveled to her earlobe to suck.

"No, come on," she pleaded. "I recognize this guy. I saw him earlier at the festival. He even said something to me after I left you. He said, *he's telling the truth*. I had no clue what he was talking about."

Caesar examined the screen. "I don't know him."

"He was selling smoothies. Apparently, he's into all this angel and ghost business. He's written a few books and wrote this article. We should talk to him. Maybe he can help us figure this out."

"Okay." He began to nuzzle her neck. "But I want to make love to you first."

She wanted to let him. He was bringing back desires she'd long ago locked away. She glanced at the clock. "The festival will be going until midnight. But we should leave now and try to find him."

"We have plenty of time," he protested. He sat up, tossed the box of pizza on the floor, placed her laptop on the nightstand, and then began tugging down her pants.

"But he might not be there until the end."

He parted her legs and slid his head full of beautiful curls between them. The festival was immediately forgotten as he pressed kisses to her thighs. Heat flowed through her body. Along with a need that she hadn't felt in a long time. He began licking her most intimate parts. When his tongue flicked across her clit, she gasped, and when he sucked on it, she lost it. Her body shook with a powerful orgasm.

He laughed lightly. "I guess we can go since I made you cum."

She looked down at him, smiling between her thighs, his chin wet with moisture from her pussy. "I came so fast."

"Yes, you did. Are you ready to leave?"

"No." She was breathless. "I need more."

"Good. Because I'm still hungry. And you taste so good."

His mouth went back to work. She moaned and lay back against the pillow, relishing the pleasure. No wonder the women he left in his wake still talked about how much they loved him.

"Caesar?" Her voice was barely audible.

He crawled out from between her legs and hovered over her. "Is it time for me to stop?"

She took his hard cock in her hands. He sucked in his breath as she moved her hands over him.

"Do you want me?" The liquid chocolate voice.

"Yes."

"Tell me."

"I want you, Caesar."

His mouth pressed soft kisses against hers. She tasted herself on his lips and loosened the grip on his cock. When he slid between her thighs, she spread her legs wider. He found her opening and entered slowly. Her wet walls collapsed around his hardness, and once again, she was shaking with a release.

Caesar had always known how to move on stage. Sensual movements that worked in perfect harmony with his sexy voice. Those moves served him well now as he swiveled his hips into hers. Her body quaked with every thrust he made.

His lips left hers. "Look at me."

She opened her eyes and was soon drowning in those dark pools.

"What are you thinking?" He slid his lips along her jawline.

"You're so beautiful." She caressed his cheek.

"So are you." He kissed the palm of her hand.

She'd never thought of herself as beautiful. Pretty, maybe. But she wasn't someone who'd ever turned heads. But hearing Caesar say it, suddenly it made her feel like the most beautiful woman in the world. Something inside her was awakening! Feelings she'd buried long ago.

Kissing him again she made a move to roll over. He went with it, and she took control. He entwined a hand into her hair as she moved on him.

"Let yourself go."

As she ground herself into him, his hands slid up to her breasts, where he kneaded them softly. She moaned, and her head rolled backward. He sat up and sucked a nipple into his mouth which only made her speed increase.

He smiled sweetly. "Are you going to cum again?"

"Yes," she replied, then kissed him hard. "Will you cum with me?"

His lips trailed down to her neck. "Yes."

As she slammed down harder, he pushed up harder. It was a wild frenzy of bodies clamoring to get as close as they could to one another.

"That's it, cum for me," he coaxed, reaching between her legs to finger her clit.

Her pussy tightened on him again. His mouth crashed onto hers as he rolled them back over. Her body quivered as he plunged into her again and again, the wild frenzy continuing until he finally moaned loudly, spilling himself inside her. His speed decreased, and he pressed feather-light kisses all over her face. They stared at one another smiling.

She began to laugh. "Now that was a first kiss."

"Indeed, it was." He chuckled and rolled over to his back. "And to think, two days ago, you were telling me to get lost."

She propped herself up on her elbow, placed her hand on his chest, and caressed him. "I did, didn't I?"

"It's okay." He brushed her hair back behind her ear. "I *was* an asshole, wasn't I?"

"You were."

"Once I became famous, I got spoiled. Women threw themselves at me or at least let me know they wanted me."

"Didn't mean to burst your bubble."

"I'm glad you did." He pulled her close and held her. His hands slid down her back to her butt. He squeezed her cheeks. "It made me more curious about you and why I was sent here."

"Speaking of that..." She pried herself loose. "We should go see that guy."

"But we're just getting started." He cupped her head, brought it close to his, and kissed her tenderly.

"We can start again later." Certain that she didn't have the willpower to deny him for very long, she slid out of bed.

"You're right." He sighed as he, too, left the bed and stretched. "Maybe he can give me some answers."

Chapter Three

"I'm sure he was around here somewhere." Melanie tried to get a sense of where she was. The sun had set, and everything looked so different. The festival grounds were more crowded, probably because the more popular bands were playing.

"Is it that one?" Caesar pointed across the sidewalk.

"Yes, that's it." There were a few people in line. To her disappointment, a woman was serving the smoothies. "He's not here."

"Maybe she can tell us how to get in touch with him. You said he owns the truck."

Taking her hand in his, he walked over and stood in line behind some scantily dressed teenagers.

A loud roar of applause erupted as a new band was taking the main stage.

"Can we listen to some music later?"

"Of course. I thought you might like that."

The two teen girls gawked at Melanie as if she had two heads.

"Did you say something?" one asked.

Without thinking, Melanie replied, "Talking to my friend."

"You're a bit old for imaginary friends, aren't you?" the other said rudely.

"Why are they being brats?" Caesar asked.

"They can't see you," she whispered to him.

"She's bonkers," the rude teen noted.

The two young women were given their smoothies and started to leave.

Caesar waved his hand in front of one's face. When she didn't acknowledge him, he knocked her smoothie from her hand. It landed on her friend's chest.

"What the hell, Teresa!"

Teresa grabbed some napkins and tried to help her friend clean up. "I didn't mean to. It just flew out of my hand."

Melanie covered her mouth, trying to suppress a smile as the two of them walked away arguing. "You shouldn't have done that."

"I didn't know it would work." Caesar shrugged, grinning. "Call it research."

"Two smoothies?" The woman in the window asked.

Melanie's eyes widened. *She sees him!*

Before she could answer, Caesar was ordering two bottles of water. He pulled a huge wad of cash from his pocket to pay, then told the woman to keep the change.

Melanie was confused.

"Are you alright?" the woman asked her.

"There was a man working here earlier. I believe his name is Tim Harris. He's an author."

"My husband. He's taking a break." She pointed to the right. "Went over to the picnic area down that way. It's not far."

"Thank you," Melanie replied.

"He said a young woman might come looking for him tonight. You have a ghost problem?"

She glanced from Caesar then back to Mrs. Harris. "Not really a problem. We have some questions for him."

"Head on down then. He loves talking about spirits."

"Thank you." Caesar flashed his dazzling smile.

"Wish they all looked as good as this one." Mrs. Harris winked at Caesar.

Caesar, ever the showman, blew her a kiss and bowed.

"Well now, look who's come to see me." Tim Harris sat at a picnic table alone, with an open laptop, pen, and spiral notebook next to him.

"Your wife said you were expecting me. How is that possible?"

Mr. Harris nodded toward Caesar. "Because earlier I saw *him* follow you into the shade. Then you walked out alone, looking confused and more than a bit annoyed. Figured he was the cause of that."

"You told me to believe what he said. How did you know what he said?"

"Sit down, and I'll explain as much as I can."

Caesar let her sit directly across from Mr. Harris, then he sat to her left.

"First, let me say, as soon as I saw him, I knew exactly who and what he was." Mr. Harris pointed toward where the music was coming from. "This isn't my first rodeo. I've worked these music festivals for over thirty years. I've sold everything from t-shirts to funnel cakes. Smoothies are the thing now, especially during summer."

"You're a fan of my music?"

"Caesar Blue. I'll be damned." Mr. Harris held out his hand. "I actually met you and your band years ago at one of your first shows. You bought a Hendrix shirt from me."

"Santa Barbara." Caesar nodded, smiled, and shook the older man's hand. "I loved that shirt. I still had it when..."

"Damn shame what happened to you."

Caesar seemed pained, and Melanie decided to quickly get to the point of the meeting.

"I'm hoping you can help us, Mr. Harris. Caesar's confused about why he's here. I am, too."

"Call me Tim." He shook Melanie's hand. "How did you know to come see me?"

"Melanie," she replied, smiling. "Ever since I met Caesar, all these strange coincidences have been happening. Like meeting you here, then going home and finding your website. When I saw your photo, I knew we had to come see you."

"Did you read any of the information?"

Melanie nodded. "We can't figure out his purpose for being here. And he didn't even realize how long he'd been...gone."

"That's strange." Tim rubbed his bristly chin. "Usually spirits have a clear purpose for returning to our world."

"I thought I was here to help her. To be with her. As a friend...and lover."

Tim's eyebrows shot up. "Now that's one I haven't heard before."

"How many ghosts have you talked to, Tim?" Caesar asked.

"Counting you? One."

Caesar turned to her. "You said he was an expert."

"Oh, I've done lots of research. I've interviewed hundreds of people who've been visited by spirits. People hear ghost and think of haunted houses and being terrorized. But that's not what ghost visits are usually about. Many have unfinished business or were sent back for a specific reason. To help loved ones in some way."

"But I'm not a loved one," Melanie noted.

Caesar placed his hand on her knee and kissed her head. "You are now."

She smiled. "Honestly Tim, other than being a fan of Lush, Caesar and I have no connection."

"None that you're aware of."

"Caesar wasn't even my favorite band member."

"Bet I am now." His hand slid to her thigh.

"Who was?" Tim asked.

"Johnnie Vega." Chuckling, Caesar rolled his eyes.

"Then the connection has to be through Johnnie. *If* he's the only thing you two have in common."

"I did an online search for him a couple of days ago to see if I could find what he was up to. I came up with nothing except for an article on a rehab visit he made years ago."

"You searched Johnnie Vega, right?" Tim began typing on his computer. "Did you try his real name?"

She groaned and smacked her forehead. "I didn't even think about it."

"Johnathan Smith," Caesar said.

"No wonder he changed his name." Tim smiled.

Caesar laughed lightly. "I'm the only one in the band who didn't."

Tim's brow furrowed as he stared at the screen. "Smith is going to be the devil to find."

Melanie moved to sit next to Tim. "Could you put in both names together and see if that works?"

"Good thinking." Tim typed again.

The two of them scanned the search results.

"That one!" Melanie pointed to the screen. "Oh my God! I can't believe it."

Caesar moved to their side. "What did you find?"

"I'll be damned." Tim began scribbling some information into his notebook.

"His parents live in Atlanta now." Melanie grabbed his hand and squeezed. "For twelve years. Maybe Johnnie's here, too."

Caesar sat down next to her. "Could I have gotten confused? What if he's the one I'm supposed to be helping?"

"I don't think you got confused." Tim looked from her to Caesar. "There's a definite connection between your old friend...and your new one."

"I wish I knew what it was." Melanie sighed. "We need to find out where Johnnie is."

Caesar nodded. "He might be in trouble, and I've been sidetracked with you."

Melanie winced. "I'm sorry."

"I'm not." Caesar hugged her close. "We'll find him, and I can help him."

"We can contact his parents and see if he's living here."

"Seems like a logical starting point." Tim was still searching through webpages. "I don't see much else here. He seems to have a long history of drug and alcohol abuse. If he needs help, I bet it's related to that."

"We'll talk to them," she assured Caesar.

Caesar nodded.

Melanie turned back to Tim. "We have another question. Why is it that some people can see him, and others can't?"

"That's a weird phenomenon," Tim began. "Based on my research, for a person to see a spirit, the person must believe in the possibility of spirits. Some folks see spirits, but not many are able to make contact, like you've done with Caesar."

"But a few days ago, I wouldn't have believed any of this."

"Then I'm positive you have some connection to Johnnie Vega. You shouldn't be able to see him unless you believe...or you're the subject of the mission he's been given."

Melanie was perplexed. What was the link between her and Johnnie?

"Let me know what happens." Tim grabbed his wallet from his pocket and slipped out a business card. "I'm curious and willing to help if I can."

"Thank you," Melanie said. She rose from the table, pulled out her own business card, and gave it to Tim.

Caesar stood as well and shook hands again with Tim.

"Great to meet you." Tim beamed.

Caesar took her hand. "C'mon, faster."

Melanie squealed with delight as they sprinted toward the main stage.

"There's so many people." She marveled as they stopped behind the thousands of fans gathered on the lawn. On the outer edges many were sitting, but toward the front people were on their feet dancing. "There weren't this many people earlier."

"It's probably the top-billed band. Let's get closer."

She let him lead the way, weaving expertly in and out of the crowd. A few people stared at them. *Can they see him?* If so, were they noticing how much he looked like a famous rock star they once knew?

They paused for a moment, as he tried to figure out a way through another thick throng of fans.

"What's the biggest crowd Lush ever played to?"

"Some super-fan you are!" He laughed as he wrapped his arms around her, moving their bodies to the music. "You should know that!"

She ran her hands through his thick curls. "Well, I'm sure it was the Rose Bowl, but I don't know the numbers."

"Close to one-hundred-thousand." His lips went to her neck, where he started kissing her. "Which is how many times I plan to kiss you before the night's over."

"Promise?"

He answered by bringing his lips to hers. She opened her mouth, and his tongue plunged inside. His hands went to her butt, pulling her closer. She could feel his erection pressing into her hip.

When a guitar solo began, Caesar abruptly stopped.

"What is it?"

"It can't be." He grabbed her hand, pulling her through the crowd again. This time with urgency.

About fifty feet from the stage, they were forced to stop. The crowd was too thick. But they could clearly see the band.

"Do you know this band?" he asked.

"It's not a band. It's a singer. Sam Dean. The band backs him up. He's pretty popular."

Caesar ran his hands through his hair, pulling it off his face and out of his eyes. "He's got a helluva guitarist."

Melanie watched the guitarist playing behind the soulful singer. He was facing the rest of the musicians, his back to the audience. When he turned around, she gasped. "Is that..."

A wide smile stretched broadly across his face. "It's Rhett."

Suddenly, she was chilled to the bone. Shivering, she began to wheeze. *A panic attack.* She hadn't had one in years. Not since she'd come to Atlanta. But today's events were too overwhelming. This was one mystery...one coincidence too many. She felt suffocated by bodies with no way out and with the air getting thinner.

"Are you alright?"

She opened her mouth, but no words emerged. She shook her head. Caesar kissed her forehead, grabbed her arm, and led her out of the crowd. As the crowd was thinning out, she felt lightheaded. Everything went black as the ground hit her in the head.

When she came to, she was lying on a cot, her mouth covered with an oxygen mask. *Where's Caesar?* She looked around. She was in the first aid tent. Alarmed, she began to breath heavily.

"Calm down." A woman in scrubs patted her arm. Her name tag said she was a nurse named Jane. "You're fine. Just a fainting spell. Probably got overheated."

Overheated? No. That wasn't it. She'd seen Rhett and panicked. The enormity of all that had transpired over the last few days had rattled her.

She pulled the mask from her face. "I need to find my...my friend."

"No one was with you when they brought you here."

Melanie started to sit up. *Where can he be?*

Jane shook her head and placed a gentle hand on her back. "You need to lie back down and rest some more."

"I have to find him!"

"Your purse is here. Do you have a phone? You can call or text him and have him meet you here."

She sighed heavily. "He didn't have his phone with him today."

The nurse handed her a bottle of water with electrolytes. "At least drink this before you try to find him."

Melanie sat up to drink it. She needed time to think anyway. *Where would Caesar go?* Maybe back to Tim's truck. Or perhaps he was trying to see Rhett. *Or maybe none of this had really happened.* Maybe it was her imagination. She'd come with Lori and Kristy. Maybe she'd gotten overheated and passed out. Perhaps she'd dreamed it all. No. She'd seen Caesar at the store two days ago. *And these are not the clothes I was wearing earlier when I came to the festival.*

"Hello, are you feeling better?"

Melanie nearly spit the water out of her mouth. She swallowed hard instead. "Rhett Star?"

"You've heard of me? That's comforting to know."

Rhett was classically handsome. An Irishman with reddish blond hair and green eyes. He was more conservative looking now than he'd been when he played with Lush. He still wore a ripped t-shirt, jeans, and steel-toed boots. But his hair was shorter, and if he were wearing a suit, he'd look like a banker.

"Of course, I've heard of you. Lush was my favorite band. I'm Melanie."

"Then you have my apologies."

"What for?"

"For not keeping an eye on Johnnie and Caesar."

"It wasn't your fault. Things happened."

Rhett sat down on the end of the cot. "We knew those two were up to no good. They'd been arguing all day. We shouldn't have left them alone."

"Caesar doesn't blame you."

"That's sweet of you to say. Not a day goes by that I don't wish he was still here. Such a talent. Playing with Lush...those were the best days of my life. I still see Kurt on a regular basis, but Johnnie...he seems to drift around too much for anyone to pin down."

Melanie heard the melancholy in his voice, and it pained her. "You seem to be doing well."

"It pays the bills. But Sam Dean is *so* young. His crew is already out partying. Not my scene anymore. I thought I'd come see anyone that might have gotten sick or injured. Try and pep them up a bit."

"That's sweet of you."

"My mum always wanted me to be a doctor." He smiled. "Guess it's a good compromise."

"Well, as a fan, I can say there were many times your music made me feel better."

"Ahh. I like you." He stood again. "I'm going to talk to a few more patients. Take care of yourself."

Melanie stood up, too. She felt woozy and stumbled.

Rhett held her arms. "Are you sure you're well enough to get up."

"I'm fine." She smiled.

Rhett sniffed the air, then moved in closer. He pulled her arm up to his face, pressing his nose against it. He then ran it all the way up to her neck. His fingers went into her hair, and he sniffed that as well. He stared at her, shock on his face.

Who knows what I fell into when I fainted. "What is it?"

"Caesar." He pressed her palm to his face. "His scent is all over you."

She put her other hand close to her nose and inhaled. *Vanilla.* "Perhaps my perfume is like something he wore."

"What perfume is it?"

Oh crap! "I don't remember. My mom gave it to me for Christmas last year."

He inhaled again and frowned. "Damn. He bought this vanilla oil when we were in some remote village in Thailand. When he ran out, he flew all the way back to get more. He wore it all the time. Walked around smelling like sugar cookies. I'll never forget that."

"I'm sorry it makes you sad."

"No." He kissed the back of her hand. "It's not you. This week was the anniversary of his death."

"I know." She hung her head.

"I've been thinking about him so much lately. And today…"

"Did something happen?"

He shrugged. "You'll think I'm crazy."

"I promise I won't."

"I thought I saw him. My mind playing tricks on me. I swear the guy looked just like him though. If I'd been closer, I would have run after him just to make sure. Even though I know damn well Caesar's gone."

"I understand. You guys were like brothers."

"And now I meet you, smelling like sugar cookies."

Melanie thought he might cry, so she hugged him tight. At first, he held her, but then he pushed her away, taking a few steps back.

"I'm sorry…it's too much. I haven't smelled that scent in sixteen years. Nothing close to it. It's overwhelming."

"I understand."

He leaned in and kissed her cheek quickly. "Take care of yourself, Melanie. Go home and get some rest."

"I will."

She watched Rhett stop and talk to another patient before she left the emergency tent. The concert was over, but people were milling about. She wanted to be away from everyone, so she could think. *I have to find Caesar. Where would he go? Why would he leave me passed out on the ground?*

She went to where the food trucks had been parked earlier. Most were gone, including Tim's. A rush of cool wind swept around her, and she shivered. *What if he's gone?* Her stomach twisted in knots as she brushed back a tear. *This is ridiculous. How can I be attached to someone so quickly?* Another rush of wind breezed past her. He'd come into her life so suddenly. What if he left it the same way? And without a goodbye. It was crazy, but she couldn't bear the thought.

A stronger wind pushed past her, and thunder rumbled in the distance. A storm was brewing. Maybe he'd gone back to her place. He'd gotten there before on his own. Surely, he could do it again. *Maybe he's at the car waiting.*

But he wasn't. She tried to keep it together as she drove home alone in the dark.

"Caesar!" Melanie burst through the front door. There was no reply. Again, she began to doubt his existence. *A ghost? Am I dreaming? Or just crazy?*

Feeling drained, she entered her bedroom and stripped down to her bra and panties. When she collapsed onto the bed, his scent engulfed her. She rolled over, placing her face against the pillow he'd slept on earlier. She inhaled. He had been there. He *was* real. It had been a long time since a man had brought joy into her life. *And now he's gone.* Unable to hold back any longer, she wept. Was it for Caesar or something more?

Melanie had once been living a full, happy life. A husband and two daughters. Twins. She'd met Logan right after college. Her parents had taken a while to warm up to him. They felt she was settling. Before meeting him, she'd dreamed of moving to California to be a screenwriter. After they married, she worked at a local news station until the twins were born.

Logan worked hard to provide for their family. Because of his stressful job, Melanie had never begrudged him the couple of beers he'd drink before going to bed. Then an accident at work revealed he'd been drinking far more than a couple of beers before bed. When he lost his job, his drinking spiraled out of control.

When her younger brother married, she, Logan, and the girls had traveled to Nashville to attend the wedding. They slept in the morning after to prepare for the long drive home. But Logan had insisted they do some site seeing. He'd appeared sober, well rested, and most of all, happy. The girls who were four at the time were having so much fun that she hadn't had the heart to keep reminding Logan that they needed to head home.

When they finally left Tennessee, it was late afternoon. The girls passed out in the back of the car almost immediately and soon she was napping as well. Somewhere along the way, Logan stopped for gas and bought a few beers as well. Just outside of Atlanta, he'd fallen asleep at the wheel and drove their car into oncoming traffic. Two days later, she'd awaken in a hospital. Her family gone.

I can't think about this. She rubbed her eyes and slid out of bed. In the medicine cabinet, she found sleeping pills she'd been prescribed. She'd used them as a crutch for the first year after the accident. Then with the help of a grief counselor, she'd weaned herself off them. But she always kept some around...just in case. On nights like this when the past came back to haunt her, she'd take one. It was a rare occurrence. Usually, she kept herself busy with work. Keeping busy left her little time to think about the past. But tonight, the past had returned. *Why? Because of Caesar?* Because he'd made her *feel* again...made her heart and her body ache for something she hadn't had in nearly ten years. *Love.* What if it was gone? Again.

She took a pill, chasing it down with water, then crawled back into bed. The tears seemed to be never-ending, but soon she was drifting off to sleep.

Chapter Four

When Melanie's eyes opened again, the room was filled with sunlight. The scent of vanilla enveloped her. Warmth surrounded her. She placed her hand on the arm around her waist, the one holding her tightly. Fingers entwined with hers. *He's back!*

Caesar nuzzled his face against the back of her neck. "Are you finally awake?"

She turned over to face him and ran a hand along the side of his face. Tears welled up once more. "What happened? Where did you go?"

"I'm not sure." His hand drifted through her hair. "When you passed out, all these people surrounded you, trying to help. I felt like I was floating away. I could see what was happening but couldn't reach you or talk to you. I was there, and not there. When I was finally able to come back to you...you were sleeping."

"I thought I'd lost you." She hugged him tightly.

"Never."

"Can you promise me that?" She pulled away, staring into his eyes.

He seemed pained by her question and sat up. The blankets fell from his naked body.

She rose and scooted close to him, placing her head against his back, her arms around his waist.

"I can't, can I?" He turned and cupped her chin. "All I can promise is that I'll do whatever I can to never leave you. And if something like that happens again, I'll do whatever I can to get back to you."

Their lips met. Soft, tender kisses that set her soul and her body on fire.

"I'm scared, Caesar. I'm getting too attached to you already. We just met, and technically you're not even real."

Gently, he pushed her back against the pillows. He kissed her over and over while his hand cupped a breast and kneaded it. He lightly squeezed her nipple until it was hard, then replaced his hand with his mouth. When his hand traveled further down her body, she spread her legs. He caressed her core, lingering on her clit, before slipping two fingers inside of her. She became impossibly wet.

He withdrew the kiss. "You feel very real to me." His fingers came to his mouth. "You taste very real."

"Caesar." She moaned.

"Tell me."

He kissed her neck sending shockwaves through her body. She felt she might cum as he returned his hand to her clit. She pushed it away.

No?" he asked. "You don't want me?"

"I want you inside me."

His hand went back between her thighs.

"No," she protested.

"What do you want?" He laughed. It was a sexy, husky laugh. He knew exactly what he was doing. Making her crazy. Making her beg. His fingers once again found her wet opening. She groaned, writhing beneath him.

"I want your cock inside me."

"Why didn't you say so?" That sweet, charming smile.

He withdrew his hand and covered her with his body, his mouth once again attached itself to hers. When her lips parted, his tongue dove inside her mouth. His cock probed between her legs, then finding her wetness, he slipped inside. He ground his hips slowly into hers, taking his time, making love to her leisurely all the while kissing her, touching her, whispering to her. Telling her that she was beautiful...that she was sexy.

And Melanie felt it. That long-gone thing was returning. Her sexuality. She wanted to be fucked...to be taken. She wanted him to make her scream in ecstasy. But there was something else there, too. An ache in her heart, as it, too, began to reopen and let life back in. Maybe this *was* his purpose.

"You feel so good," he murmured next to her ear.

She wrapped her legs around his hips, those wonderful hips that so sexily danced across countless stages, thrilling so many women. "So do you."

"Tell me what you want. I'll give you anything you desire."

She pushed him away and flipped over. Moving to all fours, she raised her ass.

"That's hot," he told her, positioning himself behind her.

It wasn't his cock he entered her with, but his hot tongue. He fucked her with it, moving it in and out, lapping at her wetness, driving her crazy once again.

"Caesar, please fuck me," she begged.

True to his word, he gave her what she desired, driving his cock into her. She began to slam her body back against his. He grabbed hold of her, stopping her moves, and began to slow the pace down, grinding those hips back into her. He reached around her to touch her clit.

"I'm going to cum." She panted.

"I'm going to cum with you." And he did, groaning as he released himself inside of her.

After another bout of lovemaking, the two of them lay on their sides, facing one another.

"Why do you have sleeping pills?" Caesar softly stroked her arm.

Melanie sighed as she rolled onto her back. "How did you know?"

"I couldn't wake you when I came back. I thought maybe they'd given you something after you passed out. I saw them on your counter and flushed them down the toilet."

"What? Why?"

"You don't need them. They're dangerous."

She turned back to her side. "Not if you use them correctly."

When he rolled to his back, she remembered that Johnnie had overdosed on sleeping pills. He'd been revived, but it had been a close call. Caesar had been the one to find him and get him help just in time.

She lifted herself, looking at him. "I'm sorry. I forgot."

"That was one of the scariest moments of my life, finding him like that."

"You saved his life."

"Not really. In the right place at the right time."

"Yet even after that, you two still continued to take drugs." She frowned.

"We both tried to stop. I didn't want anyone else overdosing. But then I died anyway."

She wanted to tell him about her own loss. Her daughters. But she wasn't ready. No one she worked with knew. Only family and a few close friends back home. Even though she'd gone to the counselor, she'd never wanted to talk to anyone else about it. It was too painful.

"I was so upset when I couldn't find you. I wanted to sleep and forget that I might never see you again."

He kissed her. "I'm sorry I worried you."

"Caesar, I have to be honest. Being with you, even though it's only been a day, has made me very happy. And the sex...I haven't wanted anyone in so long. It's like I'm feeling all these emotions that have been buried for so long."

"I hope that's a good thing." He ran his fingers through her hair. "I only want to make you happy."

"It is good, but it's also scary. I've worked so hard since coming to Atlanta. My job has been my life. I have my parents and my brother, but I don't have friends. Not close ones."

"That's not good."

"I know it isn't. Part of the reason I went to the music festival was to get out and try to be friendly with people I knew from work."

"I'm glad you did."

"Yeah, but they ditched me."

"Wasn't that a good thing? I mean you met me."

She looped one of his curls around a finger. "It was the very best thing. And guess what? Guess who I met tonight."

He shrugged.

"Rhett. He came to the medical tent to say hello to people."

"Did you say anything about me?"

"I didn't have to. He did. He took one whiff of me and said I smelled just like you. I played it off, told him I must have perfume that was similar, but he insisted it was the same as what you wore. He was really freaked out by it."

"Imagine if he'd seen me."

"He did," she told him. "He thinks he did anyway. Said he saw someone at the festival that looked just like you."

"I wish I could have talked to him."

"Me, too. He said he's been thinking about you a lot."

"Maybe it's him I'm supposed to help."

She shook her head. "He seems to have his act together. He was really sweet, too."

"But not as hot as me."

Melanie laughed, picked up a pillow, and hit Caesar over the head. "You're full of yourself sometimes."

"Been told that a few times." He grabbed her and wrestled her down onto the bed. "Mostly by my best friend and your big crush, Johnnie."

"That was a long time ago."

He began tickling her. "What if he were in this room right now? And you had to choose between the two of us?"

She giggled as she pushed his hands away. "Given his history with addiction that would be a no-brainer."

"What if he were sober? Who would you pick?"

"I'd let the two of you have one another and run off with Rhett or Kurt, since they're the ones that don't seem to be in a constant pissing battle with one another."

Caesar fell back against the pillow. He laughed so hard he turned beet red, and tears were streaming down his face.

He's like a big kid. She loved it. "What's so funny?"

He wiped his face. "Kurt won this pissing contest we had once. And I mean a real pissing contest, as in who could piss the farthest."

"You're kidding." She laughed as well. "When was this?"

"Don't remember the year, but it was while we were filming a music video in the outback. We had to drink so much water, which then made us need to pee constantly. So we had a contest, and Kurt beat us all by two feet."

"And I bet Rhett was fine with that, while you and Johnnie kept demanding rematches."

He stopped laughing and stared at her. "How did you know?"

"Super-fan, remember?" She laughed.

"Yes, you're a fan, and you *are* super." He kissed her tenderly.

She turned her gaze away. "As a fan, and now as your friend, I have to know..."

"No...he didn't. It was an accident."

She looked at him again, eyes wide. "But when we met...you said..."

"You rattled me. I had to rattle you."

"You did." She pouted.

"I'm sorry." He kissed her. "It was a terrible thing to say. Johnnie would never hurt me. We were the best of friends."

She snuggled close to him.

"Are we going to contact his parents today?"

"I can contact them from work tomorrow," she said. "Make it a work call. Tell them it's for a story about the band."

"And if they say no?"

"I'll do some more digging." She slid her hand across his chest, caressing him. "I have some connections in the entertainment business, and I can ask around."

He smiled. "What exactly is it that you do?"

"I'm a news writer."

His grimaced. "Sounds dreadful."

"Really? You're a writer, aren't you? You write songs."

"I started out writing poetry. Met Johnnie, and later we met Rhett and Kurt. When we started the band, I turned some of those poems into songs."

"I used to write poems and stories." Melanie sighed. "In school, I loved creative writing. But journalism pays the bills."

He sat up quickly. "I want to read your poetry. Do you still have it?"

"There's a ton of stuff packed away in the attic."

He slid out of bed and took her hand. "We have all day. Let's look."

"You're not hungry?" She sat up and scooted to the edge of the bed. "I thought you might want breakfast."

He opened her legs and knelt between her thighs. "I could eat."

Placing her foot on his shoulder, she gently pushed him. "That's not what I meant."

He fell to the floor in a dramatic fashion. She went to a chest of drawers, pulled it open, and withdrew a pair of sweatpants. He was a few inches taller than her, but leaner, so they would fit him.

She stood over him and dropped them. "Put these on."

He pushed his bottom lip out. "You don't like me naked?"

"I like you too much naked." She pulled on a maxi length, knit nightie. "It's distracting."

Caesar came up the folding ladder behind her and poked his head into the attic. He handed her a basket that she'd filled with fresh fruit, cream cheese, and bagels. There were two bottles of water in it as well. He climbed into the space and looked around. "You were right. There's a lot of boxes up here."

"I should get better at throwing things away." She went straight to some boxes stacked in a corner. "All my stuff from high school is in these."

He pulled the top one down and opened it. As she spread a blanket on the ground for them to sit on, he took out the contents. Inside were her journals from when she was a teen and notebooks full of poetry and story ideas. He sat down and flipped through a notebook. She sat across from him, took the food out of the basket, and placed it on the blanket. Then, she grabbed an old diary.

"I can't believe I wrote this." She laughed as she read an entry about a boy she was crazy for back in seventh grade.

Caesar was silent, reading intently. When he finally looked up at her, he appeared surprised, his eyes full of wonder. "This is good stuff, Melanie."

She scooted closer to him. "What is it?"

"A story about a guy who wants to be a rock star." He handed the notebook to her, then grabbed another for himself. He flipped through those pages, stopping to read a page here and there. "I don't understand why you never pursued this. You're a fantastic writer."

She shuddered. *Should I tell him?*

He must have sensed her hesitation. "So, what happened?"

I'm not ready. I need to know he's sticking around. "Life. I got sidetracked with other things. I moved to Atlanta because the job writing news was too good to pass up."

"But you could be writing novels in your spare time."

She sighed deeply. "I always wanted to be a novelist...or a screenwriter."

"Then why aren't you?" He opened a bottle of water and sipped.

She spread some cream cheese on a bagel and held it up to his mouth. "I don't know. I guess I got caught up in my career...climbing the ladder...making my mark."

"Is writing news what you want to do forever?" He took a bite of the bagel.

"I still dream of moving to California and writing for television or the movies."

He kissed her forehead. "Let's do it then."

"You make it sound so easy."

"It is." He grinned.

"Maybe you can whizz around the world and go where you want, but I can't."

"Why not? If you want something bad enough, you find a way to make it happen. When the guys and I first got together, we were broke. We traveled all over the States in a beat-up old van, playing any gig we could get. It was tough to get by sometimes, but those were the best days."

Melanie rubbed the scar over his left eye. It went into his eyebrow leaving a trail of hairless skin. "I bet it was amazing."

"Don't give up your dream. If you want to go to California, I'll help you."

"Are you going to rob a bank? California is expensive."

"You forget I have money."

"*Had* money."

He frowned, and she felt awful for reminding him that he was no longer alive. He rubbed his bare chest before resting his hand over his heart. She took his other hand, turning it over and caressing his palm. He seemed so real. So alive. Lightly, she stroked his wrist where his pulse should have been. But there was nothing.

He snatched his hand from her.

"I'm sorry." She moved her hands through his hair, unraveling one bouncy curl. "When I stop and think about it, I don't know how to feel. It's so strange."

"Then don't think about it." He pulled her closer, wrapping his arms around her. "I only want us to experience happiness together. Nothing else matters when I'm with you. Please tell me you feel the same."

She gazed into his dark eyes and felt herself falling deeper under his spell. His heart might not be beating, but his soul was alive in those eyes. Everything about him was there. His essence lay in those eyes. Her heart was beating wildly as she pressed her lips softly against his.

"Do you?" he asked.

"Yes."

His lips went to hers and then moved to her neck and shoulders.

"Do I make you happy?"

She smiled. "Very happy."

"I get the feeling you haven't had much happiness in your life. At least not for a while." He picked up one of the spiral notebooks. "You haven't been true to yourself. This is what your soul wants. This is your dream."

"It wouldn't be easy."

"Nothing worth having is." He lay down and pulled her on top of him. "I believe I still have money. You can have it. All of it. My house in California, too."

She moved and lay next to him. "Caesar, when you died, I'm sure everything went to your family."

"And my friends."

"You had a will?"

He took her hand. "I did."

"Then your things were given to whomever you left them with."

Again, he escaped into his thoughts. "I hid some money away. In a secret place at my beach house. If no one found it…"

"It's been a long time. The house might have been sold."

"No." He squeezed her hand. "I left my two homes to Johnnie. There's one in London, too."

"If his drinking and drug use got worse after your death, then who knows what he might have done with the properties."

He rolled to his side. "I knew about his problems when I wrote my will. I specifically said he could have the houses and everything in them. But he couldn't sell anything. I wanted him to have a place to live, even if he lost everything. He did the same for me in his will."

"So, your house is still there." She rolled to face him. "Johnnie probably is, too. And by now he's probably found any money you hid away."

"It was in a small safe, under the floorboards beneath my bed. He didn't know about it. No one did."

"Someone could have found it by now."

He moved in closer, brushing another kiss against her lips. "There's only one way to find out."

"What? You want me to go to California and find your hidden money?"

"Yes." He chuckled. "Let's do it. Together."

"Am I supposed to break into the house?" She sat up and took a drink of water.

"You forget that I can get into places pretty easily."

"And if Johnnie is living there?"

"Maybe he'll be able to see me." Caesar sat up and smiled.

"And if he can't?"

Gently, he caressed her face. "You're a beautiful woman. He gets one look at you, and he'll let you in."

"So, I waltz in and tell him the ghost of his best friend sent me to look for hidden money?"

"Why not?" Caesar shrugged. "Knowing Johnnie, he'd get a kick out of it. And he might be able to use some of the money as well."

She dipped into quiet thoughts. *What if the money is still there?* Was she ready to move cross-country and begin a new life? There was a reason she'd chosen to live in Atlanta. Her children had died here. The life she'd once known had died here, and she'd begun a new one. Was she ready to leave it behind? She knew no one in Los Angeles. *I don't know anyone here either.*

"What do you think?" He lay back down.

She laid back down as well. "I think you're crazy."

He cuddled her, pressing kisses all over her face. "Crazy about you."

He doesn't even know me. And what did she know about him? Only what had been in the press back when he was alive. He was a free spirit, wild at heart, full of life and love. And he'd given away a lot of love back in the day. He'd had several high-profile romances with actresses, models, and fellow singers. All of them beautiful and glamorous. *And what am I? No one. Plain and ordinary.*

He was nibbling on her neck and suddenly stopped. "What is it? You're quiet."

"Thinking."

"About..." He slid the strap of her nightie down and ran his tongue along her shoulder blade and collarbone.

"Do you fall in love easily?"

He propped himself on his elbow. "Are we talking about love now?"

"I don't mean you and me." Her face warmed. "It's just that you've had quite a few hot and heavy romances."

He ran a finger across her bottom lip. "There's no need for you to be jealous."

"Not jealous. More like insecure. They were beautiful women."

"As you are."

She smiled. "You really *are* crazy."

"And you're crazy to think you aren't just as good as them."

"You could probably visit them."

"Why would I want to?" he asked.

"The one you were dating when you died. The model. Shelise. You two seemed to be so in love."

"The only place I want to be is with you."

"I know." She sighed. "I'm your mission."

"You are so much more than that." His hand gripped the back of her neck. "From the moment I saw you, I wanted you."

She rolled her eyes. "I must have been so sexy, trying to choose a toothpaste."

"That wasn't the first time I saw you. Remember, I followed you for a couple of days. Although it wasn't much following. You went to work and home, so I only saw you get in and out of your car. I was thrilled when you stopped to go shopping. I finally had the chance to talk to you."

"And put your moves on me?"

His brow furrowed. "Now that I think about it, maybe I'm the one who should feel insecure. You wanted nothing to do with me."

"Come on, look at you. You're gorgeous. Millions of women would agree with me."

"And yet there's only one I give a damn about." His lips touched hers, then he ran a soft hand along her cheekbone. "Your skin is flawless, and I could stare into these blue eyes forever."

He lifted himself up and over her, pulling down the other strap of her nightie, exposing her bare chest. He rubbed one nipple gently while he took the other in his mouth. Warmth flowed through her veins, creating that increasingly familiar need to fuck him.

"You have fantastic breasts. Your nipples are a beautiful shade of rose."

She could only stare at him as his hands and eyes traveled over her body. He tugged the nightie down to her thighs. His lips left a trail of kisses from her breasts to her belly. Then he ran his tongue down her side to where her waist nipped in and her hips curved outward.

"I love your curves," he continued, pushing her nightie further down. She bent her legs slightly, and he slipped it off.

She moaned as he pressed kisses from her calves up to her thighs. He teased her there, and she became desperate for release from the desire that was eating her up.

"I love your pussy," he purred before running his tongue from the bottom to top of it. When she whimpered, he repeated his lapping a few more times. Then he pushed the sweatpants down over his hips, freeing his hard cock. He crawled back over her, hovering, staring into her eyes. "You know why?"

"No," she answered softly.

With ease, he slid two fingers inside her. "Because it gets so wet for me. Because it wants me. Because *you* want me so bad. Don't you?"

"Yes." She raised her hips to meet his fingers as they slid in and out of her wetness.

He replaced his fingers with the head of his cock. Little by little, he slipped inside and filled her. "You feel so good. We're a perfect fit, don't you think?"

Instead of answering, she pulled his head down to hers and devoured his mouth with her own.

"Fuck me," she managed to say between kisses. As he pumped harder, she once again raised her hips, meeting each of his thrusts.

He took her hands in his and raised them above her head. He began to slow his pace, grinding into her slowly, sensually. "You *are* beautiful. Don't ever doubt it."

And she felt it. Her beauty. Her sensuality. Caesar *made* her feel it. They rolled over, and it was her turn to grind herself on him. She gazed into his eyes as she rode him. Cupping a breast, she squeezed a nipple into a hard bud. Her other hand went into her hair.

"You're incredibly sexy." He moaned.

When she slipped off him, he pouted. She stood and beckoned him with her finger to follow. He smiled slyly before doing so. She leaned against a wall and moved her hair to one side. He came up behind her, kissing her neck, sliding his cock back into her wet walls.

"Make me cum," she murmured.

His hand went around her hip, parted her folds, and began touching her clit.

"How's this?"

"Oh, Caesar, yes." Her body began to tighten around him. He picked up his pace, pushing her over the edge.

He held her close as her body shivered with orgasmic tremors. "Should I cum now?"

"No." She pulled away, turned, and knelt.

"Mmm, Melanie." His hands wrapped in her hair as her mouth went to his cock.

"I want you to cum in my mouth," she told him. She cupped his balls gently in her hands as her mouth slid up and down the length of him.

"I plan to." He bit his thick bottom lip, groaned, and released himself.

Chapter Five

"You seem happy today," Susan Greene, Melanie's supervisor, noted as the two women passed in the hallway.

"Do I?" She *was* happy. After their early afternoon lovemaking session, she and Caesar had walked around the park together and visited the zoo. Then they'd gone grocery shopping, so she could prepare a big Sunday meal. She hadn't cooked like that in ages. Over dinner, they once again discussed her moving to California or at least traveling there to see if she could find Caesar's hidden treasure. She could use the money to get her own place, they'd decided. She'd agreed to ask for time off, so they could go on their adventure.

"Yes," Susan told her. "Perhaps you should take days off more often. You're glowing."

She smiled. "I did have a great weekend. And actually, I'd like to speak with you about taking more days off."

"Let's go to my office."

Melanie followed her down the hallway. As Susan shut the door behind them, Melanie took a seat.

"So, you'd like more time off?" Susan asked, as she sat down across from Melanie.

Melanie felt guilty. She'd never requested special days off, even though it was something granted to her in her benefits package.

"I do have vacation time saved up."

Susan nodded and laughed. "That's an understatement. I mean, I appreciate the hard work you put into your job, but you've never actually taken a vacation, have you?"

Melanie shook her head. "A few days here and there. To visit my family in Florida."

"Please thank *him* for me."

"Thank who?" she asked, puzzled.

"The man who finally turned your head away from work."

"What do you mean?" Her cheeks burned hot.

"I know the look." Susan leaned forward in her chair. "You're head over heels for someone. In the eight years you've worked here, I've never seen you smile as much as you have this morning."

"It's that obvious?" Melanie stared into her lap.

The older woman tapped her hand lightly against the desk in front of Melanie. "Don't be ashamed. You're a grown woman. You're allowed to enjoy time with a man. And if he wants to whisk you away on a little vacation, then go for it. Believe it or not, there are people around here who will step up and fill in for you just as you've done for them."

Melanie looked up again. "Thank you."

"Where are the two of you going?"

Melanie laughed softly. "You should know, it's always been my dream to live on the west coast and write screenplays, maybe even novels."

Susan appeared surprised. "I've known you all this time, and you've never told me."

"I sort of lost track of my dreams."

"People tend to do that."

"I'm going to L.A. to look at property there and in the surrounding areas as well."

"And *he* put you up to this?"

"Yes, he encouraged me."

Susan smiled. "A man who wants you to pursue your dreams? Sounds perfect."

"He is." She sighed, dreamily. *Well, except that he's dead.*

"When you get things sorted out and know the dates, just let H.R. know. I promise you, it won't be a problem."

"I will. Thank you."

Melanie stared at the phone number on her notepad. Being a member of the press meant the information hadn't been hard to come by, but she felt hesitant about calling Johnnie's parents. Did she want to disrupt their lives with talk of the band? Surely, it was a sore subject. *Unless.* Maybe Johnnie was clean. Perhaps he was living a normal life as Johnathan Smith, working in a music store or teaching kids to play drums. And if he was in Atlanta, she wouldn't feel as nervous about going to Caesar's place to look for the money.

She rubbed her forehead. It was too easy not to answer a phone. Everyone had caller ID these days. An unfamiliar number meant she'd probably be leaving a message to strangers who would most likely not return her call. But she had to try. *For Caesar.*

A man's voice was on the message. Charles Smith. Johnnie's father.

"Excuse me for calling you, Mr. Smith. My name is Melanie Davis, and I work for Citizen's Network News. I'm calling to see if you'd be willing to speak with me about your son. I'm planning a piece on Lush, and I'm trying to locate him. I know it's a painful subject, but if you're willing to speak with me, please call me."

She left her number and hung up, hoping she'd get a call before her workday ended. She wondered what Caesar was doing. He'd wanted to come to work with her, but she'd convinced him that would be a fiasco. Some people might see him, while others wouldn't be able to. And how could she get any work done with him around? She'd left her laptop with him and taught him how to stream movies on the television. *Hopefully, that keeps him busy.*

A little after noon, she opened her lunch tote. She found a note inside.

What will I do all day without you? Perhaps I'll lie in bed, thinking of you and wishing I was inside you. Please hurry home so I can taste you. So, I can make love to you again. And again.

As she read the words, she felt an ache between her thighs. It was the pain of him not being between them. *Two days and I'm crazy about this man.*

Suddenly, her lunch of leftovers seemed bland. And her small office seemed smaller than ever. She decided to go out for lunch, something she rarely did. But she needed to get out. To breathe in the fresh air. To feel alive.

She passed by Susan's office as she was leaving. "I'm going out for lunch. Would you like me to pick you up something?"

"You're going out? I'm liking this man more and more."

"I'm not meeting him. I just need fresh air."

Susan crossed her arms in front of her as she leaned back in her chair. "If I didn't know any better, I'd say you were in love."

Melanie felt her embarrassment return. She'd not talked like this with anyone at work before, let alone her boss. She kept her private life to herself. And why not? She didn't have a private life. Until Caesar, what had her life been? Working nearly every day, coming home, taking walks in the park, watching movies alone. Well, all that was about to change.

"I don't need anything." Susan waved her off. "Enjoy your lunch."

"Thank you."

Melanie found a nearby diner which specialized in healthy fare. She ordered a fruit smoothie with extra protein added. Then she took a walk, window shopping, as she sipped her drink.

She stopped in her tracks when a beautiful vintage style dress caught her eye. She knew the deep red color was Caesar's favorite and wondered how she would look in it. *Only one way to find out.*

"You put a push-up bra on, and you'll have every man fawning over you," the sales associate told Melanie. "That dress is fabulous on you."

"Are you sure?" She twirled in front of the mirror. "I've never worn this style before."

"You should wear it more often. It looks great on women with your curves and small waist."

Melanie smiled as she thought about Caesar's reaction. The dress really did hug her in all the right places.

"I'll take it," she told the saleswoman. "Do you have push-up bras?"

"Of course. We have a full line of lingerie."

She walked out with two new bras with matching panties as well as the dress. She'd spent nearly four hundred dollars but felt no guilt. She worked hard, and she rarely spent money on new clothes that weren't for work. *I deserve this.* And besides, she couldn't wait to see Caesar's reaction to the dress and what would be waiting for him underneath.

It was nearing five o'clock when her cell phone rang. She saw the number and quickly returned to her office for privacy.

"Mr. Smith. Thank you so much for calling me back."

"Normally I wouldn't have, but you sounded polite in your message. I thought I should at least call and tell you that we're not interested in doing any interviews."

"I'm sorry to hear that. But I could do the story without interviewing you. I've been trying to locate Johnnie, and it hasn't been going well. I spoke to Rhett on Saturday, and even he didn't know how to reach Johnnie."

"I can't help with that either. He lived with us for a while, but that was years ago. Since then he's been in and out of our lives, so it's difficult to keep track. The last time we heard from him was a few months ago. He was in London then."

Melanie sighed. "I'm sorry to hear that."

"Yes, I suppose it doesn't help you get your story."

Is that rudeness in his voice? "It's not about that, Mr. Smith. I was a big fan of the band when I was in high school and college. The story is not that important. It would be enough to know he's alright. I know he took Caesar's death very hard."

"His problems with drugs and alcohol started before then." Mr. Smith sounded bitter.

"I was hoping you'd tell me that he put that behind him."

"I wish I could. But as far as I know, he hasn't."

"Mr. Smith, I do appreciate you calling me back."

"If you find out anything will you call me? It would make his mother happy."

But not you? "Of course."

After hanging up, Melanie felt sad. She'd have nothing useful to tell Caesar about his friend, and she knew he would be disappointed. Caesar's purpose for being there still wasn't clear. Perhaps he *had* been sent to give her a sex life. She smiled at the thought.

Goosebumps dotted Melanie's skin as she unlocked her front door. It had been a productive day at work, but the thrill she felt now, coming home, knowing Caesar would be waiting for her, was powerful. She couldn't wait to put on her sexy new things and give him a show.

"Caesar?" she called out when she didn't find him in the living room or kitchen. She walked back to the bedroom and saw that the attic's ladder was down.

"Are you up there?" she asked, standing at the bottom rung. When she received no answer, she climbed up.

Yesterday, they'd only opened a couple of boxes. The ones with her journals and notebooks, mementos from her high school years. Now all the boxes were open. Her cry of distress caught in her throat as she saw what he'd pulled out. A photo album turned to pictures of the family she'd lost. The girls' stuffed animals and favorite toys were scattered around, along with their clothing.

Sitting in the middle of all these heartbreaking reminders of her former life was Caesar. In one hand a photo of the girls, in the other a teddy bear. When his gaze met hers, she saw that his eyes were red and swollen.

"Why didn't you tell me?" His voice was barely a whisper as he choked back tears.

Melanie couldn't find the words. Her chest heaved up and down. These memories were never meant to be unpacked. They were to stay locked away forever. Why had he let them out? Frantic, she grabbed a box and stuffed toys into it.

His voice grew louder. "You had two children. Why didn't you tell me?"

She ignored him. *I have to box it up again.* All the pain. All the sadness.

Caesar scrambled to his feet and grabbed her arm. "Melanie?"

She yanked free and—in a frenzy—kept packing. *These* ghosts had to be put away.

Her agitation caused him to take a step back. "I was bored. I thought I might find more of your writing. But instead, I found all these kid's things and the photos. Why didn't you tell me?"

She narrowed her eyes, her face hot with anger.

He reached out and stroked her cheek. "I saw the death notices. The newspaper clippings about the accident."

"Shut up!" She dropped the box and covered her ears.

He tugged her hands down. "Melanie, please talk to me."

Tears streamed down her face. *Why is he doing this? We're supposed to be happy. Not thinking about the past.*

"This is why you quit living."

Furious, she kicked an empty box across the floor. "You know nothing about me!"

"I know you work too much. Your social life is nonexistent." He rubbed her shoulders. "Tell me, before I showed up...when was the last time you had sex? Or a relationship of any kind?"

She walked away, refusing to answer him.

"Now I know why I was sent here. To bring you back to life. To help you let go of this."

She whirled around. "You want me to forget my children?"

"You'll never forget them, but you've got to move on. You're hiding all their things up here, but you carry it with you...in your heart...in your mind. It's always there. You're so full of grief that you can't embrace life."

She ignored him and returned to packing the clothes and toys back into their boxes.

"Have you forgiven your husband?"

Her gaze met his again. *Forgive Logan? Is he crazy?* "He's dead. And because of him, they are, too."

"You're eaten up with anger...guilt...grief. You need help."

Hadn't her parents been telling her the same thing for years? She'd sought out counseling right after the accident but eventually stopped going. Then, she'd moved to Atlanta. She felt closer to them here. Even though they were buried in Jacksonville, this is where they died.

"I saw a psychologist for over a year. I'm fine."

He picked up a box of toys. "Good. Then we're going to take the next step and get rid of these things. We'll donate them to other children."

"Are you out of your mind?" She tried to take the box from him, but he held tight. "Put it down. You will not touch *my* things."

"Things...Melanie...things." He held up a doll. "Keep the photo albums, a few special items like first shoes, but everything else must go."

"Everything stays!" She snatched the doll. "Except you. You can go!"

His mouth dropped, and genuine horror filled his eyes. "What?"

"You heard me. I want you to go away. You're not real."

He grabbed the back of her head and kissed her hard. Feverishly, she returned his kisses before coming to her senses and pushing him away.

"That didn't feel real to you?"

She placed a hand on his heart. No pulse, no beating. "You're not alive. This cannot continue."

"I'm here to help you. To love you."

"If you wanted to help...if you truly loved me...you'd bring *them* to me."

"If I could...I would."

"Bullshit!" She struck him in the chest with a closed fist. "I need them...not you!"

He enveloped her in his arms. "You need me more than you know."

His vanilla scent made her burn for him. She struggled to get away, but he held her tightly. "Let go of me."

"Not until you calm down."

She rested against him, giving him what he wanted, feigning calmness but inside still seething with anger...with pain. Finally, he let her go. She backed away then stomped down the ladder.

He followed her. "Where are you going?"

She wanted to scream. *How can I get rid of him? How do you make a ghost leave?* She went to the kitchen, opened a drawer, and took out a butcher knife.

His eyes went wide. "Melanie, what are you doing?"

She plunged the knife into his shoulder. He appeared stunned by her actions and even more shocked when she pulled the knife out. *No blood. No open wound.* His skin was as smooth and enticing as always. Next, she grabbed the scissors. While he was still rubbing where she'd stabbed him, she grabbed a lock of his hair and cut it. The thick, curled piece tumbled to the ground, but the hair left behind replaced itself perfectly as if no damage had ever been done.

"You're not real. And you need to go."

He pulled her close again. "What I'm feeling is real. And I know you feel it, too. When we make love..."

"Caesar, shut up and go. I don't want to see you ever again. I don't need this! You're dead, and you need to stay that way."

He backed away, clearly in pain, hurt by her words. "I love you."

"Go away!" she shrieked.

His bottom lip shook, and tears slid down his beautiful face. "You don't mean it."

"Go!"

He reached out, and she closed her eyes as a gentle hand caressed her cheek. Then his touch was gone. Her eyes flew open. She searched every room, but she knew. He was gone. In the kitchen, she picked up the lock of hair. As she walked to her sofa, she held it to her nose. Sugar cookies. Everything warm and sweet. That was Caesar. But he was no more. She collapsed on the sofa and sobbed.

Three days later, she was still on the couch, intermittently crying when she wasn't sleeping. She hadn't gone to work or even called in. She'd done nothing but wallow in misery. *Time to stop.* Somehow, she had to find a reason to keep going, just as she had done when she'd lost her family.

She sat up and stretched. Her muscles ached. *He's not worth all this pain. He's not real.* Her eyes were drawn to his hair lying on the coffee table. She pressed its silky softness against her cheek, remembering how his curls would dance across her face when they made love. *He was real. And he was everything.* He'd been sent to help her, and she'd pushed him away when he'd tried to complete his mission.

"I have to complete it for him," she said aloud. "I can't live like this anymore."

First things first, she needed a shower. Looking in her bathroom mirror, she was horrified. Her hair was a mess, her face swollen and red. She turned on the water, stripped off her clothes, and stepped in. Instantly, her mind filled with the memory of Caesar surprising her in the shower. She closed her eyes, dipped her head under the water, and remembered his hands in her hair, lovingly washing it for her. She'd give anything to feel his hands on her again.

But she didn't.

She washed up, dried her hair, then dressed. When she retrieved her phone to call Susan, she found the dress she'd bought, along with the lingerie lying next to her purse where she'd left them. Maybe she could return them. *Why should I?* They made her feel good, and she looked good in them. Someday she might have the opportunity to wear them. She took the items to her room and put them away. *Someday.*

"Melanie, where have you been? We've been worried sick about you." Susan sounded relieved.

"It's a long story."

"Does it have something to do with this new man of yours?" Susan asked.

"It's more than that. Can I meet with you in person to discuss it?"

"It's almost lunchtime. Care to meet for lunch?"
"Yes, I can leave now."

"I remember covering that story." Susan frowned. "It was a terrible tragedy."

Melanie squeezed her eyes closed, willing herself not to cry. Susan was the first person outside her family and grief counselor she'd talked to in detail about the accident. But she had to make Susan understand why she'd sunk into such despair.

"I came here to be closer to where they'd died. But once here, I didn't deal with my grief. I threw myself into work and pushed all those sad thoughts away. When he opened those boxes, he reopened all those old wounds."

Susan reached over and patted her hand. "I can't even imagine what you've gone through. Surely he understands why you were so upset."

"It doesn't matter. I told him that I didn't want to see him again."

"Call him and work it out. From what little I know, he seems like a remarkable person."

"He is." Melanie sighed and took a sip of iced tea. "It's better that it ended. I'm going to move to Los Angeles."

"Now?"

"It's why I wanted to meet with you. To put in my notice."

"Listen." Susan shook her head. "Don't be too hasty. Why don't you take the time off you wanted? Go to California and see if it's really what you want. You'll have time to find a place to live and look for employment. But if it doesn't work out, you can come back, and your job will be here."

A tear slid down Melanie's left cheek. "That's so generous. Thank you."

"No. Thank you. You've busted your ass for me the last eight years. It's the least I can do."

Melanie nodded and wiped at her tears.

The waiter came, and Susan asked for the check. "It's on me. To celebrate your new adventure."

Melanie smiled and thanked her again.

Susan opened her wallet and handed Melanie a business card. "This is the salon I use. Before you leave, I want you to pamper yourself. Get a new haircut, a manicure, pedicure, facial...the works! You'll arrive in California feeling like a million bucks."

"That sounds wonderful."

Melanie arrived home a few hours later. After squaring away her vacation with Human Resources, she'd called a realtor to see about putting her condo on the market. The realtor assured her that the property was highly desirable and would sell in no time. Melanie was glad. She would use the profit from the sale to buy something in the Los Angeles area. She'd also made her salon appointment for the next day.

After changing into comfortable clothes, she stood at the bottom of the ladder leading to the attic. Taking a deep breath, she climbed up. She was surprised to find everything organized. All the twin's belongings were once again packed away. The boxes were all stacked in one corner by themselves, separate from all the others. Only one person could have done this.

An envelope sat on the floor in front of the boxes. With trembling hands, she picked it up and slipped the letter from the envelope.

I've separated everything. What you should keep is in the box with the hearts. Everything else should go. Don't hate me for doing this. I only want to help. Melanie, you've mourned long enough. It's time to move on and live the life you're meant to have. My house is yours. The address is 2532 Beach Road. You'll love it. It's right off the Pacific Coast Highway near Malibu. You'll be on my private beach with plenty of peace and quiet to write. My spare keys are inside a dragon statue that stands in the succulent garden. Don't forget the money. If the bed has been moved, find the floorboard with my initials carved into it. The combination to the safe is 4-29-18. It's all yours, Melanie. If Johnnie has taken up residence, tell him I said hello and that he's not responsible for my death. I'm sorry for hurting you. I only wanted to love you. Two days was not enough time to give you all the love you deserve. If there's ever a chance I can come back to you, I will.

Eternally yours,
Caesar

Hearts. He'd drawn two, like a Venn diagram, interconnecting. Opening the box, she found her photo albums. Also inside, were the clothes the girls had worn home from the hospital after they were born. Their first shoes were there, as well as their favorite books. The blankets and the stuffed animals they took to bed with them each night were also there. The things he'd chosen all had special meaning. *How did he know?* She picked up the box and carried it to the pile with her other belongings. She didn't bother with the other boxes. The other clothes and toys she would donate, just as Caesar had suggested.

Back downstairs, Caesar's letter in hand, she retrieved her laptop. She typed in the address of his house. Shocked, she leaned back on the sofa. *Oh wow!* It was gorgeous. Large glass windows were facing the ocean. A deck built across the back of the house. A jacuzzi. Four bedrooms, three bathrooms, private beach access. In one image, Caesar appeared. He was standing against the railing of the deck, his hand raised, lifting a drink. He seemed to be smiling right at her, toasting her.

"Thank you, Caesar." She smiled at his photo. "For giving me life again."

Chapter Six

"Do you have the security code to get in, Ma'am?" the cab driver asked her.

Melanie stared at the large wrought iron gate and groaned. *Did I fly cross-country for nothing?* Caesar hadn't mentioned a gate or a code. She removed his letter from her purse. Maybe she could try the safe's combination. When she opened it, something immediately caught her eye. At the bottom were two numbers. Next to one, it read gate, the other read alarm. The hair on her arms stood on end. *These weren't here before.*

"I've got it." She reached her arm out of the window and pressed the code into the system. Luckily, Johnnie hadn't changed it, and the gate slowly opened.

"Leave all the bags at the front door." She stepped out of the cab. "I'll get everything in on my own."

"Are you sure?"

"I'll be fine." She stared in awe at the two-story house. She could hear the crashing surf nearby.

"Make sure you lock the gate behind me."

She snapped back to reality. "Yes. Thank you for reminding me."

When the driver left, she searched for the succulent garden. The lawn and the plants all appeared to be overgrown and in need of maintenance. Perhaps that meant Johnnie hadn't been there in a while. She easily found the dragon statue. She'd been expecting something small, but this was about three feet tall. She searched the yard to see if she could locate another, but this was the only one. She pushed it over, looking for an opening but found none. There was something inside rattling around. *No wonder he was so sure the keys would still be here.*

"How am I supposed to open this?" she muttered. She bent and picked it up. It weighed about twenty pounds. *Sorry, Caesar.* She hurled it toward the concrete walkway. It broke into a few large chunks. And there were the keys. A couple of them. And something else.

"You've got to be kidding." She pushed the garage door opener. Inside the garage, Caesar's *Mercedes* and his motorcycle, a *Triumph Classic.*

Immediately, she jumped into the *Mercedes* and tried to start it up. It was dead. No telling how long it had been sitting here unused. She got out and locked the doors behind her. More proof Johnnie wasn't around.

"Maybe I won't have to get my own place. I'll stay here." She squealed and happily danced all the way back to the front door.

Her elation jumped another level once she pushed the front door open. The musty smell couldn't detract from the house's beauty. The floors and walls of the living room were made of wood giving the place a rustic feel. The huge fireplace was made of slate. The kitchen had marble countertops and ceramic tile floors. Her favorite part was the deck facing the ocean. The view was stunning. Caesar was right. This would be a great place to write.

Next, she darted upstairs, wanting to see Caesar's room. Without even thinking, she flipped on the lights and walked into the huge master bedroom. Suddenly, she stopped in her tracks realizing for the first time that the electricity was on in the house. Not to mention the security system was up and running as well. *Who pays the bills?*

She ran her finger across the chest of drawers and left a trail in the layer of dust that had obviously been accumulating for some time. If Johnnie lived here, he hadn't cared to keep it clean.

As she approached Caesar's closet, she trembled with anticipation. *Will his clothes still be here?* She slid the door open and instantly caught a whiff of vanilla. Not fresh and clean like Caesar, but a staler odor that had been sitting around for a while. Grabbing a white button-down shirt, she pressed her nose against the cotton fabric and inhaled. The vanilla scent was on everything. These were his clothes. She began rifling through the closet, checking out every item.

"Unbelievable." She held up a Jimi Hendrix t-shirt. *Is this the one Tim sold him years ago?* It had to be. Caesar said he still owned it when he died. She decided to mail it back to Tim. Surely, he would appreciate the sentiment.

She also made up her mind that Caesar's room would now be hers.

On the way to retrieve her bags, she stopped in the kitchen and opened the refrigerator. Even though it was running, there was nothing inside except bottles of beer. *Okay, maybe Johnnie has been here.* She smiled. There was some canned food in the cupboards but nothing she was willing to risk trying.

"Groceries are definitely first on the list."

After she hauled her luggage upstairs to Caesar's room, she searched for a laundry room. She found it just past the kitchen. There was soap and fabric softener as well as other cleaning supplies.

"Please work," she begged as she pressed a button to turn on the washer. It started right away. "This is too good to be true."

Back upstairs, she stripped the linens off Caesar's king-sized bed. Once she had them washing, she grabbed her laptop. First, she found a mobile car repair service that could come out and inspect Caesar's car. She made an appointment for the next day. Next on her list was the jacuzzi. She knew nothing about them. She found a place that serviced them and made that appointment. Then, she found a landscaping service that could come out and tidy up the yard. Finally, she located a market nearby that delivered. All she had to do was create a grocery list. She laughed as her list got longer and longer.

They'll think I'm having a party. Once that was done, she went upstairs and changed into some shorts and a tank top. It was time to get busy cleaning this place from top to bottom.

"I need music," she said as she gathered the cleaning supplies she would need. She set everything on the kitchen island. In the living room, she found the stereo system. It was a bit outdated but still worked. Caesar had an extensive vinyl and CD collection, but she decided to go with the radio. She turned the system to radio and began searching for a station. One caught her attention. A station that announced it played older hits. She turned it up loud, then began opening all the windows in the house. It was time to let the fresh ocean breeze flow through.

Six hours later, she was soaking in Caesar's large bathtub. She'd swept, dusted, and mopped every room, cleaned the bathrooms and the kitchen, and washed all the linens. The kitchen was fully stocked with food.

The house looked lived in again. Her original plan had been to stay a couple of weeks...to give Los Angeles a feeling out. But she was already in love with the house and L.A. was not far away. Her mind was made up. She was staying.

She sighed, feeling lucky that most everything in the house was in good working condition. She wouldn't have to spend a lot of money to get started here.

"Oh my God!" She pulled the plug to let the water drain out of the tub, then jumped up and began drying off. "How could I have forgotten?"

Quickly, she slipped on her pajama pants and a tank top. *The money!* It hadn't once crossed her mind since arriving. Not even when she'd swept and mopped in his room earlier.

Caesar's bed was large, but luckily the frame and headboard were not as heavy as they looked. With some effort, she was able to push it to one side of the room. She got on her knees to search for his initials carved into a board, and when she found them, her heart thudded hard in her chest.

How do I get through the boards? It looked like she was going to have to grab a hammer and begin demolishing again. But when she pushed on the board, she could tell it was loose, and she was able to pry it from the surrounding boards. Once she'd removed it, she was able to get the others loose and removed them as well. She ended up taking apart a two-foot by two-foot section of the flooring. The safe looked heavy, and she decided not to try and lift it out. Instead, she put in the combination and opened it from its resting spot beneath the boards.

"Oh shit!" She couldn't believe her eyes as she began pulling out money. Stacks and stacks of bundled one-hundred-dollar bills. She'd been expecting a few thousand dollars, not a few hundred thousand. Half a million to be exact. *How has no one found this?* Caesar said no one knew. Only her. This was hers. Tears streamed down her face. She could live several years on this. It would give her time to find the perfect job. Or even create the perfect job for herself.

In the middle of the stacks of cash, she found a box made of mahogany. Opening it, she was surprised to find several pieces of gold jewelry, a pearl necklace with matching earrings, and a diamond ring. Women's jewelry. There was also a note from Caesar's father, telling Caesar that his mother would have wanted him to have these. Melanie shut the box, and set it aside, not wanting to disturb these precious items. Caesar's dad was still alive. *Perhaps he might want these back.* Maybe she could send them and say they were from Johnnie.

She stuffed the money back into the safe. She'd have to find a branch of her bank here so that she could make a deposit. Once she placed the money back, she returned the boards to their place, then slid the bed back into place. She took the mahogany box, opened a dresser drawer and slipped it inside. There was a bottle of oil there. *It can't be!* But when she took a whiff, she knew that it was. *The famous vanilla oil!* Well, it had been. Sitting in a drawer all these years had not been kind to the scent. She threw the bottle in the garbage. *Sorry, Caesar.*

Weary from all her work, she walked downstairs to shut things off for the night. On the deck, she took one last look at the ocean view, before heading back into the living room. As she was about to turn off the stereo, the radio station began playing another song. From the first few beats, she knew it was Lush. One of their slower love songs. Her blood ran hot hearing Caesar's silk and sex vocals. Yet, another coincidence, she thought, as she began dancing slowly around the room. She took it as a sign. *I'm home.*

"I'll send you the paperwork via overnight FedEx, and you can sign everything. Make sure to return it to me as soon as possible."

"Sure thing," Melanie told the real estate agent who'd sold her condo. "I'll be looking out for it."

When she hung up, Melanie lay back on the couch and sighed. She'd been in Caesar's house nearly a month now, and everything was falling perfectly into place. She'd been back to Atlanta only once...to turn in her resignation letter and to pack up her belongings. To trim down her load, she'd had a yard sale and sold most of her larger pieces of furniture. What didn't sell, she donated to charity. Everything else had been packed into her car and a small U-Haul trailer to make the cross-country drive back to California.

She'd loved the freedom of the open road. It made her think of Caesar and what he'd said about the band's early days. Traveling around by van, playing gigs with his friends. She understood now how thrilling it must have been. Every stop a new adventure, a new audience waiting to be conquered. It had to be like what she was feeling these days. She had yet to spend any time job hunting. Getting the house in order and closing up loose ends in Atlanta had kept her busy, but she had been rewriting some of her old stories.

After a late dinner, Melanie sank down into the warm waters of the jacuzzi. She ended every night that way. Staring up at the stars, sipping on a glass of wine and enjoying the sounds of the ocean. She smiled as she saw a star shoot across the sky. Closing her eyes, she made a wish. *Caesar.*

Nighttime was when she missed Caesar most. Being in his house meant part of him was always with her. The things he'd decorated his home with, his platinum albums hanging on the wall in the living room, his motorcycle that she knew he loved, were all pieces of his spirit that had been left behind.

She'd also found among his things, home movies and hundreds of photos of the band. Seeing him on screen so full of life, like the man she'd known for two blissful days was like porn, and she spent many nights cumming to thoughts of Caesar and their time together.

As she finished her wine, she smiled thinking tonight would be another of those self-love nights.

Chapter Seven

Johnnie Vega

Sunlight was drifting into the horizon, and into the bedroom window when Melanie stirred and lazily opened her eyes. *Why can't dreams last forever?* She'd been having the most amazing dream about Caesar. They'd been lying on the bed, his body spooning hers, his cock rock hard against her butt.

What? It can't be. She smiled and pushed her body backward, getting closer to him. His arm wrapped around her waist, pulling her even closer. It wasn't a dream. Last night, she'd wished on a star, and now Caesar was back.

"I've missed you so much." She sighed.

He snuggled his bristly chin against her neck.

Wait! Caesar doesn't have stubble! She inhaled. No vanilla. A citrusy scent mixed with...*Alcohol!*

"Oh my God!" Like lightning, she scrambled out of the bed.

"Where are you going, baby?" Grinning wickedly, Johnnie Vega sat up and patted the bed beside him. That damn smile she loved so much was mocking her. "Come back. We were just getting started."

"You're not Caesar." Remembering she was naked, she grabbed the comforter and wrapped it around herself. Problem was, that left him naked. And he didn't seem to care that she was seeing every exposed inch of him.

Hands supporting his head, he lay back against the pillow. "Sweetie, if you're expecting Caesar, you're in for a big disappointment. But I promise...with me...you won't be."

She turned away, not wanting to see his body, even though his thick, hard cock would forever be seared into her brain. Part of the blanket fell away from her, leaving her exposed again.

"Nice ass, babe."

"Stop looking at me!" She wrapped the blanket around her twice this time, creating a cocoon. "Can you please pull up the sheet or put some clothes on?"

His laugh was low and husky. "You break into *my* house and have the nerve to tell me what to do?"

She stood with her back to him, not knowing what to say. Technically, he was right. "Please."

"If you insist," he told her. The sheets rustled around. "Okay. Done."

She turned around. He had draped a small section of the sheet over his cock, essentially pitching a tent. The rest of him was still exposed to her. Quickly, she turned away again. "Johnnie, please."

"Do I know you?"

"If you cover yourself completely, we can talk."

"Damn woman. You're fucking bossy."

More rustling and Melanie peered over her shoulder.

"I see you peeking." He was standing, slipping on a pair of jeans. "Alright, done."

She turned back around.

He threw his hands over his eyes. "Oh, please cover yourself. My eyes are burning! I'm melting!" Then he doubled over laughing hysterically at her.

Frustrated, Melanie picked up her pillow and threw it at him.

"Oh, you want to play games?" He grabbed the pillow off the floor, ran to her side of the bed, and began pelting her with it.

She tried to block the blows and stay covered at the same time. "Johnnie, stop!"

Grabbing the comforter, he yanked her close and wrapped his arms around her waist. "Who the hell are you?"

"My name is Melanie." She wriggled, prying herself loose. "If you wait for me downstairs, I'll be right down to explain everything. I promise."

"Yes, boss man." He saluted, then marched down the stairs.

Or so she thought.

"Mmm...nice tits, too." He was in the doorway, watching her.

"Johnnie!" Again, she pulled the comforter around her. *What is wrong with him?* He was behaving like a teenage boy instead of a forty-four-year-old man. "Go. I'll cook breakfast as soon as you let me get dressed."

That smile spread across his face again. "Now you're talking."

She heard him scamper down the stairs this time, but to be safe, she went into the bathroom and shut the door. As she dressed, she took a few deep breaths, trying to collect her thoughts, trying not to have a panic attack. Johnnie Vega, her schoolgirl crush, the man who'd decorated her headboard with his beautiful smile, his mischievous blue eyes, was downstairs waiting on her. And she'd just seen him naked. And he'd seen her. His naked body...his erection...had been pressed against her. *What would Caesar think?*

Caesar had sent her here, knowing Johnnie might be here. They were best friends, so he knew what kind of person Johnnie was. The naughty boy of the group. *He hasn't lost that persona.* And despite his addictions and his age, he looked amazing. *Is this part of Caesar's plan? His mission?* She'd sent him away, but that didn't mean the wheels hadn't already been set in motion.

Suddenly there was loud banging on the door. "Hey! I'm waiting on breakfast, and I'm starving. Hurry up!"

He might be attractive, but he's irritating as hell. She slung open the door. "Who's being bossy now?"

He grinned, then laughed loudly. "I'm starting to like you."

She stomped past him and down the stairs. He followed on her heels. While she went into the kitchen, he went into the living room. As she was pulling out the ingredients for waffles, he walked past the kitchen, dragging a suitcase. A large duffle bag was over his shoulder. He headed upstairs with everything.

"I'm going to take a shower and freshen up," he yelled down. "It was a long flight. Maybe once I smell better, you'll let me cuddle with you again."

Melanie groaned as she poured the mix into a bowl. The devilish charm she once admired in Johnnie was now throwing her for a loop. Was he hoping to have sex with her? Or was he purposely trying to get under her skin? *Maybe both.*

She was slicing fruit when he came back down wearing swim shorts and a tank top. His hair was wet, and he was running his hands through it. He still wore it short, and she knew it would curl into soft waves when it dried.

"Hope you don't mind I borrowed your razor." He rubbed his clean-shaven chin, then sat on a bar stool by the kitchen island and grabbed one of the strawberries she hadn't yet cut. "And your toothpaste...your deodorant...your shampoo...your soap...and your hairbrush."

"You don't have your own?"

"I didn't feel like unpacking yet." He popped the strawberry into his mouth.

She looked up at him. "My toothbrush?"

He grinned and shrugged.

Shaking her head in disbelief, she opened the waffle iron to pull out the cooked waffles. Her thumb touched the hot iron, and she snatched it back quickly, sucking in her breath. "Ow!"

"Be careful. It's hot." He chuckled.

"No shit." She shook her thumb.

Johnnie zoomed over, grabbed her hand, and examined the burn. "It's not too bad."

"It hurts." Feeling uncomfortably close, she stepped away from him. Her back hit the counter behind her.

"Poor, baby." He came closer, pressed his lips against her thumb, then blew softly. "Feel better?"

Next thing she knew her thumb had disappeared into his mouth and he was slowly sliding his mouth up and down it. Hadn't Caesar done the exact same thing when they'd met? Had they come up with this flirtation technique together? She imagined them as teenage boys in school discussing how to turn a girl on and this was what they'd come up with.

She burst out laughing.

He smiled. "Aww...it's working."

That smile. Her laughter immediately stopped, and her knees weakened. His body was pressing against hers. She stared into his stormy blue-grey eyes, and he stared right back. She thought he might kiss her or maybe she just hoped to feel his lips on hers. They were almost as thick as Caesar's. They looked delicious.

She snapped out of it. She couldn't do this. Not with Johnnie. He was still an addict as far as she knew. Like her husband had been.

"The waffles are getting cold." She put her hands on his chest.

He pressed his forehead against hers. "But you're getting hot, aren't you?"

Her cheeks burned as she pushed past him to get the juice out of the refrigerator. He grabbed two glasses out of the cupboard, and she poured juice into them. He sat back down on the bar stool. She pushed the plate of waffles toward him, then the bowl of fruit. She'd already put powdered sugar, whipped cream, butter, and syrup out on the countertop.

"Help yourself," she told him.

"You're not joining me?"

"Not sure I can stomach being around you."

He grinned and took several waffles. He put powdered sugar, whipped cream, and syrup on them, then topped them off with blueberries and strawberries. "It looks yummy...like you."

"Are you always this bold?" She crossed her arms in front of her.

Instead of answering, he shoveled waffles into his mouth. Blissfully, he closed his eyes as he chewed, then shoveled in a few more bites. He drank some juice to wash it all down.

"Tastes yummy." He chuckled. "Do you?"

She rolled her eyes. "I'll be on the deck getting some fresh air."

She walked away, but he bounced up and grabbed her arm. "Don't go. I'll behave...promise."

"Is that even possible?"

He stuck his bottom lip out and tugged her back toward the kitchen. "Come on. It's not fair that you did all this work and you're not going to eat."

Reluctantly, she followed him.

He grabbed a bar stool and placed it next to his. When he patted it, she sat down. He then put a waffle on her plate. "What do you want on yours?"

She sighed. "Powdered sugar and some fruit."

"Excellent choice." He sprinkled sugar on it, then carefully laid out the fruit to make a face. Banana slices for the eyes, a strawberry nose, and a smile made from blueberries. "Here you go."

She covered her mouth, trying to hide an uncontrollable smile. *Irritating one minute...charming the next.*

He sat back down and again ate with gusto.

Melanie daintily picked at her food. "When was the last time you ate?"

"Like this? It's been awhile." He took another bite. "We should've cooked bacon, too."

"There's none in the house. I don't..."

84

"Oh, not again!" He dropped his fork loudly on the plate. "Don't tell me you don't eat meat."

She shook her head. "I'm not vegan though. I can cook eggs if you'd like."

He groaned. "Just like fucking Caesar."

"Speaking of fucking Caesar."

His eyes went wide before he grinned again. "Who's being bold now?"

"What?" She was confused, then realized his meaning. Her gaze dropped to the floor. "No, that's not what I meant. I mean, well, yeah...that did happen."

"You fucked Caesar?"

She looked at him again. "I'm trying to explain how I got here."

He pointed his fork in her direction. "And it has something to do with fucking Caesar?"

"Well, yes, but..."

"Alright. Back up to the beginning and tell me everything." When she looked at him as if he were crazy, he started laughing and shook his head. "Uhm no. Not the fucking part. Just how you came to be here...in *our* house."

"Well, I lived in California until I was about six, then my family moved to Florida."

He crossed his arms back and forth in front of him. "No, no. Not *that* far back."

"Well, I wanted you to know I was living in Atlanta before I came here."

"Atlanta? My parents live there."

"I know."

He eyed her suspiciously. "Did they send you?"

"What? No. I've never met them." It was true. "I read online that they lived there."

He still looked skeptical. He didn't believe her.

"I met Caesar a long time ago obviously." She'd been rehearsing a story in case this situation ever arose. "I was on break from college and came to California to visit old family friends. I met Caesar at a grocery store."

His eyebrows shot up. "Caesar? At a grocery store? Without causing a mob scene?"

She bit her bottom lip. "Well, it was more like a farmer's market."

"If you say so." Johnnie shrugged.

Is he believing this? "So, we met…"

"And then you blew his fucking mind in bed. He fell in love with you and gave you the keys to his house."

"I didn't say that."

"No. I said it." He pointed the fork her way again. "Because as many women as Caesar slept with, he never gave the keys to his house to any of them. Only me and the guys had the spares."

Her heart warmed. Johnnie's statement made her feel special. "I have the keys to the Mercedes and the Triumph, too."

"No fucking way! He wouldn't even give those to us. You definitely have to tell me the rest of this story."

She folded her hands in her lap, so he wouldn't see them shaking. *Will he believe me?*

"So you met him at the market…and…"

"We hit it off. And we spent a weekend together. That's it."

"A weekend? Damn you must give good head."

"Oh my God."

"Hey, don't get mad at me. Caesar said he'd marry the girl who could make his toes curl while sucking him off."

She shook her head. "Well, we didn't get married. I told him I'd always dreamed of living in California again and that after college I wanted to write screenplays for television or the movies. So, he gave me the keys and said if I ever came to town, I could stay here. He was doing me a favor, giving me a place to stay while I looked for a job and a home of my own."

Johnnie grew silent, staring hard into her eyes. *What happens if he doesn't believe me?* After a minute or two though, his eyes changed. They seemed sad.

"Caesar died sixteen years ago. You've been in college all this time?"

She took a deep breath and exhaled. "I met him a couple of years before he died. His death was pretty devastating."

"And you flunked out of college?"

"No," she replied. She knew he was getting impatient. But she had to work around the story of her family. "I met a man, right after I graduated and ended up marrying him. When that didn't work out, I moved to Atlanta and worked in the news field. I worked my way up and was making good money, but I still had my dreams."

"So, after sixteen years, you suddenly decide to take Caesar up on his offer?"

"Something like that. I was turning forty and realized I'd never pursued my dreams. I knew it was time to try."

Johnnie rose and began clearing away the breakfast mess. "Forty, huh? I know how that feels. When I hit it a few years back, I tried to make a few changes as well."

She wondered if he meant getting clean. *Tried.* "Did it work out for you?"

He put a hand on her shoulder. "You know that wine you had out on the counter?"

Her gaze zipped to where she'd left the bottle after pouring her glass. It was missing. "It was a new bottle I'd just uncorked."

"Keyword...*was.*" He shrugged.

"That's why you reeked of alcohol." She blushed.

"I had a few drinks on the plane, too."

"It's all I smelled when I woke up." Melanie cringed. He wasn't that different from Logan. And that had ended in devastation.

"Speaking of reeking." He held some of her hair to his nose. "Did you take a bath in Caesar's vanilla oil?"

"What? No. I threw it out. After all these years, it had gone bad."

He sniffed her hair again. "Well, you smell like it."

"Terrible?" she asked, pulling some strands to her nose. "I just washed my hair."

"No. Not like sixteen plus years vanilla oil. More like fresh, he just bought it, vanilla oil."

"Oh." What could she say to that? "That's strange."

He ran his hands through her hair. "It's probably from being in the house. Around all his stuff. That was some powerful oil."

"Like sugar cookies."

"You remember."

She smiled.

He seemed to get sad again. "Did you love him?"

"It was only two days."

"A lot can happen in two days."

"Yes." She nodded. "I loved him. I still do."

"Me, too."

Knowing all too well the pain of losing loved ones, Melanie wrapped her arms around his shoulders and drew him close. He held on tightly as she slid down from the stool. They continue to hug until he finally pulled back and stared at her. *He's going to kiss me this time.* And he did. On the cheek. She wondered if her disappointment showed.

"Johnnie, I don't have to stay here. I have money. I'll get a place of my own, and you'll never have to see me again."

"What if I want to see you?"

"This is your place, not mine. I heard about Caesar's will, so I wasn't sure what I'd find when I came...if you might be living in the house. But it looked like no one had been here for a while. That's the only reason why I stayed."

"I have the house in London, too," Johnnie explained. "I usually come here for fall and winter because it's so cold there. It's been nearly six months since I was here."

"I came at the end of July. I cleaned and fixed things up for the first week or so. And I've been writing a lot. But now that you're back, I should try to find my own place. If I could stay here for a week or two longer until I find something..."

"No. Absolutely not."

His directness wounded her. "Okay. I'll start packing my things."

"No. You're staying. For some reason, Caesar wanted you here, and that's enough to convince me you need to stay put. Besides, you've got the house and yard spotless, and your cooking is great, so I hope you'll stay and keep that up."

She wrung her hands, trying to decide. Being here meant dealing with him. He was being nice now, but earlier he'd been a jackass. And he was an addict. Logan had hidden his problem from her. And she'd been too naïve to catch on. Johnnie was at least up front, but she still didn't know how bad things might get when he was under the influence.

"I'm sorry about earlier." He took her hands in his. "I was a total jackass."

"That's an understatement."

"A lot of that was the alcohol talking."

She frowned. "Is that what I have to look forward to if I stay?"

"I'll stay in the downstairs bedroom. That'll give you more privacy."

"Privacy? Like when I woke up next to you this morning?"

"Again, the alcohol."

"It's not an excuse."

He nodded. "You're right, it's not. It's a nasty habit I've been trying to kick for years. One of many. In fact, living with you might be a good thing."

"I'm not planning on distracting you with sex."

His mouth dropped, and he chuckled. "A few hours with me and you're already corrupted. That's not what I meant at all. But if you're here, I won't be alone. Alone is when I'm most vulnerable to falling off the wagon."

"You used to be in a band. You weren't alone then, and that didn't stop you."

"I wasn't trying to be sober back then."

"And you are now?" she asked, confused. "You just said you were drinking most of the day yesterday."

"Before yesterday I hadn't drunk or popped any pills for a couple of weeks. But the damn flight was so long, and I hate flying."

She remembered reading that long ago. "Pills?"

"I don't do it a lot. Not like I used to. And I've been off the hard stuff for over ten years."

Hard stuff? She rubbed her temple. "Johnnie, I don't think I can deal with that."

"I understand. But you showed up after all these years because Caesar told you to. There has to be a reason for that."

He seemed to be thinking like her. That this was some sort of master plan. *Would he believe the real story? How could he?* She scarcely believed it herself. It seemed so long ago. Her two blissful days with Caesar. She missed everything about him. Except one thing was right here. And it wasn't his clothes or his mementos. It was a living, breathing person. His best friend. When she and Caesar had talked to Tim, they'd discussed a possible connection between her and Johnnie, one that had made Caesar come to her instead of his friend who obviously still needed help.

"Think about it, please." He pulled her close again. "I can't explain it, but for some reason, you being here makes the house feel alive again. I feel his spirit. And I haven't felt him in a long time."

"Because ever since he died, you've been numbing yourself with drugs and alcohol."

He pulled away quickly, and in his eyes, she saw pain. Real pain. Her comment was callous. He'd lost his best friend. She knew what loss felt like, how empty it made you feel. She'd battled with that same sort of depression; only she hadn't numbed herself from it. Instead, she chased people from her life, including Caesar.

"I'm sorry." She touched his cheek gently. "That wasn't nice."

"No. It wasn't."

It was as if his entire demeanor changed. The bold man with the crass mouth was now like a wounded animal.

"Forgive me?"

And then the naughtiness was back. He teased, "You can make it up to me tonight."

She couldn't help smile. And feel a bit turned on as well. She rubbed his arm.

"Cook me a steak for dinner." When her mouth dropped, he laughed at her. "Oh, you thought I meant sex. Sorry, I never went for Caesar's sloppy seconds."

"Sloppy?" It was her turn to be shocked and hurt.

"Ha! Gotcha!" He grinned, took a step back, and let his gaze caress her from head to toe. "Melanie, you are definitely not sloppy. More like very sexy seconds."

"And you're like...very crazy."

"Always have been." He kissed her cheek again. "I'm going to swim a bit and leave you alone. Think about staying. I really want you to."

She watched as he bounded toward the linen closet. He grabbed a beach towel then headed to the deck, where the steps leading to the ocean were. At the back door, he stopped, glanced at her, and flashed that devilish grin. "And after sixteen plus years, it really wouldn't count as sloppy seconds, right?"

Before she could reply he was rushing outside and down to the beach.

Despite his crudeness, Melanie found herself humming happily as she washed the dirty dishes. Afterward, she stood on the deck, leaning against the railing, watching Johnnie swimming in the ocean. He and Caesar were so different. *How did they ever become friends?* But as she watched Johnnie splashing around in the surf like a big kid, she remembered Caesar's playful side. Johnnie finally noticed her, smiled, and waved. As the tide rolled back from the shore, she realized he was swimming nude. She spun away, her hands flying to her mouth. Then, she laughed loudly. Maybe they were more alike than she realized. *Only one way to find out.*

Chapter Eight

Melanie bolted upright in bed. *What's that noise?* A slow, mournful wail. She'd heard that there were coyotes around but hadn't seen or heard any sign of them thus far. She looked at her phone. Three in the morning. *Should I wake Johnnie?*

After his swim, she told him she'd stay, with the condition that he kept his clothes on when she was around. They'd spent the rest of the afternoon getting to know one another. Melanie never laughed so hard in her life.

He'd been surprised by the boxes of old videos and photos she'd found. When the first tape began, he'd fallen into complete silence, and Melanie had wondered if his journeying back in time was a good thing. He'd been so engrossed that she'd felt like an interloper, so she'd run into town to buy groceries, including steak and bacon for him. But when she returned, he'd gone to bed. A note on the refrigerator door read, *jet lag.*

When the howl came again, Melanie feared the animal might be wounded. That would make it even more dangerous. She slid out of bed, slipped on her pajamas, and went downstairs. She'd look in on Johnnie. Maybe the sound had woke him as well. His door was still half open, and she peeked in.

The wail came again, only this time she easily pinpointed the source. It was Johnnie. He was flailing around on the bed, mumbling to himself, then another moan. He was having some sort of night terror.

Quietly, she approached his bed and whispered, "Johnnie?"

He didn't wake.

Instead, he shrieked. "Caesar!" More inaudible mumbling came after that.

He was probably naked under the sheets, and she hoped that waking him wouldn't give him any wrong ideas. But she couldn't let him continue having this awful dream.

She crawled onto the bed and lay down beside him. She touched him softly on the arm. "Johnnie, it's Melanie. Wake up."

Deep in sleep, he thrashed again. "You idiot! Get down."

"Johnnie, please wake up. You're having a bad dream." Gently, she caressed his face, then ran her fingers through his hair which was slick with sweat.

He started crying. "Don't leave me."

"I won't." She felt awful. *I shouldn't have let him watch those videos.* She stretched out beside him and drew him closer. She kissed his forehead as she cradled him to her chest. "I'm here."

He continued to cry, and when his arms slipped around her, hugging her, she realized he was awake. She thought for sure he'd make some sort of sexual advance, but he didn't. This wasn't the rude, crass Johnnie. This was a wounded man, haunted by his dreams. And by the sound of it, dreams of Caesar.

She moved slightly. His tears glistened in the moonlight that shone through the window. She wiped them away. "You're okay."

"Stay with me." He squeezed her.

"I told you I would."

He entwined his fingers with hers. "I mean stay here in my bed. Don't leave."

"Johnnie, I..."

"I'm not asking for sex. Just sleep with me. Let me hold you."

She turned to her side, away from him. *Can I do this?* Caesar had reawakened her sexual drive. And now she was being asked to lie next to a man she found incredibly attractive. One she'd already seen naked. Twice. How could she lie here and not think about how thick and hard his cock had been this morning?

"I get that you don't trust me." She felt him leave the bed and heard him shuffling around in the dark. "I'll put on my pajama pants. Will that make you more comfortable?"

He slid in next to her. "Okay, they're on. You can check for yourself."

She flipped onto her back and reached over, thinking she'd check by touching his thigh. Instead, her palm brushed up against something else. She gasped, as she snatched her hand away.

"Sorry, I can't help it. You're a beautiful woman. It'll go away soon."

He thinks I'm beautiful. She didn't know how to respond. She didn't want his erection to go away. *I want it inside me.*

"Are we cool?" He turned to his side.

She couldn't answer as she tried to think of something other than his cock. She turned to face him. "Do you have nightmares often?"

"Yeah, I do."

"About Caesar?"

"How did you know?"

"You were talking in your sleep." She caressed his face. "You said his name."

"What else?"

"Something like *get down* and *don't leave me.* We're you dreaming about that night?"

He frowned. "I don't remember."

"You were screaming earlier. It was awful. I thought there was a wild animal outside."

"Sorry I woke you." He rubbed her arm.

"I'm sorry I showed you the videos. I should've known they'd be too painful for you."

"I loved seeing them. Next time watch them with me. I'll tell you stories about the band."

She rubbed his arm in return. "I don't want you having more nightmares."

"The only thing that seems to help is drinking or taking something that will knock me out cold."

"If that's the case, I'll get used to the nightmares."

He chuckled. "If I'm sober prepare for many sleepless nights."

"Does sex help?"

He laughed louder. "Are you offering?"

She pushed his chest gently, then rested her hand against it. Unlike Caesar, his heart beat strongly. "I was just wondering."

"Scientific research?"

"I thought men who were sexually satisfied slept well."

He took her hand in his. "I suppose that's true for some."

"I was thinking since you had a hard-on, that you could masturbate, and it might help you sleep better."

"Oh, is that what you were thinking?"

"Sorry. It probably sounds stupid."

"You thinking about my dick is definitely not stupid." He squeezed her hand. "But that particular theory was disproven because I jerked off before I went to bed."

Her face warmed. Had he been thinking of her?

"You're not jumping out of bed and running away, so perhaps you're getting used to my naughty mouth."

Instead of answering, she snuggled closer. She kissed his cheek. "Guess what?"

"What?"

She could see his smile in the moonlight. Her heart raced. "I did the same before I went to bed."

He laughed and kissed her forehead. "Did you think about Caesar?"

"Maybe." She smiled now.

"Only maybe? Perhaps you were thinking about me then?"

"Maybe," she whispered into his ear.

"Damn, woman." He moaned. "You intrigue me. I'm starting to understand how you captured Caesar's heart."

"Can you tell me how the band came together?" she asked, wanting to change the subject. She knew if she didn't, things were going to get more heated.

"You want to hear *that* story?"

"Yes."

"Are you sure you don't want to hear the one about Caesar and me in a hotel room with twenty women?"

"Definitely not!"

He laughed lightly. "Somebody's jealous."

"Somebody's not interested in hearing about your sexual escapades."

"But they're Caesar's, too."

She scooted away. "I *don't* want to hear them."

"What about yours and Caesar's?"

"That's between me and him."

"Good." He grinned, grabbed her around the waist, and pulled her back. "Because I don't want to hear it."

"Somebody's jealous."

"You better believe it. And he would be, too, if he saw us in bed together. We were so competitive with one another. Seems so stupid now."

Caesar said the exact same thing. Melanie shivered, and Johnnie pulled the comforter around her. Caesar had teased her about liking Johnnie. Now Johnnie was doing the same about Caesar. It was surreal.

"Hey, did you fall asleep?" He hugged her close. "Alright then, the band's origin story? We met in high school..."

Melanie enjoyed hearing the story. He was so animated and full of life as he talked. It seemed to take his mind off the nightmares, the alcohol, the pills, and any other problem he might have. And it took her mind off the fact that despite this being Caesar's best friend, she wanted Johnnie. She let him talk and talk, until wrapped in one another's arms, they both drifted away to sleep.

Chapter Nine

Melanie awoke the next morning to the aroma of bacon. And smoke. As she left Johnnie's bed, she heard quite a few colorful words coming from the kitchen.

She padded down the hall and stood in the doorway. Johnnie appeared to be having quite a time with the stove.

"Damn it all to hell!" he yelled as he scraped burned eggs into the garbage bin.

Not wanting to interrupt the fun of watching his cooking attempt, she covered her mouth so that she wouldn't laugh out loud. He was racing around, bare-chested in his pajama pants, trying to do too many things at one time.

A dish towel he'd left too close to the burner caught fire. "Johnnie, behind you!"

He turned and grabbed the burning towel. "Oh shit! What do I do with it?"

She rushed into the kitchen and yanked his arm toward the faucet. When she turned on the water, he dropped the towel, and the fire was extinguished.

He seemed agitated as he ran his hands through his dark hair. He pointed at the frying pan which was filled with burned bacon. "Fuck! I really wanted to cook you breakfast."

"It was your bacon." She smiled. He turned from her, obviously frustrated. Maybe this wasn't about breakfast. She rubbed his shoulder. "It's okay. I can make us something."

"I know I said I wanted you to keep cooking and making things nice around here, but that's not really why I want you to stay. I don't need a maid."

"You were teasing me. You did a lot of that yesterday."

"I wanted to show you I could take care of myself." He started pacing. "But I fucked it up."

Melanie grabbed his arm. "It's okay. We can cook breakfast together if you want. I'll show you."

He refused to look at her.

"What is it?"

He pulled from her grasp and stared out the window above the sink. "Do you have any more wine?"

"No. I'm sorry." A wave of sadness crashed into her. This was the side of Johnnie that would be difficult to deal with.

He turned and leaned against the counter. "That's good."

"Oh?"

Finally, he looked at her. "Trust me. I'm craving something to drink. But this is good. I don't need it. I need something to distract me, so I don't think about it."

"Then let's do some cooking." She smiled.

He turned to the mess on the stove. "This cooking thing is what stressed me out in the first place."

"It'll be fun if we do it together."

"I'm over it."

This calls for drastic measures. She lifted her tank top off. Instantly, her nipples hardened.

"What the fuck are you doing?"

"Distracting you."

"You don't have to do this, Melanie."

"All we're doing is cooking."

He stared at her breasts. "Topless?"

"You're topless."

"My chest is not nearly as amazing as yours."

She moved closer and touched his chest. There was a sprinkling of hair across it. "To me it is."

"Alright, I see what this game is." He pulled his gaze from her naked chest and stared at the ceiling. "Distract me by confusing the hell out of me."

"I'm not trying to confuse you."

"Really?" His gaze locked onto hers. "Because right now I cannot figure you out. Yesterday you were appalled by my potty mouth and sexual innuendos, and today you're coming on to me."

"I flirted with you last night."

"And now you've graduated into full-blown taunting."

"Taunting?"

"Waving around what I can't have right in my face."

"Who says..."

His hand flew up to cover her mouth. "Don't say it. Please. Don't say another word."

Melanie wanted to cry as he retrieved her tank top and slipped it over her head. He claimed to be confused, but she was just as baffled by *his* behavior. *What happened? He doesn't want me?*

"I feel so stupid." She walked away as the first tear slid down her cheek. She wiped it away hoping Johnnie hadn't seen it. By the time she reached the beach, there were too many to wipe away. She sat down in the soft sand and watched the waves gently roll in.

Several minutes later, she heard Johnnie approaching. Then, a flood of pamphlets rained down onto the sand surrounding her. She gathered them into a stack.

"Those are all the treatment facilities I've stayed in. And a few of them...I never made it through the front door even after I'd scheduled and paid for treatment. A sick collection, huh?"

Melanie flipped through them. Thirteen in all. Some she'd even heard of. Places where celebrities and those with money went to get sober. There was even one for the place in San Diego.

He plopped down beside her, stretching his legs out in front of him. "Every one of those damn places will tell you not to get involved with anyone while you're in recovery. Even though I failed miserably at getting through their programs, I know that the shit makes sense."

"Yesterday you acted as if you wanted me."

"You think I don't want you? I've been walking around with a hard-on since I met you. You saw that yourself."

She blushed. "But not now?"

"You want to touch my dick and see?"

"When I took off my shirt..."

"This happened." Grabbing her hand, he brought it to his crotch. He was fully erect. "Just because I want you, doesn't mean I can let it happen."

"Because of what the programs say?"

He nodded as he gazed at the horizon in front of them. "Because of how I hurt the people I care about. My friends...my parents...the few girlfriends I've managed to have. I don't want to put you through the shit I put them through."

"You barely know me. One day is all it's been. At this point, it would only be about sex."

"Didn't you tell me you loved Caesar after two days with him?" He looked at her again and brushed her hair back, tucking it behind her ears. "I know I'm not Caesar...but I know enough to see you're someone I'd want to get close to. Last night when you came into my room, held me, and talked to me...I realized you were even more special than I thought. There's no way it would just be about sex."

"What do we do then?" She shrugged. "Should I leave? I don't want to make your life any more complicated than it already is."

He picked up some sand and let it drift slowly out of his hand. "If you want to go, I'll understand. I'm a mess. But I'd like you to stay. I want to be friends. I haven't had a good friend in a long time. Not one I could trust, and I feel like I can trust you."

Melanie closed her eyes and thought about what he was saying. Being only friends would be difficult. Already he was stirring feelings inside her that went beyond friendship. He made her laugh, *and* he made her horny.

"I meant what I said about feeling closer to Caesar with you here. There's something about you I can't quite figure out. Not only do you smell like him, you're very calming to have around. Just like he was."

"Having twenty women with two men in a hotel room was calming?"

"Still jealous about that?" He laughed. "We got into some crazy situations together, but he was the calm one of the group. Rhett was the forgetful one and sort of a loner. Kurt was the perfectionist and so organized it was annoying. I was the wild, crazy one. Caesar was chill. He let things roll off his back and rarely got angry for any reason."

She remembered how her temper had chased Caesar away. "I can get angry."

"I got a peek of that feistiness." He smiled and picked up a stick that was lying near him.

"I wish you weren't dealing with this, Johnnie. I know you were involved with drugs before Caesar's death but losing him couldn't have helped."

"I wanted to stop using everything...for him." He began pushing the stick around in the sand. "If I hadn't been involved in that shit, he'd still be alive. But every time I get sober, those nightmares come back, and they escalate until I can't take it anymore."

She put her arm around him and rubbed his back.

"Sometimes I think I see him and it scares the shit out of me."

Melanie took a deep breath and let it out slowly. "You see Caesar?"

"I know it sounds crazy. It was probably whatever I was drinking or taking at the time."

"You don't believe in ghosts?"

He looked at her. "Do you?"

Oh crap! She didn't want him to think *she* was crazy. "I'm open to the possibilities. Is anyone really sure about what happens to us when we die?"

"I suppose not." He poked her in the ribs with the stick. "If I see him again I'll send him your way."

Leaning back in the sand, she tilted her face toward the sky. Her mind filled with images of making love to Caesar. She sighed. "Yes, please do that."

"You'd like that wouldn't you?"

"You wouldn't?"

"Would I like hearing you fuck the ghost of Caesar Blue every night and day? No thanks."

Melanie's pulse quickened. They were so close to the truth. *Should I tell him?* "I meant having your friend back."

"I'd give anything to have him back. But a ghost. No thanks. I don't need a reminder of how I killed my best friend."

"You didn't kill Caesar."

"Were you there?" He grouched. "No. It was me and him. Rhett and Kurt were content to hang out by the fire at the lodge, but I convinced Caesar to climb a fucking mountain with me. A couple of drunk as fuck dumbasses."

"The investigators said it was an accident."

"No one knows what happened. And the way we were always horsing around, I probably shoved him off that ledge."

She remembered what Caesar said about Johnnie not killing him, but she didn't know how to relay the message to Johnnie. He needed to believe that Caesar might have actually visited him. And her.

"There's no way you could hurt Caesar."

"I wish I could remember."

She sat up and hugged him, wondering if it might be a good time to tell him *her* story. *It might be too overwhelming.* If he thought he killed Caesar, he'd definitely not want to hear about her alcoholic husband being responsible for the death of her children.

Her stomach growled.

Johnnie rubbed her belly. "I still owe you breakfast, don't I?"

"Why don't we find a restaurant nearby?"

"I know a few great places."

"Will you show me?"

He smiled. "I'd love to."

Chapter Ten

Melanie sat on the couch nervously watching Johnnie's reactions as he watched more of the home movies. They'd had a great afternoon together. After eating breakfast, they'd visited the nearby farmer's market where they'd bought fresh vegetables to go with his steak. She'd fallen in love with some homemade lavender soap, and he'd bought her a few bars. Then they'd come home and swam in the ocean, laughing and splashing one another until it was time to cook dinner. After he'd stuffed himself, he suggested they watch the videos together.

"Okay, this is one of the first interviews we did. It was for a local television station in Philly," Johnnie explained. He stretched out on the couch, placing his head in her lap. He began to laugh. "Look at Caesar's hair. He looks like a damn poodle."

She smiled, loving the sound of his laughter. She'd wondered if watching the videos would be a good idea. But so far, he was animated and joking around about what they were viewing.

She sighed and without thinking said, "I love Caesar's hair."

Johnnie glanced up. "No shit. You and every other woman in the world. My hair curls, too, you know."

"Somebody's jealous." She ran her hands through his hair. Because he kept it short, there were only waves, and if he didn't put some type of product in his hair, it would be in complete disarray. When he was younger, he always wore it slicked back with gel or spiked it up.

"Do you love *my* hair?"

She looked down in awe, and her body tingled with heat. "I always have."

"Wait." He sat upright and stared at her. "What do you mean? *Always?* We just met."

"I told you I liked the band."

"Really?" His eyes narrowed. "How much?"

Her cheeks burned. She hadn't yet mentioned her teenage obsession with him.

"Can I show you?" She pushed his head from her lap, stood, and held out her hand.

He took her hand and stood. "Didn't we agree earlier that this wasn't a good idea?"

"For the record, you decided for us. I'm going along with it. But the fact that you keep thinking about sex with me makes me wonder, because that is *not* what I want to show you."

"Then what?"

She tugged his arm. "Come with me."

"Cum? There *you* go again with the sexual innuendo."

She rolled her eyes, let his arm go, and walked to the stairs. "You're impossible."

He laughed.

Melanie went upstairs to the spare bedroom that she was using to store what was left of the boxes she'd once had in the attic of her condo. She'd gotten rid of a lot of things, but in doing so, she'd discovered things she now treasured more than ever.

Johnnie followed her in and scanned the room. "What's all this?"

"What I brought with me from Atlanta. Things I couldn't part with. She walked over to two boxes that were labeled *Lush*. "Ta-da!"

"What's in them?"

"Look and see."

He sat on the floor next to one and opened it. Melanie sank down next to him.

"You're fucking kidding me." He began pulling out all the memorabilia. "All of this is yours?"

"Yes. I became a fan when I was fifteen, so there's no telling what you'll find in there. I collected everything."

"I'll say." He pulled out a few t-shirts.

"Check out this poster." She pulled it from the second box and unfolded it. It was a large poster of a photo shot from above. All four band members were lying naked on a bed, a sheet draped over their private areas. They looked like they were sleeping. Johnnie was wearing sunglasses and held his drumsticks in one hand.

Johnnie groaned and shook his head. "All Caesar's idea."

"He wanted you guys to be sex symbols."

"Apparently it worked."

"Yes, quite well." Smiling, she stared at the poster.

"Did you stare at this hanging on your wall and get all hot and bothered?"

"It was a bit risqué for a teenager at the time. I hid it from my parents until I went to college."

"And then what?"

"It hung above my bed."

"Aww," he teased. "So, you'd go to bed and think about being in bed with all of us."

"Not all of you."

"Oh right, just Mr. Poodle Head."

She grabbed a large scrapbook from the box. "Maybe you should see this. You'll find it particularly interesting."

"Oh! A whole book of Mr. Poodle Head...how sweet." He opened it and began flipping pages. Then he gawked at her, obviously surprised. "What's this? Did you make one for all the guys?"

"There's another one here with everyone else and the band shots."

"This whole scrapbook is just me?"

"Yep." She smiled. "I had even more photos of you, but they got ripped when I pulled them from my headboard."

"You had *my* photos on your bed?"

"A collage of them...glued to my headboard," she explained. "Is that surprising?"

He seemed confused. "Kind of."

"Why?" She playfully pushed his knee. "You were very popular, and you were my favorite band member."

"But you slept with Caesar."

"Not when I was fifteen. I was twenty-one when I met him."

He pouted. "I wasn't your favorite anymore?"

"You were always my favorite." She stroked his cheek gently.

"But you slept with Caesar."

Melanie didn't understand why he seemed hurt. "It wasn't planned. I didn't pursue him. He actually pursued me."

"Did you happen to mention to him that I was your favorite?"

"Actually, I did."

"And he never said, *oh let me introduce you to him?*"

She bit her lip, not knowing what to tell him.

"Of course he didn't." Johnnie sprang to his feet, crossed his arms in front of him, and walked over to the window. "Because as soon as he knew you liked me, he wasn't going to let me have you. He took you for himself."

She eased herself off the floor and went to him. *How can I smooth this over?* "Johnnie, I didn't meet him as a fan. He was a good-looking guy at the market. I didn't even tell him how much I liked you until after we'd slept together."

Johnnie huffed as he stared out of the window, refusing to look at her.

"I don't understand why you're so upset, or why you're so jealous of him. You were gorgeous then, and you still are."

"He got to have you and I can't."

She placed a hand on his arm and kissed his shoulder. "You were the one who said we shouldn't be together as anything other than friends."

He finally looked at her. "Yeah, and it's pissing me off right now."

"How do you think I feel?"

He shrugged.

"You met me yesterday. I've been lusting after you for a lot longer." She grabbed a spiral notebook out of a box and shoved it in his direction.

He stared at it. "What's this?"

"Read it."

Reluctantly, he took it.

"I'll be downstairs."

She was lying on the couch watching the rest of the videotape they'd put in earlier when he walked into the room and sat down. He pulled her feet into his lap. He was holding the spiral notebook which was now open.

"I think about Johnnie all the time," he read. "I've never even had sex, but I'm always imagining what it would be like with him. He'd be on top of me, flashing that amazing smile of his, grinding his hips into mine. I would wrap my legs around him, forcing him to go deeper."

"Stop!" She covered her face with her hands. "That's enough."

"But there's so much more." He grinned, flipped to another page, and began reading. "I stare at his lips. They are so thick...so luscious. I want them on me. I imagine them on my nipples and get wet."

She tried to snatch the notebook from him, but he held tight.

"You said to read it."

"I forgot how embarrassing it was." She groaned.

"This means if you'd met me instead of Caesar, I'd have been the one to fuck you, right?"

"Maybe," she said coyly, rubbing his thigh with her foot. "And then what would have happened?"

He went quiet for a moment. "I would have broken your heart. I was and still am an ass."

"You're not that bad."

He pointed to a photo of himself in her notebook. "This is the guy you wanted, Melanie. I'm not a rock star anymore. I'm not Johnnie Vega."

"Who are you, then? Johnathan Smith?"

He winced. "Oh God, I hate that name."

"Because it's too boring. Your personality is larger than life. Always has been. It is now. Nothing's changed about that. You *are* Johnnie Vega. And you always will be."

He ran his hands through his hair. "See the grey?

"And?"

He pinched his belly. "See the gut?"

She shrugged.

He pointed to the corners of his eyes. "Wrinkles?"

"What's your point? You got older. I did, too."

"I'm no school girl's fantasy anymore."

"I could put on a school girl outfit and pretend you are."

"You did not just say that." Loudly, he groaned and smacked both hands against his forehead. "Damn! Why did you put that image in my head?"

"Because you're being stupid. I can't believe *you* of all people are this insecure."

"Maybe because it's been a while since a woman has given me so much attention and so many compliments. I'm enjoying it."

She eased closer and caressed his face. "I love your eyes. And when you smile, I feel weak."

"Like I feel when you talk to me like this." His forehead touched hers. His voice was low and husky. "I want to kiss you so bad. But if I do, I won't be able to stop."

"Did I mention I love your lips, too."

"I believe you said you wanted them on your nipples." His hand came up in front of her chest. She thought he would touch her and the anticipation of it, made her nipples harden instantly.

He must have noticed. "Magic hands."

She smiled. The band had always said that regarding his drumming ability.

"And this is our drummer, Johnnie Vega. The man with the magic hands," an on-screen Caesar declared.

Both their heads turned toward the television. It was another television interview. This one when the band was established. Caesar was holding Johnnie's hands up so that everyone in the audience could see.

"Did that just happen?" He grabbed the remote and turned up the volume.

Another one of those strange coincidences. And unfortunately, it ruined the moment.

When Melanie awoke later that night, it wasn't Johnnie's nightmares calling her from slumber but his movements from the living room. *Why is he still awake?*

She found him sitting on the floor, his back against the sofa, surrounded by piles of tapes, photos, posters. Even her things were in the mix. He had a pen in hand and was writing in the back of her notebook where there were still blank pages.

"What's going on?" she asked as she approached him. "Do you know what time it is?"

He lifted his gaze. "I told you...sleepless nights."

"Did something happen? Nightmares again?"

"I wish it were just that." He took her hand, and she sat on the sofa. "I got antsy. The cravings started. I needed a distraction, so I came in here to sort through all of this, organize it, and catalog it."

He held up the notebook where he'd listed everything on the tapes and a description of every photo and memento that was there. And the stories behind them.

"Is there a purpose in doing this?"

"Aside from keeping me away from the nearest liquor store or bar?"

Smiling, she brushed her hand lightly against his face. "I'm glad you didn't go out."

"I was sitting here thinking about something specific though." He tapped the pen against her knee. "You said you worked for a news station, and you wanted to possibly write one day."

She nodded. "I've been fleshing out some old stories I wrote long ago. To see if I can maybe turn them into full-length novels. But then you arrived...and I've been a bit distracted."

"Listen to my idea and see what you think." He moved to the sofa, and they sat face to face. "Would you be interested in putting together a documentary of the band?"

"A documentary?"

"We've got tons of material here." He lifted a shoe box and opened it. Inside were cassette tapes. "Caesar recorded himself on these. He's singing...talking...rambling on about life."

Melanie picked up one of the tapes. *He's on to something.*

"No one has seen this stuff, and if they have, it's been years ago."

She put the tape away and picked up a stack of photos. She spread a few on the couch. "Who took these? A photographer? We'd have to get permission to use them."

"There might be a few that were taken by family members or friends, but the majority we took ourselves. Caesar always made sure to bring a camera with us everywhere we went. Same thing with the videotapes. Aside from the interviews, it was all shot by us. Except the gigs. We'd get someone on the road crew to do that."

"Do you still talk to Rhett and Kurt?"

She saw his pained expression before he shifted his gaze from her.

"Not on a regular basis."

"I met Rhett at a music festival back in July."

He turned back to her, his brow furrowed. He appeared upset. "Did you sleep with him, too?"

"What? Of course not!"

"So, sleeping with the whole band is not on your bucket list?"

Infuriated, she shot off the couch before she hit him for saying something so insane. She walked over to the large picture windows that overlooked the ocean. The sky outside was black and full of stars. "I can't believe you said that."

"What am I supposed to think?" He followed her over. "You show up here out of the blue, telling me how you and Caesar had a fling and that he invited you to stay here. Then you made it clear that you want me. And now you drop a bomb and tell me you also met Rhett? Have you talked to Kurt yet?"

She took a deep breath and slowly exhaled. She wanted to call him an ass, but when she thought about it from his point of view, maybe it did look suspicious. Hell, the fact that she was withholding so much of her story was justification enough to let him slide.

"I was at a music festival in Atlanta. It was very hot that day. There were so many people, all crowded tightly together. I ended up having a panic attack and passed out. When I woke up, I was in the first aid tent. Rhett came by after playing to say hello to everyone. We talked about the band a little, but then he moved on to the next patient."

He stared hard at her, his mouth twitching slightly. He seemed at war with himself over whether or not to believe her.

"For the record, I've never met Kurt. But if we create this documentary, we're going to need their input."

He stood his ground for a few more minutes, then said, "Atlanta is hellacious hot in the summer. Why would they hold a festival in July?"

"I wondered that myself." She smiled.

"Rhett was playing with a band?"

"Playing for a pop singer. Sam Dean."

"Did he say anything about me?"

"Just that you and he had lost touch. He said he still sees Kurt."

Johnnie nodded. "They were good friends."

Melanie grimaced and looked away.

"What?"

She took his hand. "You know how you were blaming yourself for Caesar's death? Rhett apologized to me, as a fan, for not being there with you guys, watching over you two. Sounded like he blames himself for what happened, too."

A tear drifted down his cheek, and she drew him close. They hugged one another tightly. His face was pressed against her hair. Melanie felt his cock grow hard against her hip. His hands slid down her back and cupped her butt. He squeezed gently before sliding his hands back up her back. She moved her hands down to his butt and squeezed.

"Not quite as shapely as yours." He chuckled then sniffed at her hair. "I swear you still smell like Caesar."

Melanie wondered why his scent was still lingering on her after all this time.

"If I find that oil, I'm dumping it," he declared.

"I swear I already did."

He sniffed around some more, then whispered in her ear. "You smell like cookies. Good enough to eat."

Goosebumps pricked her skin as he pressed kisses against her neck. *Is this going to happen now?*

His lips were on her jawline, making a trail to her lips. Suddenly, he pulled away.

"I'm sorry." He ruffled his hair. "Damn, I'm giving you mixed signals, but this is so hard."

She rubbed his cock through the fabric of his shorts. "Yes, it's very hard."

He took her hand away. "We can't do this. I can't. I'm sorry."

Before she could express her disappointment, he zipped out the back door. Why was he so scared of starting something with her? Was it really the addiction? She sat on the sofa again, thinking of Logan. He'd hidden his drinking problem for a long time. She'd rarely seen him drunk. But once he'd lost his job, he'd boldly flaunted his drinking in front of her. He became loud, obnoxious, and at times very angry with her or their daughters. He'd even hit her once. It was at that moment she knew her husband was lost to her. She'd been making plans to leave and had even talked to her parents about moving in with them until she could stand on her own feet. When Gary's wedding came up, she'd even tried to convince Logan he didn't have to go. But he'd insisted. And why not? The booze would be flowing at the reception. Logan had surprised her by being on his best behavior throughout the day of the wedding. Even her father had asked her if she was sure Logan had a problem.

She drifted back to the window and stared at the ocean. In the moonlight, she could see Johnnie's silhouette at the water's edge. *What's he thinking about?* Yesterday, when she'd first met him, he'd been obnoxious and silly but hadn't appeared angry at all. *Is he capable of explosive behavior? Like Logan?* Could that be why he was afraid? He'd mentioned hurting girlfriends. Was it with bad behavior...or had it been worse? He didn't seem like the type to be physically violent, but then again, yesterday he'd only been slightly inebriated. She had yet to see him completely smashed, or high on something.

She wasn't sure when he'd return to the house, so she headed upstairs to bed. It was close to four in the morning. She sat on the edge of the bed and grabbed her phone. Looking in her contacts, she found Johnnie's parent's number. She'd promised to let them know anything she found out. Quickly, she composed a message.

Located Johnnie. He's okay. We're going to be working on a project together about the band, and he's excited. I'll keep you posted.

As soon as she pressed send, Johnnie was at the door.

"Are you texting someone at this hour?"

"A former coworker," she lied as she put the phone on the nightstand. "He works in the editing department. We need to get both the audio and video tapes put into a digital format so that we can work with them on a computer. He can do that, and I trust him not to leak anything."

Johnnie came into the room and kissed her forehead. "We'll talk about it later. Get some sleep."

"Do you want to sleep with me?" she asked and when he grimaced, she added, "In case you have a nightmare."

"It's probably best if I don't lie in a bed with you."

"I understand."

He kissed her cheek this time. "I'm sorry about earlier."

She caressed his cheek. "It's okay."

"I'll see you later. Sweet dreams."

"You, too."

"I'll dream of you." With that, he was gone.

Completely confused, she shed her clothes and slipped beneath the covers. Talk about mixed signals. *Will he really dream about me?*

Flipping to her side she smiled, knowing she'd definitely dream about him.

When she awoke again, it was nearly ten in the morning. The house was silent, and for a moment she worried that he might have gone out to buy the alcohol he'd been craving. But when she peeked into his room, she saw that he was still sleeping. Quietly, she closed the door to let him rest.

Back in the living room, she examined his work from the previous night. The photos seemed to be in chronological order. She was amazed as she looked at his notes. He had taken his list of videos and rewritten all of them in chronological order as well, giving specific details like dates, locations, and the event. It amazed her.

But despite how meticulous he'd been, this was still a huge undertaking. She retrieved her laptop and turned it on. She really did need to talk to someone about putting everything in a digital format. She texted her former coworker, Sidney, to see if he could take on an extra project. She also asked him advice on editing equipment that she could purchase to create a full-length movie. Immediately he became curious and asked her for more details. She told him the project was in its infancy, but she was excited about where it might go. He reminded her that the network sponsored documentaries and she should talk to that department about getting a green light to do it under Citizen News Network's production company.

Melanie quickly typed. *It's about a rock band. I doubt they'd be interested.*

You never know unless you ask.

Melanie thought about it. *You're right. Maybe I will. But let me get started first and put some type of proposal together.*

Sounds good. And since you're a friend, I'll give you a discount price on transferring all your media to digital.

You haven't seen how much it is yet. You may change your mind.

She took a photo of the items she'd be shipping to him, then sent it.

LOL. I'll give you a good price.

Melanie smiled. *Thanks. I appreciate it.*

And of course, I'll be getting a credit?

Definitely. Melanie paused then began typing again. *But right now, this is all confidential. Nothing can be leaked.*

Now I'm even more curious. When can you get it to me?

I'll ship it out tomorrow to the station.

Alright. I'll be on the lookout.

"Good morning." Johnnie came into the room, rubbing his eyes. He stretched then plopped down on the couch next to her. "Whatcha up to?"

Melanie showed him the laptop's screen.

"If we're doing this project, we're going to need bigger and better equipment. This laptop is not going to do the job. My friend in Atlanta sent me his recommendations, and I was doing some research of my own, too. This won't be some haphazard, thrown together project.

To be done professionally, I'm going to need the right editing program. But something not too complicated since I'm new at this."

"This is starting to sound like an expensive undertaking."

"It will be, but I can manage." She hadn't yet touched Caesar's money. It was all sitting in her bank account. But this seemed like something Caesar would want her to spend it on. It would be propelling her toward a future in film. She'd have to be both writer and director for the documentary. Johnnie could help with the editing and music portion of it.

"I want to help if I can."

"Trust me, you're going to. In fact, get dressed, we're going shopping. Then when we get back, you're packing up all this stuff so we can ship it to Atlanta tomorrow."

"You're not going to feed me breakfast first?"

"First off, you said I was not a maid. And secondly, it's lunchtime. We can get something while we're out."

"Sounds like a plan."

"Yes, your plan." She waved her arm around the room, noting the work he'd done last night. "Now we put it into action."

Chapter Eleven

"We've got to contact Kurt and Rhett soon," Melanie said as she relaxed in the jacuzzi with Johnnie. "Let them know what we're up to, maybe send them a script, and ask them to get involved with us."

He sighed. "Yeah, I know. But I'm not sure where to even start."

"With their management companies?"

He nodded, and she wondered if she'd be the one to take on the task. He seemed reluctant to talk to them.

For the last few weeks, she and Johnnie had fallen into a familiar rhythm. When they woke in the morning, they went straight to work. Melanie had created a script with Johnnie once they'd figured out what story to tell about the band. As Sidney uploaded items, he'd send her the files, and together she and Johnnie had started piecing together the story of Lush. It was slow going since they were both new to moviemaking.

In the evenings after dinner, they'd take a walk on the beach and discuss ideas. Afterward, she'd work on her novels, while Johnnie would either plan for the next day or watch tutorials on movie editing. Around eleven they'd meet in the jacuzzi to unwind.

Stretching her leg across the water, she poked him in the ribs with her toes. "Tell me something. Why did you quit making music? Rhett and Kurt still work as musicians...why don't you?"

"Isn't it obvious?" he grumbled. "I got too fucked-up. Too angry. After a while, people in the business no longer wanted to deal with me."

Melanie frowned. As long as Johnnie kept busy, he didn't dwell in the past and get sad about it. But in quiet times like this, she noticed he fell into a melancholy mood that sometimes he couldn't shake. He still had trouble sleeping, and often she'd wake up to find him writing notes or reviewing the work they'd done so far. When the nightmares woke him, she'd lie next to him, holding him until he got settled into sleep again.

"You're not fucked-up now."

"That's what you think."

"You've been sober for a few weeks."

"Doesn't mean I've stopped thinking about drinking or getting messed up."

She frowned. They'd seem to be doing well together, working and creating, enjoying one another's company. But it was stupid of her to think he'd been miraculously cured by her presence.

"Where are all your drums?"

His eyes narrowed. "Why do you care?"

"Because it's something you loved doing. And you were one of the best. Seems like you'd want to keep playing in some capacity."

When he said nothing for several minutes, she moved over to his side and sat next to him. "You could play for fun if nothing else."

"I don't have my drum kits anymore."

"Oh? That's too bad."

"Want to know why?" he asked snidely and skimmed his hand across the water, causing it to splash in her face.

He'd done it on purpose. *He's cranky tonight.* But she wasn't going to return the rudeness. "If you want to tell me."

"Sold them. In fact, I sold almost everything I own. Lost everything else. Addictions cost money."

It's why he and Caesar had willed each other their houses. Both knew it might come to this. Losing everything and having no place to go. Only Johnnie had two houses. Places he could at least live in.

"Caesar was a wise man." Johnnie smirked. "He knew we might fuck up all our success. He had us write wills giving each other our homes and an allowance to live on."

"You get an allowance?"

"Not much. Enough to get by."

"I'm sorry." She put her arm around him and drew herself closer to him. "I didn't know."

"Not something I wanted you to know." He rubbed her knee beneath the water. "Doesn't exactly make me desirable, does it?"

His statement pained her. "You think I want you for your money?"

"Seems like most people are working some sort of angle."

"Really? And what's your angle with me?"

He sighed heavily. "I need a friend."

"And you think I don't? I just moved here and don't know anyone."

"It's easy to go out and socialize...meet people. It's different when you want to have a real friend you can count on. One you trust. One you love."

Her heart warmed. "Are you saying you love me?"

"I'd think that was obvious." He grabbed her legs and brought them over his lap.

"Because you've always got a hard-on?" She giggled as she felt his erection beneath her thighs. "That's lust. Not love."

"You honestly think we're just two people who lust after one another? Because if that were the case, we could have banged and gotten it over with weeks ago."

"Over with?" She moved her lips close to his ear. "No way. If we made love, you'd want to keep doing it again...and again."

"Someone seems confident in her skills."

"That's not what I meant." She ran her hands through his hair, straightening it. "We'd both want to keep doing it. It wouldn't be over. It would be the beginning."

"You're a hopeless romantic. Like Caesar." He smiled now. "How come no man has snatched you up?"

Melanie winced before turning away. It was something they still hadn't discussed. Her past. Unlike Caesar, Johnnie hadn't gone through her things to discover more about her. He never pried, and she did the same with him. Things came up in a casual, natural way and she liked that.

Johnnie put a hand under her chin and brought her gaze back to his. "He broke your heart, didn't he?"

Her lip trembled as a few tears escaped. She didn't know how to talk about Logan with him, so she only nodded. He wiped a tear from her left cheek and then kissed her there.

"If he was here, I'd beat his ass for you."

"If he *was* here, *I'd* beat his ass."

"You would, wouldn't you." He ran his finger over her top lip. "You're one feisty woman. One of the many things I love about you."

The words flowed out of his mouth so easily, but they didn't make her feel better. If he loved her, why not give a relationship with her a chance?

"I know what you're thinking, Melanie." He shook his head. "It wouldn't work."

"Is there someone else you haven't mentioned?"

"Are you kidding? I've avoided women like the plague for years. Well, at least ones that were worthy enough to be in a relationship with."

"So, you do sleep with women?"

"Do I fuck *some* women? Yeah. Been a few months but, yeah, I do. You, Melanie, are not just *some* woman."

Why had Caesar been so anxious to share her bed, but not Johnnie? *Caesar's a ghost, you idiot!* He wasn't thinking about relationships or a future with her. Or had he been?

"Caesar said he loved me, too."

Johnnie rolled his eyes. "Caesar fell in love with every woman he fucked. Or at least he thought he did. Then again, he did give you the keys to his house, so maybe he did love you."

He seemed put off by her bringing up Caesar. *Why is he so jealous?*

"Guess it was those mad skills you claim to have." His hand went to her inner thighs, brushing up against her most intimate spot. "Do you have a magic pussy?"

Mixed signals again. She'd play the game right along with him. "Wouldn't you like to know?"

"I would *love* to know." He stroked her lightly, but it was enough to set her body on fire.

She pressed a soft kiss against his neck, and when he didn't protest, she pressed a few more there. She nipped his earlobe, then sucked on it.

"Melanie." He moaned and slid the crotch of her bathing suit to one side.

"Johnnie." She gasped as he began to explore. She moved her body over him, straddling his lap, giving him easier access. His thumb rubbed her clit and then two fingers invaded her. When she started to cry out, his mouth covered hers. Her body shuddered and tightened on the fingers that were still working magic inside her.

"Take this off." He lifted a shoulder strap and slid it down freeing one breast.

As she stepped out of the jacuzzi to pull off her wet bathing suit, he got out and spread a towel onto the deck. He folded another, creating a makeshift pillow.

"Lie down," he instructed before shedding his swim trunks and lying down beside her.

His lips were all over hers then. The kisses were long...deep...his tongue delving into her mouth. They were both panting with passion as he left her mouth and blazed a trail down her body. She writhed, her body aching with need as he stopped to lick and suck each nipple before heading further south. As he reached the juncture between her thighs, she spread her legs. He ran his tongue over her pussy a few times before fucking her with it.

"Johnnie, I'm going to cum again." She pulled his hair as her body shuddered with release once more.

He kissed his way back up to her mouth and lay on top of her. "I knew you'd taste like heaven."

"I love you," she confessed, feeling the thick head of his cock at her wet entrance.

Without hesitation, he jerked himself off her. He sat, turned away, and sunk his head into his hands.

Not again. They had been so close.

She scrambled up next to him, reached into his lap and took his cock in her hand.

"Melanie, no," he told her as she moved her hand on him.

"Why not?"

"You know why," he muttered, then let out a groan of pleasure.

"Doesn't it feel good?" she whispered into his ear. "You made me cum twice. Let me at least return the favor."

When he started to protest again, she covered his mouth with her own.

"With my hand?" she asked as she pulled away. "Or my mouth."

"You don't have to do this."

"I want to do this." She locked eyes with him. "I want to suck your cock."

"Please suck my cock," he gave in.

"Watch me." She smiled, feeling triumphant when he smiled as well. He leaned back, propping himself up on his elbows.

"Damn." He moaned as she cupped his balls, and pressed kisses up and down his shaft.

Her eyes never left his as she began to slide her tongue over him. He studied her intently. Only when she took him fully in her mouth did his head drop back, their gazes parting for a moment before he lifted himself back up to watch again.

"I'm gonna cum, babe." He grunted and released, then appeared surprised when her mouth stayed put. She swallowed all of him.

"Forget about magic pussy." He laughed as he lay down on the deck, pulling her into his arms. "You have a magic mouth. Guess you did make Caesar's toes curl."

His mentioning Caesar pained her. She wondered if in his new world he could see them. Did he know they were together? How would he feel about it? It was still hard to completely let go of the memories of him, even though she knew she should.

Grinning, Johnnie turned to his side and caressed her face. "Of course, I still want to find out about that pussy someday."

She was confused. "Someday? Why not now?"

"Shit," he grouched and rolled to his back. "I fucking did it again."

Sitting up, she grabbed her towel and wrapped it around her. "Let me guess...this is where I get the speech about this being a mistake, and we can't be together because you're so fucked-up."

"Melanie, this was amazing...but I shouldn't have let it happen. I'm not good for you."

In her heart, she knew it was true. He was an addict, like Logan. But she still hadn't seen that side of him. All she knew was the good, and the good was what she was in love with.

He sat up and ran his hands through his hair, clearly frustrated. "I love everything about you. I love being with you. I love the work we're doing."

"Then why can't you give us a chance?" She pouted.

"I don't want to hurt you."

"This is hurting me, Johnnie. You pull me in...then push me away. I can't just be your friend when I feel so much more than that."

He stood, and she couldn't help staring at his naked body. "You don't know the things I've done in the past. The way I've hurt people. The way I'll hurt you if I get too close."

"You said you loved me earlier. How much closer does it get?"

"You're right." He picked up the other towel and wrapped it around him. "Maybe I should leave...go back to London before things get too complicated."

Her eyes went wide. *Is he going to run away?* She jumped to her feet and stormed away, tears coursing down her face.

He caught up with her in the living room, grabbing her arm, then twisting her around to face him. "I'm sorry. This is not good for either of us."

"Then I'll leave."

"No. You've got the computer equipment all set up, and things are progressing well with the documentary. I can work with you from London. I'll get a computer, and we can talk online. It'll work out."

"Fuck you, Johnnie." She pulled free, ran upstairs to her room, and locked the door behind her.

He rattled the door handle. "Melanie, open the damn door!"

"Go away. You want to leave, then go!" She buried her head in a pillow and cried.

A couple of hours later, she woke, still wrapped in her towel. Slipping out of bed, she went to her door and slowly opened it. The house was silent, and no lights were on. Johnnie was probably sleeping. Quietly, she went into the master bathroom and took a quick shower to freshen up. After putting on pajama pants and a tank top, she walked downstairs for some water. A loud crash startled her. Her heart thudded heavily in her chest. It had come from the deck. She went to Johnnie's room to get him so that he could investigate, but he wasn't there.

Instead, he was on the deck, sitting in a lounge chair, dressed in shorts and a t-shirt, a bottle of beer in his hand. His bout of soberness was officially over. *It's my fault.* She opened the back door.

"Care to join me?" He grinned and held the bottle up in her direction. There was one empty bottle beside him on the ground and another smashed bottle about five feet away, near the stairs that led to the beach. Another full six-pack sat on the picnic table next to the half empty one. Seems he was just getting started.

"Where did you get it?"

"At the store."

"This late at night?"

"An alcoholic can always find what he needs."

"You were doing so well." She sat at the foot of the lounger. "Is this because of me? Because of what we did?"

"Don't flatter yourself." He took a long draw from the beer in his hand. "I was fucked-up long before I met you."

When he finished the bottle, he slung it hard to the deck floor, causing it to smash as well.

Lightly, she smacked his leg. "Is this what we're doing? Breaking bottles? We run around barefoot out here."

"You run around barefoot. I'm leaving, remember?"

"I don't want you to leave."

He squeezed his eyes closed. "I don't want to leave."

"Why can't we both stay?"

His eyes opened. "I can't stay and not touch you."

She ran her fingertips down his leg. "I want you to touch me."

He grabbed her arm. "Is this what you want, Melanie? A drunk? An addict? A man with no money who can't take care of you? You can't depend on me. I'm nothing...and you deserve something. Someone better."

She stood and walked a few feet away before turning back to him. "You are not nothing! You are Johnnie Vega, a rock superstar, drummer for one of the best-selling bands of all time..."

"That guy is gone."

"No." She pointed at him. "He's right here in front of me. You've pushed that part of you away, but it's who you are. You're a musician. You should be making music, not wallowing in misery."

"That's what you think I'm doing?"

"What else can I think? I only know that when you're being creative, working on the documentary, you're alive, driven, and full of passion. When we're working together, I see a man who's ready to conquer the world. But next thing I know, you're putting yourself down and telling me what a horrible a person you are."

"Because I *am* a horrible person." He opened another bottle.

"I need a drink," she told him. He handed her the bottle. Instead of drinking, she turned it upside down and drained the bottle. She then threw it as he had earlier.

"You think that will stop me?" He reached for another.

With lightning speed, she got to it first, this time not even bothering to empty it as she threw it across the deck to destroy it.

"Here." He handed her the other six-pack. "Want to get rid of these, too?"

She took it from him. She poured each one of them over the railing of the deck while he watched, chuckling.

"I can buy more." He shrugged. "I should find a real liquor store though."

She walked back over to the lounger. "Let's do something to distract you."

He unzipped his shorts, pulled out his cock and began stroking himself.

She sighed heavily. "I meant go upstairs and work on the documentary."

"The only thing that will distract me from drinking right now is having you sit on this."

She watched, mesmerized as his hand slid up and down his thickness. She forced herself to turn away. "And when we're done, you'll tell me what a huge mistake it was...how it can never happen again because you don't want to hurt me."

He grumbled before zipping up his pants. "You're right."

Melanie crawled into the lounger with him. He scooted over, allowing her room to lie next to him. He wrapped his arms around her, hugging her tightly.

"I'm not perfect. I have baggage, too."

"Did you ever cheat on someone you were in a relationship with?"

"No, but..."

"I did. And more than once. I've never been faithful to any of the women I was supposedly in love with."

"But you weren't sober. If you got sober..."

He brought her hand to his mouth. "I would love to be sober for you. But the thing is, I've tried and failed so many times. It's hard. I need to do it for myself, and so far, I haven't."

"Because you don't think you're worth it. You put yourself down all the time. I see all the good qualities you have, but you don't see them at all. You need to believe in yourself. Love yourself."

"What do you see in me that's worth saving? All I see is a has been rock star who has nothing and no one who even gives a damn about him...except you apparently."

"You could still play music if you wanted to. I know you must miss it."

"I miss my friends."

"They're still out there."

His mind seemed to drift for a moment, and Melanie knew he must be thinking of the old days.

"Not Caesar. And he's not here because of me."

She kissed his cheek and put her hand over his heart. "It was an accident."

"Everyone blamed me. The media. The fans. Rhett and Kurt."

"Is that why you won't contact them?"

"The last time we talked it was a huge battle." He frowned. "I said some shitty things."

"Then apologize." She rubbed his chest.

"What if they don't accept that? What if they want nothing to do with me?"

"Then it's their problem, not yours. You've got to let this baggage go and get over it."

"We haven't even begun to discuss my parents and how I've screwed them over so many times."

"When was the last time you spoke to them?"

"Called them from London months ago but haven't seen them in years."

"I'll have to go to Atlanta to do the proposal for the documentary. You could go with me and visit them."

"Not a good idea. I tend to get them upset. Even gave my dad a heart attack once. And I mean literally."

"What?" She sat up, shaking her head. "No. I'm sure it wasn't your fault."

"I lived in Atlanta with them for a while. Trying to get sober. I was doing alright, too. One day he accused me of taking some pills they had in the medicine cabinet. I hadn't taken anything, but he wouldn't believe me. We argued, and right in front of me, he clutches his heart, doubles over, and passes out."

"I can't imagine how scared you must have been."

Johnnie rubbed her back. "The worst part was seeing my mom upset. She'd cleaned out the medicine cabinet and had tossed out old prescriptions. She felt terrible thinking she'd caused it all. He almost died. They had to resuscitate him twice."

Melanie lay against him and pressed a soft kiss against his cheek. "I'm sorry you had to go through that."

"Hey, I remember something." He smiled and brushed back the hair from her face. "You'll like this because it's something good I did."

"Tell me," she said, wanting him to feel good about himself for a change.

"While we were at the hospital waiting for word on my dad, these nurses came around. They were looking for someone with O negative blood type. There was an accident. A dad and two kids were killed. The mother was barely alive and needed a transfusion, but they didn't have enough on hand. Since I was O negative, I donated. The woman survived. Although I'm sure she was devastated at losing her family."

Melanie felt her breath being sucked out of her. She sat up, trying to slow her breathing, fighting against the panic attack. *I'm O negative. He's talking about me.* "When was this?"

Apparently, he sensed her anxiousness and sat up beside her. "What's wrong?"

"Do you...remember the date?" Wheezing, she stood and took a deep breath of the night air, letting it out slowly, trying to calm herself.

"No, not the date. It was about ten years ago." He stood and held onto her as she teetered. "Melanie, what's happening?"

She patted her chest. "Can't...breathe."

"Melanie? Baby, look at me." Were the last words she heard before falling to the wooden deck floor.

Bright lights burned Melanie's eyes. Her head ached. An oxygen mask covered the bottom of her face. Glancing around the room, she knew she was in a hospital. *Where's Johnnie?* She found the call button and pressed it. A few seconds later, a nurse came in.

"It's good to see you awake." The nurse smiled and checked Melanie's blood pressure and heart rate. "Are you feeling better?"

She nodded and tapped the oxygen mask. The nurse removed it. "My friend?"

"He's sleeping in the waiting room. I'll get him. The doctor will be in to check on you as well."

The doctor arrived first. She was a petite woman with silvery grey hair. "Hello. I'm Dr. Barnes. You were brought into the ER after passing out. You hit your head on a chair on the way down. We checked everything out, stitched up your wound and you seem fine. There were no drugs or alcohol in your system. You aren't pregnant. Do you have any idea why you might have passed out?"

Johnnie walked in and smiled uneasily. His eyes were red-rimmed.

She smiled, then turned her attention back to the doctor. "It was a panic attack. Something upset me, and I couldn't breathe."

"Do you have these attacks often?"

"I used to get them a lot, but that was years ago."

"Why do you think you had this one?"

She started to cry. "I was reminded of what happened all those years ago."

"May I ask you what you were reminded of? I don't mean to pry into unpleasant events, but we need the information for our records."

She glanced at Johnnie and began to cry harder. He walked over and held her hand.

"I was in a car accident ten years ago. My husband and children were killed. I almost died myself."

Johnnie's hand slipped from hers. He backed away from the bed and sat in a nearby chair. Tears slid from his eyes.

"I'm sorry." The doctor patted her arm. "I'm going to let you stay a few more hours. Just to be sure you're stabilized. You can rest some more. Then we'll get you checked out to go home."

Melanie took the doctor's hand when she held it out to her. "Is he allowed to stay?"

The doctor looked back at Johnnie. "Technically, visiting hours are over. But I think we can fudge on the rules this one time."

"Thank you."

"If you need oxygen put the mask back on."

She nodded. The doctor smiled, then left.

"Johnnie, please come here."

He seemed shell-shocked as he approached. His eyes were wide, his mouth slack. "It was you? All those years ago? In Atlanta?"

She nodded, unable to speak. Immediately, he sensed trouble and put the mask over her mouth. She took a few deep breaths, then counted to ten to calm herself. *This is the connection. I have Johnnie's blood.* Tim had talked about it, a connection between her and Johnnie. It's why Caesar had come to her. To help her...and in doing so, help Johnnie as well.

"I saved your life?" Johnnie caressed her hair.

She removed the mask. "Yes."

Shaking his head, he sat on the edge of the bed. "I can't believe it. How crazy is this?"

Melanie wanted to tell him about Caesar, to tell him the truth of how she had come to be with him. Everything was connected. It would blow his mind, just as it was blowing hers right now. *Will he even believe me?*

Chapter Twelve

"I can walk, silly." Melanie squealed as Johnnie lifted her into his arms and walked toward the house. "I'm too heavy. You're going to drop me, and we'll both end up in the hospital this time."

He set her down at the front door then rubbed his back. "You might be right."

As soon as he unlocked the door and they stepped inside, he lifted her again. "But we'll find out for sure."

"Johnnie, you're crazy!"

"That's what you keep telling me." He carried her upstairs, dropped her on the bed, then fell to the bed himself.

"Oh!" She rubbed her forehead near where her stitches were. "Now my head is aching."

He kissed her just below the bandage. "Sorry."

"How's your back?"

"Broken but I'll live." He grinned.

"Turn over, and I'll massage you."

"Sure you don't want to rub this side?" He pointed to his crotch.

She groaned. "Roll over or forget it."

"Yes, boss." He slipped out of his shirt, then rolled to his stomach.

Melanie smiled, happy that the emotional turmoil of last night was over. Today, they seemed to be in a better place with each other. She wasn't sure why the change had come about...if it was her trip to the ER or because he was fully sober. Whatever it was, she didn't care. She'd enjoy the lighthearted time with him.

She ran her hands over the smooth tan skin of his back and thought of Caesar's inked skin. "Why don't you have any tattoos?"

"Was never my thing." He sighed. "Preferred my needles with heroin, not ink."

Melanie shivered. "I'm glad you stopped doing that."

"Me, too."

As she continued to caress him, she marveled at his body. For someone with so many unhealthy habits, he'd managed to stay in great shape. "Do you work out?"

"Admiring my assets?"

She popped him on the butt. "Be serious. You're in excellent shape for someone..."

"So old?"

She smacked his butt again. "Someone..."

"So fucked-up on drugs and alcohol."

"Yeah. I suppose that's what I was thinking."

He rolled back over and pulled her down next to him. "The times when I tried to get sober, I'd work out. Treadmill mostly. I took yoga classes for a bit but quit when I messed up my sobriety. What about you?"

"What about me?"

His hand roamed down her side. "How did you get this fantastic body of yours?"

"Lots of pizza!" She laughed.

He turned her over and popped her butt. Then mimicking her voice said, "Be serious!"

"I walked mostly." She lay on her back. "I lived near Grant Park. I went there a lot after work and on weekends. It's a peaceful place and pretty there."

"I remember going there a few times myself. And the botanical gardens."

"I love it there, too."

"Do you think we were ever in those places at the same time?"

Overcome with a surge of emotions, Melanie covered her face with her hands and began crying.

"I'm sorry, babe. What did I say?" He drew her closer, holding her tight. Her tears dampened his chest, but he didn't let go.

After a few minutes, she edged away, and grabbed some tissues off the nightstand.

"Are you alright?"

She nodded as she sat up to blow her nose. "Everything's been so emotional."

"Tell me about it." He caressed her face. "When you passed out...I've never been so scared in my life...and the blood."

"Type O negative." She lay back down beside him.

Johnnie grasped her hand, brought it to his mouth, and pressed several kisses against the back of it. "Can you tell me more about your family? About what happened?"

She bit her bottom lip, and a tear slid from her right eye.

"You don't have to."

"Can you go into the room with all my boxes and get the one that has two hearts drawn on it?"

"Sure." He bounded out of the room to retrieve it.

She sat up and propped several pillows behind her. He came in a few minutes later with the box and set it down next to the bed. His brow furrowed as he traced the outlines of the hearts. The ones Caesar had drawn.

"What is it?"

"You drew this?"

Her heart raced. "A friend of mine did. Why?"

"Strange. It looks like something I've seen before."

Caesar's artwork. He recognizes it!

"There's a photo album inside that you can hand to me."

He opened the box and brought out the album. Then he sniffed something in the air and crinkled his face.

"Oh no. Tell me something did not crawl in there and die."

"It's not that. It's Caesar again. It smells like vanilla oil inside."

"Maybe I set it in some when I was putting things away."

"Maybe." He joined her again on the bed.

She took the album from him and sat it in her lap. Closing her eyes, she took a deep breath. She hadn't looked at these photos in years.

"We don't have to do this, Melanie. If it's too painful..."

"I need to." She put her head on his shoulder. "It's time."

The first page was their birth announcement, their footprints, and the hospital issued baby photos.

He inhaled sharply. "Twins?"

"Yes." She swallowed hard. "Leila and Lily."

Melanie felt the tears begin again. She hadn't said their names aloud in a very long time. They were always *the girls* or *the twins* if her parents ever brought them up. And her parents had stopped bringing them up years ago. They'd always tried to tiptoe around the issue knowing how painful it was for her.

"They're beautiful." Johnnie flipped to the next page where there were photos of her parents holding them and of course, Logan.

"This is your husband?"

She nodded, then blew her nose.

"You said a man broke your heart. You meant him, didn't you? Not some recent guy, but this one."

"He was a good man. As far as I know, he never cheated but..." She stopped herself, still scared to tell him the truth. He would see himself in Logan. Her husband had been a drunk and had destroyed her world because of it. Johnnie thought he would as well which is why he would not let himself get close to her.

Johnnie kept turning pages, viewing the progression of her daughters' lives. Then after their fourth birthday, the photos abruptly ended. She hadn't even added the ones from her brother's wedding. He went back a few pages, examining one photo.

"What caused the accident?" he asked.

She cried harder now.

He slid the photo from the album, then placed the album back inside the box. "Tell me."

Instead, she turned away from him. "I can't."

"Why not?" he asked, gently stroking her arm.

"I'm afraid of losing you."

He scooted closer, brushed the hair back from her shoulder, and kissed her there. "I'm not going anywhere. Tell me."

She shook her head.

"He was driving drunk, wasn't he?"

"What?" She turned to him, her mouth open. "How did you know?"

He sat the photo in her lap. Logan was with the girls sitting on the couch. Next to him on the end table were several beer bottles.

"This doesn't mean anything."

He lifted her gaze to his. "Except it does, doesn't it?"

She couldn't speak as her tears fell full force. She nodded.

He flopped back on the bed, tears of his own starting to fall. "I'm so sorry."

"It's not your fault."

"Why the fuck would you even want to be with someone like me after what you've been through?"

Hadn't she known he would say that? She wiped at her tears. "I can't explain it. But given everything, how we came to be together, it feels like it was meant to be. As if we're being pushed together by some force greater than us."

Gently, he stroked her face again. "I felt something the day I met you...and then all these connections we seem to have..."

"Are we crazy?"

"I'm not." He tweaked her nose. "But the jury's still out on you."

She shook her head. "You *are* impossible."

"Come here." He gathered her back into his arms. He kissed the top of her head, then began rubbing her arms and back.

"My head hurts."

"I bet." He kissed her forehead. "We need to get you focused on something else, something less sad, before you pop those stitches open. I'll get you some water so you can take one of your pain pills."

"Can you bring my purse? I need to check my phone."

"How about some food? Are you hungry?"

"Maybe a few crackers to take with the pill."

He first returned with her purse and a glass of water. When he left to go back downstairs, she took out her prescriptions, popped one pain pill, then washed it down with water. She stared at the bottle of pills. *Should I hide these?* They would be a temptation for Johnnie, but she wanted to trust him, so she set them on the nightstand next to the antibiotics. She found her phone, saw that she had no calls or text messages, and set it next to the bottles. Knowing the pill would knock her out soon, she took off her clothes and slipped under the covers naked.

Johnnie returned with a plate of cheese, crackers, and sliced fruit. He also had her laptop bag. He set the plate down on the nightstand, then got her laptop out and turned it on.

"I thought we could watch a movie." He lay down beside her. "You know, *Netflix* and chill."

"Which I've heard is dating code for *let's have sex.*"

"Except when you have eight stitches in your forehead, or you've been up half the night worrying about the person with the eight stitches in their forehead. Then it means *Netflix* and chill."

She smiled and ate a few crackers with cheese while he looked for a movie to watch.

"How about this one?" He pointed to the screen. "About a haunted house."

"Evil ghosts? No thanks."

"What would you like?" he asked. "Wait. Let me guess. *The Notebook*?"

"Is that on the list?" She smiled. "I love that movie."

"Figures." He continued scrolling.

She jabbed him in the belly with a finger. "Have you even seen it?"

"Hell no."

"Then how do you know if you'd like it or not?"

Now he jabbed her belly. "Romance was Caesar's realm, not mine."

"Really? This coming from a guy who used to play beautiful love songs."

"Caesar wrote the lyrics, remember?" Then he winked. "We played a lot of songs about sex, too."

"They can go hand in hand you know." She yawned. "Watch what you want. I'll be asleep soon. This medication is making me drowsy."

Signaling victory, he raised both hands skyward. "Porn it is then."

"Knock yourself out." She rolled her eyes. "As long as you wait until I'm asleep."

"Deal." He bit into an apple slice.

"Don't get cum all over my comforter."

"How about if I get it under your comforter." He jumped off the bed and pulled back the covers. "Why are you naked? Do you have plans you didn't mention?"

She threw a pillow at him. "You know I always sleep naked."

"I do?"

"I was naked when we first met."

He grinned. "You were, weren't you."

"We both were."

"You've always worn clothes since then. When I have the night terrors, and you sleep with me."

"True. But in my bed, I wear nothing."

"Perhaps I should wear nothing as well. Seeing as how I'll be jerking off to porn while you sleep."

"Suit yourself." She was too tired to play his silly game with him. She yawned again and flipped to her side, away from him. "I'm going to sleep."

When she awoke again, he was under the covers, cuddled close, and as naked as she was. Unlike the first time she'd woke to find him in bed with her, this time she was happy to be snuggled up with him.

Her laptop was between them on top of the comforter. She smiled when she saw that he'd been watching one of her favorite romantic comedies, *P. S. I love you.* She closed the computer and set it down on top of the box by the bed. She felt warm all over, seeing him like this, sleeping so peacefully, when often his body and mind never settled into rest easily. Like Caesar, he was a beautiful man, one who had aged gracefully. Gently, she caressed his dark brown hair. Yes, there were a few greys tucked in here and there, but it only added to his character and went well with his blue-grey eyes. She envied his long eyelashes and high cheekbones. And those lips. Her hand traveled to them, and she ran a light finger over them.

Johnnie pressed kisses against her fingers, then her palm.

"You're awake."

"No, baby. This is a dream." He caressed the side of her face as his eyes locked onto hers. "A beautiful dream."

She was unnerved by the intensity of his stare. Her cheeks burned. It was clearly written in his eyes. He wanted her.

His hand left her face and traveled down her neck to her chest. Softly, he skimmed his palm over her nipple bringing it to life. His eyes never left hers as he then kneaded her breast. Her hand went to his chest where his heart pounded as hard as hers.

Grabbing the covers, he flung them backward and off, fully exposing their bodies to one another. They'd seen one another naked before. They'd slept together. They'd even made each other cum out on the deck. But for some reason, she felt vulnerable, frightened of the possibilities. And excited by them as well. *This is happening!*

He moved over her, and his lips were on her neck, then her mouth. Their kisses grew longer and harder as their hands explored one another's bodies. His cock ground painfully into her belly, then her hip. She parted her legs, inviting him in.

He hovered over her, staring down. "You scare the hell out of me, Melanie. But I can't fight how I feel. I love you, and I want to be inside of you. I *need* to be inside of you."

"I love you, Johnnie." She pulled him down on top of her and ran her hands down his back, from his shoulders to his butt. She spread her legs further apart. "Make love to me."

They continued to gaze into one another's eyes as the thick head of his cock found her wet opening. He pushed himself inside, and she let out a little cry, one of pleasure...and relief that they'd finally gotten here. They were one.

"Shit," he muttered and stopped. "You feel too good. I'm going to explode already."

"Magic pussy." She smiled, causing him to chuckle. "You can cum as many times as you like."

"Right now, I want you to cum." He withdrew his cock.

She pouted. "Don't stop."

He slid down her body until his head was between her legs. "Magic tongue, remember?"

"Refresh my memory."

His tongue *was* magic. She moaned loudly as he fucked her with it. When he began flicking it across her clit, she grabbed his hair. "You're going to make me cum."

"You're going to make me bald." He laughed and stretched his body back over hers.

"You're stopping?"

"Thought you wanted my cock." He slid into her again. She was even wetter than before. He ground his hips into hers. "I want to feel you cum."

Wrapping her legs around him, she panted. "Make me cum."

His pace increased as his lips found hers again. A hand came to her breast, teasing her nipple, pinching it.

"Suck them," she whispered.

"Is that what you like?"

"Yes."

He shifted their position, bringing her to his lap while he sat. Her legs were bent on each side of him, her nipples right in his face so he could feast on them.

"Johnnie," she moaned and tossed her head back.

He swirled his tongue around one nipple, then sucked on it. Then he teased her with a laugh. "Should I stop now?"

"Please don't."

He grabbed her hips and helped her grind even harder into him. "Cum for me."

As his mouth latched back onto a nipple, her body tensed and shuddered. He pushed her onto her back once again and drove into her, making her body quake and tighten its grip on his cock. She ran her hands down his back to his butt. She squeezed as he pushed into her over and over.

"I fucking love you, Melanie," he admitted before releasing himself inside her.

As he lay on top of her, breathing heavily, she caressed his back. Then he propped himself up on his elbows and smiled down at her. "Magic."

She laughed. "Magic together."

"Indeed." He began moving inside her once more, hardening again.

She ran her hands through his hair. "No regrets."

"About loving you?" He kissed her. "Never."

Chapter Thirteen

"Oh my God, this is exactly why I don't have a damn phone." Johnnie grouched when Melanie's ringtone began playing.

"Sorry," she mumbled, waking up from slumber. "I thought it was on silent."

"And you had to have *that* song playing."

She lifted herself from the crook of his arm. "I love this song."

"You would."

It was a Lush hit from early in their recording career. One where Caesar's voice was all breathy and teasing. A song about wanting and needing sex. It seemed perfect given the fact they'd spent the last two days in bed making love nearly nonstop.

"Stop being jealous and hand me my phone."

"Ignore it," he said before nipping her neck.

She tapped his arm. "It might be important."

The ringtone stopped.

"Good. And now that we're awake, let's get back to business." His ran his hands all over her.

The song started again. Johnnie cursed, and Melanie laughed. "Hand it to me."

"I'll get rid of them." Johnnie grabbed the phone and hopped out of bed. Without even checking who it was, he answered. "You're interrupting some excellent fucking."

"Johnnie!" Melanie hoped it wasn't her parents.

His eyes widened, and he stared down at the screen. His surprised gaze then turned to her. His chest pumped up and down as he threw the phone on the bed.

"Who is it?" As she reached for it, he pulled on his pants and stormed out of the room.

"Hello?" she asked. "Are you still there?"

"Was that Johnnie?" A woman's voice. Melanie checked the number calling. *Oh shit!*

"Mrs. Smith?" Melanie scrambled out of the bed, grabbed a sundress, and slipped it over her head.

"Was that Johnnie?"

"Yes, it was."

"Put him back on, please."

She hurried downstairs but couldn't find him anywhere. "Mrs. Smith, I don't know where he is. He picked up my phone, but when he realized it was you, he got upset."

"I got your message. Where are you two? In Atlanta?" Mrs. Smith sounded as if she were crying.

"In California. At Caesar's beach house."

"I need to speak with him. It's an emergency."

"Did you tell him that?"

"I tried to, but I'm not sure if he heard me."

Melanie walked over to the windows overlooking the ocean. "He may be outside on the beach. I'll find him and have him call you."

"Please do. I was so happy to get your message. His father mentioned talking to you a couple of months ago. We've been very worried about him."

"He's fine, Mrs. Smith."

"His father isn't. He's in the hospital. It's his heart again."

"I'm sorry." She walked outside onto the deck. When she saw the broken glass, she went back inside to slip shoes on. "I'm going to look for him now."

"Thank you."

Melanie hung up and started across the deck to the stairs. She saw blood. *He isn't wearing shoes.* She followed the bloody footprints out to some rocks which were about five hundred feet down from their private beachfront. Johnnie was sitting on top of a large rock...obviously waiting...knowing she would come.

"You're bleeding. Come back to the house so we can clean that up."

"I'm fine. I pulled the glass out."

"But the blood." She lightly touched the arc of his foot where the cut appeared to be.

He snatched his foot away and tucked it under him. "Don't touch me."

"Johnnie, I can explain. But we need to clean that cut. It looks deep."

He jumped off the rock, landing on both feet. He grimaced, obviously fighting the pain. He closed in, his face inches away from hers. "You lied to me. You said you didn't know my parents. You said they didn't send you."

"They didn't."

"But you know them."

"No, I don't. I talked to your dad once about possibly doing a story on the band. That's it."

"How am I supposed to believe you?" he raged and quickly moved away. He shook his head. "No wonder there are so many coincidences between us. It's a huge fucking set up, isn't it?"

"I don't even know what you mean by that." Her head began to pound. "Let's go back to the house and talk. You need to call your mother back. She says your father's in the hospital."

"You think I believe you? Or her for that matter? My parents and their stupid interventions. Always trying to get me into rehab. Did you know they even tried that damn reality show? The one where the counselors show up and take you away? My own parents, knowing how famous I am, tried to pull that on me. It's why I don't visit them anymore."

"That's not what this is. I swear I've never met them."

He stared up at the sky and chuckled. "I've got to hand it to them. This is some creative shit. Sending me a beautiful woman, hoping she'd distract me from my problems. It almost worked, too. The last couple of days, making love to you...I haven't thought once about drinking. I didn't even look at those damn pills of yours."

"Johnnie, they did not send me."

"I don't believe you." He put his hands on his hips and paced around in circles. "I knew you were too good to be true...that there had to be a catch."

"There's no catch, Johnnie. I haven't lied to you." She grabbed his arm and blocked him from moving. "At least not where your parents are concerned."

His eyes narrowed, and his face turned red. He jerked his arm away. "Really? What *have* you lied about then?"

"The things about Caesar. About meeting him before he died."

"What does that make you then? Some crazy fan who broke into our house and took up residence, hoping to seduce me if I ever showed up?"

"Not at all."

"Then what?" His eyes started to water. "Explain this shit to me. What are you lying about?"

She didn't know where to begin. How could she explain Caesar and what they'd shared? Johnnie would never believe her, and he'd only end up hating her.

He started to walk away, then turned back to her. "Were you lying when you said you loved me?"

"No." She went to him and touched his face. "I do love you."

He grabbed her arms roughly. "Then tell me the truth! All of it!"

"I don't know how."

"Start at the beginning."

"You won't believe me."

He shoved her away and stalked back toward the house.

"Remember when you said you sometimes see Caesar?" She followed him. "That you thought you were seeing his ghost? You said it was one of the reasons you did more drugs and alcohol...to get rid of those visions."

He turned around and crossed his arms over his chest. "I'm an addict. I see, say, and do stupid shit all the time. If I saw Caesar, it was because I was high."

He continued toward the house, but she ran ahead and stood in front of him. "Well, what's my excuse then?"

"What the fuck are you talking about?"

"I don't get drunk or high. But I saw Caesar. I met him. Nearly two months ago. Right before my birthday."

"Now I've heard it all." He laughed and pushed past her. Stepping around the glass, he climbed the stairs. Then, he stopped and turned around. "You should forget the documentary. Stick to writing those fiction novels you work on at night. Because your imagination is pretty wild."

He stormed into the house. Frustrated, Melanie sat down on the top step. *How can I make him believe?*

Opening the door of Johnnie's shower, Melanie stepped in.

He jumped slightly. "What the fuck are you doing? We're done. You need to start packing your shit so you can go."

She stood under the water, dousing herself. "I'm not going anywhere. Caesar said I could stay here."

"Yeah, Caesar's ghost. Not sure that will hold up in a court of law."

Ignoring him, she scrubbed her body, using his body wash, then she ran it through her wet hair, scrubbing her head with the suds.

"You're getting your stitches wet," he grumbled.

"I don't care!"

"Trying to get the smell of me off your body?" He cupped her crotch, slipping a finger inside her. "Want to wash all the cum away?"

Her heart pounded. "I'm trying to put your scent on me. I want to prove something."

"What? That if you smell like a man, I won't want you." He pushed her against the tiled wall of the shower. He breathed hot and heavy on her neck. "You smell like Caesar all the time, and I still fucked you."

She stared hard at him, letting him know she wasn't intimidated by his anger. "Are you going to fuck me now?"

"Do you want me?"

She turned and pushed her butt toward him. He got the message and shoved himself inside of her. There was no tenderness to their lovemaking now. He slammed into her over and over.

"I guess if my parents are paying you," he snarled sinisterly in her ear. "I should make sure they get their money's worth."

She reached behind her, grabbing his head and bringing it closer. Her lips went to his, kissing him. "No one has to pay me to fuck you, Johnnie. I love fucking you."

He withdrew, and she was afraid he was going to leave her there, unsatisfied. Instead, he spun her around and dropped to his knees. He parted her, and his tongue danced over her clit. She put a foot on his shoulder. It didn't take him long. Not with that magic tongue.

"I need you inside me."

He stood and pushed her against the wall again. Then he slid into her. His mouth locked onto hers and his hands came to her breasts, pinching her nipples. She let out a loud moan as she came, her pussy clamped onto his cock, trapping him inside her. He groaned and released inside her.

Without a word, he left the shower, wrapped a towel around himself and sat on his bed. Again, she scrubbed herself with his body wash. When she got out, she wrapped herself in a towel as well and went to join him on the bed.

"What is it you're trying to prove using up all my soap?"

"Smell me."

"I know what my soap smells like."

"But I don't smell like your soap."

She lifted the hair from her neck. He leaned over and sniffed. "You smell like Caesar. As always."

"Why do you think that is?"

"Because his scent is all over this house."

"Only in his closet, and even so, it's very faint. I scrubbed the house down when I moved in. It doesn't smell like him, but I do. You bought me that lavender soap and I've used it every day, but it never washes away his scent."

"What are you trying to tell me?"

"When I met Caesar, I inhaled that vanilla scent before I ever saw him. He'd take a shower and wash his hair, but it never went away. And when he left, I realized I smelled just like him. You smelled it when you met me. Rhett did too. He completely freaked out about it."

He closed his eyes and sighed. "I'm supposed to believe you met Caesar's ghost."

"I know it's unbelievable. It took me a while to believe it. He didn't know exactly why he'd been sent to me. He only knew he was here to help me. And he did. Before I met him, I was sleepwalking through life. I had no social life, no friends. I didn't go out with men or have sex."

His eyes flew open. "You had sex with his ghost?"

Thinking about it now, she got choked up. She willed herself not to cry as she tried to catch her breath. She nodded.

"Fucking unbelievable."

She took a deep breath to relax herself. Then she continued. "Caesar and I met with this ghost expert, so we could talk to him about why he might have returned. The man, Tim, felt that you and I had some connection. But I had no idea what it was, other than you being my pinup boy when I was younger. I'd never even been to a Lush concert or met any of you until July. I met Caesar, then Rhett, and now you. When I found out it was your blood I received in my transfusion, everything made sense. That was our connection. Caesar came to help me, but he was also trying to help you. Your parents didn't send me to straighten you out. Caesar did."

He stood, and the towel fell from him. He rubbed his neck obviously considering what she'd told him. *At least he's trying.*

"The hearts on that box," she said quietly. "You said you'd seen them before."

He turned to her. "Caesar drew them?"

She nodded.

He slipped on a pair of sweatpants. "Be right back."

He returned with the box he'd found Caesar's cassette tapes in. It was an old shoebox really, but when he flipped the lid, beneath it was a drawing of two hearts connected. Surprised, her hand flew to her mouth.

"Swear to me you didn't draw this, Melanie."

"You found those, remember? Not me."

"There's one more thing, if I can find it." He left the room again. This time she followed. Upstairs in her room, he pulled something off the top shelf of Caesar's closet. It was a rectangular shaped wooden box.

"What is it?" she asked.

He opened it and inside were papers. "Caesar's poems from when we were in school. Some eventually became song lyrics."

He pushed the box toward her, and she pulled the stack out. As she flipped through the pages, she saw that on the bottom of each page, beneath his name were the two interlocking hearts. "I suppose you could say I copied it from something he published. Something that was out there in public."

Johnnie shook his head. "He *never* put this on anything other than private stuff. It was sort of his personal logo."

"Does that mean you believe me?"

He wiped his brow. "I'm still wrapping my head around the possibility."

"He told me about the pissing contest. In the outback. Kurt won."

He stared at her, probably looking to see if she'd flinch, admit she was lying. Then suddenly, he burst into tears. She hugged him tight.

"I need to show you one more thing."

He wiped his eyes. "Why not? Keep scaring the shit out of me."

"There's no need to be scared. It was a wonderful thing...being with him."

"You weren't the one who killed him."

"You didn't either." She touched his cheek. "Help me move the bed."

Together they pushed the bed to one side.

"Look." Melanie pointed to the board with Caesar's initials. She'd kept the boards loose, and they easily popped up for her this time.

"A safe?" He studied her intently as she opened it.

The only things inside were Caesar's mother's jewelry and the letter he'd left behind. She handed the letter to Johnnie.

"Fuck me!" He sat down hard on the floor, staring at the words.

"His handwriting?"

Johnnie nodded. He seemed to be reading it repeatedly. He laughed lightly. "Well, that explains where the dragon went."

"I had to break it open."

"And the money?"

"Five hundred thousand. It's in my bank account. I've only used it to buy the new computer and editing equipment. I can give you whatever you need, Johnnie. He probably wanted you to have it."

He shook his head. "Hell no. I know for a fact he didn't. If he wanted me to have it, he would've left it to me. Him hiding it here and never telling me or the other guys means it wasn't meant for anyone but him...and now you. He knew damn well what I'd do with it."

"But you need it."

"I don't. I get by."

She nodded. "You read where he said you weren't responsible for his fall?"

He shrugged and handed the letter back. "He probably said that so you'd feel better about possibly meeting me."

The hurt in his eyes was evident, and she wished there were some way she could make him believe. If he continued to live with his guilt, he'd never get sober.

After she locked the letter in the safe again, they slid the bed back into place. She picked up her phone and handed it to him.

"Call your mother, please."

He wiped at his eyes and nodded. He took the phone downstairs. She didn't follow, knowing he needed privacy and time to think.

She went into her bathroom to comb out her hair. Her bandage was wet, so she removed it. The skin around the stitches looked red. *Probably from all the emotional stress. Not to mention the sex.* Having her head shoved into a pillow while being fucked from behind probably hadn't helped matters. She went into her bedroom and grabbed the bottle of antibiotics.

Downstairs she made toast and slathered it with peanut butter so that she could take the meds with food.

"Where's mine?" Johnnie wrapped his arms around her from behind.

She held the toast to his mouth, and he took a bite. "You have some peanut butter on your face."

"Lick it off."

She ran her tongue over the corner of his mouth.

"If I put some peanut butter on my dick, will you lick that off, too."

"Why don't you *not* put peanut butter on your dick, and I'll lick it anyway."

He kissed her neck. "Sounds like a plan."

"You talked to your mom?"

He nodded.

"Are you going to Atlanta?" She ducked away to make a slice of toast for him.

"Why would I?"

"To see your dad."

"Don't want to see him."

"Johnnie, he's your dad. You said he's had heart problems before. You need to see him. What if something happened to him and you weren't there?"

"He'll be fine."

"Your mom sounded worried, and she could probably use your comfort. They've obviously missed you very much."

His eyes flashed with anger. "You tell me you don't know them, yet you're able to tell me how they feel?"

The toast popped up. She grabbed it, put it on a plate and spread peanut butter on it. Then she placed the plate in front of him.

"If you don't want to go, that's fine."

"I don't."

"I need to present our proposal to the news network. My old boss could get us a quick meeting. We could go soon and since we'd already be in Atlanta for that, why not visit them?"

He slammed his hand on the counter. "Who said I was going with you to Atlanta?"

She frowned, hurt by his declaration. "I assumed you would. It's your movie, too."

"You can handle all that. You used to work there, so you'll be fine without me."

She sighed and ruffled his hair. "I'm sorry this has been an upsetting day for you."

"Don't feel sorry for me," he replied gruffly. "These are my issues, not yours."

"What affects you, affects me. I care about you."

"Are you afraid I'll go out and pick up some booze? Or go to a bar and get smashed?"

"I wasn't thinking that at all." *Although now I am.*

"Well, you should be. Because right now I could use a drink."

She wanted to be angry, but she couldn't. *He warned me. Several times over.* "I'm going to go lie down. My head hurts."

He gently touched her hairline right above her stitches. "Your skin's inflamed. Did you take the antibiotic?"

She nodded.

"I'll go to the market and get you some *Neosporin*."

"I don't need it."

He rubbed her chin. "*Now* you're worried I'll drink."

Huffing, she folded her arms in front of her. "Well, I wasn't until you mentioned it."

"It's reality with me, Melanie. The norm. Get used to it."

She placed her hand on his heart. "Even if I begged you not to drink..."

"I can't promise I won't. I've been trying...I haven't wanted anything the last couple of days, but that doesn't mean I won't drink again. Or take something I shouldn't. It's a day to day thing."

"I understand."

"Do you really?" he asked, sneering. "Because I'm not sure you get the enormity of my problem."

"I was married to an alcoholic, remember?"

"And apparently you stayed with him until it was too late."

She inhaled as a sharp pain stabbed her heart. "What an awful thing to say. I lost my girls."

"Exactly. You should have left him. Maybe you wouldn't have."

"You don't know anything about our situation. You didn't know him."

Johnnie rolled his eyes. "Oh, I'm sure he was a pillar of virtue."

"He *was* a good person."

"With a bad habit. Like me. Except I've never been good."

She couldn't stand to hear his self-loathing. "I'm going upstairs."

He grabbed her arm. "If you want to love me, you have to learn to deal with me."

"Maybe you're right." She nodded. "I didn't deal with his problem. Maybe it is my fault my children died."

"Shit, Melanie." He rubbed her arm as he pressed soft kisses all over her face. "I didn't mean to imply that. Fuck! See, I say stupid shit all the time and hurt people."

"But it's true. I knew his drinking was getting worse, and I thought about leaving, but I didn't. I kept thinking he'd eventually get himself together...get a new job and everything would be back to normal."

"I'm sorry." He wiped her tears away, then kissed her forehead. "Go lie down. Rest."

She was halfway up the stairs when she heard him mumble, "You stupid fucking idiot."

Why is he so hard on himself?

She grabbed her laptop and slipped under the covers. She'd watch another movie and relax.

Melanie bolted awake. She shivered, disturbed by the dream she'd had. Caesar and Johnnie both running away from her. And she couldn't catch up with them no matter how hard she tried. She couldn't have either of them.

There was a glass of water on the nightstand next to her meds. And a note from Johnnie telling her he was going out and would be back soon. *Please don't drink.*

Five hours later, he still hadn't returned. The sun was setting. She'd swept up the glass from the deck, and then hosed it down, hoping she'd gotten rid of every tiny sliver. She tried writing a bit, but it was no use. Thoughts of Johnnie filled her mind with worry. Her imagination ran wild with images of him getting drunk and crashing the car. He could end up in a hospital. Or get arrested. She hated that he didn't have a phone. *Who doesn't have one these days?* All she could do was sit, wait, and worry.

At nine, she found herself still alone, sitting in the jacuzzi, trying to relax and not panic over his absence. The moon was full, and the surf was kicking up, crashing into the shore. It was beautiful, and she wished Johnnie was here to share it with her. Or Caesar. She wouldn't mind him being here. She smiled thinking back to the day she met him. What a crazy two days! And it had put her life on a new trajectory. Which looking back, she knew was all part of his plan.

What was the plan now? Was she supposed to end up with Johnnie? Was he going to get clean? Or stay a mess? She knew he had to do it for himself not her. But she also knew Caesar had sent her here for a reason. *The documentary? A way to bring Lush back into the spotlight?* But if Johnnie wasn't sober how could he deal with all the new attention? His constant put-downs of himself worried her.

A crack of lightning sent her scrambling out of the jacuzzi and back into the house. By the time she'd showered off and put on her pajamas, it was raining outside. Her concern for Johnnie increased. If he'd gotten drunk, the last thing he needed to be doing was driving on a wet road.

She drank a glass of water and took another antibiotic pill. Her head ached a little, but she was reluctant to take a pain pill. She wanted to know when he returned, and not be fast asleep. *Then again, if I'm asleep, I won't be worrying.* She took one, went into the living room, turned on the television, and lay down on the couch.

"Hey, sleepyhead, wake up." Johnnie shook her gently, then brushed a kiss against her lips.

"Am I dreaming again?"

"Oh?" He made a space for himself to sit on the couch. "You've been dreaming about me?"

"You and Caesar."

He kissed her again. "Trying to make me jealous?"

She smiled. "Where have you been?"

"Everywhere." He crossed one leg over the other. His foot was bandaged. "Starting with the emergency care center."

She touched the bandage. "I told you it looked bad."

"I didn't listen until I was at the store picking up a few things and started bleeding all over the floor."

"Are you okay?"

"Guess how many stitches." He grinned.

She eased herself up to sit. "Eight?"

He nodded.

"You're right. Sometimes this thing between us...all the coincidences...is a bit scary."

"Are you scared of me?" He slid his index finger from the bridge of her nose down to the tip.

She slipped her hands into his hair. "I'm scared *for* you. For us."

"I didn't drink, Melanie. However, I did get us a pizza if you're hungry."

"Starving. I didn't eat lunch or dinner."

"You were *that* worried about me?"

She nodded.

He brushed back her hair. "I needed to get away and think. Run some errands."

"We need to get you a phone, so we can call or text one another."

"We will. Let's eat some pizza." He grabbed her hand and pulled her up from to couch.

"Tell me more about Caesar." Johnnie cuddled closer to her as they lay in bed. "I want to believe you, but I need to hear more."

Melanie sighed. Thinking of Caesar made her both happy and sad. Being with him was thrilling...it was such a brief time that it felt like a vacation fling. A romantic getaway that's over too soon but leaves a lasting impression. Carefree and wild. The way she ended things, still hurt. She'd apologized to him a thousand times in her head, but it still didn't feel like enough. She'd love to see him again, but where would that leave her and Johnnie?

"Hello?" Johnnie chuckled and waved his hand in front of her face. "It's okay. I promise not to get jealous."

She turned to face him. "Nothing to be jealous of."

"You said you loved him and you had sex with him. Plenty enough for me."

She pouted. "You just said..."

"Let me rephrase. I'll *try* not to get jealous."

"Then let me say again. Nothing to be jealous of. We were together for two days. And then he was gone. Besides he was a ghost. Real, but not real."

He entwined his fingers with hers. "Explain."

"It was real. It happened...but it couldn't last forever. Not like you and me."

"Forever? You think this might last forever?"

Why did I say that? "Well, we have a better chance than me and Caesar."

Johnnie grunted and sat up. "You were probably better off with him."

Melanie winced. *Not again with this self-loathing.* "Maybe so. At least he was sure of things...sure that he wanted to be with me."

"Really?" Johnnie snatched his hand from hers. "Then where is he?"

"We argued, and I sent him away."

"He let you go without a fight? Typical Caesar. Ready to move on to the next woman."

"He fought hard for us, but me stabbing him didn't help."

His blue eyes widened. "You stabbed him?"

"With a butcher knife."

"Okay, back this up. How did *that* happen?"

Melanie explained, telling him about the afternoon she'd come home to find Caesar going through her things, trying to get her to talk about her daughters when she'd not been ready to face that tragedy. "And he said I needed to get rid of their things."

"Ten years is a long time to hold onto grief and let it control your life."

Melanie sat up. "Says the man holding onto guilt for the last sixteen years...letting it eat him alive."

"Touché."

"I know Caesar was right, but at the time, I wasn't ready to hear it. So, I pushed him away. Told him he wasn't real. Stabbed him to prove it. The knife went in, but when I pulled it out, his wound healed like it had never been there. I cut his hair, and it grew right back."

Johnnie raised an eyebrow. "Interesting."

She scooted off the bed and went to one of her jewelry boxes. When she returned, she held the curl, tied together with ribbon, out to Johnnie. He recoiled.

"Why didn't you show this to me earlier?"

"You were upset, and I wasn't sure you even believed me. I was afraid you might destroy it or flush it down the toilet."

He laughed lightly. "You're getting to know me pretty well."

"Speaking and acting out on emotion without thinking seems to be your forte."

He grinned.

"Take it," she pushed the curl closer. "Smell it."

He refused. "Vanilla, right?"

"Of course." *Why was he hesitant?* She didn't want to force him, but she wanted him to believe.

"You said he wasn't real. That looks real."

She nodded. "Even if I hadn't sent him away, I'm not sure he could have stayed with me forever."

Johnnie turned his hand over, and she placed the hair into his palm. He brought it to his nose, then ran his finger over its softness.

"When you first saw him...what did you think? Were you scared?"

"I thought he was some guy who looked like him. And that he was a jerk."

"Like me?"

Melanie smiled. "Actually, a lot like you. He propositioned me for sex in the middle of a store."

"And..."

"You think I took him up on his offer?"

"Right...you thought he was a look alike." Johnnie playfully poked her belly. "You didn't have sex until you were convinced he was Caesar."

"Well..."

"Am I right?"

"Sort of." She shrugged. "But that's not the reason why I had sex with him."

"Why did you?"

"It just happened. He showed up at my house and next thing I know..."

Johnnie fell back on the bed laughing hysterically. "Oh yes! Sounds just like him. Irresistible Caesar. Not a woman could say no to him. Not even you."

She pouted. "I did at the store."

"Because you didn't think it was him."

"It wasn't planned. I was taking a shower and next thing I knew he was there with me..."

"Hmm...seems like there are perks to being a ghost. Show up in a beautiful woman's shower and seduce her."

Sitting back on the bed, Melanie frowned. *He's right though.* Caesar had seduced her. And she hadn't been able to say no once he'd gotten her turned on with the hair washing.

"Do you think he was lying when he said he loved me?"

Johnnie sat up beside her, lifted her hair and slid Caesar's curl against her neck. "He had a habit of falling in love with beautiful women. So, I don't doubt it at all."

Hadn't she thought the same thing? How easily Caesar fell in love and seemed to love so effortlessly? Somehow hearing it from Johnnie hurt though. She wanted to think that what she and Caesar shared was special.

Johnnie must have sensed her hurt feelings. He kissed her neck as he stroked her face lovingly with the hair. "But remember, you're the only one he ever gave his house to."

"He gave it to you first. Because he loved you."

"And he sent you to me. Better than any house."

Melanie kissed him tenderly, then suddenly remembered something. "Did he run around naked a lot?"

Johnnie grinned. "We were always pelting him with clothes, telling him to put them on. He was a born nudist."

She laughed then frowned. "He had no idea how long he'd been dead. He's forever twenty-eight."

"Oh. I see," Johnnie teased. "A younger man."

"That's not why I slept with him. Although that's one of the reasons I first said no to him."

"I wish I could've been there for that. What a blow to his ego."

"He's not the least bit egotistical."

"You're right, but he was used to getting any woman he wanted."

"I know. He told me. He was much nicer the second time we met."

"Naked in the shower?"

"No. At the music festival."

"The same one where you met Rhett?"

"Yes, but I met Rhett later that day when I went back to the festival." She told him about returning to meet Mr. Harris and about the panic attack.

"Rhett said he'd seen Caesar, too?"

Melanie nodded. "Then he smelled me and got upset."

"I bet." Johnnie waved the curl back and forth in front of his nose. "I guess we should get in touch with him and Kurt soon."

"I've got the numbers to their agents."

"You do?"

"I've got great connections." She smiled.

"Since we're up, we could get some work done on the video. Do a little more editing, so it will be ready for you to take it to Atlanta."

"Already done. And I sent my former boss a meeting request, too. I'll be flying out soon I imagine. Are you sure you won't go with me?"

He shook his head. "I'll let you take care of it."

Melanie was disappointed.

He lay down and pulled her to him. "Close your eyes."

"Why?"

"Just do it."

"Alright." She closed them. Then she felt a soft caress against her nipple. *Is he rubbing Caesar's hair on me?*

"Do you like that?"

Her mind remembered making love to Caesar, his hair caressing her skin, as his lips traveled down her body. "Yes."

He brushed it against her belly. "Maybe I should let my hair grow longer."

She opened her eyes and stared at him. His hair was already longer than when they'd met a month ago. It was starting to curl at the ends. She wondered what it would look like if he let it grow as long as Caesar's.

"You're thinking of Caesar, aren't you?"

"It's hard not to when you're rubbing his hair all over me."

"Do you miss him?"

"Don't you?"

He winced as he placed Caesar's hair on the nightstand. "Every day."

"I'm sorry that you lost your best friend." She reached up and caressed his face. "I can't imagine what it must have been like. And then to have all the media attention focused on it."

Melanie saw the pain in his eyes, but he didn't respond. Instead, his lips found hers. He slipped inside her and then turned them over so that she was on top of him.

"Make me feel better," he said as a tear slipped from the corner of his eye.

Slowly she began to move. He placed his hands on her hips, and their gazes met and held as she sensually ground her body into his. He pulled himself into a sitting position, wrapping his arms around her.

"I miss him so much." His voice cracked as he began sobbing.

She held his head tightly against her breasts, and his tears wet them.

"Please don't stop," he told her and continued to cry.

Keeping him cuddled against her, she began her slow grind again. "Damn it!"

"Is it not good?"

He pressed desperate kisses all over her face. "The more I fuck you, the more I want to fuck you. Harder, longer, deeper. It's never enough. I can't get enough of you, babe."

She laughed, feeling delighted. "Is that a bad thing?"

"You've become my new addiction."

"Isn't it better than your others?"

"No, because if you break my heart, it will be the death of me."

Melanie kissed him even harder.

"I know it's not romantic, but I really want to fuck you from behind. Can I do that?"

"Yes," she said breathlessly. "I love when you do that."

"I love you." He kissed her.

She eased off him, then turned to face the other direction. He rubbed the head of his cock all over her pussy, spreading her wetness.

"Do you want me?" he asked, placing his cock just outside her entrance.

"Yes, Johnnie." She moaned. "I want you."

"I want to fuck you hard."

"Then fuck me hard."

All gentleness was gone as he shoved himself into her. He pulled her body back into his as he forcefully slammed into her body over and over. Melanie pushed her body back against his, meeting his thrusts so that he was as deep as he could possibly get. Reaching between her legs, she touched her clit, helping herself along.

"I'm going to cum," she told him.

"Yes, cum on me."

Her body tensed, then shuddered in release, tightening around his cock. He pushed her into the mattress and then began to slow his strokes, grinding his hips into her butt. Her body continued to spasm, and then his did as well.

Finally, he collapsed on top of her. "That felt so good."

"Do you feel better?"

He rolled to the side of her. "I always feel better with you."

"Which is why you should come with me to Atlanta."

"Dead horse, babe."

"You'll be here all alone."

"A few days. I can handle it."

"Don't you think you should see your parents?"

"That's what this is about, isn't it?" He crawled out of bed and slipped on his pajama pants. "Not me being with you for the proposal but getting me to see my parents."

"It's for both." She sat up. "Why do you hate them so much?"

"I told you why. Always interfering in my life."

"Trying to help you get sober?"

"Trying to force me to get sober."

"You said when you lived with them, you were doing pretty good. How bad could it have been?"

He ran a hand through his hair. "My mom's cool. My dad not so much."

"Then visit her at least."

"I can't. She'll see me, and I'll just be a big disappointment."

"I doubt that seriously."

"You know nothing about my life."

"Then tell me. I want to understand."

"Let's just say I've done nothing but disappoint my parents for a long time. It's better if I stay away."

"But Johnnie..."

"Stop! Drop it! Please." He threw his arms out to his side, then turned and left the room.

Melanie watched him go. *What is it with his parents? Why won't he open up to me?* It was frustrating to have him tell her he loved her, and then to shut down completely. She was trying to be patient. Obviously, this was part of his pain, the pain that had led him to drugs and alcohol. She wanted desperately to understand it all so that she could help him.

Chapter Fourteen

"You look fabulous! You're so tan." Susan hugged Melanie tightly.

Melanie beamed. "Been spending a lot of time on the beach."

"Sounds fantastic. Did you find a job yet?"

"I've been working on the documentary and writing a novel. I saved plenty of money when I was working here so I could afford the luxury of taking time off."

"Yes. The film department was raving over your work. And they couldn't believe you had access to all the film footage and photographs of this band."

"I was lucky enough to meet one of the band members. I'm working with him, and we'll soon meet with the other guys, so we can get them involved."

"Sounds exciting." Susan checked her phone. "Let's get you down to the meeting room. It's almost time."

Three hours later, Melanie was back in her hotel changing out of her business suit and into jeans and a blouse. As soon as she was casually dressed, she dialed Johnnie's new cell phone number.

"How did it go?" he asked right away.

"Fantastic. They want to buy the rights to the documentary and air it when we're done with everything. I told them about having all the band members on board, and they were thrilled. I left messages with Rhett and Kurt's agents to see if we can meet with them soon."

"Already?"

"Things are going to move fast from here."

He sighed. "I see."

"How are things there?" she asked.

"Missing you."

"I'll be back in a few days. My parents are excited that I'm visiting. They're throwing me a party since we didn't get together for my birthday."

"Sounds like fun."

She sat down on the edge of the bed. "Would be more fun if you'd hop on a plane and come with me."

"To meet your parents?"

"I realize it's a big step."

"One I'd like to wait on."

"That's fine," she replied, trying to hide her disappointment.

"You can tell them about me." He chuckled. "If you want to."

"If I don't they'll be trying to set me up on a date."

"Oh really?"

"Jealous?" she purred.

"Nah. You only want me. Oh, and Caesar."

She laughed now. "You're crazy."

"That's what people tell me."

"Well, I'm getting hungry. I'm going to do a little shopping and find some lunch."

"Hey, I've got another idea for a project we could work on together."

"Let me guess." She groaned. "Get naked on Skype?"

"Uh no. I was thinking we could write an autobiography of the band."

"Really? That's a great idea," she told him. "Are you ready to go there, though? I mean we're just getting started with the documentary. We haven't included Caesar's death yet. That's going to be tough to handle."

"I'll be fine as long as we're doing it together. It might actually be cathartic."

"It would be." She smiled. "Why don't you start doing an outline and writing some things down?"

"Already on it."

"You amaze me."

"The feeling is mutual," he replied. "Now about this Skype thing."

"Tonight?"

"It's a date."

Melanie stopped by the dress shop where she'd found her red dress a couple of months ago. She hadn't had an occasion to wear it yet, but she wanted to see if there were anything else she might like.

An hour later, she was paying for two new dresses, when her phone rang. She assumed it was Johnnie and answered right away.

"I thought we were going to talk later."

"Excuse me." A woman was on the other end.

"I'm sorry, who's this?"

"Mrs. Smith. Johnnie's mother."

What are the odds? "Oh. Can I help you?"

"Is Johnnie there?"

"No. I'm not in California at the moment."

"Do you have a way to reach him?" His mother sounded distressed.

"Has something happened?"

"His father's had another stroke."

"I'm sorry."

"Can you let him know?"

Melanie took a deep breath and let it out slowly. "I can. But Mrs. Smith, I'm in Atlanta on business. Is there any way I can stop by and see you? Maybe take you to lunch?"

"That would be nice. I don't leave the hospital much these days."

"I understand. I can meet you there, and we can eat some place nearby."

Melanie followed the directions given to her by the front desk and took the elevator to the third floor. She'd picked up a flower arrangement on her way in and signed the card from both her and Johnnie. He'd hate it, but it wasn't like he'd ever see them. She was still trying to figure out how she would tell him she'd met his mother.

"Patients in ICU aren't allowed flowers," a nurse explained.

"Could you keep them here, then? His wife can take them home with her."

The nurse nodded and set them aside. "Who are you here to visit?"

She hesitated. *Should I be doing this?* "Charles Smith."

"Are you a member of the immediate family."

"No, but I'm taking his wife to lunch."

The nurse smiled. "I'll get her for you. She needs to get out for some fresh air."

When the nurse returned to her station a short, older woman was following her. Mrs. Smith had dark brown hair like Johnnie and the same grey-blue eyes. It was clear where he got his good looks. The woman looked amazing for her age and for someone who'd been stuck in a hospital worrying about her husband.

"Melanie." Mrs. Smith wrapped Melanie in her arms. "I'm so happy to meet you."

"It's good to meet you," she greeted. "I'm not allowed in the room, so if you're ready for lunch, we can go. I saw a few places nearby if you don't mind walking."

"Not at all. After all this sitting around, I could use a nice walk."

"Tell me how you met my son." Mrs. Smith folded her hands on the table in front of her.

Melanie set down her glass of iced tea. She hadn't planned on explaining that one. Then again, she was getting good at telling tales around Caesar.

"I contacted him about doing a story on the band and as we were talking he mentioned that he was looking for someone to help take care of the beach house since he spends a lot of time in London."

"My husband told me you contacted us about doing an interview about the band."

She nodded. "I wanted your input."

"I hope you understand why we said no. Anything to do with the band has caused us a great deal of grief regarding our son."

"I understand. And it worked out for the best. Johnnie loved the idea and in fact, decided to help me put together a documentary instead. It's why I'm back in Atlanta. Presenting our project to the news network I worked for. We're selling the rights to them, just as soon as we get Rhett and Kurt on board with us."

Mrs. Smith seemed surprised. "A documentary?"

"Yes, and now he wants to write an autobiography as well."

"Are we talking about my son?"

Melanie's mouth stretched into a wide smile. "He very excited about it. He's so creative and talented."

"Did he get sober?"

Suddenly, Melanie felt uncomfortable. Her smile faded as she fidgeted with the napkin in front of her.

"He didn't, did he?"

"He's trying. I've known him nearly a month, and in that time, he's only had a few beers."

Mrs. Smith smiled warmly. "Because he's on a love high."

"What do you mean?"

"He's in love with you, isn't he?"

Her face grew hot. "Mrs. Smith...I'm not sure..."

"You can tell me. He already did."

"He did?"

"When we spoke on the phone."

"Oh."

"Has he not told you?"

"He has." Melanie squeezed another lemon into her tea. "But I'm surprised he told you."

"Why is that?"

"It doesn't seem like he has the best relationship with his family."

"We've made some mistakes." Mrs. Smith sighed heavily. "Johnnie's made many."

"He wants to get sober, and I want that for him."

Mrs. Smith reached across the table and took Melanie's hands. "He's a very sick man, Melanie. Don't let him fool you. When the cravings get strong enough..."

"You don't have faith in him?"

"I want to. But I've been dealing with this since he was a teenager."

Fighting back tears, Melanie bit her bottom lip. "Do you know why he started?"

"My father was an alcoholic, so Johnnie has the genetics. Being in a band didn't help. It was a culture his father did not approve of."

"But they're so talented."

Mrs. Smith nodded. "It was evident when they first began playing together. Johnnie was drinking already, and I thought the musical interest might help keep him busy and away from it. At first, he never let it interfere with the band. But when they began getting paid, the temptation to do other things began. It didn't affect the others like it did him."

"I've not seen him completely wasted, so I don't know what to expect."

"He can be violent."

Her stomach twisted into knots, and she felt sick. To her, Johnnie was this tortured soul. A sweet, crazy soul who didn't have a violent bone in his body.

"I haven't seen that side of him."

"Hopefully you won't." Mrs. Smith squeezed her hands. "I haven't myself, but the boys did. He trashed a few hotel rooms along the way. It made Caesar get sober. He wanted to help Johnnie. It tore him up when Johnnie overdosed."

"Caesar was sober?"

"Apparently no one knew that."

"But it was reported he did peyote that night of the accident."

The older woman nodded. "After almost a year of being clean."

"I've never heard anything about him getting clean."

"He confided in me but kept it a secret from most people. He'd seen too many other musicians clean up, then mess up again. He didn't want to disappoint anyone if he failed."

"Do you know why Johnnie is so self-deprecating? He constantly puts himself down. It's why I couldn't get him to come to Atlanta. He said he'd disappoint you."

Mrs. Smith drew her hands away and wiped at a tear that had slid down her cheek. "I'm sorry to say his dad did that to him. Charles was never kind to Johnnie."

Melanie's heart ached. "His own son?"

"We have three sons. Johnnie's the youngest. His two brothers are the manly type. They love sports, fishing, hunting, camping, and roughhousing. Johnnie's the complete opposite. Creative and artistic like you said. My husband couldn't relate to that, so he didn't spend a lot of time with him. And he was very critical of Johnnie when he didn't do well in school. When Johnnie dropped out to pursue music, they didn't speak for a long time."

"Did he give Johnnie any credit for becoming a success?"

Mrs. Smith shook her head, then stared out the window. "For his father, the drugs and alcohol overshadowed that."

"I'm glad he had Caesar to look out for him. Giving Johnnie his houses and money."

"If my husband passes away..." Mrs. Smith met her gaze again. "I'll give Johnnie his money back."

"What money?"

"He didn't tell you his father took control of his money?"

Melanie shook her head. "He told me he lost it all."

"I suppose that's one way to look at it. He got very bad after Caesar died. The band's manager asked us to intervene before he lost everything. He got him into a rehab facility, then helped us legally take control of his money. Johnnie signed the papers. It's in a trust, building interest."

"Why haven't you given it back?"

"Do you know how many times he's been to rehab?"

Melanie nodded.

"It's never been a good time. He was getting that allowance from Caesar's estate which helped him live minimally and not get into too much trouble. When he lived with us a while, we thought about giving it back, but his father wanted him sober for five years. He got to two. Then he took off, and we haven't seen much of him since."

"Does he see his brothers?"

"No. They're career military, and they've traveled a lot over the years. I'm waiting for them to arrive from Fort Benning before we decide whether or not to take Charles off the machines."

Melanie rested a kind hand on Mrs. Smith's arm. "I'm sorry."

"I was hoping Johnnie would visit. Thought you might be able to convince him. He hasn't told me he loves someone in a long time."

"He was reluctant to begin a relationship."

"He's afraid of hurting you."

Melanie nodded.

"Are you afraid?"

"I worry for him."

Mrs. Smith patted Melanie's hand. "You must look out for yourself. It won't be easy to love him, and he *will* hurt you. Don't be afraid to leave to protect yourself."

Melanie forced a smile. "I'll remember that."

Mrs. Smith smiled and picked up the dessert menu. "How about dessert?"

"I could eat a bit more."

"I've enjoyed meeting you, Melanie. And I hope this won't be the last time I see you."

"I hope not either."

"What are you up to?" Melanie asked as Johnnie appeared on the screen of her laptop.

"I'm thinking about you, what else?" He smiled as he tugged his pajama pants down a bit. "My dick is hard, and you're not here."

"You're always hard."

"I wasn't until I saw you looking so delicious."

Melanie smiled. He was in a good mood. She wouldn't ruin it by talking about his parents or anything she'd learned from his mother.

She opened her legs giving him a peek at her new white lace panties.

"Damn, why aren't you here with me?" He began to stroke his cock.

"Taking care of business."

"I should have gone with you. That bed looks cozy."

"And I have it all to myself." She slid the panties off.

"Touch yourself."

"Here?" She rubbed her nipples, pinching them into hard buds. Then she moved a hand in between her legs. "Or here."

"Fuck!" He groaned, and cum began to shoot from his cock. He grabbed some tissues and wiped himself. "Sorry, babe. It's so hot seeing you like this."

"You left me hanging."

"If I were there, my magic tongue would be all over you. Make yourself cum. I want to watch."

She leaned back on the pillows and continued to touch her clit. She put a finger inside herself.

"I wish that were my tongue."

"Me too," she whispered, feeling very close to the edge.

"Imagine it's my tongue tasting you. Fucking you."

"Mmm...yes."

"My cock is hard again. I want to make love to you." He was stroking himself again.

"Please."

"I'm inside you. Your nipple is in my mouth." His hand slid up his length. "Cum for me, baby."

She let out a loud moan as her body began to shiver.

"That's it, baby. I'm cumming again."

"If I were there I would lick up every drop."

He inhaled sharply as he came again. Then he grinned and blew her a kiss. "I love you."

"I love you."

"It's late there. You'd better get some sleep."

"I should. I have a long drive tomorrow." She'd rented a car to drive down to Jacksonville. From there, she'd take a flight back to California.

"Will you leave your camera on. I want to see you."

"Sleeping?"

"I love watching you sleep. I do it all the time."

"You do?"

"On my sleepless nights. Does that creep you out?"

"A little. But then I've watched you when you sleep late."

"I'm going to do some writing. I can leave this camera on, too."

"Will you?" She yawned. "In fact, tell me a band story. It'll help me fall asleep."

"Because we were such a boring bunch?"

"No...because I love the sound of your voice."

"I don't like you driving when you're on the phone," Johnnie told her.

"I've got you on speaker phone."

"Well, be careful. I need you back safe and sound in two days."

"Of course." Melanie smiled. She'd been waiting for the right time to bring up his mother. *Is there a right time?* She knew it was going to upset him.

"Johnnie, I need to tell you something."

"I already know."

Melanie was confused. "How? Did you call your mom?"

"My mom?" he asked. "What are you talking about? Wait. Did you talk to her again?"

"She called me."

"I told her not to do that."

"Johnnie, your dad had a second stroke. He's in ICU hooked up to machines keeping him alive. She wanted to reach you, so she called me. Your brothers were headed to Atlanta, so they can make the decision to take him off the machines."

"What?"

"I'm sorry. She wants you to be with the family. She wanted me to convince you."

"And you think you can?" He sounded angry.

"Of course not. I understand if you don't want to be there, but you should call her and let her know."

"Is that all you talked about with her?"

She wanted him to be more open, so how could she justify keeping something from him? "I met her yesterday for lunch."

"You met my mother? Whose idea was that?"

"Mine. It made sense. I was in Atlanta. She was reaching out."

"To me. Not you."

"I didn't think it would be a problem," she lied.

"I need to go. I can't talk right now."

She became frantic. "Are you upset? Talk to me."

"I'll call you later." He hung up.

What the hell?

Almost immediately, she received a text notification.

I love you.

She wasn't sure whether to be worried or not.

"Tell me about this guy you're dating." Melanie's Aunt Lynn passed the dinner rolls her way.

"She won't tell us." Melanie's mother laughed. "What makes you think she'll tell you?"

Melanie's face warmed as she took a bite of her roll. Everyone was gathered around a large picnic table in her parent's backyard. Her immediate family was there, as well as a few family friends. They'd all brought covered dishes so there was plenty of food. She wished Johnnie had come. Her heart was aching from this brief separation especially with him now being upset with her.

Her mother and aunt had been hounding her all day for information about her new life in California. "Who says I'm dating anyone?"

"It's written all over your face." Her dad chuckled. "You're glowing."

"Maybe she's pregnant," her cousin, Maggie, remarked.

Melanie's mouth dropped. She hadn't been thinking about pregnancy and Johnnie hadn't brought it up either. They'd been careless. She was starting a new life. He needed to get sober. She'd have to get back on the pill as soon as possible.

"I'm not pregnant," she told the twenty-six-year-old who'd be having her first in a few months. "And I don't want to be. I'm forty and beginning a new career path. A lot of exciting things are happening."

"Including a new man?" her aunt asked.

Her cheeks burned again. "There might be a new man."

"I knew it." Her mother patted her hand. "Tell us about him."

"Well, we started out as roommates." Her heart raced. She'd forgotten how exciting it was to share news like this. She hadn't had a new boyfriend to brag about in a long time. "I moved into a beach house that was once owned by Caesar Blue."

"Why does that name sound familiar?" her father asked. "Is he an actor?"

"Remember all those photos I had on my walls when I was in high school? Of my favorite band? Lush?"

"I remember." Someone on the other end of the table called out.

Melanie looked at Paul, a guy she'd known most of her life. They'd grown up together, and her family had once thought they'd be a couple. But she'd never felt anything other than friendship. Unfortunately, he still seemed to be carrying a torch for her, and she'd felt uncomfortable around him all day. Every time someone had taken a photo of her today, he'd been right next to her. He and his wife had divorced a few years ago, and he was obviously on the prowl for something new.

"Is he the one who died?" an older cousin asked.

"Yes, Dave, he died sixteen years ago."

"And you're living in his house? That's so creepy." Maggie's face twisted. "It's not haunted is it?"

I wish. Melanie sighed. "No. He didn't pass away there."

"Yeah, he fell off a mountain in Arizona," Paul explained. "Well, some people think that. Others think his best friend pushed him. What was his name? Johnnie Vega? Both of them were messed up on drugs."

"I remember," her mom interrupted. "You were crazy about that guy, Johnnie. Had his photos up on your headboard."

"So, she could dream about him every night," Paul taunted. "Instead of a real man, she imagined herself with a drug-addicted rock star."

Melanie's eyes narrowed. *What an ass!* "I don't have to imagine any longer since we live together."

"Wait." Paul took a swig of his beer and stared at her. "Are you saying your new man is Johnnie Vega?"

"Sometimes dreams come true."

"I bet reality isn't as good as the dream." Paul huffed.

"Why would you even say that?"

"Come on, his exploits with drugs and alcohol are well known."

"Melanie, you're not dating a man with an addiction problem, are you?" her dad asked. "Not after Logan."

Damn Paul! She didn't want to lie to her parents, but she also didn't want to reveal Johnnie's problems. Not yet. "Dad, that was the past. He's not a rock star anymore. That's not his life. He's creative, like me. We're working on a documentary of the band, and I'm going to be a co-writer of the band's autobiography."

"Who the hell wants to hear about a has been rock band?" Paul grouched.

"Someone apparently does. My old news network is buying the rights to our movie."

"That's wonderful." Her mom smiled.

"You always said you were going to write for the movies." Her dad kissed her forehead. "I'm proud of you."

"Thanks, Dad."

Dave's five-year-old son ran to the table. "Is it time for cake yet?"

"Is there cake?" Melanie picked him up and placed him on her lap. "Birthday cake for you."

"Will you help me blow out the candles?"

"Yes!"

Melanie kissed his cheek.

"Better have your kid tested," Paul muttered to Dave. "No telling what sort of diseases he could contract if she's screwing Johnnie Vega."

"Someone's got a severe case of jealousy," her aunt whispered into her ear.

"Maybe you need to lay off the beer," Dave told Paul. "Because if you keep acting like a jackass, we're going to ask you to leave."

Paul tipped his beer in her dad's direction. "Your daughter seems to have a thing for addicts."

Her dad stood, and Melanie knew Paul had pushed one button too many. "It's best you leave, Paul. We're celebrating Melanie's birthday, and we're proud of how well she's doing. I'll not allow you to ruin her homecoming."

Paul stood and glared at her. "Enjoy your life."

"Is he driving home?" Melanie asked as Paul stalked away. "Someone should stop him."

"I'll make sure he gets home," Dave said, then followed Paul.

"Sorry about that." Her dad rubbed her shoulder.

"It's not your fault."

Her dad nodded. "Yeah, it is. I sort of hyped him up about you coming home. Thought maybe the two of you..."

Melanie sank her head into her hands. "Dad, me and Paul are *never* going to happen."

"I see that." He chuckled and hugged her. "This Johnnie better treat you right."

She smiled thinking how lucky she was to have a great family who had always loved and supported her. *Unlike Johnnie.*

Melanie set her phone down on the nightstand in her old room. She squeezed the bridge of her nose, trying not to cry, trying hard to think about something other than the fact, she'd called Johnnie a dozen times without receiving any answer. She'd left one voicemail telling him she'd made it to Jacksonville, but after that, she'd just hung up. She'd sent a few texts but had yet to receive a reply. *Maybe I shouldn't have met with his mother.* Then again, she'd learned more about Johnnie's past in that one short meeting than she had from him in a month. Why did he want to keep his past to himself? To be part of his life, to support him, she needed all the pieces to the puzzle.

She thought about changing her flight, rescheduling so she could leave tomorrow instead. But her parents were so happy to see her, and she didn't want to disappoint them.

In the morning she woke to her phone buzzing. A text from Johnnie's mother.

Thank you for having Johnnie call me. His father died around ten last night. This may send Johnnie into a downward spiral. Please be careful and remember what I said. Get out if you need to.

That explained why he hadn't returned her messages. Or did it? Shouldn't he want to reach out? Unless he was drinking. Then he'd avoid her. To protect her. *Should I go home? Or leave him to deal on his own?* What would he want? He was ignoring her which meant he probably wanted to be alone.

"Damn it!" She slung the covers back, slid out of bed, and began packing her things.

Chapter Fifteen

Relief washed over Melanie when at last she was dropped off at the gate of the beach house. It had been a frustrating process getting back home with last minute notice. She'd had to make several stops. It was nearly three in the morning. *I should have just taken my scheduled flight.* Johnnie had still not answered any of her messages, and her dread had only escalated as she'd crossed the country.

She pushed the security code and then pulled her rolling suitcase behind her as she entered the yard. No lights were on. *Please be sleeping.* It had been over twenty-four hours since his father died. Too much time alone with his grief. And his anger with her for meeting his mother.

She set her luggage and purse by the front door, then removed her shoes. The house was eerily quiet. He was a night owl and usually awake. *Maybe he's not here.* She did a quick check of the deck where she'd previously found him drinking. Feeling dehydrated herself, she went into the kitchen for water.

"No, Johnnie," she said aloud when she saw an empty bottle of whiskey lying in the sink. She grabbed a bottle of water from the fridge and took a few sips, trying to calm herself. *I finally get to see his bad side.* She went to his room and flipped on the light.

He wasn't alone. A woman lay next to him sleeping. Another bottle of whiskey stood on the nightstand. Quietly, she slipped back into the hallway, her heart thumping in her chest. She took a deep breath and slowly let it out. She'd never expected this. *He warned me.* Instead of sadness, she felt anger. Anger at herself for not heeding his warnings and for falling in love.

Her fists balled tightly as she walked into his room again. She went to the woman and shook her gently. When she didn't wake, Melanie became more forceful.

"What is it?" The woman opened her eyes, blinked a few times, and stared at Melanie.

"Get dressed, get your stuff, and leave," Melanie ordered through clenched teeth.

The woman sat up and rubbed her eyes. "Who are you?"

"His girlfriend."

"Oh, shit."

"Oh, shit is right. I need you out of my house."

The woman scrambled, picking up her clothes that were scattered on the floor. "I rode with him."

"He drove drunk?"

"He only had a couple at the bar," the woman told her. "We picked up more on the way back."

Melanie motioned for the woman to follow her. When they got to the kitchen, she turned to her and said, "I'll get you a ride."

The woman slipped on her high heeled pumps. "I'm sorry. He never mentioned having a girlfriend."

Melanie retrieved her phone to request a ride. "Did you even ask?"

"I asked if he were married. He said no."

"Well, he wasn't lying about that," Melanie told her. "Your ride will be here in ten minutes. You can wait outside the gate."

The woman shifted nervously from one foot to the other. "Thanks for not kicking my ass."

"We still have ten minutes." Melanie wanted badly to hit the woman, but what would that accomplish? Johnnie was at fault. Not her.

"If it makes you feel any better, it was just one time. And it didn't last long. He was too drunk and couldn't stay hard."

Melanie stared at her phone. "Nine minutes."

"I'll wait outside."

Once the woman was gone, Melanie grabbed a blanket, wrapped it around her, and headed down to the shore. Gazing out at the dark expanse of water, she wondered what she should do. *Wake him or wait?* She wanted him to be sober, so he'd understand the impact of what he'd done. Then again, she was furious and wanted him to know it.

Finally, the tears came. She sat in the soft sand and wept. She thought she'd found the purpose of Caesar sending her here, and now nothing made sense. Caesar must have known that Johnnie might hurt her, yet he'd sent her straight into the lion's den.

"Why Caesar?" she whispered into the sea breeze. She pulled up her knees, wrapped her arms around them, and cried harder. How could she ever be with Johnnie again? She'd never be able to trust him. And what would happen to the documentary? The book? These were projects they'd both been excited about, and now there would be nothing.

"There's love."

Melanie lifted her head. "Caesar?"

His voice. Or was it? Was she imagining things? *Wishful thinking?*

She felt an electric current flow through her. It was like what she'd experienced the day she met Caesar. The hair on her arms stood straight. Scrambling to her feet, she frantically looked around in all directions. "Caesar? Are you here?"

A strong gust of wind snatched the blanket from her hands. She chased after it. When she grabbed it, a dolphin leaped out of the water and landed with a huge splash. At least she thought it was a dolphin. She strained to see in the dim moonlight. And then the dolphin jumped again. Any other time it would've thrilled her, but all she felt now was despair.

"Caesar, please come back. I can't handle Johnnie. Not if he's going to hurt me. You know I've been hurt too much."

Melanie stayed there awhile, silently waiting for any sign Caesar was listening. But there was nothing. If he had been there, he was gone now. Spreading out the blanket, she lay down and stared at the stars. The night was beautiful. She should be making love to Johnnie not figuring out a way to leave him. She began to cry again.

The heat of the sun's rays woke Melanie. She yawned and stretched. *When did I walk to the deck?* She was lying in the lounger but had no memory of getting there. *Did Johnnie wake up and carry me? Or...was Caesar here last night?*

When she eased out of the lounger, she saw that she was covered in sand. As if she'd been rolling in it. She ambled over to the outdoor shower and stripped off her clothes. Then she stepped inside the stall and rinsed the sand from her hair and body. Her nipples grew hard as she remembered that first shower with Caesar.

"I want you."

There it was again. Caesar's voice. But he wasn't here. Was her mind playing tricks on her? Was it trying to ease her heartbreak over Johnnie by bringing Caesar back into her thoughts? Frustrated, she groaned loudly and smacked the wooden stall. As much as she wanted to believe Caesar was near, the fact was, he wasn't. Johnnie was. Right inside the house. And it was time to deal with him and the nightmare to come.

After getting dressed, Melanie went to his room. Seeing Johnnie still passed out in bed, refreshed her anger and when she spied a used condom on the floor, she knew she couldn't wait any longer. In the kitchen, she plunked ice cubes into a pitcher and then added water.

"Mother fucker!" he screeched, leaping from the bed. His eyes went wide when he saw it was her. "Melanie, what the fuck are you doing here?"

"Dry yourself off, and we'll talk." She snatched the bottle of whiskey from the nightstand and headed to the kitchen to pour it down the sink.

He followed her. "What day is it?"

She whirled around. "You don't know what day it is? How much did you drink?"

He shivered as he tried to smooth back his wet hair. "You weren't supposed to be home until tomorrow."

"It is tomorrow. I'm home early because I spent all day yesterday jumping from plane to plane to get back here because I was worried about you."

"Why? Did you talk to my mom again?"

"She messaged me about your dad. Even though you weren't answering my calls or messages, I thought you might need me."

"What time did you get here?"

"Early this morning." She placed the bottle on the counter next to the empty one. "Very early."

He leaned against the island and sunk his head into his hands. "Shit."

"I was wrong. You didn't need me. You found someone else."

His head shot up. "What are you talking about?"

"The woman who was with you in bed."

"I don't remember anything." He sunk his head again. "I must have been trashed."

She folded her arms in front of her. "She told me you had two drinks at the bar where the two of you met. And that you didn't get drunk until you came back here."

"What do you want me to say?" Like a wounded puppy, he glanced up. "I fucked up."

"Yes, you did. And what's worse. You fucked *us* up." She closed her eyes, trying to be strong. Trying not to cry.

"I warned you." He smacked his hand hard on the marble countertop right next to her.

Remembering his mother's warning, she swiftly ran upstairs. She had to get away from him. *Just in case.* She closed and locked her bedroom door.

"Melanie, talk to me, please!" He pounded on the door.

"There's nothing to talk about." She sniffed. "We're done. I'll leave as soon as I find a new place."

"No! You belong here." He pounded harder. "Come on. Let me in so I can see you."

She flung the door open and stood in the doorway. "Nothing to see, except me crying over you just as you predicted."

He reached out to touch her, and she smacked his hand away. "You smell like her."

"I'll take a shower."

"What difference does it make, Johnnie?"

"We can talk."

"What is there to say?"

He stared at the floor. "You're right."

She closed the door, leaned against it, slid to the ground, and began sobbing.

There was a soft tapping right behind her head. "I'm sorry, Melanie."

Melanie didn't respond, and finally he walked away. After a few minutes, she quietly slipped out of the room and went to the kitchen for water. Her throat was dry and sore from crying. She immediately noticed the whiskey bottle had disappeared from the counter. She stomped to his room. He was in the shower, the bottle in his hand.

She opened the door. "Give it to me."

"Why should I?" He took a swig.

"Fine then." Exasperated, she threw her hands up and turned to leave. "Get drunk. Stay drunk. I can't care anymore."

"Here," he said, shoving the bottle in her direction. "Take it."

Without looking his way, she held her arm out. When he placed it against her hand, she grabbed hold of it, then quickly dumped the rest down the sink.

He turned the water off and stepped out. "Look at me."

"No."

"Please." His breath was warm on her neck.

The stench of whiskey made her nose crinkle. She turned to him then looked away again. "Put some clothes on, or a towel."

"You've seen me naked."

"I don't want to see you naked anymore."

"Afraid you'll want me?" he taunted.

She looked at him. "I know I want you. But we're done."

"You want to know why I started drinking?"

"I know your father died." She walked back into his room. "But that's no excuse. Not for what you did. Not for sleeping with someone else."

He wrapped a towel around his waist, then grabbed her arm and pulled her toward the door. "I need you to see something. And explain it to me."

He took her upstairs to their workroom. With a few clicks of the computer's mouse, the computer came to life. It was on her Facebook page. There was a photo of her with Paul.

"What the hell." She plopped into the chair and scrolled down her page. Paul had posted several photos from her party. And he'd tagged her in all of them. He was lurking close in every one, making it seem as if they were together. His posts described her as his old flame. There was even a photo of them together as teenagers.

"I can't believe this jerk," she seethed as she began untagging herself.

"Who is he?"

"A friend I grew up with. Nothing more. My parents invited him over. Apparently, he got it in his head to try and get close to me. He wasn't too happy when he found out I had a boyfriend, especially when he found out it was Johnnie Vega."

"He calls himself your ex-boyfriend."

Furious, she stood and stomped across the room. "So that's your excuse for drinking...for fucking someone else? You couldn't call and ask me about it? No, you couldn't. You were too busy being mad at me for meeting your mother."

"Did she tell you all about me?" His eyes narrowed. "Me and my problem?"

"She told me more than you have."

"She had no right telling you anything!" Johnnie jabbed a finger in her direction. "And you shouldn't have met with her. Were you trying to dig up dirt on me?"

"Dig up dirt? I was trying to understand you better, so I could help you."

"And what wonderful insights did you discover about me?"

"This is ridiculous." Melanie headed for the stairs. *I need fresh air.* She slid open the back door. He followed her out.

"I'm tired of them meddling in my business. And it seemed like you were doing the same thing."

"Guess I shouldn't have paid a driver to take your date away. Wasn't my business to meddle in your sex life."

Melanie started for the beach and instantly skidded to a halt. *Why didn't I notice these before?* Sandy footprints on the deck. From the steps to the lounger where she had awoken. Too large to be hers.

Stunned, she glanced back at Johnnie. Should she tell him what she suspected?

"What is it?"

He doesn't need to know. "I meant what I said about leaving. I'll start looking for another place."

"And I meant what I said. Caesar wanted you here. I'll leave. I have the London apartment."

"Fine." She huffed. "Until then, stay away from me."

His arms flew around her, pulling her close. When he kissed the top of her head, she felt his erection rub against her butt. "Melanie, I love you so much. I never wanted to hurt you. I swear."

Tears stung her eyes once again. She started to pull free of his arms but instead rubbed them. They were strong, muscular, honed to perfection from years of playing drums. She loved being in them.

His body heaved against hers as he began crying. "I don't know how I'm going to live without you."

She squeezed her eyes tight. "You've lived a long time without me. You'll be fine."

"I've lived, but I've never been happy. Not until I met you."

She turned to face him. "You warned me. You told me you'd do this. And I still gave you a chance."

"I know. And I fucked up."

"Yes. You did." She slipped out of his arms. "Now please, leave me alone."

Melanie sat on the beach for a while, staring out at the ocean. No dolphins came, neither did Caesar's voice. Except for the crashing waves, she was engulfed in silence. She'd come to love this beach and Caesar's house. She didn't want to leave, but if Johnnie didn't go, she knew she'd have to. It would be too easy to forgive him, to fall back into his bed. She craved his body and missed him being inside her. But she couldn't give in. She knew it would be an endless cycle of him loving her, then hurting her. Rinse. Repeat. She'd been a distraction, but she wasn't a cure for what ailed him.

When she returned to the house, he was gone. A quick look around his room let her know it wasn't permanent. As far as she could tell, his things were still here. Which meant he most likely had left to find alcohol. *Or another woman.* She was relieved to find both cars in the garage. At least he wouldn't be driving.

In the kitchen, she grabbed an apple and a bottle of water, along with her phone and went upstairs. She scrolled through a few emails on the computer, then checked her voicemail. She was surprised to hear Rhett's voice telling her he was interested in hearing more about the documentary. Without thinking, she quickly dialed his number. He answered on the third ring.

"This is Melanie Davis, you left a message."

"Hello. My agent told me about your documentary on Lush. I wanted to hear more about what you're working on."

"First off, I have to say that I met you a couple of months ago in Atlanta. You were playing with Sam Dean. I passed out, and we talked in the first aid tent."

"I talked to a few folks there."

"You said I smelled like Caesar. It seemed to unnerve you."

Silence.

"Rhett. I know this will sound crazy, but I'm living in California now. In Caesar's old house...with Johnnie."

More silence.

"Are you there?"

"I'm here. A lot to take in. How the hell did you end up with Johnnie?"

"Uhm...well, I always wanted to move here. He was looking for a roommate. Like I said, it's a strange coincidence. When he found out I was a writer, he told me about his idea of putting together a documentary."

"Is he there?" Rhett seemed excited. "Can you put him on the phone?"

"I'm sorry. He's out right now. And frankly, I'm not sure if he's coming back or what shape he'll be in if he does."

"Guess he hasn't changed."

Her voice started to falter. "We...we sort of had a falling out."

"You broke up with him."

She sighed heavily. "Yes."

"Don't feel bad. Kurt and I broke up with him, too. And we knew him for much longer."

She wiped at her eyes. "He told me you guys parted on bad terms."

"Yeah, well, given the shit that went down with us, bad terms were all we had."

"I understand," she told him. "I can send you what we've put together so far. We basically compiled a lot of old video and audio that Caesar had here in the house."

"I wouldn't mind coming to the house and seeing it there with you and Johnnie."

"Honestly, I'm not sure if he's going to be here. He said he was going back to London. I don't know if he's going to be helping on the project anymore. We have most of it completed, but we wanted you and Kurt to have some input."

"Why don't I let things die down for you? Give it a couple of weeks before coming up? By then you'll know what's up with him."

"That may be best."

"Don't be sad. If Johnnie's not sober, you're better off without him. He'll break your heart over and over. He did mine. Caesar seemed to be the only one who could rein him in, and when he died, it really put Johnnie in a bad way. Frankly, I'm surprised he's still with us."

Melanie shivered at the dark thought, but she knew it was true. Given his addictions and self-loathing, Johnnie was living on borrowed time.

"I'm sorry for saying that," Rhett told her. "It's clear you have feelings for him."

"I understand. You know him better than I do."

"Give him my number. He can call me anytime."

"I will," she promised.

"I'll be back in touch soon. Kurt and I both will."

"Thank you so much."

Melanie clicked open her document file containing the photos of the band. She opened a photo of Johnnie and Caesar. They were sitting on a park bench in Paris. Both were laughing hysterically. The next one she opened was them lying in the sun on the beach. Caesar's smile was closed, while Johnnie wore his trademark toothy grin.

She touched the screen, and tears began to fall again. "I love you both."

On the desktop, she discovered a new file. It was titled *Autobiography*, and she opened it. *When did he write all this?* She'd only been gone a couple of days. Soon she was engrossed in Johnnie's words. This wasn't an autobiography of the band. This was his life. And it wasn't pleasant.

By the time she finished reading, the sun was setting, and she was in tears again. She rose from the desk, stiff and in need of fresh air, so she headed down to the beach to watch the sky change its colors.

Johnnie's written words disturbed her. His father hated the interest Johnnie had shown in music. Johnnie had started out playing the piano but switched to drums thinking his dad might appreciate the more masculine instrument. Mr. Smith had been tough on Johnnie just as his mother had said. Only Mrs. Smith neglected to tell her how often the man went out of his way to belittle Johnnie. His older brothers had played sports, but Johnnie hadn't had any interest, and that bothered his dad. Mr. Smith had tried to toughen him up, but all he'd done was make Johnnie an angry young man ready to fight at the drop of a hat. Then Johnnie had befriended Caesar. His musical kindred spirit. And things got even worse.

Caesar was the quiet, thoughtful, artistic type. A poet. He was different and ended up the target of relentless bullying by the tough guys...the jocks...which included Johnnie's brothers. Even though girls fluttered around Caesar, he'd been labeled gay by his male peers. Johnnie, who ignored high school politics, hadn't paid much attention to Caesar's plight until one day he'd walked into a school restroom to find Caesar surrounded by several guys who were mocking him. Johnnie tried to mind his own business, but when they pummeled Caesar to the ground and smeared makeup on his face, Johnnie stepped in. He threw a few good punches before facing a few himself. By the time a teacher discovered what was happening and stopped the fight, Johnnie's eye was swollen, his nose bleeding. Caesar survived with a few bruises, and the two of them bonded over ice packs and hydrogen peroxide in the nurse's office.

Overnight, Johnnie became the butt of the jokes. He and Caesar were boyfriends according to the assholes at school. Of course, Mr. Smith didn't care for Caesar. His son's new friend was too feminine for his liking. Mr. Smith was also convinced his son was gay, even though it was Caesar who'd helped him lose his virginity to a girl Caesar had also slept with. With Caesar by his side, Johnnie had more girls than his two macho brothers put together. But his dad didn't see it. He only saw a son who was a disappointment.

Things got better for Johnnie once they connected with Rhett and Kurt, two fellow musicians who wanted to start a band. Johnnie spent more time at Caesar's house rehearsing, and Mr. Smith seemed glad to have him out of his hair. When Johnnie announced he was dropping out of school, his dad told him he couldn't live at home anymore. Caesar's father had allowed Johnnie to stay at their house. Mr. Blue even helped the boys convert the garage into a rehearsal area and bought them the old van that they used to travel to gigs.

Melanie stood at the water's edge, sliding her big toe back and forth in the water. *Johnnie saved Caesar. Caesar saved Johnnie.* But the last thing Johnnie had typed was *I killed my best friend.* How could she make him believe he wasn't responsible for Caesar's death?

She groaned and walked toward the rocks. "What am I thinking?"

It wasn't her place to convince him. Not anymore. She wished they could be friends so that they could continue to work together. She wasn't sure how that was going to play out. They had something good going with the movie, and she hated to let it go. *Can I do it by myself? Of course, I can! But do I want to?* Maybe after meeting with Rhett and Kurt and getting their perspectives, she'd decide.

She sat on the same rock Johnnie had sat on after cutting his foot. His dried blood was still there. Rubbing her fingers across a streak of it made her heart ache. How could any parent treat their child so cruelly? No wonder he constantly degraded himself. *I wonder if he'll come back?*

A loud splash made her look up. Dolphins. Three of them. Smiling, she watched them play. How wild and carefree they were, she thought. *Like Caesar and me.* There were moments with Johnnie when she'd felt that wild freedom as well. But she'd been foolish to think she could change him. He had to do that himself. And he wasn't ready to move forward. As one dolphin jumped and spun into the air, she felt a sense of exhilaration. *But I am.*

She strolled back to the house under a blanket of stars. The cool breeze felt amazing against her skin. It was as if she were being enveloped by the atmosphere. That's when she knew for sure. Caesar *was* here. He was in the sand beneath her feet, the cool Pacific waters, the happy dolphins, the shining stars. He was everywhere because he was in her heart.

Chapter Sixteen

Melanie returned to her pre-Johnnie routine. She closed off the workroom where the computer and editing equipment were, streamlining her creative focus to herself. Not Johnnie. Not Caesar. Not Lush. Soon, she'd completed her romantic tale of rock and roll dreams come true. She sent proposals to publishers and soon had three who were interested in the book.

As she was researching each publisher, trying to decide which offer to take, her phone buzzed. It was a message from Rhett.

Johnnie crashed here last night. He was pretty messed up. I'd hoped to talk to him today, but when I got up, he was gone.

Melanie wasn't sure how to feel. It had been nearly two weeks since he'd left, and she'd not received a call or text from him. She hadn't contacted him either. Instead, every time she'd gotten the itch to try, she'd taken a walk on the beach.

She sent a text to Rhett telling him thanks for letting her know and that it was the first news about Johnnie that she'd received since he'd left. He responded quickly.

He loves you. He kept mumbling your name in his sleep. What's this about Caesar's ghost?

Melanie couldn't help laughing. *I'll tell you when we meet.*

I look forward to that story. Take care.

She sent a smiley face to end the conversation and set her phone aside. Quickly, she pushed thoughts of Johnnie out of her mind. She couldn't let thoughts of him ruin the good vibe she'd had all day.

Closing her laptop, she began to think about dinner. She'd not had anything since this morning, and her stomach grumbled as she opened the refrigerator and looked inside. She'd not been shopping since Johnnie left, but it was getting late, and she didn't feel like going to the grocery store tonight. Maybe she'd go out to eat instead. In fact, she felt like getting dressed up and going out on the town. Drive into L.A. and maybe see a movie or go out dancing.

Not wanting anything to spoil her good mood, she turned on the stereo and found a radio station playing music from the 50s and 60s. She turned up the volume until the music blasted through the house. She danced in the shower and continued to move to the familiar beats as she blew out her hair, applied her makeup and then dressed. For the first time, she put on the red dress she'd bought in Atlanta. It was even more amazing against her tan skin.

She sprayed her hair one last time to keep it in place, grabbed her clutch, and headed back downstairs.

Grooving to James Brown, she slid over to the stereo. It was such a good song, so she decided to keep the radio on just a bit longer. She sashayed to the back door and locked it, then turned on a table lamp. Johnnie was sitting in the corner of the room, in a plush chair, watching her.

Surprised, she shrieked and stumbled, but somehow maintained her balance. "Damn it! What are you doing? You scared the shit out of me!"

Still shaken, she turned the stereo off.

"Leave it on. I like watching you dance."

Her eyes widened as her gaze caressed him. There was something feral about him. He was a mess. His hair...his clothes...all dingy. His eyes were swollen and red. She wondered if he'd been living on the street. *Or had drugs done this?* When her eyes fell to his lap, her heart nearly stopped. *Where did he get a gun?*

"Don't be scared, Melanie. I'm not here to hurt you. I'm not going to hurt you or anyone else ever again."

A tear slipped from her eye as she realized his intent. She couldn't panic. She had to remain calm. Keep him calm. *Maybe I can talk him down.* "Johnnie, where have you been? I've missed you."

He smirked. "In that dress? Dancing to music?"

"I wanted to go out for dinner. I've been cooped up finishing my novel. I received three offers to publish it. Go get cleaned up and come with me. We can celebrate together."

"You look beautiful," he said as his own tears slid down his cheeks, smudging the dirt on his face. "I wish I could be the man you deserve."

Feeling helpless, she wrung her hands. "Johnnie, no matter what's happened, I love you. Nothing has changed those feelings."

"Save them for someone else." His hand patted the gun. "I saw Rhett. He's single, and he's been clean a long time."

She shook her head. "I'm not interested in being with someone else. It will take me awhile to get over you, Johnnie. And if you hurt yourself because of me, I don't think I'd ever get over it."

"This isn't about you. It's about my fucked-up life."

She shifted her weight from one leg to the other, then back again. "I read your autobiography. I know some of the things you've been through. We'll get you help, and I'll be there for you. I promise."

He brought the gun to his temple. "I don't want help. I want it to be over."

"Johnnie, please don't." She was sobbing as she knelt beside the chair. "I love you so much."

"I love you, too. But you've been hurt enough."

"Please." She rested her head on his knee.

"It's alright. I'll be with Caesar."

Caesar! She shot to her feet and looked wildly around the room. "Caesar if you're here, I need you right now!"

"What are you doing?"

"Caesar, please come back! Johnnie needs help. I can't do this without you!"

"Stop yelling!" Johnnie ordered. "Or I'll do it!"

She spun in a circle, looking skyward. "Caesar, please!"

"Shut up! He's dead!" Johnnie rose from the chair, the gun still to his head. "He's not coming back! I killed him!"

Suddenly, the gun flew across the room and landed near her feet. *Caesar!*

"What the fuck?" Johnnie scanned the room, clearly confused.

Melanie took his moment of bewilderment to snatch the gun from the floor. She pulled open the cylinder.

He grabbed her from behind. "Hand it to me!"

"No!" She grunted as he wrestled her for the gun. The bullets dropped to the floor.

He threw her to the couch and raised his fist. Closing her eyes, she lifted her hands to protect her face from the blow.

"Don't you dare hit her."

Melanie opened her eyes and saw Caesar standing next to Johnnie, gripping the hand that had been about to strike her.

Johnnie's eyes went wide, and Caesar released his hand. He looked from Caesar to her and then back to his dead friend again.

"You're not real." He blinked a few times, then pushed Caesar. Hard. "You're not real! You're dead!"

"Johnnie, stop!" She yelled, standing again. "It's Caesar."

Johnnie cried as he continued to shove Caesar. "I killed you. Get the fuck out of here."

Caesar said nothing, allowing Johnnie to take out his frustrations, his anger, his hurt on him. When Johnnie started to throw a punch, Caesar ducked, and threw one of his own. It struck Johnnie squarely in the jaw and down he went.

"Oh my God." She ran to Johnnie, knelt, and gently touched his face.

"He'll be alright." Caesar picked up the bullets and slid them into the pocket of his jeans. He grabbed a pillow from the couch and lifted Johnnie's head. "He needs to sleep this off."

Melanie rose to her feet, and Caesar straightened. He pushed the curls back from his face and stared at her. Those deep, brown eyes made her feel weak, just as they had the first time she'd seen him.

"Melanie." His voice was a mere whisper. His bottom lip began to tremble. "I missed you."

She fell into his arms. His lips crashed into hers as he wrapped her up tightly in a hug. He kissed her over and over, his lips traveling softly over her face, her neck, her shoulders.

"You smell delicious." He smiled.

She laughed. "I smell like you. It's never gone away."

He cupped her chin and kissed her again. "And I'll make sure it never does."

He lifted her over his shoulder and carried her to the bed that was once his.

Chapter Seventeen

Johnnie and Caesar

The next morning, Melanie was cooking breakfast, humming one of Lush's biggest hits when Johnnie hobbled into the kitchen, rubbing his bruised face.

"Good morning." She smiled, full of cheer after spending the night in Caesar's arms.

"Maybe for you," he grouched, sitting on a stool at the kitchen island. "I feel like I was run over by a freight train."

She placed two aspirin and a glass of water in front of him.

He swallowed the medicine. "Got any coffee?"

"I'll make you some." She hummed once more as she began preparing a pot.

Johnnie seemed confused. "Aren't you supposed to hate me?"

Staring out the window above the sink, Melanie took a deep breath. *He doesn't remember.*

"Damn! My head is pounding."

She returned to the food, divvying it out onto three plates. "Hangover?"

"A bender," he explained as she placed a plate of eggs, toast, and bacon in front of him. He rubbed his jaw again. "Whatever pills I took must have been something. I was seeing things."

"What things?"

He dipped into his thoughts, then smiled. "You were in this gorgeous red dress and dancing. Damn...you were sexy. I was watching you, then Caesar came in and ruined everything."

A shirtless Caesar was coming down the stairs behind Johnnie. Melanie held up her hand signaling him to stop. "You saw Caesar?"

"Figures you'd be thrilled." He shoveled eggs into his mouth.

"Is that all you remember?"

"Somehow I made it back here last night. But I must have fallen and hit my face on something."

"Perhaps the pillow you woke up on."

Johnnie narrowed his eyes, and appeared to be thinking, trying to remember. "Did you put that pillow under my head?"

Melanie smiled as Caesar strolled up behind Johnnie. "No. He did."

Johnnie twisted and—in his surprise—turned over the stool beneath him. He ended up on the floor. "Holy fucking shit! Am I still hallucinating?"

"No. She tried to tell you before. Didn't you listen?" Caesar held out his hand.

Hesitantly, Johnnie grabbed it, and Caesar helped him back to his feet. Johnnie stared at him, blinking his eyes repeatedly. He reached out and touched Caesar's face, yanked on his curly hair, then poked him in his bare chest several times.

"Are you real?"

Melanie laughed lightly. "I know it's hard to believe."

"I had to show her my tattoos and my premonition skills before she believed me." Caesar patted Johnnie on the back.

"Premonition?" Johnnie looked at her. "She never mentioned those."

"I forgot. He has to try and use them, and he never really had to once I realized he was really Caesar."

"You can see into the future?" Johnnie set the stool upright and sat on it.

"Only if I want to." Caesar nodded, then frowned. "Your foot's infected. You need to see a doctor."

Melanie zoomed over to check it, but his shoes were still on.

"It does hurt." Johnnie shrugged. "I left my meds here."

"And you've been walking around on it a lot, haven't you?" Caesar asked.

Johnnie nodded.

"Eat your breakfast," she told Johnnie. "As soon as you take a shower, and get all that dirt scrubbed off, I'll drive you to the clinic."

"Speaking of showers." Caesar grinned and grabbed her around the waist, pulling her close, pressing kisses along the side of her neck.

The distress on Johnnie's face did not go unnoticed. Melanie felt terrible. She lifted Caesar's hair and whispered, "He's not ready to see us together."

Caesar glanced over at Johnnie then kissed her cheek. He sat down on a stool across from his best friend. "I'm starving. Let's eat."

They ate in silence. Melanie could feel Johnnie's scrutiny. *But he slept with someone else.* They'd broken up because of it. How upset could he be that she was back with Caesar? Mad enough to try and kill himself again? He didn't even seem to remember what happened last night.

When Caesar tried to hold her hand, she pulled it away.

"It's alright." Johnnie dropped his fork loudly on his plate. "I get it. I screwed up, Melanie. You have every right to be with him again."

Caesar smiled at him. "She loves you, too."

"She shouldn't." Johnnie stared at her. "I'm a fucked-up mess."

Caesar pressed his head against hers and stared back at Johnnie. "Get unfucked."

"I've tried."

"I know." Caesar took a sip of juice. "I'm sorry about your dad."

"He was an ass, and you know it."

Caesar nodded. "Your mom's planning on giving you back your money. She'll also give you a letter from your dad. He'll apologize for his behavior and tell you how proud he's been of you. He'll also say he hopes you'll stop hurting yourself because he knows it's because of him that you do it."

Johnnie glared at Melanie. "What did my mom tell you?"

"Just the money part."

"This is beyond weird." Johnnie's brow furrowed. "Can you not look into my future?"

"Let's talk about the past." Caesar pointed a fork at him. "Specifically, last night."

"I don't remember much. Mostly Melanie looking delicious in that red dress."

Caesar smiled slyly. "She looked even more delicious with it off."

Johnnie grinned at her and winked. "It sure is a shame to put clothes on *that* body."

Melanie's cheeks burned, and she continued eating, trying to ignore them as they continued to talk about her. Both pair of eyes were on her. Both pairs glazed over with passion. They both wanted her. Things were getting more complicated by the minute. The two of them admitted to being competitive. Were they going to compete for her?

"Back to last night," she interrupted.

"I'm going to take a shower," Johnnie announced. He kissed Melanie's cheek, then lingered near her ear to whisper, "I'm hard as a rock. Gotta take care of it. I'll be thinking of you."

Her gaze followed him down the hallway. "He's avoiding the subject."

"You can join him if you want."

Her gaze whipped back to Caesar. "What?"

"He wants you. You want him. I'm okay with that."

"He cheated on me."

"Forgive him." Caesar rubbed her back gently. "You still love him, don't you?"

"I can't. Like he said, he's a mess. He tried to kill himself last night, and he almost hit me..."

"We'll help him get better."

Irritated, Melanie threw her fork down on her plate and went into the living room. Caesar followed.

He came up behind her and gently caressed her arms. "What is it?"

She turned to face him. "I thought you loved me."

"I do."

"Why would you tell me to be with Johnnie?"

"I love him, too."

Melanie was confused. "You and he aren't..."

"No." Caesar smiled. "Nothing like that. He's my brother. I loved seeing the two of you together."

"You saw us?"

"More like...felt you." He pushed her hair back, then caressed her shoulders. "I felt what you were feeling for one another. It's powerful."

"I feel like that with you, too." She mindlessly played with his curls.

"I know. But I don't know how long I'll be here."

She placed her hands on his chest. "I don't want you to leave."

"I don't want to leave you. But this is about helping Johnnie. I'm going to get him straightened out once and for all. You're a part of that remember?"

"Because of the blood."

"What?"

"I have Johnnie's blood. He donated years ago when I needed a transfusion after the accident. That's our connection. Why you were mistakenly sent to me."

He pressed his lips softly against hers. "There was no mistake, Melanie. This was supposed to happen. All of it. I found you and sent you here. You and Johnnie found one another. He needs you."

"And I need *you*." She grabbed a single curl, untangling it with her fingers. "And I want you."

He smiled that charming smile. He took her hand and placed it against his crotch. "Johnnie's not the only one with a hard-on."

"Take your pants off," she purred. "Sit down on the couch."

As he sat, she slid down her panties and stepped out of them. Hiking up her dress, she straddled his lap, impaling herself with his long, hard cock.

"You feel so good," he murmured in her ear as she began to move on him. "You're so wet."

"From all the cum you put into me last night."

"Are you sure it's not from wanting me so much?"

"That, too." She smiled.

He slid down the straps of her sundress, then her bra, freeing her breasts. He licked one nipple and nipped another lightly with his teeth. She wound her hands into his long thick curls, holding on tightly as she continued to grind.

"Do you want me to put more cum inside you?" he asked, rubbing her nipples into tight buds.

"Yes, please." She picked up her pace.

"I'm gonna cum, babe, but I want your mouth on me."

She lifted herself off him and immediately wrapped her lips around his cock, stroking him with her mouth. His body shook, and his hot cum was released. Her mouth stayed on him, drinking every drop.

"Your turn." He pulled her to the couch and laid her down beside him.

"Caesar." She gasped as he sunk his tongue deep inside her, fucking her with it.

Johnnie walked into the room. "I'm ready to go Melanie and…"

Melanie sat up fast and adjusted her dress.

Ignoring Johnnie, Caesar lay on her and replaced his mouth with his hand.

"Caesar, no," she protested.

Caesar nuzzled her neck. "He can go away. I need to make you cum."

"Guess I have to get used to this." Johnnie turned his back on them. "Even though you have a bedroom, not to mention two spare bedrooms."

"Sorry." Melanie pushed Caesar away and scrambled to her feet. "Let me get my purse, and we can go."

"Don't forget these." Caesar smiled, twirling her panties on his finger. He handed them to Johnnie. "Maybe you'd like to help her get back into them."

She and Johnnie stared at one another before Johnnie handed them to her. In the bathroom, she slipped them back on. After grabbing her purse, she returned to the living room.

"Let's get going," she told Johnnie.

"Hurry back." Caesar grabbed her, kissed her, and ran his hands up and down her body, stopping at her butt to squeeze her cheeks. "I want to make love to you all day."

Melanie sat in awkward silence as she drove Johnnie to the closest clinic. She wanted to talk to him, especially about last night, but when she glanced over, he was staring out the window. He remained quiet during the drive, something she wasn't used to. Normally, she couldn't shut him up. She wanted him to say something, anything…even yell at her, but he stayed tight-lipped. She was at a loss as to what to say to him.

While she waited in the clinic, she sent a text to Rhett to let him know Johnnie had returned home. She didn't mention the gun and

Johnnie's threat of suicide. *Because then I'll have to explain Caesar.* Rhett responded almost immediately.

I'm glad he's safe at home. Kurt and I will figure out a date to visit. I'll let you know.

She messaged him back to say she'd keep it a secret for now and let the two of them surprise Johnnie. *They'll be surprised as well!* Rhett had already thought he'd seen Caesar. She wondered if Kurt would be as open to it. It would be wonderful to see them reunited.

Melanie was startled when a doctor approached her. Immediately, she rose to her feet to greet him.

"I believe you're Melanie. I'm Dr. Johnson."

She shook his outstretched hand. "Is Johnnie okay?"

"The nurse is bandaging his foot. We had to stitch up the wound again. He's in a lot of pain but refusing medication."

"Did he tell you he's an addict?"

Dr. Johnson shook his head. "I thought he might be. I gave him a shot of powerful antibiotics which will hopefully clear up the infection."

He handed her a bottle of pills. "He needs to finish the full cycle of antibiotics this time."

"I'll make sure he does."

He pulled a business card out of his pocket and scribbled something on the back. Then he handed it to her. "An old friend of mine owns a store that sells herbs and natural medicines. I've written down a few things that will help with Mr. Vega's pain. It's not addictive."

"Thank you so much."

Johnnie walked out of the exam room using crutches.

The doctor patted him on the shoulder. "Most importantly, he needs to stay off this foot as much as possible for a few days."

"He will." She nodded.

Melanie paid the bill and then held the front door open. Johnnie limped to the car.

"The doctor told me about a place where we can get herbal medicine for your pain." She started the car.

"I can deal with it." He moved the seat back to stretch out his leg.

"You shouldn't have to."

"Whatever." He waved his hand in the air and stared out his window.

They drove in silence to the herbal medicine shop. Johnnie refused to go in, so she went in alone to get the items the doctor suggested. The heavy silence remained on their way home. She thought she might go crazy if he didn't say something.

"Johnnie, I'm sorry."

"For what?"

"Caesar and me."

He shrugged. "No biggie."

"It is. You and I just..."

"You and I are finished." He looked at her. "Right?"

She fell silent, again not knowing what to say.

"I'm sorry for what I did." He frowned. "Hurting you. You didn't deserve that."

"Do you think it's weird that Caesar wants us to still be together?"

"What's fucking weird is that Caesar is dead, and I can see him."

"I suppose it is. I didn't know him when he was alive, so it's different for me."

Johnnie shifted in his seat, angling his body toward her. Then he simply stared.

Melanie shook a finger at him. "Don't you dare."

"What?" He shrugged with a hint of a sly smile.

"I know *exactly* what you're thinking."

Now the full, fantastic smile. "What the fuck are you talking about, woman?"

"You're going to ask me who's better."

"No, I wasn't."

"Yeah right." She rolled her eyes. "I know you two."

"Did *he* ask you?"

"Well, no."

"Right. Because he already knows who's better. Me."

Melanie laughed and lightly swatted his chest.

He grabbed her hand, holding it against his heart. "Are we done? Really done?"

"Caesar doesn't think so."

"Fuck Caesar," Johnnie whined, then teased, "wait...you already are."

She cringed. "Johnnie, I feel bad enough."

"Really? So those were moans of *feeling bad* I heard?"

Her face burned.

"Didn't think so." Johnnie kissed her hand. "He left you hanging, right? You didn't cum."

"Were you watching us?"

"I'm not a glutton for punishment."

"You aren't?"

"So maybe I am." He slid her dress up her thigh. "But he didn't take care of you."

Her skin dotted with goosebumps. "I'll be fine."

His hand slipped between her legs. She wanted to close them tight, but it was as if they had a will of their own and spread further apart instead. One of his fingers lightly touched her panties. She shuddered.

"I want to make you cum." Two fingers now, rubbing her over the cotton fabric.

"Johnnie," she whimpered.

"Do you want me to stop?" He pushed the fabric aside with his thumb, and his fingers eased into her. "Tell me to stop."

She swerved the car, then righted it. "Johnnie, I'm driving."

"Pull over." His thumb was on her clit.

She turned the car into a beach access road and drove off to the side.

"Turn to me," he ordered. She did, and he pulled her panties off.

Melanie knew she should stop him but couldn't find the words. She put one leg up on the back of the seat, spreading herself wide as his head dove between her thighs. His tongue darted across her clit, and his fingers delved inside her again.

She grasped his head, keeping it pressed against her. Then she remembered what Caesar had told her. "Johnnie. We should stop. Caesar said he could feel us. Our emotions. What we're doing."

Johnnie peeked up at her, grinning, his mouth glistening with her wetness. "Let him feel this, then."

His mouth latched onto her clit. His fingers stroked her g-spot. She let out a cry of pleasure as immediately her body reacted. She shuddered uncontrollably. And with her orgasm came tears as well.

She scrambled out of the car, slammed the door, and leaned against the hood. *How could I do this after he cheated?*

Johnnie exited the car and teetered over to her. He rubbed her arms. "I didn't want to make you feel bad. I'm sorry."

Sobbing, she fell into his arms. "I love you so much. Why did you have to mess everything up? Why did you bring that woman home?"

"I wish I could take it all back. I hate that I hurt you. My insecurities, the shit with my family, were all playing with my mind. I wanted to make it stop. I started drinking at the house. When I saw you and that guy together, I left and went to a bar. It was stupid, and there's no excuse. But this is my life. I'm a horrible bastard at times."

She ran her hand through his dark, wavy hair. "You can also be a wonderful man who's creative, talented, and a great friend. That's the Johnnie I want."

He grinned. "What about the guy who's the best lover you ever had?"

Melanie's mouth dropped in surprise. Then again, this was the wisecracking Johnnie she loved. "Caesar? I already have him."

"Caesar huh?"

"You asked for that." She playfully pushed him.

Pouting, he let her go, leaned against the hood of the car, and crossed his arms in front of him.

She caressed his cheek. "Are we going to talk about the gun?"

"I was hoping you'd forget."

"As if that could happen." She put her head against his shoulder. "Johnnie, you were going to kill yourself. Maybe you think that would have ended your pain, but it would've only been the beginning of mine."

He stroked her hair. "Guess it's a good thing Caesar came back when he did."

"What if he hadn't?" She lifted her head, and her lip trembled as she stared into his eyes. "Johnnie if you're suicidal you need help."

"I need you." He took her hands in his.

She glanced away. "I can't be your crutch...or your babysitter. I can't save you from yourself. I don't have that kind of power."

He squeezed her hands. "You'd be surprised at the power you have over me."

She looked at him again. "I want you to love yourself and be happy. Even if you're alone."

"Why? Are you going somewhere? Running off with Caesar?"

"We're not going anywhere." She smiled. "We love you very much, and we want you to be well."

"I can't be well if I don't have you." He wrapped her in his arms. "Do you have any idea how much it hurts to not be with you?"

"Of course. You betrayed my trust, but that doesn't mean I don't still love you."

"I ache for you, Melanie." He pushed her away, then placed her hand on his crotch. "All the damn time."

"I want you, too."

He threw his arms out to his side. "What are we going to do?"

"I want you to get counseling, Johnnie. You have to heal your emotional wounds. I had to do it when I lost my girls. There were times when I wanted to die, so I know what that kind of pain feels like."

Johnnie stared at the ground and kicked a stone with his non-injured foot. "If I agree to get help, will you give me another chance?"

Tears slid down her face, and she wiped them away. "Yes."

He stared at her. "And Caesar?"

"What about Caesar?"

"What are we going to do about him?"

"Aren't you glad to see him?"

"Like I said it's weird. And we haven't really talked since he's been too busy banging you."

"There's no reason for you to be jealous."

Johnnie threw his head back and winced. "I can't believe you said that."

"He said he's okay with me being with the both of you."

"And you think I'll be okay with that?"

She placed a gentle hand on his arm. "Why can't we just enjoy our time together? It'll take you a while to get well, so in the meantime..."

"In the meantime, I get to hear the two of you fucking all the time."

"We'll be more discreet."

"Really?" He brushed her hand away. "You who screams like a banshee when she's being fucked."

"I thought you liked that."

"I do. But only when it's me who's making you scream."

"You told me once it was stupid that the two of you were always so competitive with one another."

"I don't believe we were discussing you at the time."

Melanie rubbed her temples. *What are we going to do?*

Johnnie glared at her. "You don't want to give him up, do you?"

"When you and I met, I told you how I felt about him."

"And then you fell in love with me."

"I never stopped loving him."

He turned and smacked the hood of the car. "Take me home."

She touched his back. "Please don't be angry."

"I said take me home." He limped back to the passenger side of the car.

"Show me the work you two have been doing," Caesar insisted when Johnnie came into the kitchen.

Melanie looked from Caesar to Johnnie. The tension in the air was thick, but Caesar didn't seem to notice. He was always cheerful. Johnnie was moody though. After they'd come back from the clinic, he'd retreated to his room to eat lunch and then had fallen asleep. Meanwhile, Caesar had been all over her. She'd explained Johnnie's feelings about the situation, but all Caesar had said was, *he'll come around.* Then he'd taken her outside and made love to her on the beach.

"Why don't you show Caesar the documentary? I'm sure you two can come up with some ideas for additions and edits together."

"I thought it was *our* project." Johnnie placed his dirty plate and glass in the sink.

"I have some things I need to work on," she explained. She hoped to get them alone together so that they could rekindle their friendship without her in the way. "And I want to go to the market."

"We could have gone on the way back from the clinic," Johnnie grumbled.

"I got distracted." She picked up her purse. "Remember?"

He grinned. "Yes, I do."

"Is there anything special you want for dinner?"

He grinned again and winked.

Her face warmed. Typical flirtatious Johnnie.

Caesar swept up beside her. "I only want one thing to eat."

She watched Johnnie immediately look away, appearing uncomfortable as Caesar began kissing her neck and grinding his hips into hers.

She kissed Caesar. "Later. Spend time with Johnnie. You two have a lot of catching up to do."

Caesar wrapped his arms around Johnnie. "Yes, we do man. Come on let's go check out this project of yours."

Melanie smiled as they headed to the stairs together. Caesar turned and blew her a kiss. Then he wrapped Johnnie's arm around his shoulders, so he could help his friend navigate the stairs with his injured foot.

When she returned to the house a couple of hours later, Johnnie and Caesar were on the deck, sitting in chairs beneath the big umbrella. They didn't even notice she had returned. She watched them for a few minutes laughing and joking around. Johnnie slapped Caesar's back, and Caesar threw playful punches in his direction. The two of them seemed to be getting along well. She breathed a sigh of relief and went into the kitchen to pour them each a glass of lemonade.

Johnnie went quiet when he saw her coming out the back door.

"I brought cold drinks," she said, handing them each a glass.

Caesar took his, then wrapped a hand around her waist and pulled her closer. "Isn't she fantastic?"

Johnnie raised his glass. "That she is."

"Did she tell you how we met?" Caesar pursed his lips, then smiled wickedly.

"She did." Johnnie nodded. "Perhaps you'd like to hear how we met?"

"I bet you were surprised to find her living in the house."

"Not as surprised as she was to wake up next to me in bed."

Caesar doubled over laughing. "Was she appalled? She hated it when I hit on her at the store."

Melanie shook her head as they continued to compare stories. "I'll be in my room, working on some things."

She bent to meet Caesar's lips.

"Aren't you going to kiss Johnnie?" Caesar asked when she started to walk away.

Melanie took a quick glance at Johnnie.

"I'll pass." Johnnie sneered at Caesar. "You know I've never wanted your sloppy seconds. Except for that time I lost my virginity."

Melanie frowned. It hurt much worse hearing that a second time. He was still upset. What did he want her to do? Tell Caesar to get lost? She couldn't. Not only because she loved Caesar but because Johnnie needed his friend. Maybe she was the one who needed to get lost. They'd been fine until she'd come out on the deck.

"That's not nice." Caesar pushed Johnnie's knee.

"No, but it's typical." She went back into the house.

Sitting at her computer, Melanie went over the three book offers again. Then, she did further research on the publishing houses. Once she was sure which one seemed like the best fit and the best opportunity, she sent an email to them. Then she sent another email to Susan to inform her she'd be meeting with the entire band soon and getting their input on the documentary.

After getting caught up with emails, she tried working on another fiction story, but her mind kept wandering. To Johnnie. He was so complicated. She knew he wouldn't be happy until they were back together. But she wasn't ready to trust him again. He needed to work on being sober. For himself. Not for her. Or anyone else for that matter. *What else will make him happy?*

She opened the file which held all the photos of Lush. She found one of Johnnie smiling as he pounded away on his drums during a concert. *Drums!* Was it true that he'd sold all his equipment? Even if it wasn't, there were no drums there. Quickly, she did a search for Johnnie Vega and drums. Several articles came up, including one from a drummer's magazine. In it, he talked about the brand of drums he always played, and it had a diagram of his set up, along with photos. She printed the photos and searched for the drum manufacturer's website. Once she'd found a phone number, she called and placed an order for an exact replica of the kit featured in the magazine. She wouldn't tell him. This would be another surprise, like Rhett and Kurt's visit.

Chapter Eighteen

Startled from sleep, Melanie sat straight up in bed. Caesar who had his arms wrapped around her, began to stir.

"What is it?" he asked groggily.

"Johnnie's having one of his night terrors."

Johnnie hadn't had nightmares in a while. Had Caesar's presence caused it? Or was it her absence from his bed?

Caesar sat up beside her. When they heard another moan, he kissed her shoulder. "Go to him."

"This isn't about sex. I need to hold him. It comforts him."

"If you want to have sex with him, you can."

She groaned, got out of bed, and slipped on a tank top and pajama pants. "He's not having a wet dream. He has nightmares about your death. About killing you."

"Did you tell him he didn't kill me?"

"You think he believes me?" When another loud wail came from downstairs, she dashed to Johnnie's room.

She clicked on the small table lamp, then sat down on the bed and touched his forehead. "I'm here, Johnnie. It's okay."

His moans turned into sobs. She lay down and pulled him close. "Let me hold you."

His eyes opened, and he eased closer. "Melanie?"

"I'm here. Try to sleep."

"Where's Caesar?"

"Upstairs."

"He's not dead?"

"He is. He's come back to help you."

"I killed him."

"No." Caesar sat down on the end of the bed. "You didn't."

Johnnie sat up. "We were arguing, and I pushed you."

Melanie gasped.

"That's what you think happened?" Caesar asked.

"It's what I remember."

"Then I'll help you remember what *really* happened." Caesar held out his hand. "Grab hold."

"Why?" Johnnie's eyes widened. "What are you going to do? We're not going to fly around or some crazy shit like that, are we?"

Caesar tossed back his head of curls and laughed deeply. "This isn't *The Christmas Carol.* Hold my hand."

Johnnie reached out his hand. Caesar took it and scooted closer to his friend. Then Caesar reached out to Melanie. "You, too."

She grabbed the offered hand.

"Johnnie, take her other one."

They sat in a little circle, the three of them, holding one another's hands.

Suddenly, Caesar's grip tightened. It was almost painful. "Close your eyes and don't let go. No matter what."

Johnnie looked at her, shrugged, and closed his eyes. She glanced at Caesar. He mouthed *I love you* and shut his eyes.

When she closed her own eyes, it was as if she had been transported to another world. The air was chilly, and she rubbed her arms as she walked along the path in front of her. She marveled at the setting sun. The sky above her was filled with what seemed like a hundred colors, and stars dotted the horizon.

"Come on, we're almost to the top."

It was Johnnie's voice. She walked faster, trying to catch up to him.

Then she heard gagging and the sound of someone vomiting.

"Geez, you can't handle a few drinks?"

Now Caesar's voice. "It's been a year since I've had anything. You should've known I'd get sick."

Melanie caught up with them. "Slow down."

Johnnie trudged on. "Wait until we get higher."

"Why? What's up there?" Caesar asked.

Johnnie laughed loudly. "You think I mean climbing?"

"Caesar wait!" she called, but he kept going, not even acknowledging her.

They can't see or hear me. She was watching their experience.

When she caught up with them again, Johnnie was sitting on the edge of the mountainside, his feet dangling. *This isn't the Johnnie I know.* He was younger. Caesar looked the same. She realized, she had become a part of their past. Of that night.

"I brought peyote."

"Why are you messing me up?"

"Come on, I bought it just for you." Johnnie held up a small plastic bag. "You've always wanted to try it."

"I said that years ago." Caesar stood, glaring down at him, his hands on his hips. "Aren't you tired of being high and drunk all the time? We should be back at the lodge writing songs, not doing this shit."

"You're getting to be a drag with this health kick of yours."

"Yeah, well maybe you shouldn't have overdosed. That scared the hell out of me. I don't want to lose you."

"Why don't you lecture Rhett or Kurt like you do me?"

"All they do is smoke weed and have a few beers. They're getting tired of this shit, too."

"What are you guys going to do? Find a new drummer?"

Caesar squatted beside Johnnie. "Of course not. We'd like to keep you around forever, but we might not be able to if you keep doing this crap."

"This stuff is natural." Johnnie took a dried button and chewed. He held the bag up to Caesar. "Come on, try it. At least once."

Caesar grabbed the bag from Johnnie, examined it, then threw it on the ground. He started to get up.

"Chicken shit." Johnnie pushed him playfully.

Caesar started to shove Johnnie back but lost his balance and began sliding down the side of the mountain ledge.

Melanie screamed and ran to help, forgetting that this scenario had already played out years ago.

Caesar was holding onto a rock that was jutting out about four feet down. His body dangled precariously as he strained to hold on.

"Caesar!" Johnnie yelled. He lay down and held out his hand to his friend. "I'll get you."

Johnnie's fingertips met Caesar's hand that was clinging to the rock. He had to get closer, so Caesar could grab him with his free hand. He shimmied over the ledge, easing himself closer to Caesar, but also putting himself in grave danger of falling.

Finally, he reached Caesar's hand and grabbed his wrist. He tried to move backward to see if he could hoist Caesar back up. Instead, the dirt and rock beneath his waist began to give way.

"Johnnie, go get help." Caesar managed to put his other hand on the rock. He held on with two hands now.

"I can pull you up. Grab my arm."

More sand was shaken loose from the mountain's edge. It fell into Caesar's eyes. "Johnnie we can't do this. You're going to end up falling with me."

"No. You *will* grab my arm, and I *will* pull you up."

Caesar had tears coursing down his face. His knuckles were white. "I can't hold on much longer. It hurts."

Johnnie moved his arms to his side and found the bag of peyote. He scooted back over the ledge. "Take some of this. You won't feel pain."

He dropped some pieces toward Caesar's mouth. Caesar managed to grab a larger slice between his teeth and quickly ate it.

"Tastes like shit!"

"Grab my arm now!"

Caesar grabbed his arm with both hands, and Johnnie's body slid forward, his upper torso hanging over the edge now. He was being pulled over by Caesar's weight.

"You've got to let me go," Caesar pleaded.

"Hell no!" Johnnie tried desperately to pull Caesar upwards. More sand and gravel fell as Johnnie continued to slide forward.

"We can't both die." Caesar took one hand off Johnnie's arm.

Johnnie started to panic. "You can't leave me!"

"Tell my dad I love him. Rhett and Kurt, too. I'm going to miss you."

"No Caesar hang on. Please. I don't want to live without you. Let's go together."

Kneeling on the ground, Melanie continued to watch, feeling completely helpless. Tears streamed down her face.

"Your time here's not done."

"It should be me...not you." Johnnie's voice cracked as he choked back tears. "You're the good one."

"I love you, man. You *are* worthy. You just don't know it yet. One day you will."

"Shut up! Give me your other hand back. We're doing this!"

"I'm ready, Johnnie. Let me go."

Johnnie frantically tried to pull Caesar up, but he only inched closer to the edge himself.

"Johnnie, look at me. Look at my wings. I can fly. I'll be okay."

Melanie wondered if Caesar was hallucinating or hoping that Johnnie was by now.

"I'll fly away with you."

"No Johnnie, you're needed here."

"No, I'm not."

"You can't save me. But you'll save someone else someday."

Melanie's heart raced. *Does he mean me?*

"I can't do it."

"You can." Caesar let go of Johnnie's arm.

Johnnie desperately tried to hold on to his friend, but Caesar was slipping away.

"No!" Johnnie screamed in agony as he lost his grip. Melanie buried her head in her hands, unable to watch as Caesar's body fell onto the rocks below. She hoped he'd had enough peyote to feel little pain and to imagine he was indeed flying.

Johnnie obviously hadn't had enough, and he continued to sob. He pulled himself onto solid ground and curled into a fetal position. She lay down beside him, curling herself around him, holding him close.

Melanie woke the next morning across from Johnnie in his bed. He appeared to be sleeping peacefully, and she simply couldn't resist lightly touching his hair.

His eyes opened, and he smiled. *I love his smile.* And after last night it was wonderful to see.

They stared at one another for several minutes.

"I could look at you all day, beautiful." He brushed the hair back from her face. "Can I kiss you?"

"I'm not sure I could stop at one kiss."

He ran a finger over her bottom lip. "I know damn well I couldn't."

"It's probably best we don't, then."

Johnnie frowned. "Where's Caesar? Is he still here?"

"I heard some banging pots and pans earlier. Maybe he's cooking."

"We're in big trouble." Johnnie slid a hand up and down her arm.

"Why is that?"

"His cooking is worse than mine."

"Is that possible?" She laughed lightly.

"Wait and see."

She gently stroked his face. "How do you feel about what he showed us?"

"What did you see?"

"I saw everything that happened that night. I was there with the two of you. Only you couldn't see or hear me."

"Same here. It was like watching a movie starring myself." Johnnie squeezed his eyes tightly shut.

She moved closer and kissed his forehead. "It was an accident. You tried to save him."

"I shouldn't have taken him up there."

"You had no idea what was going to happen. Stop blaming yourself. Caesar doesn't blame you."

Johnnie's eyes opened again. "I'm trying, Melanie. I've missed him for so long."

"Then you should spend time with him today. Work on the documentary."

"How long do you think he'll be around?"

"I don't know. I forced him to leave last time."

"Promise not to do that again." He took her hand and kissed it.

"I won't." She smiled. "But you have to promise me the same thing."

"Why would I ever want him to leave?"

"Why would I?"

"Your magic pussy might get sore." He grinned.

"It was fine with you."

"True. And I am the better lover and all..."

An oven mitt flew across the room and hit Johnnie in the head. Caesar was at the door. "Care to make a wager on that?"

Johnnie slid from the bed and pulled on his pajama pants. "She won't tell you the truth anyway. She's too nice to hurt your feelings."

Johnnie hugged Caesar tight. They stayed wrapped up in each other's arms for a while, and Melanie realized they were both crying.

"I love you, man." Caesar pulled away and grabbed Johnnie's face. "Stop hating yourself because of me."

Johnnie nodded, wiping at his tears.

Caesar flung himself on the bed and hugged her. "Now let's eat breakfast."

"You cooked?" Johnnie asked.

"I made pancakes."

"So, your plan is to poison us?"

Caesar threw the oven mitt at Johnnie again. "I promise they're delicious."

"Do ghosts learn to cook properly or something?" She smiled as she and Caesar left the bed.

He kissed her cheek. "It's one of my ghostly superpowers."

Johnnie's eyebrow raised. "Like your supposed sexual prowess?"

"I've always had prowess, and you know it." Caesar wrapped an arm around Johnnie's shoulder. "And it's a million times better now."

"Oh really?" Johnnie laughed as the two of them walked out of the room together.

She followed, shaking her head. *They're impossible!*

"Well, look who I'm fucking."

They both glanced back at her.

"I'll give you that one." Johnnie nodded, grinning. "Got that magic pussy *and* that magic mouth."

Melanie smacked Johnnie on the butt, then Caesar. "Stop talking about me like I'm not hearing every word you say."

Caesar playfully pushed her into Johnnie who grabbed her around the waist. Caesar closed in on her, causing her to back into Johnnie and press him against the wall. Caesar grabbed the back of her head and brought his lips to hers. The hair on her arms stood straight as she realized she was sandwiched in between two hot men, both of whom she was madly in love with. She eagerly returned Caesar's kisses and felt his hard cock press into her groin. Johnnie maintained his grip on her waist, and his thick cock pressed against her butt. Her pussy began to throb. *I want them both!*

She reached back and encircled Johnnie's head. Caesar lifted her tank top and squeezed her breasts before attaching his mouth to one.

Johnnie whispered in her ear. "Is this what you want?"

Tilting her head back, she answered him with a kiss. His mouth parted hers, and his tongue invaded. Caesar worked his mouth down her belly. When he tugged her pants to the floor, she widened her stance allowing him to slip his tongue between her legs.

Johnnie's continued kisses swallowed up her moans of pleasure. His hands were on her breasts now, teasing her nipples as Caesar's tongue teased her clit. This was beyond any pleasure she'd felt before, and it didn't take long for her body to begin tightening.

"I'm going to cum," she panted.

Caesar took his mouth from her and looked at Johnnie. "Should I do the honors, or would you like to?"

Instantly, Johnnie pushed her aside. "She's all yours."

When he limped away, Melanie wanted to go after him.

"He's not ready to share you yet." Caesar stood. His fingers took over for his tongue. "He'll come around."

"I feel terrible. He's hurt seeing us together."

"He's alright." Caesar closed his eyes. "He's on the beach...going for a swim. Trying to cool himself down."

"But his foot..."

"The saltwater will be good for it."

She frowned, still worried.

"We can go talk to him." Caesar took his fingers from her.

She faced the wall. "I'd rather you fuck me."

He pulled her hair aside and pressed kisses against her neck. She shivered as a bolt of energy spread to her pussy.

"Please, Caesar, now."

He laughed playfully as he pushed the waistband of his pants down. He spread her butt cheeks and shoved into her from behind. He continued to kiss and suck her neck as he moved inside her.

"How is it that you're even more wet?" He pulled out wiping the head of his cock on her opening. Then he slipped easily inside her again. "You must have really wanted Johnnie, too."

She didn't respond but instead envisioned both of them making love to her.

"You're getting wetter by the second. You're thinking of him, aren't you?"

"I'm trying not to."

"I want you to." Caesar withdrew and grabbed her hand. "In fact, come with me."

He led her to the large picture windows facing the beach. She could see Johnnie in the water. He'd taken his clothes off and was playing in the surf.

"Watch him while I fuck you." Caesar once again entered her from behind.

She pressed her palms against the glass of the windows and watched Johnnie. He was knocked over by a wave and came up sputtering, smiling, pushing his dark wet hair from his face. He hobbled out of the water, and his thick cock came into view. He was still hard.

"You want him, don't you? He still wants you. Imagine it's him who's fucking you, Melanie."

She bent slightly so that Caesar could drive in deeper. Johnnie came up the stairs of the deck and went into the outside shower. When he turned his back to the spray of water, he began to stroke his cock unaware that she was watching.

"Caesar," she moaned. "You feel so good. I love you so much."

"And Johnnie?"

"I love him, too."

"You want him?"

"Yes." She shuddered, close to her pinnacle.

Caesar wrapped his arms around her, pulling her upright again. He withdrew from her. "Go to him."

"But he and I made a deal that he would get counseling first."

"He's going to. He'd do anything for you."

Reluctantly, Melanie went outside and stood in the doorway of the shower.

"What are you doing?" Johnnie's cock slipped from his hand. "We decided this shouldn't happen until I get help."

Her hand slid up his chest and to the back of his neck. "I can't stay away from you."

"Where's Caesar?"

"Probably watching us."

"Wanting to pick up some tips?" He grinned. That sexy, mischievous smile that turned her on even more.

She bit her bottom lip. "I think he enjoys seeing us together."

"He's going to beat off while watching? Is that it?"

"If you want me to go back to him, I will."

"In the hallway." Johnnie sighed heavily. "You didn't think that was strange?"

"It felt right."

"Maybe to you. For me, I'm not sure." He cupped her cheek. "I don't know if I can share you."

"We're alone now. No sharing."

He grabbed her butt with one hand, and the other went between her thighs. Fingers began exploring. "Damn. You're dripping wet. Guess he prepped you for me."

"He asked me to think of you. Had me watch you swimming."

"Did he now?"

She brushed a kiss against his lips.

"I don't want to fuck you."

"I understand."

He grabbed her arm as she started to leave. "I want to make love to you. Like that first time we were together. Just you and me in bed, making love for days."

"You want it to be sweet, is that what you're saying?"

"I don't know what the fuck I'm saying. I can't believe I'm turning you down."

"Especially when you were so adamant yesterday about finishing me off when Caesar didn't."

"I'm sure he'll be happy to finish the job today."

He turned his back to her. His rejection stung, but she knew it was for the best. *Hadn't they agreed to wait? What am I doing?* She honestly didn't know. These two men were making her crazy.

Caesar was standing at the kitchen island eating pancakes when she wandered in.

"That was fast," he said, licking syrup from his fingers.

She shrugged, pouting.

"Don't tell me he turned you down."

Instead of answering she grabbed a pancake from the stack and put it on a plate.

Caesar grabbed her arm and tugged her toward him. He hugged her tight, pressing kisses all over her face. When his lips found hers, the passion inside her raged again. His mouth never left hers as he lifted her to the kitchen counter. She freed his cock from his pants, then wrapped her legs around him. He eased into her wet walls, then slid out slowly, so she could savor every inch of him.

She moaned, and her head lolled backward.

"Like that?" he asked repeating the slow push and pull.

"I love it." She kissed him softly. "And you."

"I love you." He kissed her harder, parting her mouth, exploring with his tongue. "Are you going to cum for me, baby."

"I'm so close."

He swirled his tongue around her nipple. He sucked it into his mouth, pushing her over the edge. "Let me feel you cum on my cock."

Her pussy tightened, and she let out a long moan of ecstasy. He pushed harder and faster into her, causing her body to spasm and clutch his cock even tighter.

"Why am I not surprised?" Johnnie limped past the kitchen, catching them in the act. "Wipe down the counter when you're done."

"Someone's jealous," Caesar whispered, as he pulled her back to the floor, turned her around and entered her from behind.

Placing her palms against the side of the counter, she met each of his thrusts, slamming her butt against him.

"Yes, Melanie. I love that. I want to get as deep as possible."

He reached around her hip and in between her legs to touch her clit.

"I'm going to cum again." She felt her pussy tighten once more.

"Cum with me." He groaned and let loose inside her.

Melanie and Caesar were eating when Johnnie reappeared.

"I suppose the food's cold now."

Caesar grabbed a plate holding a few pancakes and placed it in the microwave. "I'll warm them up for you."

Johnnie opened the refrigerator door and grabbed the juice. Caesar passed him a glass to fill, and Johnnie snatched it from him.

"How's your foot?" she asked him. "You shouldn't have gotten the stitches wet."

"Oh yeah. That's right." Johnnie sat on a stool. "You watched me swimming. Did you enjoy it?"

"She certainly did." Caesar smiled.

"Are you losing your touch?" Johnnie taunted. "She had to watch me to get turned on?"

Caesar smacked him lightly on the back of the head. "Stop being jealous. She wanted you. You're the one who turned her down."

"I said no sloppy seconds."

"Stop with that bullshit. It's insulting. She loves you, and I expect you to treat her with respect."

"Fuck you."

Caesar slammed a dish towel against the counter. "Stop being an ass."

Melanie slid off her stool. "If the two of you are going to argue whenever I'm around, I'm going to go stay in a hotel somewhere. You got along fine yesterday when I wasn't here."

Melanie walked upstairs to her room. They continued to argue, and at the top of the stairs, she paused to listen. *Please stop fighting on my account.*

"Don't chase her away, man," Caesar was saying. "She's the best thing that's ever happened to you."

"Yes," Johnnie grouched. "And now she's with you again."

"She wants to be with both of us."

Quietly, Melanie crept back down the stairs to spy on them.

Johnnie shook his head. "I can't do that."

"Why the hell not?"

"Because I want her all to myself."

Caesar threw his hands up. "I don't know how long I'll be here. I could be gone tomorrow...or in half an hour...in the next ten seconds even."

"Don't say that. I want you to stay with us."

"Do you really?" Caesar asked.

"Of course."

"Then stop making every moment we spend together a conflict."

Johnnie groaned. "It's hard watching the two of you together. It's hard seeing how much she loves you."

"Bottom line, my friend. You're alive. I'm not."

"You seem pretty alive to me."

Caesar pointed to his chest. "Put your hand over my heart."

"What?"

"Just do it."

Johnnie hopped off the stool and placed his hand on Caesar's chest. "What the fuck?"

"Don't forget I'm dead. What she and I have can only go as far as I'm allowed to stay. No matter what happens, you'll always be the one who ends up with her. So, stop with the animosity and jealousy. Stop pushing her away. Let's have fun together and love one another."

"She and I agreed to wait until I got help. Some counseling."

"Do you honestly want help?" Caesar backed up and leaned against the counter. "To kick this shit once and for all? Because when I was alive, you reveled in it."

"Things changed after you died. It got very bad. Then I tried. I really did. I almost made it two years, even living with my parents, being around my dad, I did it. Now I have a real reason to get sober."

"No. You can't do it for her. Do it for yourself. You have more life ahead of you. You should be playing and writing music. Where the fuck are your drums?"

Johnnie hung his head. "Sold them. After you were gone...Rhett and Kurt...I could tell they blamed me. There was so much bitterness. They were tired of my nonsense and stopped coming around. I didn't want any reminders of that life. It hurt too much."

Caesar smiled and tossed his hair back, out of his face. "Then Melanie came along and reminded you of all of it."

"She did." Johnnie sighed. "Only it wasn't painful. The way she lights up when she hears your voice...our music. The way she talked about having my face nearby when she slept. How she fantasized about me. It was nice knowing I was part of her life, long before we met."

Melanie smiled. Her phone began ringing, and she slipped back upstairs to retrieve it. When she saw it was Rhett, she closed the door.

"Hey, how are things going? Any better?"

"Yes. And he's agreed to get counseling. Maybe if he deals with what's on his mind, he can then deal with the addiction."

"I hope it works out. I talked to Kurt, and we'd like to come next weekend if that's good with you."

"That's fantastic. It will be great to have all of you together again."

"Well, minus one."

Just you wait. "Johnnie will be happy to see you."

"We'll bring our instruments. Maybe he'd enjoy playing a bit."

"He will. I bought him a new drum set. It'll be arriving soon."

"Now that's what I need to find. Someone who buys me instruments."

"Hey, where did you go?" Caesar was yelling from the stairs.

"Who's that? Sounded like Caesar."

Oh shit! "We're working. Watching some video footage."

"Can't wait to see what you've dug up."

Caesar walked in, and Melanie immediately held a finger to her mouth to shush him.

"You're going to love what we've found. I have to go so we can keep this a surprise for Johnnie."

"Okay, see you next Friday afternoon. We'll come down midafternoon before the highway gets gridlocked."

"Sounds great." She hung up.

"Who was that?"

She held up her phone.

Caesar beamed. "No way!"

"He and Kurt are coming Friday. To spend the weekend. But don't tell Johnnie. It's a surprise."

He hugged her tight. "You're amazing. I can't wait to see them."

She pulled away. "Well, I think Rhett will see you. Not sure about Kurt though."

"Oh yeah, that's right. Let's hope though."

"We'll make him believe."

"Make who believe?" Johnnie was standing in the doorway.

"Make you believe that you need to stay out of the water, so your foot can heal properly," Melanie answered. "Did you take the antibiotics?"

"Yes, I did while I was eating cold, disgusting pancakes," Johnnie grumbled. "Told you he can't cook."

"Do you want me to make you something else?"

"I'm good, except I'd like to talk to you." He glanced at Caesar. "Alone."

Caesar nodded, smiling. "I'll go watch the documentary again."

"And don't be looking into the future to see what I'm going to say to her."

Caesar slapped him on the back playfully, then left the room.

"Important call?" Johnnie asked. "Good news?"

"Yeah, a nice surprise," she replied.

"Will you take a walk with me?"

Without thinking she slipped her tank top over her head, then tugged off the pajama pants. Johnnie turned away from her naked body.

"Sorry." She opened the closet and grabbed a sundress. Quickly, she slipped it over her head. "I'm used to being naked around you. I'm dressed now. You can look."

He smiled at her. "I love seeing you naked. You know that."

"But..."

"But I want to take a walk with you."

"Only if you put shoes on...and thick socks."

"Shoes and socks on the beach? Hope we don't run into the fashion police."

She laughed, glad that he was joking around again. "They'd be so mesmerized by those gorgeous blue eyes of yours, they wouldn't notice anything else."

"Laying it on thick, huh? Still hoping to get into my pants today?"

"You wish." They walked downstairs.

He smacked her butt gently then rubbed it. "Don't think I didn't notice you're going commando."

"So, you were watching."

"I'm always watching you." He held out his hand, and she took it.

The cool ocean breeze felt good on her skin, but having Johnnie hold her hand felt even better. He seemed lighter, as if some of his troubles had been lifted. Or maybe it was because Caesar wasn't there to complicate things.

They came to the rocks where he'd sat before, bleeding, and where she'd also sat. Instead of climbing onto the rock, he sat in front of it on the sand. She plopped down beside him.

"This is my favorite spot to sit and think."

She tucked her hair behind her ears. "It's beautiful. I saw dolphins playing here when you were gone. I walked out here and felt close to you and Caesar. Then they came, swimming and splashing."

"I've never seen dolphins. Not here or anywhere."

"I think Caesar sent them. I was upset and missing you. They showed up and made me smile, and I knew I'd be alright with or without you."

"I wasn't alright without you. When you were gone to Atlanta, my insecurities...my cravings got the best of me. And when I left...I was a mess. I thought about shooting up but didn't. I know too well how hard it is to shake heroin. I didn't want to start that shit again. Instead, I got drunk and stayed that way. I crashed with a few friends, cleaned out their medicine cabinets, and disappeared before they knew what I'd done."

Melanie rubbed his knee. "And the gun?"

"Bought it from a pawn shop." He stroked her arm with one finger. "Where is that damn thing, anyway?"

"In the safe."

"Good."

She kissed his forehead. "Don't ever scare me like that again."

"I'm sorry. And I'm sorry for the way I've been acting around Caesar. I'm edgy, coming off that bender. My system is clearing out again. The harder I fight the cravings, the crankier I tend to get."

"I can handle cranky."

"You shouldn't have to." He wrapped an arm around her shoulders. "I'm also scared of losing you."

"That won't happen. I'll always be here for you. Even if it's just as a friend."

"I don't want to be just friends."

"I don't either."

"Seeing you with him hurts. It shouldn't, but it does."

"We both love you. I love both of you. You love us."

"You two make it sound so simple." With his free hand, he picked up a small rock and threw it toward the ocean. "Put yourself in my shoes. What if it were you and me, and suddenly there was another woman."

"There was another woman."

"Some random pick up. I'm talking about someone I loved. If I loved two women and I asked you to be okay with that...to share me. Could you do it?"

Melanie grimaced. "I see what you mean, but with Caesar it's different."

"Because he's a ghost? He talked to me about that. About the fact he might be gone at any time. Which also worries me. I don't want him to leave. I feel like I have to give in to make him happy so he won't go."

"When we met the ghost researcher in Atlanta, he said Caesar was probably sent here to help me. He did. But he also needed to help you. Maybe that's why you saw him before. Maybe he was trying to reach out to you."

Johnnie laughed and shook his head. "Or maybe I was just high."

Melanie rubbed his knee. "Well, I don't think he'll leave until you're sober."

Johnnie cringed. "That makes me want to stay messed up, so he doesn't leave."

"You'll have to let him go when it's time. Like you did on that cliff."

"And what about you? When will I have to let you go?"

"Never."

"I might have to. I should be in rehab. And I'd be there awhile."

"And I'd be right here."

He slid his hand along her leg. "Will you help me look for a psychologist? I want to make an appointment soon."

"Of course."

"I want that second chance." He kissed her temple.

"I believe I already gave you that today."

He chuckled. "I guess you did."

"And you blew it. Turned me down."

"Make it a third chance then." He grinned, then moved his hand gently through her hair. "Will you do something for me?"

She nodded, hoping he'd changed his mind about making love to her.

"Will you take off your dress and let me watch you play in the water?"

"Only if you let me watch you touch yourself."

"It's a deal." He held out his hand, and she shook it.

She rose to her feet and shed her dress.

"You're beautiful." He unsnapped, then unzipped his shorts. His cock was already hard.

Melanie wiggled to the water's edge. She lifted her hair from her neck and peeked back at him. He was stroking himself. She dipped her feet into the ocean. When she went in about calf deep, she knelt and splashed water over her body. She went to all fours next with her ass facing him. Waves crashed around her.

When she heard him groan, she stood and faced him. She moved her hands up her sides to her breasts. She kneaded them, pinching her nipples into tight buds, then strutted back to his side.

"You're so fucking hot." He moaned.

She sat on her dress, spread her legs and began touching herself.

"What are you doing?"

"Are you the only one who gets to have fun?"

His eyebrows raised. "You haven't had enough fun for today?"

"Not with you."

"I wish I were inside you."

"I'm so wet, thinking of you inside me."

"I'm going to cum. Are you going to cum with me?"

Melanie put two fingers inside herself, got them wet, then touched her fingers to his lips. He opened his mouth and sucked on them.

He sat up on his knees and scooted closer to her. "Touch me."

She took hold of his erection, sliding her hand up and down. His hand was on her now, two fingers inside her, his thumb rubbing her clit.

"Johnnie." She gasped.

"What is it, baby?"

Her body clenched, tightening on his fingers.

"Fuck." He continued to move them inside her as she squealed in delight. "I'm cumming, too."

His cum began to erupt, and she bent her head, catching it in her mouth. When she'd caught every drop, he wrapped her up in his arms.

Johnnie grinned. "We're naughty, aren't we?"

"I'm afraid I have an addiction, too."

He sat back down, pulling her with him. "That's called codependency. Given your past with your ex, you might want to get some counseling as well."

She knew it was true but hearing him say it stung a bit. "Is it terrible that I want you all the time?"

"It is until I get sober." He rubbed her shoulders. "I don't want to ever hurt you again."

She kissed him. "Everything is better now. Don't you think?"

"Because Caesar's here?" He laughed lightly and squeezed her. "You really have it bad for him."

She snuggled closer. "Stop teasing me about him."

"But it's so much fun."

"Don't you think things are headed in the right direction?"

"So far so good." He pulled away, stood, and hoisted his pants back up. "Until we get back to the house and find out Caesar's deleted a bunch of files because he has no clue how to use a computer."

Melanie scrambled to her feet. "He might do that. We better get back."

"Let's go out to eat tonight. You and me."

"And leave Caesar alone?"

"Yep, you got it bad."

Chapter Nineteen

Melanie set aside the magazine she'd been reading when she saw Johnnie and his psychologist exiting the doctor's office. They'd chosen Dr. Radford because his website had mentioned his success in treating addiction problems.

"Ah." Dr. Radford gave a slight nod upon seeing her. "This must be Melanie. I've heard quite a lot about you today."

"It's nice to meet you." Melanie stood and held out her hand.

Dr. Radford shook it. "I'm hoping you might consider joining us next time."

She nodded. "If it will help Johnnie, of course."

They bid the doctor goodbye and went out to the car.

"I need to stop by the grocery store on the way home."

"Why don't we have lunch somewhere while we're here in L.A. I know some good places."

"I'd love that." She smiled. "You want to drive?"

"Are you going to give me road head?"

She shook her head, trying hard not to smile, and failing. "I hadn't planned on it."

"Then you drive."

"I can't believe you bought all this food. I know we have one more person in the house, but he doesn't eat much."

"We won't have to make another trip into town for a while."

"I see," he replied. "More time for fucking Caesar."

The truth was, she was preparing for Rhett and Kurt's visit. They'd be visiting soon, and she wanted to work on cleaning the house. The past few days she'd stayed out of Johnnie and Caesar's way as they worked together on the documentary. They were a great team if she kept her distance. She wrote while they worked, and at night they would show her what they'd added or tweaked. After that, they'd watch a movie together and then she'd retreat to her room with Caesar while Johnnie went to his own room.

Johnnie hadn't had any more nightmares, but now she imagined he laid awake in bed listening to her and Caesar make love. She worried about how he felt, but she wasn't going to push him into discussing it. As long as everyone was getting along, she'd decided to let it go.

"No one's stopping you from fucking me."

Johnnie rubbed his head as if it hurt. "Your bed's a bit crowded."

"I can come to yours."

"What? And leave Caesar all alone?"

"He'd be fine

"Is that why he's sitting on the front steps looking like a lost puppy?"

Caesar opened the gate, and she drove into the driveway, parking close to the front door.

"I hauled all this from the store to the car," Johnnie complained to Caesar and stalked away. "You're turn."

"Why did you buy so much?" Caesar asked as he helped Melanie unload and carry things inside.

"You know why. For our visitors."

The two of them were putting the groceries away when Melanie's phone rang.

"Can you let us into the gate. We have your delivery."

"I'll send someone out."

"Johnnie!" she yelled. "There's a delivery truck at the gate. Can you let them in?"

Johnnie walked past the kitchen and pointed at Caesar. "You didn't show him how to order stuff on *Amazon* did you?"

"I ordered something for you. So, let them in."

"Sure thing, boss." Johnnie saluted.

"I'll help," Caesar offered.

"You can't," Melanie reminded him. "If they were able to see you...see Caesar Blue...that wouldn't be good."

"I'll be upstairs then."

"That's the last box." The delivery guy handed Melanie a clipboard. "Sign here."

She did, then saw him out. Once he'd turned out onto the street, she shut the gate, then went back inside.

Johnnie was sitting on the couch in the living room, surrounded by boxes. He looked dazed.

"Are you alright?"

He stared at her. "You bought me drums?"

"I used Caesar's money." She saw that his eyes were watery. "I was hoping it would make you happy."

"It's the best gift ever." He kissed her. "I love you."

"Let's open them." Caesar had a box cutter in his hand. He and Johnnie began working.

"No way!" Johnnie held up the first drum. A snare.

Caesar patted his back. "Hey, that looks like the set you used on our last tour."

Johnnie smiled at her. "You really are a fan."

"I did my research."

He handed Caesar the snare, then hugged her. In her ear, he whispered, "This is almost as good as road head."

"You're impossible." She swatted his arm, then kissed him.

It was meant to be a short kiss, but he held onto her, keeping his lips on hers. Over and over he kissed her.

"Thank you," Johnnie said when he finally pulled away.

Caesar beamed as he continued pulling out instruments. "Let's get this together so you can play."

Later that night, Melanie sat outside in the jacuzzi with a naked Caesar. Her head throbbing. "Is he ever going to stop?"

"He's in heaven." He kissed her cheek. "You made him very happy today."

"And he's made me very deaf." She covered her ears. "We've got to give him a curfew."

"We'll set him up in the studio tomorrow."

"What studio?"

"The rehearsal studio." Caesar pointed toward the garage.

"You have a rehearsal studio? How did I not know about this?"

"Did you bother looking into the room next to the garage?"

"No. It was locked, and I never found a key for it. Johnnie never mentioned it either."

"What did you think was in it?"

She shrugged. "Dragon statues?"

He laughed. "It's a small studio. Soundproofed. So we could rehearse when the guys were here."

"Soundproof? Why didn't either of you mention it today."

"I wanted to watch him having fun. And I'm sure he wanted to make sure we could barely have a conversation."

The drumming stopped.

"Oh, thank God," Melanie said. "Maybe he's finally tired himself out."

"Or maybe he just needed a bathroom break, or a drink, or a snack."

"Don't say that."

"You should go dance naked in front of him. I bet he'd quit then."

"I don't think my ego could handle another rejection."

Caesar softly stroked her cheek. "He'll change his mind."

"Are you saying that because you're looking into our futures?"

"I'm saying that because I know he loves you…and because you're irresistible."

"So are you." She moved into his lap, slid her bathing suit bottoms over, and sunk herself onto his cock. Caesar untied her bikini top and began sucking on her nipples.

"I broke the last pair of sticks," Johnnie announced as he bounded out the back door. "I wish I knew a music store that was open this late at night."

Caesar let go of her nipple, but beneath the water, he began to stroke her clit. "Maybe you've played enough for today. We can get more sticks tomorrow."

"I can't thank you enough, Melanie." He was a bundle of energy as he paced back and forth on the deck. "Do you mind getting up early with me to get more sticks?"

Melanie couldn't help herself. Caesar had zeroed in on her magic spot. Her arms wrapped tightly around his neck as she shivered, panting loudly.

Johnnie stopped in his tracks and stared at her, his eyes wide. "Shit! Are you two having sex?"

"Sorry," she said, sheepishly. "We weren't expecting you."

Instead of getting upset or angry, Johnnie smiled. "I should have known better than to barge in on you two. I'll leave you alone."

Melanie's mouth dropped as Johnnie went back inside. "What just happened?"

Caesar's curls danced around his face as he laughed. "He's in a great mood obviously. The psychologist, the afternoon spent with you, then the drums. I'd say he had a good day."

"Since he can't play for a while, would you mind finishing this upstairs?"

When they entered the living room, Johnnie was at the drums, giving everything a once over. Caesar headed into the kitchen, while she lingered watching Johnnie admire his new set. It felt good to see him so happy.

"I'll probably need to get some extra drum heads, too," he said tapping the snare with his finger. "And I guess I should move them out to the studio."

"The studio I knew nothing about until today?" Melanie smiled. "I'm glad you're enjoying them."

"Thanks again." He kissed her. Another long, hard kiss.

"We'll be upstairs," she told him.

He kissed her again and knelt to adjust a stand. "I want to work on some writing in a bit. You might want to close your door, so you don't hear me banging on the keyboard."

She took his hands in hers.

"Aren't your hands tired?"

"A little numb, but I'll be alright once they get calloused up again."

"I like these hands." She kissed each palm. "Don't do too much damage."

"Don't worry." He grinned. "If my hands get too rough there's always my tongue."

She bent to his ear. "I love when you're naughty."

"See you in the morning." He gave her a quick kiss, then went back to his drums.

"Alright, I'm done." Johnnie barged into her bedroom without bothering to knock. "I'm trying to focus on writing this autobiography, and all I hear is you two giggling and moaning...the bed squeaking. It's distracting."

Caesar was lying down with Melanie was sitting on top of him. She scrambled off and covered herself. Caesar didn't bother.

Melanie slipped out of bed with the blanket wrapped around herself and went to the chest of drawers. "I have some earbuds for my phone. You can use them. You could even listen to the music from my laptop if you want to."

Johnnie grabbed her arm. "No, it's okay. But I miss being with you. I can't stop thinking about being inside you. So, I'm here to join you."

She looked at Caesar who smiled. She knew what he was thinking. *I told you so.*

Her gaze went back to Johnnie's. "Are you sure?"

"Like you said, we both love you." He rubbed her shoulders. "Why should he be the only one to express that to you?"

"We could go to your room."

"It's too far." He tugged the blanket from her body, then pulled her close. His hands went down her back and to her butt, which he squeezed. "I want you right now."

Melanie slid his shirt up and over his head. Then she unbuttoned his pants and slid them from his waist. She took his hand and led him to the bed.

"Now let's be clear on a few things." Johnnie shook a finger in Caesar's direction. "There will be no touching of dicks or balls. You stay on your side...Melanie stays in the middle."

Melanie slipped back into bed. "How did you guys manage to do this before?"

Caesar appeared confused. "Before? We never did anything like this before."

Johnnie slipped in beside her. "She's assuming since we were rock gods, we would've been in similar situations."

"I'm not assuming. You said you once had twenty women in a hotel room with the two of you."

"Twenty?" Caesar's eyes widened. He began laughing and couldn't stop. He laughed so hard tears rolled down his cheeks. "I can't believe you told her that."

"In my defense"—Johnnie shrugged—"I was trying to discredit you as a love interest."

"And apparently yourself at the same time." Caesar couldn't stop laughing.

"Alright, enough," Johnnie grouched. "This is supposed to be a mind-blowing sexual experience for her. Maybe you could get serious for a minute."

"Oh yes, of course. Serious." Caesar cleared his throat and set his mouth in a hard line. His face began twitching though, and he started laughing again.

"Never mind." Johnnie started to rise.

Melanie placed a palm on his chest. "Ignore him."

She ran her hand down to his cock and lightly skimmed it with her fingertips.

"I want you so bad." Johnnie sucked in his breath as she gripped him. He turned to face her. "It's been too long since I've been inside you."

His lips touched hers. Soft, tender kisses. He caught her bottom lip in his mouth and sucked on it.

Caesar covered his face with a pillow trying hard to stop laughing. Melanie reached behind her and found his cock as well. Instantly, he was hard again. She stroked both at the same time.

"Mmmm." Caesar cuddled up behind her, pressing his groin into her butt. He lifted her hair and moved his lips over the nape of her neck.

Her heart raced. *Is this really happening?* Johnnie's lips were blazing a trail of kisses down to her chest. His tongue swirled around a nipple before sucking it into his mouth. Caesar's hands traveled to her butt. He parted her cheeks and slipped two fingers into her from behind.

Johnnie's hand slid to her thighs, which she parted. He found her clit at the same time his mouth locked onto her other nipple.

"Feel how wet she is," Caesar said. Two of Johnnie's fingers also invaded her. "I think she wants us."

This is what heaven feels like.

Caesar's beautiful curls tickled the side of her face as he kissed her shoulders, his warm breath on her neck. Johnnie's thumb worked her clit. She moaned, so close to her orgasm, but trying to hold off, for Johnnie...for his cock that she'd been missing.

"Johnnie." She moaned.

His lips left her breasts, returning to her mouth. "What?"

"I need you."

"Do you?" He kissed her chin.

"Yes." She cupped his balls and squeezed them gently. "Don't you want me?"

"More than anything." He took her leg and hoisted it over his hip.

She eased closer to him. Caesar snuggled closer, caressing the butt cheek and thigh of the leg that was now on Johnnie. She turned her head to Caesar, and he kissed her.

"I love you...I'm going to give you two some privacy." Caesar kissed her again. "I'll be back."

Johnnie immediately rolled her onto her back. She spread her legs, and he put the head of his cock at her wet entrance.

"Tell me again." He pressed kisses on her face.

"I need you." She writhed beneath him, trying to get him to enter. She grabbed his face between her hands. "I love you."

"I love you." He pushed hard into her, both of them crying out with relief. Her walls immediately closed tight on him as she came. He pushed into her again and again, causing her body to quake uncontrollably. He groaned and came inside her.

Caesar peaked his head into the room. "Well, that didn't take long."

Johnnie hurled a pillow in his direction. "I'm not done yet."

"I'm not either," she said.

Johnnie rolled to his back. "Get us some glasses of water. We're going to need it."

Melanie knelt on the bed and began to lick his cock. She slid her tongue up and down his shaft, then swirled it around the head.

"That feels so good." He groaned when she took him fully into her mouth. "You give amazing head."

"Magic tongue remember."

"Refresh my memory some more."

Caesar wandered in with the water. He saw her there, ass up, on all fours, sucking Johnnie's cock. "Damn, I love your ass."

"I do, too." Johnnie sighed.

Caesar set the water on the dresser and moved in closer behind her. "I'm going to fuck you, baby."

Melanie's body trembled as Caesar entered her from behind. Without detaching her mouth from Johnnie, she looked into his eyes. He was paying no attention to Caesar. His focus was on her as she worked her lips up and down him. Caesar slowly worked her from behind. She loved when he did that, letting her feel every inch of him. His cock was long and hard. Johnnie's wasn't quite as long, but it was thick, stretching her, filling her when they made love.

"This is so hot." Caesar groaned and let loose inside her.

"That didn't take long," Johnnie mocked him.

"I'm not done yet." Caesar slid his cock from her. "Switch places."

"You guys are going to wear me out." She smiled as Caesar climbed onto the bed. Johnnie stood behind her.

"It's strange seeing his cum dripping out of you."

"It's not just his...it's ours."

Johnnie slid inside her. "Damn, you feel so fucking good."

Caesar knelt in front of her, and she brought his cock back to life with her mouth. He grabbed her suddenly, pulling her away from

Johnnie, and into the bed next to him. He motioned for Johnnie to join them on the bed again and then covered her mouth with a deep kiss, pushing his tongue in between her lips.

Johnnie's hands were caressing her body...from her thighs up to her breasts, squeezing them, teasing her nipples.

Caesar let her come up for air and looked at Johnnie. "Let's drive her absolutely wild."

When Caesar held up his hand, Johnnie gave him a high five. Then Johnnie's lips were on hers, kissing her deeply. When he broke the kiss, Caesar took over. Johnnie's mouth was on her shoulders, her chest. Caesar finished his kiss and then Johnnie was pressing his lips against her neck and then back up to her lips.

"Want to watch?" Caesar grabbed two pillows and stuffed them under her head, propping her up.

Then he was on her nipple. Johnnie worked his way down, too. Each one at a breast. She saw them eye one another and then watched as they synchronized their tongues to tease the tight buds with little flicks. Her pussy ached with desire as they began to each suck the nipple they'd claimed.

Hands replaced mouths on her breasts, and their tongues began to glide down her belly. Knowing their intent, she spread her legs, but instead of going right to her pussy, they swept their tongues along her inner thighs. They licked the crease between her thigh and her core. She thought she might die from anticipation.

Her hands tightly clutched the blankets beneath her as she moaned both in pleasure and frustration. "Please."

Caesar laughed lightly. "Please what?"

Johnnie began to softly blow air against her pussy. "Yes...what should we do now?"

Caesar blew as well.

It was maddening.

"Whose mouth do you want?" Johnnie asked as he spread her folds. He touched her clit softly with his tongue. "Mine?"

"Or mine?" Caesar ran his tongue along the sides of her pussy.

The two of them looked at one another and smiled. Then both their tongues ran up the sides of her pussy together

"Or both?" They said in unison.

She shuddered. "How is this even a question?"

They went to work together. Taking turns at her clit...taking turns fucking her with their tongue. Each of them slipped a finger inside her, then curled them upward to work her g-spot. Caesar latched onto her clit and slid another finger inside her as Johnnie returned to her side to kiss her.

"Do you like this?" He caressed her face.

She stared into his stormy gaze, and her heart beat even faster.

"I love you, Johnnie."

"I'm going to get better, Melanie. For you *and* me. So, we can always be together."

A tear slid down the side of her face and Johnnie kissed it away. She didn't even realize Caesar had stopped what he was doing.

He lay down beside them. "Make love to her."

Johnnie's gaze never left hers as he entered her slowly. She took his face in her hands and ran her fingers through his hair.

"He wants to be deeper inside you," Caesar whispered in her ear.

Johnnie ground his hips into hers. She ran her hands down his back to his butt, and she pressed him deeper into her. She lifted her hips to meet his thrusts, forcing him even deeper.

"She feels amazing, doesn't she?" Caesar smiled. "She's so tight and wet. She wants you so much. She loves you so much."

"And I love her." Johnnie's own tears were falling onto her cheeks.

Caesar kissed her shoulder. "Feel that thick cock inside you, Melanie?"

"It feels so good."

"You want to cum on it, don't you?" Caesar asked.

"Yes."

"Johnnie wants to feel that magic pussy of yours cum on him."

"I do. I want to make you cum, Melanie."

Johnnie sat up and pulled her into his lap. She straddled him and took his cock inside once more. She rode him now, and her pace quickened when he bent his head to suck on her nipples once again.

Caesar pressed kisses on her back. "Ride him, Melanie. Make him cum."

She was worried Johnnie might get annoyed by all of Caesar's instructions, but he didn't seem to mind. Instead, like her, he seemed turned on by his friend's encouragement. She doubted Johnnie could do the same thing...tell Caesar what to do to her. But there was just something about Caesar's voice, the sensual nature of it, that silky chocolate, that turned her on further, making her body tingle...making her want to be fucked even harder.

With Caesar's sexy prodding and Johnnie gently sucking her nipples, she picked up her pace. Johnnie's hand went to her clit, and he caressed her softly.

"Johnnie, yes." She ground her hips harder into his.

His mouth went to hers again. "Cum for me."

"I love you." She moaned loudly, and her body tightened on his.

"Oh baby, I love you, too." He grunted and pulled her against his cock, shoving himself even deeper as her body quaked on his. "I'm cumming."

He held her tightly to him, kissing her over and over as he came.

Caesar threw his arms around them both. "And I love you, both of you."

"Caesar, your dick is touching my leg." Johnnie smiled at Melanie, and the two of them began laughing. Caesar joined in. All three of them collapsed onto the bed in a fit of laughter. Caesar hit Johnnie with a pillow again, and soon the trio were racing around the house naked as a full-fledged pillow fight ensued.

Chapter Twenty

"Why are you up so early?" Johnnie sauntered naked into the kitchen where Melanie was cleaning the countertops. "I woke up and thought I was cuddling you. But it was Caesar's head on my chest."

Melanie laughed as he wrapped his arms around her. "I have a lot of cleaning to do today."

"Come back to bed," he begged, pressing his groin into her butt. His hands cupped her breasts. "Who gives a shit about cleaning?"

"I do. So, if you're up, I need your help."

"Part of me is awake."

"I see." She turned to him. "But if I stop what I'm doing to make love to you, then I'll never get this done."

He cupped her chin, kissing her as he removed the sponge from her hand and tossed it into the sink. His hand slid into her yoga pants. "Again, who cares about cleaning? All I want to do is get dirty with you."

"Johnnie," she protested as he slid her pants down. He knelt in front of her and wiggled his tongue in between her legs. She sighed. She wanted the house spotless for Rhett and Kurt's visit. But Johnnie knew how to work her clit. How to make her forget everything but his mouth on her.

"Good morning." Caesar strolled into the kitchen. He kissed her softly, letting his lips linger on hers. He appeared awestruck as he stared into her eyes, tenderly stroking her jawline. "I love how you look right now. Completely turned on. Your body on fire. Ready to cum."

"I was trying to clean." She whimpered as Johnnie's fingers now found their way inside her. Then she whispered, "You know...for the surprise later. He won't let me."

"Once you cum I bet he will."

Johnnie removed his mouth from her and smiled. "No, because then I plan to take her back to bed and make love to her all day."

"Caesar, please help me. You know how important this is."

Johnnie stood and eyed them suspiciously. "What are you two up to?"

"We have visitors coming," Caesar blurted out.

"What visitors?" Johnnie asked.

"Some book people...about her book," Caesar lied. Technically not a lie since she *was* going to work on an autobiography with the band soon.

"Why didn't you tell me?" Johnnie ran his hands through his hair.

"I wasn't sure how you'd react to visitors. You seem to keep to yourself most of the time."

"Maybe. But I'd help you get the house straightened up." He kissed her. "Where should I begin."

"Can you move the drums out to the studio?"

"Of course, we will." Caesar nodded. "In fact, why don't you go take a long, hot bath and relax."

"Good idea," Johnnie agreed. He gently rubbed between her legs as he kissed her. "You're probably sore as hell. Not to mention nervous about the meeting. Go relax. We've got this."

"If you say so." Melanie kissed him back. "My muscles are a bit sore."

"A hot bath will do you good." Caesar kissed her now.

Melanie sank down into the bubble bath. The water was steaming hot and felt so good on her muscles. Three days of nearly nonstop lovemaking with two men was hard on the body. But she'd relished every moment of it. A few times they'd repeated the threesome they'd begun, but other times Caesar would watch her and Johnnie. When it was Caesar's turn to be with her, Johnnie would often take a break to get food or something to drink. She knew it was still difficult for him to share her, but he wasn't complaining, and he seemed happy they were back together. She knew she should still be upset about the cheating, but she also knew it was a symptom of his addiction for which he was now getting counseling. And since he'd been reunited with Caesar, he hadn't had any alcohol or taken anything. Besides, it was just too hard for her to stay away from him. She loved him too much.

Her phone alerted her to a text, and she saw that it was Rhett. He told her they'd arrive around three in the afternoon. She hoped Caesar and Johnnie could get the house somewhat in order by then.

Melanie responded quickly. *Do you think you could find a music store and pick up a few pairs of sticks for Johnnie?*

You've got him playing again? Fantastic! I'll get some.

"What time is the meeting?" Johnnie asked her. He and Caesar were sitting on the bed watching her race around the room getting ready.

"They said they'd be here at three." Melanie tugged on a pair of jeans, then began looking through the closet for a blouse to wear. "You left the gate open?"

"Yeah, took care of it." Caesar swept up beside her and grabbed a sky blue, bohemian style tunic. "This would look great on you, and I don't think it would be too big. I bought it in India."

She pulled it over her head and turned to Johnnie. "What do you think?"

"It looks great with your eyes." Johnnie sat up. "But it's a bit casual for a business meeting, don't you think?"

"It is a home visit." She checked her reflection in the mirror on the back of the door. "I think it'll be okay."

"Where should I hide out? Up here?"

She nodded. "It shouldn't be for too long."

"I'll take a nap, I think."

She bit her lip as she looked from Caesar to Johnnie. "I'll let you know if anything changes."

"Sure thing." Caesar kissed her forehead. "I can't wait."

"I'll hang out in my room," Johnnie told her. "Stay out of your hair."

"You should be with her," Caesar said. "For support."

"I might say the wrong thing or do something stupid."

The doorbell rang.

"They're early!" Melanie ran into the bathroom. She grabbed her mascara and dabbed it on her eyes. Then picked up her lipstick.

"I'll let them in." Johnnie smiled and kissed her cheek. "I can handle that much."

She smiled. "You can do anything."

After Johnnie trotted off downstairs, she covered her mouth and looked at Caesar. "This was a hard secret to keep."

"It sure was." Caesar kissed her softly. "Go downstairs and record this reunion. Hurry."

She grabbed her phone and scurried downstairs after Johnnie.

"No fucking way!" Johnnie yelled when he opened the door.

"Long time. No see." Rhett hugged him tightly.

Melanie held up her phone, capturing the moment. When she saw that their backs shook from genuine sobs, she found herself tearing up. Kurt stepped into the foyer, joining in the hug and the tears. After a few minutes, the trio finally withdrew from one another, wiping at their eyes.

Johnnie looked at her. "Did you do this?"

She nodded, and he came to her, kissing, then hugging her.

"This is Melanie." Johnnie beamed as he presented her to his friends. "She's met Rhett apparently."

"Just briefly." Rhett took her hand but then pulled her close for a hug. When they parted, he had a strange look on his face. "You still smell like Caesar."

"Is it her I smell?" Kurt asked as, he too, hugged her. "Wow. That's crazy. Is there still some of that vanilla oil lying around the house?"

"I believe you said your mother gave you some vanilla perfume."

Johnnie shook his head. "She's been rolling around in Caesar's bed for a few months."

Rhett nudged him and grinned. "What? You mean she isn't rolling around in your bed?"

Melanie was surprised when Johnnie's cheeks turned red. "Speaking of rooms and beds. We can put your bags in the downstairs rooms."

"How did you hurt your foot?" Kurt asked Johnnie as everyone relaxed on the deck after dinner.

"While he explains, I'm going to get dessert and more lemonade." Melanie excused herself from the table. "Be right back."

She found Caesar in the kitchen eating some of the salad she'd prepared. "You're supposed to be in the bedroom."

"I got hungry. And bored. When are you going to tell them about me?"

"It has to be the right time. I don't want to scare them away or have them think I'm crazy."

He bounced up and down like an impatient child. "I opened the upstairs window so I could listen in on the conversation. I want to talk to them so bad."

"I know." She kissed him. "I'll try to work you in soon. I promise."

"Who are you talking to?" Kurt wandered into the kitchen.

Damn! He can't see Caesar. "Mumbling to myself."

"Thought I'd come in and help."

"Thanks." Melanie grabbed some dessert plates and forks and set them on the counter. Then she grabbed the second pitcher of lemonade out of the refrigerator.

"What do you see in Johnnie?"

Melanie was surprised by Kurt's question. "So many things. Why?"

"He tends to wreck everything in his path."

Melanie glanced at Caesar, who didn't appear happy with Kurt's words. "Lush didn't seem like a wreck. You guys were very successful...he was a big part of that."

"When Caesar was around, it was different. Johnnie was messed up, but Caesar was there to smooth things over, straighten things out, keep Johnnie from going too far. Johnnie was always self-destructive, but losing Caesar made him even worse."

Don't I know all this? "I'm sure it was hard on all of you."

"He said he wants to get straight once and for all. I'm not sure if he can do that with you in his life."

"I appreciate your concern. I understand what I'm getting into with Johnnie. When he's ready to get into a program, I'll let him go. I only want what's best for him."

"It's clear he's in love with you. But that doesn't mean he won't hurt you."

Frowning, she turned from his gaze.

"He already has, hasn't he?" Kurt leaned against the counter next to the stove. "What was it? Drugs? Drinking? Another woman? All of the above?"

One of the dessert plates fell to the floor, shattering...saving her from having to answer Kurt's inquiry.

Kurt picked up the bigger pieces. "How did that happen?"

Melanie mouthed 'thank you' to Caesar as she retrieved the broom from a nearby closet and began sweeping up the shards. "I'll get the rest. Take everything out to the guys."

Kurt picked up the tray with the pie and plates.

"I'm glad you came to visit him." Melanie bent to sweep the shards into the dustpan. "He really needed to see you two."

"It's been too long."

"I know it's not easy."

Kurt nodded and gave half a smile. "We're not getting any younger. Time to get over old grudges."

"Does he not like me?" she asked Caesar once Kurt was gone.

"He's always been very direct." He kissed her. "He's going to question your motives about the band so be prepared."

"He can't see you."

"Make him believe. I know it will be hard, but I have faith in you."

"We're in for another beautiful sunset," Johnnie announced as he poured himself more lemonade.

"It was always gorgeous here." Rhett nodded and then took a bite of his key lime pie. "This is delicious. My compliments to the chef."

"A Florida specialty." She smiled and took a bite herself.

"When do we get to see this documentary you two have been working on?" Kurt asked.

Melanie hadn't realized it before, but since the kitchen, she'd noticed Kurt studying her. Kurt had always been all business, very serious-minded. Of all the band members, he was the one who'd always kept a steady girlfriend in their younger days. He'd married, too, but divorced after a few years. He and his current wife had been married for eight years. He was handsome with dark blonde hair and hazel eyes. He wore thick-rimmed glasses that reminded her of Buddy Holly.

"We have plenty of time." Rhett smiled. "Let's relax and watch the sunset. Then we'll help clean up since Melanie cooked us such a delicious dinner."

Johnnie took her hand, brought it to his mouth, and kissed it.

"I find it strange that you met Rhett in Atlanta. Then you moved here and met Johnnie. And now the two of you are working on a documentary about the band. And Rhett mentioned the possibility of an autobiography as well?"

Melanie knew it seemed overly coincidental. But was Kurt thinking she'd set all this up by design? He didn't trust her, and she supposed she could understand why. It still stung a bit though.

"I know what it must seem like. Even Johnnie was suspicious at first. But honestly, it was just a series of amazing coincidences."

"We only met briefly when she passed out at that music festival," Rhett chimed in. "We didn't talk too long...mostly about how she smelled like Caesar."

"Another coincidence it seems," Kurt remarked.

Melanie bit her lip and decided to steer the conversation to where she needed it to go. "Rhett, do you remember telling me you saw someone at the festival who looked like Caesar?"

"Oh yeah, I still remember that guy." Rhett nodded. "I wanted to run after him but lost him in the crowd."

"You didn't mention seeing Caesar's ghost again." Kurt took a sip of lemonade.

"Because you always give me grief about it."

Melanie looked at Johnnie and squeezed his hand. "Was that not the first time you thought you'd seen Caesar?"

Kurt chuckled. "He claims to see his ghost from time to time. Usually around the anniversary of his death, right?"

"Yeah." Rhett rubbed his chin. "And it seems so real."

"Who's to say it's not?"

Kurt laughed louder now. "You're kidding right, Johnnie? You don't believe in ghosts, do you?"

Johnnie shrugged.

"Wait, don't tell me. You've seen Caesar, too?" Kurt rolled his eyes and slapped his knee. "With some of the shit you've taken, it doesn't surprise me."

"Fuck you, Kurt."

"Yeah, lay off him," Rhett ordered, then turned to Johnnie. "Have you really seen Caesar?"

Johnnie nodded.

"Obviously you don't believe in ghosts," Melanie commented to Kurt.

"Do you?"

"I do now."

"Because Johnnie told you to?" Kurt sneered. "You don't strike me as a woman who'd believe something just because a man told her it was true."

"The plate that fell on the floor in the kitchen was real."

"You're saying Caesar's ghost did that?" Kurt asked.

"He was upset with the way you were talking about Johnnie."

Kurt huffed. "He should be mad at Johnnie for making him a ghost."

Johnnie cursed under his breath, and she squeezed his hand again.

"Do you know what happened on that mountain ledge?" Melanie's voice rose. "Were you there?"

Kurt went to stand by the deck's railing. "Good thing I wasn't. He might have pushed me off, too."

Johnnie jumped from his seat. "I did not push him off!"

Rhett got up and wrapped an arm around Johnnie, obviously trying to calm him.

"Do you even know what you did that night?" Kurt threw his arms out to his side. "No, because you were too wasted. You were *always* too wasted!"

Angry, Melanie stood as well, her fists balled at her sides. "He didn't get wasted until after Caesar fell. And only because he was so distraught over what had happened."

"How the hell do you know?" Kurt glared at her.

"Caesar slipped. He was able to grab onto a rock. Johnnie tried to pull him up, but he couldn't. He started to slip himself, and Caesar told him to let go. Johnnie didn't want to, he even told Caesar he'd die with him, but Caesar insisted that he let him go."

Kurt stormed over, closing in, his face inches from hers. "Who are you? How do you know all of this?"

"I showed her." Caesar strolled out onto the deck.

"Oh my God!" Rhett pointed in his direction.

Melanie stared into Kurt's face. "Caesar showed me. He's here right now. Rhett sees him."

Kurt's gaze zipped over to Rhett. "What the fuck is going on? Is this some sick joke?"

But Rhett didn't answer. He rushed into Caesar's outstretched arms and hugged his friend tightly.

"You've all lost your minds."

"Kurt, will you take a walk with me? Please." Melanie tried to take Kurt's hand.

"I don't even know you." He jerked away, then looked at Rhett who was in tears. "Rhett, we should get out of here. She's as fucked-up as Johnnie."

Melanie placed a calming hand against Kurt's cheek. "Please come with me. We'll talk, and I promise to tell you all about myself."

Kurt grumbled and reluctantly followed her onto the beach. "Where are we going?"

"Johnnie's favorite spot. It's beautiful there."

She led him to the rocks. It was getting dark fast, and stars were beginning to appear in the sky. When they reached Johnnie's rock, she stopped and turned toward the sea.

"Isn't it gorgeous?" When he didn't respond, she looked at him. His mouth was set in a hard line. He appeared tense and unmoved by her kind manner. "Take a deep breath and then exhale slowly. Count to ten when you do."

To her surprise, he followed her instructions. She crawled up onto the rock and motioned for him to do the same. He did.

"Caesar told me to figure out a way to convince you. I'm not sure I know how, but I'm going to try."

Unmoving, he stared at the ocean as she relayed almost everything that had happened to her since that day in the store. She left out the sexual stuff for now. His face stayed void of emotion.

"I know it's hard to believe. But please try. He wants you to see him."

He ran his hands through his hair. "You have to know how preposterous this sounds."

"It did to me, too. I've never believed in ghosts. I never even thought about them until I met Caesar."

"How were you convinced?" Kurt asked.

"If he tries, he can peek into the future. He was able to warn me away from a huge traffic accident back in Atlanta." She sighed and nervously smoothed out her dress. "Tonight, he told me you had suspicions about my motives with the band right before you began questioning me."

Finally, he looked at her. "That's not perfume you're wearing is it?"

"It's from being around him. I don't know why, but it never goes away."

"Are you able to touch him?"

Melanie's face warmed. "Yes. He seems very real and alive."

"How is it you, Johnnie, and Rhett can see him, but I can't?"

"He came to me in Atlanta to help me. Now he's here to help Johnnie. And Rhett believes in ghosts apparently. You'll see him when you believe."

Kurt put his hand on top of hers. "I want to believe, Melanie. I want to see him for myself."

Melanie hopped down off the rock. Kurt followed.

"You have to really believe it...believe in him."

He rubbed his forehead. "Caesar was the best."

"Hold my hands and close your eyes." When Kurt did so, she closed hers as well. "Now I want you to think back to a good time with Caesar. Remember something that made all four of you happy. When you were smiling and laughing, not a care in the world. One of the best times you experienced together."

"Okay," Kurt said. "Got it."

"Tell me about it."

"It was our first tour. Our manager came to our hotel room to tell us our song had hit number one. It was something we'd dreamed about, and it happened. We were yelling...jumping up and down like wild men. That wild energy we felt, transferred to the show that night. It was one of our best performances. Afterward, we wanted to go out. We didn't have a lot of money back then, but we splurged that night. We all had a steak dinner. Even Caesar. He wasn't a vegetarian yet."

"I can almost see it in my mind. Your smiles. I love Caesar's smile. It's so pure and full of love for whomever he directs it at."

"It is." Kurt squeezed her hands. "After dinner, we rode around in a limousine. We had the top open and were screaming at the top of our lungs, waving at everyone we passed."

Melanie felt hands on her shoulders. *Caesar.* Images materialized in her mind. She was seeing the limousine, the four of them yelling out of the top and raising glasses of champagne to confused onlookers. Then she saw a club, the four of them at a table.

"You were dressed in suits. You went to a burlesque club that was open late at night. There was a dancer you liked. She had long black hair, a sexy red dress, and red fans. You took her back to your hotel room."

"How do you know that?"

"I showed her," Caesar answered.

Melanie opened her eyes. Kurt's eyes were wide, as he stared over her shoulder, obviously at Caesar.

He dropped her hands, took off his glasses, and wiped at his eyes.

"Am I dreaming?"

"No." Melanie took one of Caesar's hands and kissed it. "He's here."

"Thank you for bringing him to me." Caesar wrapped his arms around her neck, then pressed kisses against it.

Kurt appeared confused by their affection for one another, and Melanie knew he was wondering about Johnnie.

Rhett came running up the beach toward them. Johnnie followed, walking. Rhett let out a loud whoop and laughed hysterically. When he reached them, he threw his arms around Kurt.

"Isn't it amazing?" Rhett smiled, shaking Kurt gently. "We're all together again!"

Kurt was still staring at Caesar in disbelief. "How can this be?"

Caesar let her go and held his hand out to Kurt. "Hello again, my friend."

Kurt's hand was shaking as he moved it toward Caesar's. Caesar finally grabbed it, and then the two of them were hugging, both shedding tears. Rhett joined in the hug as well. Johnnie stood by her, apart from the three of them.

"What are you doing?" Rhett waved a hand in his direction. "Get over here."

Kurt and Johnnie locked eyes. She could see there was still some unresolved issue between them.

"He tried to save me," Caesar assured Kurt. "He really did."

"I'm sorry." Kurt nodded as he broke down. He looked to Johnnie, then back to Caesar. "I knew he could never hurt you. I was angry and lashing out."

"We understand." Caesar hugged him close.

Kurt held out his arm to Johnnie and Johnnie moved swiftly into their huddle. The four of them sobbed as Lush was reunited.

Melanie leaned back against the cushions she'd brought into the studio. Lush was giving her a private concert. They hadn't played together in sixteen years, but you'd never know it. The band sounded amazing, and she was completely enthralled. Johnnie seemed especially happy, smiling that huge toothy grin of his. Caesar mesmerized her with his sexual appeal, flirting with her as he sang hit after hit.

"Whew! I need a break." Rhett set his guitar down, grabbed a towel, and wiped his face.

"What time is it?" Kurt asked.

"When I went in to get drinks it was around one." Melanie opened the cooler she'd brought out. Inside were bottles of juice and water. "Help yourself."

"Bathroom break for me. Be right back," Johnnie announced as he walked out the door.

Caesar plopped down beside her and grabbed a bottle of water. She giggled, as he pulled her down to the floor, drizzled some on her neck, and then licked it off her.

"I'm usually inside you by now," he whispered in her ear. "Are you okay with me doing this instead?"

"Of course." She kissed him. "You're having a great time, and I'm loving it. I never got to see the band live, remember?"

Caesar returned her kiss, and they sat back up. He took a long swig of water.

Rhett and Kurt were staring down at them. Then they side eyed one another.

Johnnie returned and sat on her other side. He caressed her leg tenderly and kissed her cheek. "Enjoying the show?"

"Very much," she replied, wiping the sweat from his brow.

"Okay, I have to ask. So, you two…" Rhett pointed at Johnnie, then her. Then he pointed at Caesar. "And you two…"

"The three of us." Caesar smiled, and caressed her other leg.

Rhett and Kurt gawked at one another again.

Johnnie signaled timeout. "Nah, not like that. No balls or dicks are ever touching."

"Except this morning when I woke up in your arms." Caesar laughed.

Johnnie's eyes narrowed. "Because I thought it was her. But she left to clean up for you two."

Rhett sat down across from her. "So, you're with both of them."

"Holy shit." Kurt laughed and sat as well. "You're sharing a woman? As competitive as you two were?"

"Still are." Melanie blushed.

Johnnie grabbed some juice from the cooler. "I do quite well keeping up with him, considering I'm forty-four and he's still twenty-eight."

"This has been going on a while then?" Rhett asked.

"A few days. Caesar's only been back a couple of weeks." Johnnie took her hand and squeezed it. "When he came back, Melanie and I weren't together because I'd cheated on her."

"Is that why you're okay with her being with Caesar?" Kurt asked.

Melanie let out a little gasp. She hadn't thought of that. Was this his way of making retribution for what he'd done?

"Hell no." Johnnie grouched. "I hated her being with Caesar. But she fell in love with him first back in Atlanta. And he came back when I was in a very bad place. To help me. I didn't like seeing them together, but I accepted it because I'd fucked up what she and I had."

"Somehow you got back into her good graces," Kurt noted.

"I know it's not the best situation." Johnnie stared at the floor. "Fact is, I'm crazy about her. It's like a new addiction, being with her...loving her. I haven't ever felt like this. I have a feeling she's addicted to me, too. I certainly wouldn't have taken me back if I were her. But she did, and I'm grateful. I resisted the whole threesome thing at first, but he makes her happy. And I'm glad for this time with him. However long it lasts. We're making the most of it."

"So, this isn't a permanent return?" Rhett asked.

Caesar flipped his long hair back. "I have no idea. We're pretty sure I was sent here to help Melanie and Johnnie. To help them heal from their pasts. I've completed some of that. But I don't know when I'll be taken back. In the meantime, we're going to enjoy one another's company."

"I don't blame you." Kurt winked at her. "She's gorgeous."

"I second that." Rhett held up his juice bottle.

Johnnie shook a finger in their direction. "Don't get any ideas. Three's already a crowd. No more are invited."

Kurt held up his left hand. "Happily married, remember?"

"Yeah," Rhett said, patting Johnnie's back. "And I have a boyfriend."

Johnnie's eyes widened. "What?"

Caesar fell back into the pillows laughing.

"I didn't realize it would be so funny." Rhett frowned.

Johnnie grumbled, grabbed a twenty out of his pocket and dangled it in front of Caesar.

Caesar sat up and snatched it.

"You guys had a bet?" Melanie asked.

"I called it years ago," Caesar explained. "Johnnie never believed me."

Johnnie shrugged. "I had no idea."

"I didn't accept it myself for a long time," Rhett told him. "Until about ten years ago."

Kurt scratched his head. "How did you figure it out, Caesar?"

"He always seemed uncomfortable around women. Johnnie and I were always fucking around. You always had a steady girlfriend. Rhett seemed to be bored by it all. He had no use for women. He just wanted to play guitar."

"Yeah, you're right," Kurt nodded. "Looking back, I guess that wasn't the norm in this brotherhood."

Melanie stood up. "If you'll excuse me, I'm going to get ready for bed. It's been a long day."

Caesar and Johnnie scrambled to their feet.

"Sit back down." She smiled. "I'm capable of putting myself to bed."

"Do you mind if we keep playing?"

She kissed Johnnie. "Of course not. This is what you should be doing."

"We'll be up soon." Caesar hugged her tight, then kissed her.

"Stay with your friends. Take all the time you want with them. They'll only be here a few days."

"Sleep well then." Caesar kissed her again.

"Goodnight," she told him, before kissing Johnnie. Then she bent over and gave Rhett and Kurt each a kiss on the cheek.

"Goodnight," the two of them said in unison.

On the way out, she heard Kurt chuckle. "I still can't believe you two are sharing anything. Much less a woman."

She smiled, feeling like the luckiest woman alive.

Chapter Twenty-one

"Perfection!" Caesar yelled, and fist-bumped Johnnie.

"I believe a celebration is in order." Johnnie pulled up his musical playlist.

A few clicks later and the three of them were dancing around the room. Melanie squealed in delight as they both swiveled their hips into hers, Johnnie in the back, Caesar in the front. They had completed the documentary with the help of Kurt and Rhett. The other band members had left two days ago, and Johnnie had been editing and piecing in the new interviews and voiceovers until at last, he was satisfied. He'd shown her and Caesar the entire piece, and she was ecstatic with the results. They'd decided to only tell the early Lush story, from the time the band formed until their huge night at the Rose Bowl. Every Lush fan would love it, and surely, they'd gain new fans once the piece was aired.

The autobiography would include Caesar's death and the aftermath. She'd interviewed Kurt and Rhett alone and together to get their perspectives for the book. Caesar had already allowed her to type up his story and now she would work with Johnnie to get all those pieces put together as well. Rhett and Kurt had also suggested they put together a new album of previously unreleased music. Apparently, Kurt being the one who'd gotten clean first had inherited those recordings.

She felt her dress being lifted. Caesar slid down her panties.

She grabbed his hands in hers and pushed them away. "I can't."

Johnnie's hands cupped her breasts. His dick was hard on her ass.

"Why not?" Caesar pouted.

"Period. I started this morning."

Caesar brushed kisses against her neck. "I told you when we met...that's never stopped me."

"You win this round." Johnnie backed away. "She's all yours."

Caesar frowned. "Are you upset?"

"About what? You want blood on your dick, more power to you. It freaks me out."

"No." Caesar rolled his eyes. "Are you upset that she's not pregnant?"

Melanie's hands flew to her mouth.

"What the hell are you talking about?" Johnnie's eyes widened. "I'm not trying to get her pregnant. Are you?"

"I wish I could."

"I've been taking the pill since I got back from Atlanta," Melanie explained. Caesar appeared hurt by her announcement. She brushed his curls away from his eyes. "I'm sorry. Babies are not in my plans right now. I'm trying to begin a new life. There's no time."

"Maybe later then." Caesar kissed her tenderly.

Beads of sweat dotted Johnnie's forehead. He sat on the bed, obviously overwhelmed by Caesar's suggestion. She didn't blame him. This was big. This was a mood killer. Worse than any period.

"Was it wrong for me to bring up babies?" Caesar's gaze bounced from her to Johnnie. "I thought...the two of you are so good together, and Johnnie's never had kids...you lost yours. I'm sorry. It sounded like a good idea."

"I'm starting over. Johnnie's trying to get clean. It wouldn't be a good time. Plus, I'm getting older. It's riskier."

"Sorry I mentioned it. We were having such a good time. I screwed it up."

"No, you didn't." She pushed a hand through his curls. "It's a conversation we probably should've had already."

Caesar gently pushed Johnnie's shoulder. "You're quiet. What are you thinking?"

Johnnie stood and hugged her. "I wish I weren't so fucked-up. To have a baby with you...I can't think of anything more beautiful."

She realized he was tearing up and wanted to take his mind off baby talk. Caesar *had* ruined the moment, but she knew how to get them back on track. She tugged down Johnnie's pants, then knelt in front of him. She ran her tongue up the length of his softening shaft. Immediately, it sprang to life, and she took him into her mouth.

"On second thought, there is something more beautiful." He grinned and wiped his face.

"Don't forget me." Caesar tugged his pants down and stepped out of them.

Melanie smiled at Caesar. Keeping Johnnie's cock in her hand, she turned and pressed kisses along Caesar's. *This is so hot.* Giving both men a blow job at the same time. She hadn't been loved in so long and being loved by two gorgeous men was a thrill she couldn't seem to get used to.

As she sucked Caesar's cock, he nudged Johnnie. "Put on a condom, and you won't get blood on your dick. Or we could get into the shower together."

"Or I'll just let her make me cum with that magic mouth of hers."

Melanie switched to Johnnie's cock, taking him deep inside her mouth.

"Let's at least get on the bed where it's more comfortable," Caesar suggested.

After stripping her clothes off, Melanie stretched out on her side. Caesar laid down behind her, lifted her leg, and slid into her. Johnnie knelt in front of her, and immediately she went back to work on his cock. He closed his eyes obviously enjoying the pleasure he was receiving.

"Damn." Johnnie grunted as he came. "You're too good."

"Grab us a towel out of the bathroom," Caesar directed. "Things are about to get messy."

When Johnnie returned, both she and Caesar were kneeling on the bed, and he was still fucking her from behind. Johnnie placed the towel on the bed, beneath her.

"How about blood on your fingers?" Caesar questioned. "I could use a hand."

Johnnie knelt in front of her and kissed her. Caesar reached from behind and squeezed her breasts. Johnnie's mouth left her lips and locked onto a nipple instead. All the cramps she'd been having were forgotten as he sucked on first one, then the other.

Caesar moved his hands between her legs where he gently rubbed her clit. "Put your mouth on her. Lick her clit while I'm fucking her."

Johnnie kissed her. "Don't think I can handle that."

"The blood's not on her clit."

"It's okay, he doesn't have to. I'm sure you can make me cum, Caesar." She smiled at Johnnie, knowing he'd take that as a challenge.

Johnnie shimmied to his belly, pushed Caesar's hands away, parted her and began flicking his tongue across her clit.

Melanie reached behind her, wrapping her arms around Caesar's head. He pushed her hair aside and kissed her neck, sending shivers down her spine. His hands returned to her breasts, where he ran his palms softly against her nipples.

"How does that feel?" Caesar asked.

"Like heaven."

"Except his dick is way too close to my mouth," Johnnie complained.

Melanie was breathless. "Please don't stop, Johnnie. Make me cum."

His mouth returned to her clit, and as she felt her body tense, her hands went to his hair. It was longer now, and thick with curls.

"Tell me what you want." Caesar kissed her cheek.

She turned her head to kiss him back. "Fuck me hard, baby. Make me cum."

Caesar pulled her body into his, pounding into her. Johnnie latched on to her clit, pushing her over the edge. Her body shook, vibrating on Caesar's cock. Johnnie raised back up and kissed her over and over again as she came hard. Caesar then pushed her down on the bed. Flipping to her back, she wrapped her legs around his hips as he shoved himself into her. Her pussy quaked as he pumped into her harder and harder. She moaned loudly and screamed out his name. Her nails raked down his back, and she pushed her hips into his.

"I love you so much, Melanie." Caesar's gaze locked onto hers as he came. Then his lips were all over her face, all while his hands caressed her body. He smiled and collapsed on top of her.

She gently stroked Caesar's back. Johnnie was staring at the two of them. She waved a hand in his direction, beckoning him to her side. When Johnnie lay down beside her, she touched his lips. "I love you."

"I love you, too." He snuggled closer to her.

Caesar was falling asleep. He rolled off her and onto his back.

Johnnie held a finger to his lips. "Shh."

She smiled at him. When they were sure Caesar was sleeping, Johnnie slid from the bed. He grabbed her hand and helped her to her feet.

"Where are we going?" she whispered.

"Downstairs to my bedroom. We can take a shower there."

"We can use the one in my room."

"No. We might wake him up."

"Are you planning on making a lot of noise?"

"I'm planning on you making a lot of noise."

"What about my period?"

"I don't care anymore. I need to be inside you."

A week later, Melanie woke up in an empty bed. Glancing at the clock, she saw that she'd slept later than normal. She got up and slipped on her nightie, then quietly crept down the hallway to where she heard low voices. Caesar and Johnnie were in the workroom, probably watching the documentary again, or maybe writing. The door was slightly cracked open, and she started to knock but hearing the subject of their conversation stopped her.

"It looks like a cool facility," Caesar was saying.

"The program's hardcore." She heard Johnnie clicking the mouse. "I wouldn't be let off the grounds or have contact with the outside world for months."

Melanie sucked in her breath. *He's talking about rehab.*

"It's pretty pricey."

"It is. But when my mom transfers my money back to me, I'll be able to afford it. Then I can truly start over afterward. Rhett said he can get me some work as a session drummer."

"What about Melanie?" Caesar asked.

"You and I both know we need to let her go."

"Bullshit! You need rehab, sure. But I don't need to go anywhere."

"You honestly believe that? If I'm gone and it's only you here, what kind of life will she lead? She can't go out with you and do things. Half the people out there would see Caesar Blue walking around, and the other half would think she was crazy talking to herself. She'd be stuck here in the house."

"She could do things by herself."

"She hardly leaves the house now. Her life is just us, and it should be so much more. And it will be more once the documentary is released, and then the autobiography...her own books. She's going places, but you and I aren't. It's time, Caesar. We have to let her go."

Melanie sank to the floor. *Is this happening?* The three of them were so happy together.

"I don't...want to." Caesar's voice faltered.

"You said you came here to help us. You have. Once I'm in rehab, your mission's done. You'd probably be leaving anyway."

"I know...I know."

Melanie felt a tear slip from her eye. Johnnie was right. And hadn't she known this would eventually happen? Still, it didn't hurt any less.

"It will take me a couple of weeks to get things in order and get accepted into the program. We have a little more time together then we'll have to..."

"Shh..." Caesar interrupted. "She's listening."

Johnnie opened the door. "Melanie, what are you doing here? I thought you were asleep."

She couldn't find her voice as she choked back sobs. She scrambled to her feet, then fled downstairs, out the back door, and to the beach.

Caesar found her on Johnnie's rock. He climbed up next to her and wrapped an arm around her. "I'm sorry you overheard us like that."

She rubbed her eyes. "Johnnie's right. I hate it, but he's right. I have to let him go so he can get well."

"I checked out the website. It's one of the best facilities in the world. He'll do well there. I'm sure of it."

"And once he's gone..."

"I'll probably be gone, too."

"Maybe not. Maybe there'll be more for you to do here."

"I'd like to think that, but in all probability, my days are numbered."

"What will I do without the two of you?"

Caesar pulled her closer and kissed the top of her head. "You'll thrive. There'll be nothing and no one holding you back."

"I'll have no one to love me."

"We'll always love you no matter where we are."

"It's not the same."

"I know." He rubbed her arm. "But you're the strongest person I know. You'll get through it. You've been through far worse."

"Where's Johnnie?"

"He was calling the rehab center when I came to find you. He's ready to go, Melanie. You have to let him. I know it hurts, but you can't do or say anything to make him change his mind. He needs this."

"I know." She nodded and brushed back the tears on her face. "Do you mind if I stay here awhile...to think?"

"Of course." He kissed her forehead. "Cry it all out. Every tear. Then put a brave face on. Do it for Johnnie...please."

Johnnie was sitting on the steps of the deck when she returned.

"Take a walk with me," he said, offering her his hand.

She took it, and they walked toward the water, and then along the water's edge, hand in hand. There was so much she wanted to say but couldn't find the words.

He pulled her toward the water, going in about calf deep. "I'm going to miss it here. It's so beautiful."

She fought back tears. Caesar had asked her to be brave and she would.

"Nothing to say?" he asked, wrapping her in his arms.

She forced a smile and rested her head on his shoulder. "I don't want to think of you leaving. I know you have to go. But right now, I just want to be with you and enjoy the time we have together."

He grabbed her around the thighs and hoisted her over his shoulders. "And I want to enjoy it by throwing you in this ocean."

"Johnnie, no...don't!" She laughed as he trudged into waist deep water. He threw her in, then ran back to shore.

She came up sputtering, wiping her eyes. She shook a finger at him as she walked back to dry land. "That was evil."

He held up his hand. "Stop right where you are."

She stopped in her tracks in calf deep water.

His gaze scanned her up and down. "Damn. That's sexier than any swimsuit."

She looked down at the white cotton nightgown that was clinging to her body. Her nipples were hard and showing through the fabric, as was the patch of hair between her legs.

He untied his swim shorts and let them drop to the ground. His cock stood at attention.

"It would appear that you want me, Mr. Vega."

"I always want you." He sat down in the sand. "Now get over here and fuck me."

She walked slowly toward him, pulled off the wet nightie, and tossed it toward him. When she stood over him, he lay back on the wet sand. She straddled his body, then sank hers onto his thick cock.

"You're so sexy." He groaned.

Water droplets cascaded down her body, and he used his finger to follow the trail of one right to her nipple. He rubbed the saltwater into the hardened nub. She moved her hips in a circle on him.

"And so beautiful...I'm going to miss you so much."

With those words, her tears came. He raised himself off the ground and hugged her tight.

"I'm sorry, baby. I need to do this. For me...for us."

"I know." She sniffed.

He rolled her onto her back, staying inside her. He stared hard into her eyes as he slowly made love to her, long, lingering strokes that made her pussy even wetter.

"You feel so good." She ran her fingers through his hair. "I love your cock."

He chuckled, then kissed her. "It loves you. It craves you. Every minute of the day I want to be inside you."

"What will you do without me?"

He put his right hand in her face. "See this hand? It will be getting quite the workout."

She smiled and held up her own hand. "So will this one."

Chapter Twenty-two

"Are you nervous?" Melanie handed Johnnie his belt.

"A little," Johnnie admitted, looping the belt through his jeans. Then he pulled his new shirt over his head. "It's been awhile."

"Your mom will be happy to see you."

"She's not the one I'm worried about."

"You'd think your brothers would be glad to see you after so long."

"You don't know them." He kissed her cheek, then sat on the bed to pull on his leather boots. "Assholes like my dad."

"Obviously. I can't believe they told your mom not to return your money."

Johnnie stood and turned around in a circle, showing off the new clothes that she'd helped him select. Jeans that fit perfectly, a blue t-shirt, and a nice black leather blazer to top off the look. "How do I look?"

"Like a sexy rock star." She ran her hand through his recently trimmed hair, spiking it up a bit. Then she twirled in her new vintage style black and white polka dot dress. She sported red patent leather flats as well. "What about me?"

"Beautiful as always." He kissed her again, then checked his reflection in the hotel mirror. "Let's get going."

Melanie grabbed her purse and took his hand. Johnnie's mom had asked him to come to Atlanta so that she could give back his money. He was needed at the bank to sign some documents. When Mrs. Smith mentioned that his brothers thought he didn't deserve it,

Johnnie realized it was even more pertinent to travel to Atlanta. It had worked out well because Melanie had been able to visit her former workplace and together with Johnnie, present in person, their finished documentary, titled *Love and Lush.* Johnnie had been able to see firsthand the enthusiasm that people at the studio had for their work. And for the band. He'd signed a few autographs, and they'd begun discussing a premiere party. He'd nodded, smiling politely, pretending that he'd be around for it.

"Oh wow!" Melanie stared at her phone. "I know our driver."

When the car pulled up, Johnnie opened the door for her, and she slid in.

"Akeyo, right?" She grinned. "It's been a few months, but I remember you."

The driver studied her, trying to place her. Johnnie sat beside her. Akeyo then stared at him.

Melanie shook her head. "You only know me. We met after the big summer music festival in July. We talked about ghosts."

Akeyo grinned and nodded. "Yes, I remember now. You thought you'd seen a spirit and he told you not to get on the highway. We avoided that big accident."

"Yes, that was me."

"I don't think this is your ghost though."

"Nope, but he's a friend of mine." Johnnie chuckled. They'd told Caesar to stay put in the beach house while they were away.

As Akeyo pulled into the busy Atlanta streets, he looked at them in the rear-view mirror. "After meeting you, I spoke to my mother about ghosts and about what happened. She said the spirit had probably been sent here to help you. She said he sounded like a kind spirit."

"He is." Melanie smiled and took Johnnie's hand in hers again. "How are your studies going?"

"Very well. All A's last semester. Thank you for asking."

"Well, I moved to California and met this guy since our last ride together."

Akeyo nodded. "Did the spirit have something to do with that?"

"Yes, he did."

"Sounds like he's been up to a bit of matchmaking."

Johnnie grinned. "Let's just say he's helped the both of us."

After a short drive, Akeyo pulled up along the curb in front of Johnnie's mother's house. He turned to them, business card in hand. "Here's my phone number. Give me a call, and I'll be your personal driver while you're in town."

"Thanks, man." Johnnie took Akeyo's card, then stepped out of the car. He held his hand out to Melanie, helping her.

They waved Akeyo off, then Melanie squeezed his hand. "No going back."

Johnnie's blue eyes lit up. "I'm ready. With you by my side, I can take on the world."

She pressed her lips against his and let them linger there awhile. They were still kissing when the front door of his parents' house opened.

"Johnnie." His mother placed both hands to her heart. "Baby, it's so good to see you."

Johnnie smiled, and Melanie nudged him forward. "Go."

He met her at the steps, and they hugged for a long time. Melanie noticed two men standing in the doorway watching the reunion scene. Neither of them appeared happy.

When Johnnie broke the hug, he turned back, motioning for her to come forward. "I believe you know Melanie already."

Johnnie's mother hugged her tight. Then she grabbed Melanie's face in her hands. "Thank you so much for finally getting him here."

Melanie smiled. "His idea."

"Of course, he came, Mom. He wants money."

Melanie's eyes narrowed at the big, hulking figure standing in the doorway. His scowl was intimidating, but Melanie put her hand out to him. *I won't stoop to his level.* "Hello, I'm Melanie...are you Robert or Darren?"

"Darren."

"Nice to meet you."

He forced a smile and then the other man stepped forward to offer her his hand. "I'm Robert."

Neither of his brothers made a move toward Johnnie. There was no love or warmth between the trio and Melanie felt terrible for Johnnie. Robert finally patted him on the back, and she thought he might be the friendlier of the two.

"I'm so glad you could make Sunday dinner. Come to the dining room and sit."

Johnnie placed a hand on Melanie's back, and she entered the house. Johnnie shrugged off his blazer and took her purse, hanging them both in the foyer. Then he took her hand and led her into the dining room. She and Johnnie sat on one side, and the brothers sat on the other.

"Robert, help me bring the food in," Mrs. Smith instructed.

Immediately, Melanie popped up. "I'll be happy to help."

Johnnie stood and put his hand on her shoulder. "Sit. I'll help."

"Robert, pour everyone iced tea then."

Melanie sat back down. She watched as Robert poured tea into all the glasses. Then he sat next to his brother. "How was your trip here? I'm glad our flights were on time. Our schedule was pretty tight yesterday. Luckily we could sleep in this morning and get used to the time difference."

"We drove in from the base," Robert told her.

Darren glared at her. "We come up quite a bit to visit our mother. Unlike our baby brother."

"Fort Benning is a little closer than California." Melanie took a sip of tea before something worse came out of her mouth.

Johnnie came in carrying a few dishes filled with steaming vegetables. His mother came in with a few more. He disappeared into the kitchen again and returned with the pot roast.

"I make my own bread," his mother proudly said as she placed a platter with the bread near Melanie. Mrs. Smith then took her place at the head of the table.

"I've never tried making bread. I bet it's delicious." Melanie reached for the platter to grab a slice.

"We say grace first," Darren said sternly.

"My apologies." Melanie tucked her hands into her lap.

After the blessing, the food was sent around the table in an assembly line fashion. Melanie took a bit of everything but the meat.

"No pot roast?" asked Robert.

"No, thank you. I don't eat meat."

"Californians," Darren complained.

"I've only lived in California a few months. I moved there from Atlanta which is where I became a vegetarian."

"I'll happily eat her portion." Johnnie smiled and took a bite of the roast. "It's delicious, Mom."

"You'd get to eat more of mom's great cooking if you lived closer."

Melanie rubbed Johnnie's thigh under the table, trying to provide calmness to a tense situation.

"I've been living in London and L.A. Mom understands the situation."

"I understand, too," Darren grumbled. "Rent-free living. Must be nice to have a dead friend give you two free houses."

Johnnie leaned back and gave his brother a smug smile. "It is actually."

"If you're living rent-free, why do you need the money from Mom?" Darren asked.

"It's his money," Melanie blurted out. "Why shouldn't he have it?"

Darren sneered at her. "Guess you can't wait to get your hands on it."

Melanie's eyes narrowed. "Johnnie needs it. And he worked hard for it."

Johnnie's hand was on her leg now.

"Mom needs it, too," Robert finally spoke. "Dad's hospital bills are outrageous."

"I'll help out with those. But it is *my* money, and I'm going to need it." Johnnie looked at his mother. "I've filled out an application to get into a rehab facility in Arizona. It's one of the best in the world, but it's expensive. I'll use the money to pay for it."

His mother took his other hand. "I'm so happy to hear that."

Darren groaned. "Dad said he wasn't giving the money back until you were completely sober. And we all know that's never going to happen."

"How do you know?" Melanie snapped, annoyed with Johnnie's older brother.

"You've known him for what...a few months? We've known him all our lives."

"Really? I don't think you know him at all."

Darren laughed loudly. "I guess not. All this time I thought he was a sissy, screwing around with that friend of his, Caesar. Then again, maybe he likes to go both ways."

"We don't need that kind of talk at the dinner table," Mrs. Smith complained.

Unable to take Darren's put-downs of the two men she loved, Melanie slammed her fork down and stood. "Caesar is not gay, and neither is Johnnie!"

Darren jumped to his feet. "How come he has to have a female fight his battles?"

"Maybe because he knows he can't win with you two." Melanie pointed at Darren. "You've always been jerks to him, just like your father. It's messed up."

Darren pointed a fork in her direction. "Don't talk about my father."

"Don't talk about Johnnie. Or Caesar. Unless you have something positive to say, just shut up!"

"Guess I'll shut up then because there's nothing positive to say about those pieces of shit."

"Sounds like you're jealous." Melanie put her hands on her hips. "Despite the abuse he took from you and your dad, he still made something of himself. He became world famous and rich. Women threw themselves at him. I bet that just pisses you off, doesn't it?"

"This is not your house, so I'd advise you to shut the hell up!"

Mrs. Smith slammed her hand against the table. "Stop! All of you be quiet."

"I'm so sorry." Melanie took her seat, embarrassed by her outburst. "I shouldn't have reacted like that."

Johnnie's mother smiled at her. "Honey, I wish I had your spirit. I should have been the one fighting for Johnnie all those years ago when he was bullied by these two and his father."

"Mom?" Robert appeared confused.

"Admit it, Robert. You two followed in your father's footsteps in every way, including treating your brother horribly. No wonder he began drinking and doing drugs. He felt like his own family hated him."

Johnnie sat there, leaning back in his chair, taking it all in.

"You've got nothing to say?" Darren asked.

Johnnie shrugged, then grinned sheepishly. "I say we eat this delicious food Mom cooked before it gets cold."

Darren rolled his eyes.

"Oh, and one more thing...did I mention how much I love this woman?" He kissed her hard. "And another thing. She knows Caesar isn't gay because she was in love with him before she met me. Seems he and I have the very best taste. In women...*and* in houses."

He kissed her again. "But you should know...Rhett *is* gay. I found out recently. But I don't give a shit because he's one of the best friends anyone could ever have. Caesar, Rhett, and Kurt. They're my real brothers."

Mrs. Smith bit her bottom lip trying to suppress a smile but soon lost the battle. Melanie saw that Johnnie inherited his beautiful smile from his mother.

"Let's eat. And like Melanie said. If you have nothing nice to say, then keep your mouths shut." Mrs. Smith turned her attention to Johnnie. "Now tell me more about this rehabilitation facility."

Melanie couldn't help but gloat as she glanced at Darren. The buffoon had been shut down. He sat looking disgusted as his mother gushed over Johnnie and his decision to go to rehab. Robert looked as if he didn't know what to do. Clearly, he was a follower, doing Darren's bidding.

After dinner, Mrs. Smith invited them to the back porch which was screened in. Darren and Robert stayed inside to clean up and wash dishes.

Mrs. Smith patted Johnnie's arm as they sat down on the porch swing together. "I'm truly sorry for the way your father treated you...and for me allowing it to happen."

Johnnie wrapped his arm around his mom's shoulder. "We can't change the past, Mom. All we can do is make a better future."

"I hope you'll come visit more often."

"I won't be able to for a while, but I promise I will."

"And I promise I won't invite your brothers next time."

"It's a deal." Johnnie held out his hand so that they could shake on it.

Melanie laughed.

"She's a keeper," Mrs. Smith whispered just loud enough for Melanie to hear.

Johnnie stared at Melanie then whispered back, "I believe you're right."

"Did you really date Caesar, too?"

Melanie wasn't sure how to answer that question. She'd told Mrs. Smith previously that she moved in with Johnnie to help take care of the house.

"For a very short time."

Johnnie answered for her. "Although even he saw that she and I were a far better match."

"Did you date Melanie before? While Caesar was still alive?"

Melanie's heart beat a little faster. Was he going to create a web of lies for his mom?

"Nah, she didn't like me much the one time we met. I was surprised when she called me for an interview. And even more surprised she wanted to move into the house with me."

Mrs. Smith laughed. "I can believe that. He can be very crass until you get to know him."

Melanie smiled at Johnnie. "Yes, he can."

"Whatever. She was too hung up on Caesar to even notice me." Johnnie grinned. "Probably why she moved in with me. To feel closer to her lost love."

Melanie feigned surprise. "Well, you did tell me you didn't want Caesar's sloppy seconds."

"What an awful thing to say." Mrs. Smith smacked his knee lightly. "You were just jealous he got to her first. They were always so competitive. But still the best of friends."

Melanie sighed. "Yes, they are...I mean were."

Mrs. Smith frowned. "It's still hard to believe he's gone."

Melanie nodded.

Johnnie's mom leaned over and whispered in his ear. "I think she still has a thing for Caesar. She gets a wistful look when she talks about him."

"I believe that's called lust, Mom." Johnnie playfully winked at Melanie.

Melanie's cheeks burned.

"Honey, I don't blame you. He turned into one sexy man."

"You did not just say that." Johnnie laughed and shook his head. "Just great. My mom *and* my girlfriend lusting after my best friend."

Melanie's heart warmed. It was the first time Johnnie had used that term...girlfriend. She liked the sound of it. She hadn't been anyone's girlfriend in a long time which made it even more special to hear.

"So, I'm your girlfriend now?"

He seemed surprised by her question. Had it been a slip of the tongue?

"I guess Caesar's seconds aren't so sloppy now," his mother replied snidely.

Melanie laughed. "I see where he gets his boldness from."

Mrs. Smith rose from the swing. "Let's look over those papers. Tomorrow we'll go to the bank and get things taken care of."

"Why don't we go to the botanical gardens afterward?" Melanie suggested.

"Oh, I haven't been in years." Mrs. Smith smiled.

"It's a date then." Johnnie kissed his mom's cheek.

Chapter Twenty-three

Johnnie lay still inside her, the two of them tenderly kissing one another, over and over. They'd been making love most of the day. Tomorrow morning, Rhett was coming to drive him to Arizona. She'd wanted to be the one, but Johnnie had insisted she stay behind. He didn't want her seeing him in that setting. He felt it was better that they part at the house, on the beach...where they'd met and fallen in love.

Caesar bounded into the room. "Are you two coming up for air anytime soon?"

Johnnie never took his eyes off her. "I don't think so."

Caesar stripped his clothes off and got on the bed with them. "I'll join you then."

Melanie reached her hand behind Caesar's neck and pulled him closer so she could kiss him. He'd been quiet the last few days, leaving her and Johnnie alone for the most part, except to sleep with them at night. She knew he realized how precious these last few hours with Johnnie were. But she also knew he might be feeling the need to be with her and Johnnie. His time here might be ending soon as well. There simply was no way to know.

Johnnie must have understood, too, because he didn't protest Caesar's intrusion. "Take over for me. Bathroom break."

"Hurry back," she told Johnnie.

He kissed her and as soon as he was gone, Caesar slid inside her. She wrapped her arms around his neck.

"Miss me at all?"

"Of course. I'm sorry we've been ignoring you."

"I understand." He kissed her sweetly. "It's your last day with him for a while."

"But you love him, too. You two should be hanging out playing music."

"Maybe while you're cooking that big dinner you promised us, we'll hang out in the studio."

"He'll like that."

"Speaking of eating." Caesar eased down her body and replaced his cock with his tongue.

Immediately, she plunged her hands into his mass of curls.

"Watch it...she'll rip your hair out." Johnnie walked in carrying a plate with cheese, crackers, and fruit along with two bottles of water.

Caesar peeked up from between her legs. "Won't matter, apparently my hair grows right back."

"Oh yeah, I've heard that story. And seen the proof," Johnnie told him.

Caesar laughed. "You kept my hair?"

"She sure did. I used it once to turn her on."

Caesar shook his head. His curls bounced around his face, and lightly touched her pussy. "Like that?"

"You're silly." She smiled.

He moved back up her body, letting his curls dance all over her, lingering on her belly. It was usually a sensual turn on, but now it made her giggle uncontrollably.

"I don't think the seduction by hair is working." Johnnie sat in a nearby chair eating grapes.

"Turn over," Caesar instructed.

When she did, he covered her body with his. He pulled her hair aside and placed his curls against the side of her face. She inhaled. The vanilla scent took her back to the first day they'd met, how she'd smelled him before ever seeing him. His hard cock on her butt cheeks caused her legs to automatically part. He slipped into her from behind.

"Now close them tight," he instructed.

She did, squeezing him in the process. He had to work extra hard to make love to her like that, but it felt amazing, especially with his hair pressed up against her face. It was incredibly soft. He took her hands and held onto them as he ground his crotch into her but. She felt smothered, by his hair, his body, his love. It was an incredibly sexy feeling.

"I love you, baby. You feel so good." Caesar moaned as he came.

"Come sit in my lap," Johnnie coaxed.

Caesar rolled off her, and she went to Johnnie. Turning away from him, she sat on his lap. He stroked himself with her. Her hand traveled to her clit.

"No, no," Johnnie playfully scolded and held both her hands behind her back. "That's not allowed."

"Caesar," she whined. "Help me."

"Gladly." He knelt in front of her, and she spread her legs wide. He honed right in on her clit once more.

She panted as he flicked his tongue across it, all while Johnnie moved his thick cock within her wet walls.

"I know what you're thinking," Johnnie taunted. "You want me to let you go so you can run your fingers through his hair."

"Please?"

"No."

"What if I want to play with your hair?"

"Do you?"

"Yes."

He loosened his grip, and her hands went behind her, wrapping around his head. She pulled him closer, and then her hands were in his hair. Caesar's tongue caressing her clit was maddening, and she began to ride Johnnie harder.

"Oh yeah, baby," Johnnie murmured into her ear. He sucked on her earlobe, before nibbling her neck.

"I'm going to cum." She gasped.

Gently, he pushed her away. "Not just yet. Lay on the bed."

She did and then Johnnie dragged her to the edge. She opened her legs wide. This time it was Johnnie kneeling in front of her, lapping at her pussy. Caesar climbed back on the bed and swirled his tongue around a nipple, sucking, then nipping. Next, Caesar climbed over her and his cock was in her face. She ran her tongue over his balls and up and down his shaft. She opened her mouth, and he placed it between her lips. Then he leaned over and joined Johnnie in the tongue action. Johnnie stood and entered her again. The combination of Caesar's mouth and Johnnie's thick cock was overwhelming, and her body began to quiver.

"Damn, it feels so good when you cum," Johnnie said as he pushed into her over and over. Spasms of pleasure spread through her body. The tighter her pussy gripped him, the faster he fucked her until he also came.

When he withdrew, Caesar changed positions and stood by the bed. She sat up and took his cock into her mouth once more, sliding her lips over him slowly. When he spilled himself inside her mouth, she swallowed every drop, savoring the taste of him.

They fell onto the bed, the three of them, satisfied, sweaty, and exhausted. Melanie lay between them receiving countless kisses and caresses, until all three of them fell asleep.

"You two plant eaters don't know what you're missing." Johnnie took a bite of the thick steak he'd cooked on the grill.

Caesar held a piece of baked potato smothered in butter up to Melanie's mouth. When butter dripped down her chin, he licked it off. "I don't think we're missing a thing."

Johnnie slathered some melted butter onto his mouth. It slid down his chin. He winked at her. "Who's going to clean me off?"

Wagging his tongue, Caesar leaped from his chair and scurried to Johnnie's side of the table. "I will!"

"Get the hell away from me!" Johnnie laughed as Caesar licked his cheek.

Melanie doubled over, in a fit of giggles.

"I think he wants you to do it." Caesar sat back down beside her.

Melanie threw her napkin at Johnnie. "Here, use this."

It smacked him square in the face and Caesar laughed so hard, tears sprang up in the corner of his eyes.

"You'll pay for that." Johnnie pointed his fork at her.

"Really? How?" She stretched her foot out to his lap and placed it in between his thighs, patting his crotch with it.

"I'll throw you in the water again."

"You'd have to catch me first."

He took another bite of his steak. "I will, but right now I'm eating."

"You've eaten so much you won't be able to move." Caesar laughed again, then leaned back in his chair and patted his belly. "Same with me."

Melanie smiled. They were enjoying dinner on the deck outside. It was a beautiful evening, and she tried not to let her thoughts accelerate into the future. Instead, she would enjoy this time with them. She'd cooked a huge meal while they played music in the studio. Now she wanted to relish these last moments with them.

She sighed, unable to tear her eyes from Johnnie as he joked with Caesar. He was in good spirits, and she knew he was only thinking of tonight...not what tomorrow would bring. He caught her looking and flashed that big, beautiful smile that made her pulse race. But then sadness flickered in his gaze, and he quickly turned away. Caesar was cheerful, laughing wildly as if he didn't have a care in the world. He must have sensed Johnnie's change in mood because he placed a hand on Johnnie's shoulder and squeezed it.

"I'm proud of you," he said.

"Why don't you two go out to the studio again? I can clean up."

"You did so much work cooking all this." Caesar shook his head. "I'll take care of it. Take a walk with Johnnie."

Melanie nodded, stood, and took Johnnie's hand. They walked to his rock. Johnnie climbed up, and she followed. She sat between his legs, and he wrapped his arms around her, cuddling her close. They sat in silence, watching the horizon turn from blue to pink and gold, and then to inky black. Stars dotted the sky, and a cool breeze lifted her hair from her shoulders. He kissed one and then the other. Melanie felt like she had a million things she needed to tell him before he left, but sitting there like that with him, the two of them were saying so much without any words passing between them.

It was Johnnie who finally broke the silence. "Who'd have thought a few months ago, we'd end up here?"

She caressed the arms that were wrapped around her. "Sometimes it still feels like a dream. Like it's not real."

"I know what you mean. I'm forty-four. I've traveled the world. Earned millions of dollars. But until now, I don't think I've ever *felt* this much. For the first time I love life, and it's because of you."

She turned so that she could see him. "And Caesar."

Johnnie smiled. "Yes, I have to give him credit for sending you to me."

"To think I used to kiss a photo of you on my headboard every night before I went to bed. And now...now I get to kiss the real thing." She softly pressed her lips to his.

"Did you kiss Caesar's photo as well?"

"No. Just yours."

"We must tell him *that* story." He chuckled.

"You want to make him jealous?"

He squeezed her. "Yes, I do."

Melanie groaned. "I'm surprised you two aren't keeping tabs on how many times each of you has made love to me."

"Who says we haven't?"

"Who's winning?"

He grinned. "As of this afternoon? I am."

Melanie hopped off the rock. "I better help him catch up."

"I don't think so." He hopped down and grabbed her, hugging her close. "Let me hold this title for at least a few more hours."

Melanie wiggled free. "If I get to the house before you do, I'm locking you out of the bedroom til he catches up."

She laughed loudly as she began running, zigging and zagging in the sand always one step ahead of him. *Is he letting me win?* When she reached the house, she raced up the steps and into the house. Caesar was in the kitchen putting dishes into the dishwasher.

"Quick! Get to the bedroom!" She grabbed Caesar's arm and pulled him down the hall into Johnnie's room.

"What game are we playing?" Caesar asked when she shut the door and locked it.

"The one where she tries to get you all alone." Johnnie was already inside his room. He'd taken the screen out of the window and climbed through. "She wants to even our score."

"You told her?"

"I can't believe you two."

Johnnie cupped her chin. He brushed a soft kiss against her lips. "Really?"

"Alright, I can believe it. You two are impossible."

Caesar pressed his body into hers from behind. He rested his chin on her shoulder. "Impossibly in love with you, Melanie."

Johnnie grabbed her dress and lifted it over her head, while Caesar tugged her panties to the floor.

"Don't slap me when I ask you this." Johnnie kissed her once again.

She rolled her eyes and laughed. "What now?"

He glanced down at Caesar who was kneeling behind her, then back to her. "Have you ever had anal sex?"

Her eyes widened. *This is a surprise.*

Johnnie shook his head. "Okay, never mind, I didn't think so."

"Are you willing to try?" Caesar asked, cupping her ass cheeks in his hands. He spread them apart and ran his tongue along her crack.

She inhaled sharply when he lingered on her butthole. "I've never even thought about it."

"Forget it then." Johnnie kissed her tenderly. "Caesar had an idea is all."

Now her curiosity was piqued, and Caesar's tongue on her felt surprisingly nice. She reached back and touched the top of his head. "Tell me."

Caesar stood back up. He took off his joggers and pressed his cock into her butt. "It's a way we can both make love to you at the same time."

"You mean double penetration?"

Johnnie appeared surprised. "You know about this?"

"I used to work for a major news channel," she reminded him. "Not much I haven't seen or heard. Besides, I had a boyfriend in college who enjoyed porn way too much."

"And you gave me grief about watching it?"

Caesar chuckled. "Don't tell me you watched porn with her lying right next to you."

"Of course not. I was teasing her about watching it...to make her mad."

"Which is why I was giving you grief." Melanie caressed Johnnie's face.

"Back to my idea." Caesar gently squeezed her cheeks.

"I've never had anal sex." She looked from Johnnie to Caesar. "But we could try."

"We'll need that lube you bought," Caesar told Johnnie.

"Wait." Melanie put a hand on each chest. "You've been planning this?"

Caesar shrugged. "Sort of."

Johnnie touched her arm. "Again, we don't have to do this."

Melanie smiled. "Sounds like you're the one who doesn't want to do it."

"It does involve a very close encounter with his dick." Johnnie retrieved the lube from the top drawer of his nightstand. "And for the record, my dick isn't going to be the one going in the back door. I'm too thick and I don't want to hurt you."

She stared at Caesar. "It's probably going to hurt, isn't it?"

"I'll take things slow."

"You've done this before?"

"A few times." He took the lube from Johnnie and opened the bottle.

She looked at Johnnie.

"Was never my thing," he said. "But then again, when you're wasted sometimes you don't always remember what you've done."

"So, it's possible you *have* touched a few dicks back in the day," Caesar joked.

Johnnie narrowed his eyes, as he slipped out of his shorts.

"How do we do this?" Melanie asked.

"First we have to get you as ready as possible." Caesar knelt again and ran his hands over her butt. "Did you like when I licked you?"

"It was different but felt good."

Johnnie cupped her breasts and moved his thumbs over her nipples. His lips descended to hers. He kissed her over and over while Caesar spread her cheeks and pushed his tongue between them again.

Johnnie's hand traveled to her pussy, where he parted her and began stroking. Then he put two fingers inside her.

Caesar stood again, squeezing lube into his hand. "I'm going to try a finger. Relax, don't think about it...concentrate on our lips."

Caesar moved her hair to one side and put his lips on her neck. It sent a sexual jolt to her core, and she felt herself grow wetter on Johnnie's fingers. Johnnie's lips traveled from hers down to her chest where he wrapped them around a nipple to suckle. Caesar rubbed the lube in between her crack. He lightly touched her butthole, spreading the lube around. He placed one finger against it, then gently pushed. Again, she inhaled deeply and went up on her toes.

"Are you alright?" he asked, his finger still inside her.

Her feet rested back on the ground. "Yes."

She bit her lip when he pushed in a little further.

Johnnie scooted a chair closer to them. "Put one foot up."

When she did, he kissed her again, and rubbed the tip of his cock against her pussy, spreading her wetness.

"Do you want this?" he asked.

Caesar kissed the back of her neck. "Tell Johnnie how much you want his cock."

She wrapped her arms around Johnnie's neck and pulled him closer, pressing her lips against his. "I'm so wet for you, Johnnie. I want you inside me."

Johnnie bent his knees slightly and entered her slowly. Meanwhile, Caesar's finger delved deeper. If there was pain, she didn't feel it. The thickness of Johnnie's cock was all she could focus on.

Then, she felt Caesar slip another finger inside her.

"Still okay?" Caesar asked as his other hand came up to caress a nipple.

"Yes," she managed to say in between Johnnie's kisses.

"I'm going in," he told Johnnie.

She was disappointed when Johnnie pulled out.

"Don't want to overwhelm you," he said, rubbing her clit. He kissed her tenderly.

Caesar pulled his fingers out, slathered more lube on her and his cock, and then placed the head at her back entrance. Ever so slowly he began to enter.

"Caesar!" she cried out.

"You're alright," Johnnie cooed and put his fingers inside her once again. His thumb stroked her clit. "I've got you. Focus on me, babe. I'm going to make you cum."

"Can you lick me?"

"I would love to taste you."

On his knees again, Johnnie licked her pussy. When his tongue flicked over her clit, she shuddered. His fingers went inside, and Caesar continued to push his cock into her butthole.

"I'm in." He pressed his lips sensually against her neck. "Now I'm going to fuck you."

The painful pleasure of the sensation made her feel weak in the knees. Johnnie was sucking on her clit. She patted his head. "I need you inside me again."

"Are you sure you're ready?"

"I want to cum on your cock."

Caesar chuckled. "You're going to cum on both our cocks."

Johnnie stood and caressed her chin, then rubbed his thumb over her lips. "I love you, baby."

"I love you." She twisted her head so that she could see Caesar. "I love you, too."

Johnnie's lips met hers as he pushed into her once again. She thought she might faint from the sensation. Both their cocks buried within her...fucking her.

"Shit! This is amazing!" Johnnie smiled and wrapped his arms around both her and Caesar, pulling them in closer.

"I need to lie down," Melanie said.

Both men withdrew immediately.

"Are you all right?" Caesar asked. "Are you going to pass out again?"

When she sat on the edge of the bed, Johnnie handed her a bottle of water. "Drink some."

"Lie down," she instructed, and he did. She climbed on top of him, taking his cock inside her once more. She leaned forward, then asked Caesar, "Does this position work?"

Caesar climbed into the bed, got on his knees behind her and once again lubed himself up.

"I like it like this," she said as Caesar eased into her once more.

"Our balls are touching," Johnnie whined, then laughed.

Melanie smiled. "Focus on me, silly."

"Is her pussy wet?" Caesar asked as he fell into Johnnie's rhythm.

"Dripping." Johnnie moaned. "Fuck, Melanie...your pussy *is* pure magic."

"It loves your cock." She kissed him.

"Damn, I'm going to cum." Caesar grunted, pulled out and came between her cheeks. "Even more lubrication for you."

Melanie straightened on Johnnie's cock. Caesar sat beside the two of them, grabbed her left breast and attached his mouth to it. She gripped his cock which was hardening once again, sliding her hand up and down. She began to grind faster.

"Yeah, baby. Fuck me." Johnnie groaned.

Caesar's fingers disappeared between her legs to stroke her clit. "Feel good?"

"Yes, but don't stop sucking my nipple."

He smiled before latching on again.

"I'm gonna cum." She bucked even faster.

"Let's cum together," Caesar told her and straddled Johnnie's legs so he could enter her ass again.

"Yeah, let's do that," Johnnie murmured against her ear when she leaned forward. He picked up his pace shoving his cock upward into her.

Caesar held onto her hips and synched with Johnnie again. She felt so full with them both fucking her. Full of cock, and full of so much love for them. She cried out as her orgasm came. Her body quivered on both their cocks, causing them to push faster and deeper, until they cried out in ecstasy as well.

Caesar rolled over onto the bed. She then lay between them, holding hands with each of them. All three of them breathing hard. Then they burst out laughing.

Caesar kissed her forehead. "Thank you, baby. That was the best."

Johnnie brought her hand to his lips. "Fucking magic."

"It was, wasn't it?" She smiled.

The two of them answered by snuggling closer to her. Soon they were drifting off to sleep.

"Where are you going?" Melanie asked when she was awakened later by Johnnie's body sliding away from hers.

"Caesar and I are going to play some music. You want to come to the studio with us?"

She yawned. "How are you two not tired?"

"I'm wired. Can't sleep. As for him, I'm not sure he really needs to sleep."

"Well, I do. I'm staying here."

He sat down on the bed and caressed her face. Then, he brought his lips to hers. "I love you more than anything."

"I love you, too." She kissed him tenderly. "See you in the morning."

He closed his eyes and smiled. "Get some rest."

Chapter Twenty-four

Melanie woke the next morning with her face burrowed into Caesar's curls. She smiled as she ran her hand through them, inhaling his sugary scent.

She turned to Johnnie, but he wasn't in bed. *That's odd.* Johnnie was the heavier sleeper, and because he was a night owl, he often slept late. He'd been anxious about the journey today, so maybe he'd never come to bed. She pulled the covers back.

Caesar wrapped an arm around her waist, holding her tightly. "I love you."

She rolled over and kissed him. "And I love you. Looks like Johnnie got up early. I'm going to see where he is. I want to spend time with him before he leaves."

"Melanie, baby." Caesar held tight and pulled her closer. "He's already gone."

"What?" She wiggled free and slid from the bed. "He's not leaving until noon."

Caesar rose and grabbed her as she tried to leave the room. "He's gone, Melanie. Rhett came about six this morning, and they left. Johnnie planned it that way."

"He wouldn't leave without saying goodbye."

Caesar retrieved a letter from the dresser and handed it to her. "He did say goodbye."

"No!" She smacked the letter out of his hand, grabbed a dress to slip on, and fled the room.

The suitcase Johnnie had packed was no longer by the front door. She flung the door open and ran to the gate. Grabbing the bars, she screamed, tears racing down her face.

"Melanie." Caesar hurried to her.

"How could you let him do this? We were supposed to say goodbye." She fell into Caesar's arms, sobbing.

"I'm sorry. It's what he wanted. He was afraid if he had to say goodbye face to face, he wouldn't be able to leave."

Furious and sad at the same time, she ripped herself away from Caesar and stomped back into the house. Immediately, she grabbed her phone and called Johnnie's number. The rings of his phone, within the house, caused her lip to tremble. *How could he do this?*

Caesar appeared, holding Johnnie's phone. "He's not allowed to have it."

Her heart thudded in her chest as she rushed past him and out the back door. On the beach, tears stung her eyes. She started to panic. *Will I ever see him again? Talk to him again?* She ran all the way to his rock and leaned against it, trying to catch her breath. Her world was spinning. *Is this another panic attack?*

"Breathe slowly."

She spun around, ready to yell at Caesar but he wasn't there.

"Close your eyes. Take a deep breath."

"Fuck you!" She shrieked to no one.

She crawled up onto the rock, pulled her knees to her chest, and cried.

Melanie was jolted awake by the sounds of laughing dolphins. There were two of them playing nearby, and she couldn't help but smile when one leaped into the air, twisting its body around in a spiral.

"You're missing them again, Johnnie," she whispered into the gentle breeze and then her body was heaving again with heavy sobs.

Finally, she wiped away her tears. "This is exactly why you left without seeing me, isn't it? This is exactly what I would've done. And you would have felt terrible and stayed."

Her head throbbed from crying, and she scooted off the rock. She was surprised that Caesar hadn't come to comfort her. *Where is he?*

"No!" she cried out, then sprinted back toward the house. *Is he gone?* She'd gotten angry with him. Yelled at him. He was all she had left. *Did I chase him away?* Or maybe because Johnnie was gone, he'd had to leave, too...without being able to say goodbye.

"Caesar!" she yelled when she reached the deck. She opened the door, shouting his name over and over. No reply came. The house was eerily quiet.

"No! No! No!" She ran back to the deck wondering where he could be. Then she heard something. Muffled beats. *The studio!*

Music was blaring when she entered. Caesar was banging on Johnnie's drum set. She covered her ears. A drummer he was not. She turned down the volume of the stereo. When he looked up, she saw that he'd been crying, too.

"Melanie?" He got up from the drummer's seat.

"I thought you were gone." She ran to him and threw her arms around his neck. "I'm so sorry."

He rubbed her back. "There's nothing to be sorry for. I understand how upset you are. I'm sure it hurt to not say goodbye to him."

"Promise me you'll stay right by my side until you go."

"I'll do my best."

She broke their hug and pressed her lips hard against his. He grabbed her butt and pulled her tight against his groin, grinding his hard cock into her. As she backed up against the studio wall, she tugged his pants down, freeing his cock. With both hands she enveloped him, caressing him.

"Wrap your legs around me."

When she did, he plunged into her, using her body to stroke himself. Her orgasm was fast and powerful, squeezing his long cock within her walls.

"You feel so good." He moaned against her neck.

Their lips met again and again as he continued his strokes. He carried her over to the cushions that were on the floor and only then let her slide from his arms. He lay down, and she straddled him.

"Ride me, baby."

She ground her hips against his, tossing her head back, thrusting her chest forward. He grabbed her breasts and went to work on her nipples, causing her to buck wildly on him.

"That's it...make me cum." He smiled when her speed increased, then moaned loudly as her body tightened around him. He came with her, spilling himself inside her.

Overcome with emotions tears once again slid down her face. Caesar drew her close, kissing her tenderly, cuddling her, his tears mingling with hers. Melanie clung to him, afraid to let go, all the while knowing she would soon have to say goodbye.

"Oops, you're missing a word there." Caesar pointed to the computer screen.

"Thanks." Melanie clicked the mouse and inserted the missing word. "You're a great editor."

"I'm glad Kurt's wife knew an agent willing to shop the manuscript around for us. I know it will get picked up and published soon."

"I'm sure it will. Especially since I have the inside scoop on the band."

"The official autobiography." Caesar raised his arms up in victory.

Melanie did the same. "It will be a best seller."

Caesar wrapped her up in his arms. "And when someone asks how you got all this information on me?"

"You did leave all those tapes behind, remember?"

He kissed her as she received notification of a new email.

"Oh my God." Her heart raced. "It's from Johnnie."

"Can't be. He's not allowed any contact with the outside world for a while."

She clicked open the email. No message, just a video attachment. She clicked on the video and Johnnie appeared on her screen. The video wasn't from rehab. Clearly, it was taken in the house.

"Did you know about this?"

Caesar smiled, then kissed her cheek. "I'll leave you two alone."

When he left, she saved the video to her hard drive and then opened it again. She turned up the volume on the speakers.

"Hi baby, it's me."

Caesar, somewhere off camera, laughed. "That's obvious."

"Hold the phone steady."

Melanie smiled. The two of them together always made her happy.

"By now I'm gone. I'm sending this video to tell you again I love you. I'll be missing you like crazy locked up in rehab. It may look like a vacation resort from the website, but fact is, it'll feel like jail."

"You'll hate it," she said aloud.

"I'll be thinking about you...about us...every day I'm there. It's only been a few months, but I feel like I've been waiting my whole life for you to walk into it. Or I guess, in our case, I've been waiting for you to break into my house."

Melanie took a deep breath and exhaled slowly. It seemed like a lifetime ago that she'd arrived at the gate, eager for change and a new life.

"Caesar and I made this video a couple weeks ago, and I arranged for it to arrive after I left."

He paused for a moment, and Melanie could tell he was on the verge of tears. Then the video seemed to end but then picked up again.

"Melanie, the thought of you moving on without me...the thought that you might even forget about me...terrifies me."

That will never happen.

"I know what you're thinking, Melanie. That you'll never forget me. But fact is, I'll be away for a while. No contact with anyone. You *must* move on. Write your books, find some new projects, and explore all your possibilities. The sky is the limit, babe. You're so creative and smart...you can do anything. I want you to know that if your future takes you away from me...I'll understand. What's important is I get better, and you do the things that make you happy and bring you success."

"The battery's running low," Caesar announced.

"I thought I charged the phone." Johnnie rolled his eyes, threw up his hands in exasperation, then looked at the camera. "I love you, babe."

The video swung around to Caesar's face. "I love you, too."

And then it was over.

"Caesar?" she called out.

He was at the door. "Right here."

"Where's the letter Johnnie wrote me?"

"The one you told me to throw away?"

"Please tell me you didn't."

"It's been sitting on his dresser for two days."

"I couldn't go into his room." She rose from the chair and went downstairs. When she opened his door, his citrusy scent assaulted her. *I will not cry.* She straightened her back, walked in, and grabbed the letter from the chest of drawers. Then she sat on the bed and opened it.

"Caesar!" she yelled.

Caesar came trampling down the stairs and into Johnnie's room. "Are you okay?"

She held up a cashier's check. "Did you know about this?"

"Damn! That's funny!" He sat on the bed next to her.

"Five hundred thousand *and* one dollar!" She shook her head.

Caesar chuckled. "He just had to outdo me...as usual."

She nudged Caesar. "Between your gift and his...I'll be set for a while."

"What does the letter say?"

She bit her lip as a tear slipped from her eye. "His apology for not saying goodbye in person. Says he was having doubts about leaving all week and knew if he saw me, he would've stayed."

Caesar wrapped an arm around her. "Our Johnnie's going to be okay."

"Yes, he will."

"You've given him something to fight for."

"Is that why you sent me here?"

"Remember when I met you, I had no idea your dream was to live in California and become a writer. In fact, we decided it was a fluke. Confusion over his blood that flows in you."

"Then this is all just fate having her way with us?"

"Fate?" He winked. "Or maybe something more."

She pushed the curls off his face and kissed him. "Let's go play in the ocean."

He pulled her backward onto the bed. "We could just play here."

She leaped up and grabbed his hand. "I need fresh air. We've been inside working all afternoon. Let's go."

Melanie's moans of pleasure were caught by Caesar's mouths as his lips feasted on hers. He pumped into her harder and deeper. She grabbed his butt and squeezed to encourage him. Her hips raised off the ground, meeting every thrust. When her body began to quake, he increased his speed, pushing her over the edge into ecstasy and bringing about his own orgasm.

As they slowly slipped from their lovemaking high, he lay on her, inside her, and kissed her over and over, stopping only to stare at her. His dark eyes twinkled in the light of the full moon, and the saltwater dripping from his curls splattered across her face. The breeze was cool, but with his cock inside her, she felt full of heat.

His brow suddenly furrowed, and a look of concern registered on his face.

"What is it?"

He slid out of her and sat up on their blanket. "No...no, no, no."

Alarmed, she sat up beside him. "What is it?"

He turned to her and tears fell from his eyes.

Instantly, she knew. She rested her chin on his shoulder. "You have to go."

"I feel something. I can't explain it."

She pressed kisses across the top of his back. "You don't have to explain."

"I don't want to leave you." He turned around to kiss her.

She stared at him, trying to memorize everything. She traced her fingers over the angles of his face, over his thick lips. Then she plunged her hands into his hair and buried her nose inside it. She inhaled deeply.

"I promise I'll be fine." She tried to be brave as she fought back her own tears.

He pushed her hair behind her ears. "Now I know why Johnnie didn't want to say goodbye in person. My heart may no longer beat, but it aches."

"It's your soul." She kissed him.

He nodded. "Let's go for a walk."

She stood and slipped her dress over her head. Caesar didn't bother putting on his shorts. She didn't mind. Instead, she raked her gaze over his body, once again trying to preserve it to memory.

Hand in hand, drenched in silence, they walked toward Johnnie's favorite spot. As soon as they reached the rock, he squeezed her hand. "I love you."

And then there was no hand in hers. He was gone. She climbed up on the rock, as she had done when Johnnie had left two days ago. She stared into the ocean and saw movement. The dolphins. Now there were three of them. She smiled.

Chapter Twenty-five

Melanie

February

"Are you ready for this?" Rhett rubbed Melanie's arms, trying to help calm her nerves. They were backstage, along with Kurt. The three of them would be introducing their documentary, *Love and Lush*, to the world from the Fox Theatre in downtown Atlanta.

Melanie trembled with anticipation. "I don't know how you guys did this all the time."

"You'll be fine." Kurt patted her back. "You look beautiful and that's all most of these people will notice."

"I hope you're right." Smiling, she hugged him.

"Ladies and gentlemen," the announcer boomed in over the microphone. "Rhett Star, Kurt Rain, and Melanie Davis."

Each of the guys took one of her hands, and they walked out from behind the curtain together. There was a microphone set up in the center of the stage.

"Good evening," Rhett spoke first, and a generous amount of applause followed. Even though tickets to the event had been expensive to come by, it was obvious a lot of Lush fans were in attendance. "It's great to be here as we unveil *Love and Lush* for the first time."

Kurt scooted closer to the microphone. "But we wouldn't be here at all if it weren't for this talented woman. This was her idea...her movie...and I believe she's the most qualified to introduce our film."

More applause and Melanie felt her breath being taken away. *Oh no! The last thing I need is a panic attack.* This event was too important for the band. She closed her eyes, took a deep breath, and counted to ten. She'd give anything to have Caesar or Johnnie there. In the months they'd been gone, not a day passed by that she didn't miss them terribly. But she'd kept herself busy writing. Her first book was scheduled for release in a few months, and the publisher had also accepted the second manuscript she'd submitted. As for the band's autobiography, she'd held off accepting offers knowing the documentary would create a higher demand which would mean more money.

"You can do this."

It was Caesar's voice. Although he was no longer in her life, from time to time, she heard him. It could very well be her imagination, but she liked to think he was near. She opened her eyes and smiled.

"Good evening, everyone." She paused, taking another deep breath. "If you'd told me a year ago that I'd be on stage introducing a documentary of my favorite band...one that I'd written and produced with my favorite member of that band, I would have thought you were crazy. But in a few short months, my life took a major U-turn that lead me on this wild, creative journey. One that led me to this night. This is not just my film though. I could not have done this without my co-writer and producer, Johnnie Vega. Nor without input from Kurt and Rhett. Together, we've created a wonderful tribute to a band that left the limelight far too soon. A band with so much more to say. But without their lead singer and brother in music, Caesar Blue, it will forever remain unsaid. As much as Johnnie, Kurt, and Rhett helped make this possible, I would not be here tonight if it weren't for Caesar. His presence is deeply felt in the film, and I've felt his inspiration and love surrounding me from the moment I decided to take Johnnie up on his idea to tell the world the story of Lush."

A shout from the audience. "Where's Johnnie?"

"I knew someone would ask that," Melanie answered, and the audience laughed. "Johnnie took a monumental step a few months ago, but I'll let him tell you about it."

A video began playing on the screen behind them. It was one Johnnie had made before he'd left and had scheduled her to receive in an email. She'd gotten a video every few weeks. This video had been created for an audience that might see the documentary. Caesar had not been involved with this one. Apparently, Johnnie had balanced his phone upright on a shelf to create it.

"I have no idea who I'm talking to, but I left this video with Melanie to use as she begins promoting our movie, *Love and Lush*. Although this project was initially my idea, Melanie's incredible writing skills and vision lead us to the final product. Caesar, Kurt, Rhett, and myself were kindred spirits who found one another and became inseparable. We grew up together and traveled the world together. When we lost Caesar, not only did the band die, but a piece of my heart and soul did as well. I couldn't get over his death...and the guilt I felt ate me alive for a long time. But meeting Melanie, and working with her, brought me back to life. I'm not there with you because I'm in rehab. At this point in my life, I'm willing to do whatever it takes to get clean. I hope that you enjoy our movie because it was a true labor of *Love and Lush*. Not only did I get to honor the brothers I love...but in the process I fell in love with my beautiful and talented creative partner."

Melanie's cheeks warmed as the audience *oohed and aahed* at his declaration.

Johnnie blew a kiss toward the camera. "I want to thank our fans for their support. I love you all. I love Caesar, Rhett, and Kurt...my mom, and most of all I love you, Melanie."

Applause erupted when the video ended. Melanie waited for it to die down.

"In case you're wondering...the feeling is mutual! Now let's watch *Love and Lush*." Melanie waved as she exited the stage with Kurt and Rhett.

"Hanging in there?" Kurt asked.

Melanie nodded even though she was exhausted. After the movie, there had been a party. She'd mingled with guests who gushed over the documentary, but now she sat between Kurt and Rhett fielding questions from reporters.

"Watch out for this one," Rhett told her when a reporter rose to ask the next question. He seemed to be about the same age as the band members and was dressed in a leather jacket and jeans. "He's an ass."

"After Caesar died, he kept bugging us for interviews," Kurt explained. "He wanted to write our autobiography with us, but we refused."

"He was one of the main reporters fueling the whole Johnnie killed Caesar theory," Rhett added.

"You next." Melanie pointed at the man.

"Did I hear you correctly, Ms. Davis, that an autobiography is in the works?"

"What's your name, sir?" she asked, smiling, trying to appear polite.

"Phil Chase."

Melanie nodded. "Mr. Chase, all the band members have contributed to the writing of the autobiography. I've been helping them through the process."

"All the members except Caesar you mean." The reporter's tone was snide.

She looked at Rhett and then back to the reporter. "Actually, Caesar contributed a great deal."

"Really? How did he manage that?"

"He left behind tapes, both audio and video of himself and the guys. He kept journals as well."

"How did you manage to unearth these items?"

"Johnnie lives in Caesar's house, and that's where we found them."

Phil Chase folded his arms across his chest. "Can you explain to everyone how you managed to find yourself living in Caesar's house with Johnnie?"

"Came to California to follow my dreams. Johnnie was looking for a roommate."

"You obviously became more than a roommate."

This guy was goading her into a confrontation. She'd not take the bait. "Obviously."

"As a fan, how did you manage to fall in love with someone responsible for destroying your favorite band?"

"Listen..." Kurt began, but Melanie put a hand on his arm.

"Johnnie didn't destroy anything," she said with confidence.

"And I suppose he told you this?"

"If you're talking about the night Caesar died, let me assure you, the three of us and Johnnie are all aware of what happened that night."

"Really?" Phil Chase asked. "Because Johnnie Vega always said he didn't have a clue what happened."

"Johnnie felt tremendous guilt about Caesar dying. It didn't help having the media speculating that he'd killed Caesar on purpose."

"So, he didn't kill Caesar?"

"Of course not." Her eyes narrowed. "He loved Caesar. It was a tragic accident."

"You were there?"

"I believe Johnnie's account of that night."

Phil Chase threw his hands up. "And what happened?"

"You'll have to buy the book and find out." Melanie shot him a sly smile. "Now I think we should allow someone else to have a turn."

"Thank you so much for visiting me." Mrs. Smith squeezed Melanie's hand as they sat on the porch swing. "And for bringing the boys. That was a nice surprise. Lunch was delicious. I'd been wanting to try that place for a while."

Melanie was happy for time with Johnnie's mother. It made her feel closer to him. "I wish they could have stayed longer."

Kurt and Rhett were traveling back to California while she'd be staying another night and then driving to visit her family in Florida.

"I'm sorry I didn't make the premiere last night. My arthritis was flaring up."

"I'm glad you're feeling better today." Melanie pulled her phone from her coat pocket. "I have some photos of Johnnie and me to show you."

"These are wonderful," Mrs. Smith gushed as Melanie scanned through the photos. "He looks so happy."

She came to one of his videos. "I don't know how he managed to do it, but he filmed all these videos and scheduled them to come to me at different times. Here's one."

In this video, Johnnie was telling her what she meant to him.

"...remember how hard we fought to stay away from one another...we were trying to deny how much we wanted to fuck one another."

"Oops...maybe not that one." Melanie blushed as she quickly clicked it off.

Johnnie's mom laughed. "That's *my* boy."

"Sorry. I guess I should have better named the videos, so I could show you the G-rated ones."

Mrs. Smith patted her arm. "I lived with four males. There's nothing I haven't heard or seen. I'm surprised he didn't send you one of those...dick pics."

Melanie laughed. "I have a feeling I'll get one eventually."

"I don't care what's coming out of his mouth though. I love seeing his eyes light up when he talks about you. He loves you so much."

"I love him, too."

Johnnie's mom squeezed her hand again. "He's going to get better, Melanie. For good. I know it."

"I have faith in him."

"That's what he's needed more than anything. Someone who believes in him."

Her lip started to tremble. "I miss him so much."

Mrs. Smith wrapped an arm around Melanie, pulling her closer. "You're always welcome to stay here for a visit. Darren and Robert come up every other weekend. We could make sure you came when they weren't here."

"Thank you." Melanie smiled. "I did fly over to visit my family at Christmas...and for New Year's I went out with Rhett to an exclusive Hollywood party. Got to rub elbows with some celebrities."

"That must have been fun."

"Yes. And I made some good contacts as well."

"Are you still thinking about screenwriting?"

"I'm not sure yet. I want to see how well the books do. We'll see what happens after that."

Mrs. Smith shivered. "It's getting chilly out here. Do you mind going inside?"

"Of course not."

"Would you like to see some old family albums? Get a look at Johnnie when he was a boy?"

Melanie beamed. "I'd love that. Maybe you have a few I can use in the book."

"I bet we can find something."

Chapter Twenty-six

May

Melanie sat down at her writing desk and turned on her laptop. But instead of opening the manuscript she'd been working on, something drew her to the website of the rehabilitation center where Johnnie was living. She navigated through the pages, trying to imagine Johnnie's new life. She knew very little about the program. Johnnie hadn't wanted to discuss it. Their time together had been too precious to waste with talk of an addiction program. But now she wished she'd learned more. He had talked to the counselors there. He knew what to expect. And he'd been to rehab before. She was clueless. And she had no idea when she'd hear from him again.

Seven months. Seven long months since he'd left. In that time, she'd heard nothing. She'd moved on without Johnnie in the house. It wasn't easy. Working on getting the documentary out to the public, talking to Rhett and Kurt about the band, writing the autobiography meant that Johnnie was always on her mind...Caesar, too.

Somehow it was easier to come to grips with losing Caesar. As much as she loved him and loved being with him, he was not of this world anymore. But Johnnie was real...and alive, and very much gone. She missed his smile and the way they'd laugh with one another. And of course, she missed the lovemaking, the way he'd stare into her eyes as if she were the most exquisite thing he'd ever seen. Her pulse quickened thinking about it. A familiar yearning stirred between her legs.

A message popped up on the screen alerting her to a new email. *Johnnie.*

Another video. These mementos he'd arranged to send her, filled her with both happiness and sadness. She loved seeing and hearing him. But they also reminded her of how far away he was. And the uncertainty of when, or even if, they'd be together again.

The videos weren't the only things Johnnie had arranged for her to receive. Her hand instinctively went to her neck. A gold necklace with angel wing charms attached. Three sets of wings inscribed with the names Leila, Lily, and Caesar. Her Christmas gift from Johnnie. Roses had arrived on Valentine's Day with a card that read, *I love you.* He'd managed to find time before leaving to make sure she knew she was remembered on these special days.

Filled with nervous excitement, she downloaded the video file to her computer wondering what message she would receive. It was larger than other files he'd sent.

Her breath caught when the file opened. *He did not!* But he had. It was a video of the two of them making love. Caesar must have taken it. *How did I not notice?* She sat mesmerized watching her and Johnnie rolling on the bed naked. Watching his butt tighten as he pushed into her time and time again was a turn on. He rolled over and let her take control. As she rode him, the camera moved. Suddenly Caesar appeared in front of it.

"This is so hot," he whispered. Then the camera moved again. His long cock came into view, and he was stroking it. "It's making me hard."

The camera moved again, and it appeared that Caesar had set the phone down because he was now joining them on the bed. He lay beside Johnnie, and she eased off him and began to ride Caesar instead.

Even though she'd experienced the real thing, seeing it on video aroused her even more. She reached under her dress, slid her panties off and touched herself. She watched as the three of them changed positions again. This time Caesar fucked her from behind as she sucked Johnnie's cock. Her fingers slipped inside her wet pussy. In the video, Caesar started to cum, and he pulled out so she could finish him with her mouth. Then the two of them had her on her back, licking her. When she started to cum, Johnnie fucked her, pushing her over the edge and beyond until he was cumming, too.

"Johnnie...Caesar ..." she panted as she came. But with her orgasm came tears. *I miss them so much.*

The next afternoon, Melanie was working on edits to her latest novel when her phone rang. It wasn't a number she recognized. *Is it him?*

"Hello," she greeted.

"Melanie Davis?"

"This is she."

"We sort of met in Atlanta. Phil Chase?"

"How did you get my number?"

"I'm sure you know that when you're with the press, you can get access to many things."

"And as you know most people would think this was an invasion of privacy and hang up on you."

"You'd do that?"

She hung up. He had some nerve.

She got a text message from the same number. *What does he want?*

I'd like to talk to you and Johnnie. Can I interview the two of you?

What is he trying to do? He knew Johnnie was in rehab. What angle was he working? Just as she went to block him from further texting or calling, there was one last message.

Do you even know where he is?

She blocked him. *Why did he say that?* Now her mind was whirling with doubt...questions. Was Johnnie at the center? Or had he left like he'd done in the past?

There was only one way to find out.

She dialed the number of the rehab center. She'd never wanted to before but was compelled to now. Still, she felt like she was intruding on his life...on his recovery...something she knew was very personal.

"Hello. My name is Melanie Davis, and a friend of mine is currently residing in your facility. I was hoping I could find out how he's doing and when he might be released."

"Are you a family member?"

"We live together," she explained.

"He hasn't contacted you?"

"No. He told me he'd have no contact for a while. But it's been seven months, and I wanted to check in."

"I'm sorry. We can't release any information on patients unless it's to family members."

"But anyone could call and say they were a family member."

"Our residents give us a list of people who are allowed information should they call."

"Again, I could just pretend to be his mother. Or I could have her call instead."

"Why don't you give me the name of the resident and I'll see if he's put you on the list?"

"Johnnie Vega...or perhaps Jonathan Smith. That's his birth name."

"Hold and I'll check." A few minutes passed. "I'm sorry. There isn't anyone under those names on site."

"Are you sure?"

"Positive."

"But you have records of him being there, right?"

"Again, I cannot discuss that with you."

"I'll have his mother call you then. Maybe you'll be able to tell her something."

Twenty minutes later, Johnnie's mom was calling her back.

Melanie was an anxious wreck. "Were you able to find out anything?"

"Melanie…" Mrs. Smith sighed.

Her heart nearly stopped, and she had to sit down. "He left?"

"He did…but not because he quit. He finished the program."

"Why hasn't he called me? I don't understand."

"I'm sorry. I wish I could tell you what he was thinking."

"What exactly did they say?" Melanie asked.

"It was somewhat good news," his mother told her. "He left and went into a sober living facility. That was about a month ago."

"Did they give you the name of it?"

"Yes, I called to see if I could talk to him. But he left about two weeks ago."

What does this mean? Is he sober? Did he give up? Why hasn't he called?

"Melanie?"

"I'm here." She willed herself not to cry. "Just stunned."

"I'm sure he told you part of recovery is to not get involved in relationships."

"We were already involved."

"He needs more time. To make sure he's ready to be the man you need. Don't lose faith in him. He loves you."

"I miss him so much." Her voice cracked as the tears finally came. "I've tried so hard to not think about him. But that reporter's call put me over the edge."

"Do you think he knows something we don't?"

"Maybe." Melanie sighed. "Rhett and Kurt don't trust him. I blocked him from contacting me."

"If they don't trust him, it's better to stay away. Kurt has a good sense about these things."

Melanie remembered how Kurt had questioned her motives. At the time, he'd been looking out for his bandmates. The two of them were friends now, and she'd visited him a few times. He and his wife had a horse ranch where they were raising their two children.

"I'll call the guys and let them know. Rhett's in Europe. Maybe he can stop by the house in London and check there for Johnnie."

"Good thinking," Mrs. Smith replied. "If you find out anything, let me know. And if you need to come for a visit, please do."

"Thank you."

Melanie said her goodbyes and hung up. Quickly, she texted Rhett and let him know the situation.

Are you alright?

Tears fell again. *Not really.*

The phone rang immediately.

"You didn't have to call," Melanie said. "Isn't it almost show time?"

"Yeah. But I know you must be hurting. As soon as I get to London, I'll go by the house. And when I get back home, I'll visit. Just hang in there."

"Not much else I can do."

"No last-minute edits on the autobiography?" Rhett asked.

"Still waiting to hear from the editor on the last ones I sent back. We should be going to print soon."

"Let's have a big release party...for the book and the new album. Planning that will keep you busy."

"Sounds like fun." She pushed back tears. *Johnnie should be here. These are his ideas.*

"I've got to go."

Her voice started to falter as she said goodbye.

"Hey, he'll reach out soon," Rhett assured her. "Don't worry."

"Thanks."

She set her phone down on the kitchen counter and walked into the living room. It was a beautiful day, and she should be out enjoying it. Inside the house...inside her heart was a feeling of complete emptiness. *I must keep busy, or I'll go crazy worrying.*

Slipping on sneakers, she headed outside. She watered and weeded the garden. She'd planted new flowers last week, and so far, they were growing well. She'd even found another dragon statue, this one holding up a bird bath. Which led her to also hang a bird feeder.

When Melanie returned the garden tools to the garage, she felt compelled to visit the studio. Sitting down on Johnnie's stool, she picked up his sticks. She hit the snare drum a few times. It was too much. Too many memories came crashing into her mind. The band playing for her, Johnnie and Caesar playing on his last day home, and then she and Caesar making love the next day. Her heart ached, but something else was bubbling beneath the surface. Anger. He *should* have contacted her. If he loved her. If he wanted to be with her...make a life with her. Isn't that why he'd gone to rehab in the first place? She'd waited patiently for his return. Working, putting his absence out of her mind, and focusing on her goals. And their goals. She deserved a phone call. Or a letter. Something to let her know he was alright.

Letting out a shrill scream, she threw the sticks hard against the wall. When she stood, she pushed the drum stool over and onto the ground. She started to send the drums crashing to the floor as well but stopped herself. She stomped out of the studio and back up the garden path to the house. Inside, she went to Johnnie's room and slipped out of her clothes. After showering, she pulled open a drawer and held a pair of his pajama pants to her face. The scent was faint but unmistakably his. She slipped them on, then rifled through his drawers holding up t-shirts and smelling each, trying to find one that held something stronger. The house was full of Caesar's scent, but there had to be a little of Johnnie somewhere. Opening the closet, it hit her. The scent of citrus that was as familiar to her as vanilla. This was Johnnie's cologne. She found a grey hoodie made of soft cotton and slipped it on. Another wave of sadness washed over her. This time she didn't fight it, but let it take her. She curled up on his bed and cried herself to sleep.

Laughter woke her. Kids playing. A strong, cool breeze rushed in causing the curtains to take flight. She sat up, her head aching. *Too much crying.* Laughter wafted through the window again. Another breeze. *Did I open the window?* She couldn't remember. Lifting herself from the bed, she walked to the window, wondering who was trespassing on Caesar's private beach. But from Johnnie's window, she couldn't see anyone. She headed downstairs and to the back door. She would let whomever it was know that they'd have to leave. Or maybe she'd let them stay awhile depending on the circumstance. It might be a nice distraction to watch kids playing.

She stood at the railing of the deck and looked both ways along the shore. There was no one. Was her mind playing tricks on her? In Caesar's house, there was no way to be sure.

Her stomach growled, reminding her she hadn't eaten dinner last night. As she reopened the back door, she heard the children's laughter again. She turned toward the sound.

As she walked down the steps, a strong gust of wind swept past, chilling her. She strained her eyes, trying to make out the three figures she saw strolling along the beach, heading her way. One was obvious. The headful of bouncy curls immediately gave his identity away. The other two were little girls with blonde hair that flowed behind them as they ran and skipped around Caesar.

"Oh my God!" Melanie sprinted toward them. When Caesar saw her, he began running. She ignored him, her mind set on one thing. To reach the girls. Her girls. *Lily and Leila.*

Caesar grabbed her around the waist and held tight.

She struggled fiercely. "Let me go!"

"Melanie...shh...calm down. Let me talk to you first."

"Leila! Lily!" she cried out. The girls didn't respond but kept playing their game.

Caesar enveloped her in his arms. "They can't see you, baby. I brought them for you to see, but they can't see you. I'm sorry. It's the best I could do."

He released her, and she ran to them anyway. They skipped in circles and chased one another, ignoring her presence. She sank to the sand, tears flowing.

Caesar knelt beside her. "I wish they could see you and talk to you. I wanted to make you happy, not sad."

She turned to him. "They're so beautiful."

He held her face, brushing the tears from her cheeks with his thumbs. "Yes. They look like you."

She stared in awe as the girls blissfully zoomed around the two of them. "Thank you."

"We've always been close. But when I felt your sadness last night, I knew you needed me."

She kissed him softly.

"I'm afraid we can't stay long."

Leila ran over and held out her hand. "Look what I found, Caesar."

Caesar's eyes widened. "A starfish! Cool! But you should put it back into the water so it can find its way home."

Leila ran back to the water's edge and dipped her hand in the waves to let the starfish go. Lily stood right beside Melanie, and she longed to hold her daughter.

"Who were you talking to?" Lily asked Caesar. "Is it Mommy?"

Melanie gasped. "They know I'm here?"

Caesar nodded, then turned to Lily. "Mommy's here."

Leila waltzed back over. Lily whispered in her ear.

"Mommy?" Leila looked around.

"You can't see her, but she sees you," Caesar told them. "And she can hear you."

"We love you, Mommy." They said in unison.

Melanie teared up again. "I love you so much, babies."

"She loves you, too." Caesar smiled, ruffling the hair of each twin. "She misses you."

"We miss you too, Mommy," Leila said.

"Don't worry, Mommy." Lily patted Caesar's head. "Caesar takes good care of us."

Shocked, Melanie stared at him.

"I've kept them close since I found out about them."

She kissed him again. "Why didn't you tell me?"

"I knew you'd want to see them, and I wasn't sure I could make that happen. I didn't want to disappoint you." Caesar stood and held his hand out to her.

She stood and brushed the sand from her bottom. Caesar helped, patting her butt, filling her with a familiar desire.

"Caesar, can we go play?" Leila asked.

"Yes, I'm going over there." He pointed to the house. "It's where I used to live and where your mom lives now. Stay close by."

They ran ahead, laughing loudly. Caesar grabbed her hand, and they strolled back to the house. They sat on the steps to the deck.

"Can you see into the future for me?"

"Unfortunately, no. I'm not supposed to be here. I only came back to cheer you up. I thought I might be able to tell you something about Johnnie, but I can't see or feel anything related to him."

"Maybe it means he's sober...that he's not hurting anymore."

"It has to be." Caesar squeezed her hand. "I believe in him...and you. You two will be together. I know it. That I do feel."

"Can you feel how much I want you inside me right now?"

"Definitely." He kissed her neck. "You smell like him."

"It's his clothes. I still smell like you."

"Caesar...Caesar! Look what we found."

Lily was holding a young, screaming ginger kitten.

"Is it alive...or?" Melanie asked. There was no telling with three spirits surrounding her.

"Alive," Caesar answered.

"They can see and hear a kitten but not me?"

Caesar shrugged. "I wish I could explain it to you."

She watched Leila stroke the kitten's head while trying to shush it. "Maybe because it needs help?"

"Perhaps." Caesar nodded.

"Can we keep it?" Leila asked.

Caesar rubbed Leila's head gently. "I'm afraid not."

"Can Mommy keep it for us?" Lily asked, gently shaking the baby, trying to comfort it.

Caesar looked at Melanie. She smiled and nodded.

"She can. Did you see any more kittens? Or was this the only one?"

"There was another one...a big one...but it's not moving."

The four of them walked to a wooded spot where they'd found the kitten. The cat, obviously the mother, was lying dead in the bushes. Melanie reached out and touched it. It was not completely stiff.

"I think she may have died recently. The baby is probably starving, though."

Caesar rubbed her shoulder. "Looks like you've been given a new project to work on."

"I need to take it to a vet soon."

"Yes."

"Will you be here when I get back?"

"I don't think so." Caesar frowned, and a tear escaped his eye. "But we'll always be close. Don't ever forget that."

She threw her arms around him. "I love you so much. Thank you for bringing them to me."

"I wish it could have been more." He kissed her forehead.

She hugged him tightly.

Caesar knelt close to Lily. "You have to give Mommy the kitten now. She needs to take it to the animal doctor and make sure it's okay. And she has to get milk for it."

Melanie reached out to take the kitten. When her hand touched Lily's, the hair on her arms stood on end. As soon as she had the kitten, it settled down and stopped crying.

"It has a new mommy now," Caesar told them. "He'll be fine."

The two of them cheered, then ran off toward the water.

"I love you, Melanie." He brushed a soft kiss against her lips. "And so does Johnnie."

"I love you and him." She smiled. "I better get going."

She watched him walk toward the girls, and then she rushed into action, taking the kitten inside, finding a box to put it in, and then getting dressed to leave.

When she returned a few hours later, the kitten was in a carrier. The vet had estimated it to be about a month old and a male. He'd checked it over and then sent Melanie to the nearest pet store for kitten formula and other supplies.

"CJ." She smiled as she looked in the carrier. He was sleeping now having been fed at the vet's office. She set his carrier on the floor and brought in all the other supplies to put away.

Caesar had left a note on the kitchen counter.

We buried the mother in the garden beneath the new flowers you planted. The girls said their prayers and then we had to go. We are always close, Melanie. Always loving you. Keep your heart and mind open, and you'll see and feel us.

Eternally yours,
Caesar

At the bottom of the page, he had drawn three dolphins. Melanie smiled as she clutched the paper to her heart.

Chapter Twenty-seven

June

"Can you make it out to Phil, please?"

Melanie glanced up from the open book that had been placed in front of her. Phil Chase was standing at her signing table.

Why is he here? She wanted to scream, but that wouldn't be professional. There were other people standing in line behind him, and she needed to keep her composure.

Quickly, she scribbled his name and signed her own. Then she closed the book and handed it back with a big smile on her face.

"When are you and Johnnie going to grant me an interview?"

Her eyes quickly scanned the store. Rhett and Kurt were here to celebrate her first book signing, but she didn't see them.

"Mr. Chase, you're holding up my line, and I don't want to keep these ladies waiting."

Phil glanced behind him, then said loudly, "I bet these lovely ladies would love knowing two members of the band Lush are in the store."

Melanie heard a rumbling of soft murmurs sweep through the crowd. Several of the women looked around.

"Did you know Ms. Davis here is Johnnie Vega's girlfriend?"

More whispers now. Someone stepped up and took a photo of her with a cell phone.

"Seems the demographic to buy your book is full of Lush fans."

She rolled her eyes. *What the hell is wrong with this man?*

Facing the crowd, he yelled again. "She's helping them write their autobiography."

He was drawing a bigger crowd to the table.

Phil threw his arms out to his sides. "Apparently, she knows all the band secrets...like what really happened the night Caesar died."

"Is Johnnie here?" A woman asked. "I loved him when I was younger. What a hottie!"

"Not as hot as Caesar!" Another woman laughed.

Melanie groaned. Her book was all but forgotten as the topic of conversation turned to Lush.

Then there was a collective squeal as Rhett joined her at the table. "What's happening?"

She pointed to Phil Chase. "He started this."

More squealing as Kurt appeared.

"Is there a problem?" the owner of the bookstore asked as she approached the table as well.

"Can we get two more chairs?" Kurt asked. "And the microphone she had earlier?"

"What are we going to do?" Melanie whispered.

"Let Kurt handle things." Rhett patted her arm and sat in one of the chairs the owner brought. "He's a whiz at this."

Kurt sat down as well. The store's owner set up the microphone and plugged it in. Kurt tapped it lightly to make sure it was working.

"Seems one of our biggest fans has decided to ruin a very special occasion for a good friend of ours." Kurt held up her book. "A shame, too, because my wife has read this and loves it."

"I do, too!" someone shouted from the back.

"I'm sure Melanie is delighted to hear that. And she would like to get back to signing books if that's okay. If you have any questions about the band, we'll try to answer them the best we can."

Melanie glanced at Phil Chase knowing he was going to stir the pot some more, but he didn't. Instead, he stayed quiet, glaring at her.

Melanie, Kurt, and Rhett shook hands with everyone that came to the table. She signed more books than she'd expected to and tried to answer everyone's questions.

"Did you know Caesar, too?" one fan asked.

"Briefly." She smiled.

"Was he nice? He always seemed nice."

She nodded. "He's a beautiful person."

"Inside and out then?" The fan gushed.

"Definitely."

The woman picked up her signed book and hugged it close. Then she bent closer to Melanie, and asked, "Did you and he...you know?"

Melanie's face burned. What could she say?

Kurt knew what to do though. He grinned. "You'll have to buy the autobiography and find out."

"I can't wait. When does it come out?"

"Next month," Rhett answered. "And a new album of previously unreleased songs as well."

"We'll be having a huge release party." Melanie smiled. "Would you be interested in attending?"

The woman's eyes lit up. "Oh yes! I bet the tickets will be expensive though."

Melanie looked from Rhett to Kurt. "We're going to give some away."

Rhett pushed a pad of paper in her direction. "Write down your information, and we'll let you know. And be sure to like us on our social media pages. All the latest information will be there."

"Can I get a photo with you guys?" she asked.

"Of course." Rhett stood. He and Kurt posed with the fan.

"I'll take it for you." Melanie reached for the lady's phone.

"No. You have to be in the photo." The women handed her phone to Phil Chase. "Will you take it, please?"

Phil rolled his eyes but took the phone and snapped the photo. He had to take several more after that as everyone now wanted a photo as well as a signed book.

"Would you mind doing another signing?" The owner asked once she'd locked up behind the last customer. "We sold out of books so fast."

"I'd love to." Melanie nodded. "I'm sorry for the scene we caused. I had no idea it would get so crazy."

"You handled it wonderfully though."

Melanie glanced at Rhett and Kurt who were waiting by the front door. "Guess it comes with the territory when your friends are rock stars."

"I hope you'll bring them back when the autobiography is released."

"And all my other romance novels after that?"

"Of course." The owner held out her hand. "It was a pleasure to meet you."

Melanie shook hands, then went to join the guys.

"His mother hasn't heard anything either?" Kurt asked while cutting his steak. "And he's not at the house in London."

"It's crazy." Rhett shook his head. "You'd think we'd have heard something."

"Mrs. Smith and Caesar both told me to have faith in Johnnie, so that's what I'm doing."

Kurt chuckled. "I still can't believe I saw Caesar."

"I know how you feel." Rhett took a sip of water. "But it happened."

"It was good to see him." Kurt said. "Tell him how we feel...and say goodbye in person."

"Closure is the cure for a lot of ills." Melanie smiled.

"You seem happy." Rhett grinned.

"You don't want me to be happy?"

Rhett reached over the table and wiped tomato sauce from the side of her mouth. "Of course. But there's something different about you."

"You seem content," Kurt noted. "As if you're alright with Johnnie missing."

Rhett nodded. "Especially given how upset you were when you discovered he was no longer in rehab."

"Things are going well with my writing. Our projects are moving forward. I can't dwell on the past. Johnnie will come home when he's ready."

"You're getting counseling, aren't you?" Kurt smiled.

She laughed. "That's helping, too."

Rhett took her hand and squeezed it. "Good for you."

"There's something I need to tell you guys." Melanie straightened in her chair. "About me and my past."

"Of course," Kurt said. "You can tell us anything. We're family now."

Melanie cleared her throat and began telling them about her former life in Florida. And then in Atlanta. She told them about her marriage and her daughters. A few tears were shed, but afterward, she felt better. All of them had survived terrible tragedies.

"You're stronger than I ever imagined." Kurt pulled her closer and kissed her forehead. "If I lost my kids...I don't know how I could go on living."

"I ran from it. Locked it away. I pretended they didn't exist...that the accident didn't happen. Caesar forced me to face it. He helped me start living again."

Rhett nodded. "His purpose for returning."

"He's watching over them." Melanie took each of them by a hand. She explained Caesar's latest return. How he'd brought the girls to her.

"Wow...that's incredible." Sweat beaded on Kurt's brow.

"Caesar is fucking amazing." Rhett smiled.

She kissed the backs of each their hands. "We've got to get our story straight about my relationship with the band."

"True." Kurt wiped the sweat away. "One that doesn't involve our lead singer turning into a dolphin."

She and Rhett burst into laughter. Then Kurt entertained her with strange but true stories about Caesar, Johnnie, and the band.

It was nearing midnight when Melanie climbed into her car. The guys had wanted her to come to Rhett's place to crash, but she needed to get home. She hadn't left CJ alone this long before, and she was worried about the little guy.

A knock on her car window startled her. Phil Chase again. Ignoring him, she started the car. He knocked on the window again.

She put down the window. "Are you following me? Do I need a restraining order?"

"I'm a reporter." He sneered. "You're a pseudo-celebrity. Get used to it."

"You're harassing me."

"Johnnie's not in rehab anymore is he?"

She wouldn't let him see her sweat. "Tell me something I don't know."

"Where is he?"

"Home. Waiting for me."

"Why isn't he with you? With the rest of the band?"

"You seem to know him and the band so well. Can't you figure it out?"

"Why don't you help me?"

She huffed. "He knew some asshole like you would be hanging around, ready to make tonight about the band and not me. His presence would've been a distraction."

Phil Chase shrugged. "Rhett and Kurt aren't?"

"You know very well that the media thinks Johnnie's the big story."

"Is he planning to hide the rest of his life?"

"Once the book and new music are released, the band will be back in the spotlight in a positive way. He'll be fine then."

"Oh? That means he's coming to the release party?"

"Yes. He'll be there."

"Sounds like a fun event. I'll see you there."

"Just so you know...if you don't behave, we'll have your ass thrown out." Melanie put her car in gear and sped away.

Chapter Twenty-eight

July

"I can't believe I told everyone he'd be here." Melanie sat in the back of a limo with Rhett, Kurt and his wife, Mrs. Smith, and Caesar's dad. "If he doesn't show up, I'll be so embarrassed."

Mrs. Smith patted her hand. "He'll come. This is a big moment for the band."

"If he doesn't show"—Kurt began—"we'll make up an excuse for his absence."

Melanie nodded. Of course, they could always invent another story. She'd been doing it since the day she'd met Caesar last year.

Filled with dread, she mindlessly toyed with the angel wings hanging from her necklace. She'd needed the party to be perfect for the fans, and for the media who would be there covering the event. The band deserved this. A return to glory. The documentary had started it. Now the autobiography and new music were being released together. Interest in the band was at a new high, helped along by social media. She'd become a de facto manager, running their Twitter, Facebook, and Instagram pages. New audiences were being turned on to their music through streaming services, and they'd been asked to do some high-profile interviews. She'd been reluctant to book them until she knew Johnnie would be part of it.

Nine months since Johnnie left. Nearly a year since I met Caesar.

"If he doesn't come he'll be missing out on something special." Caesar's dad winked at her, then turned to Mrs. Smith and Kurt's wife. "You ladies look ravishing."

Kurt wrapped an arm around his wife. "They certainly do."

Melanie blushed. Mr. Blue had been flirting all night. *I see where Caesar gets it from.* He was especially friendly with Johnnie's mom, and Melanie liked the idea of them together. She knew that a long-distance relationship would be difficult though. *Maybe one of them can move.*

"This dress is gorgeous on you," Mrs. Smith gushed.

"Caesar's favorite color." Mr. Blue grinned.

Melanie smiled, remembering that as one of the reasons she'd bought it. Blood red. On her feet, she wore leopard print pumps. And she'd gone to the salon earlier with Mrs. Smith for updos. They were Hollywood glamorous.

"I'm hosting this shindig. Had to look the part." She told Mr. Blue. "Thank you for letting me keep your wife's jewelry."

"It looks better on you than it would've on me." He laughed. "Besides, Caesar would want you to have it."

Melanie turned to Rhett who'd broken up with his boyfriend a few weeks ago. "No date tonight?"

His green eyes lit up. "I thought you were my date."

"Sure," she teased. "Until some hot waiter or security guard walks by our table."

Melanie was making the rounds, greeting guests and meeting people, when a familiar scent caught her attention. *Caesar. He's here.* She had no idea where. As she made her way through the crowd, she glanced around, anxiously. *What am I thinking? He can't be here.* But as she circled the room again, she still smelled vanilla. *Where is it coming from? Is it me?* Perhaps she was thinking too much about him. He should be here. Johnnie too.

Are you coming, Johnnie? Even though she had no idea where he was, she'd emailed him the details of the party. Plus, the event had been covered extensively in the media. He had to have heard something. But that didn't mean he would come.

Rhett swept up beside her. "Have you eaten?"

"No, I've been busy."

"Sit and eat. No one expects you to work this room all night. Kurt and I can handle it from here. Go relax."

They hugged and then she headed for the buffet table.

Someone doing a horrible impression of Jack Nicholson from *The Shining* came up behind her and asked, "Where's Johnnie?"

Melanie turned to find Phil Chase. "I warned you. If you don't behave, I'll have you thrown out."

"Why can't you admit he's not coming and that you have no idea where he is?"

"Why can't you leave us alone? Seriously? What's the deal with you? Is this because the band wouldn't work with you on a book? Because that's petty."

"Is that what Kurt told you?"

"Maybe if you weren't such a jerk...trying to blame Johnnie for something he didn't do. No wonder they didn't want to talk to you."

"So they choose you instead? A no-name romance writer? Fangirl of the band? Did you fuck all of them or something? What is it about you that made them say yes?"

She tilted her chin upward. "I love this band and want only the best for them...including Caesar. But you...when you didn't get their blessing, you wrote a book anyway, which was a bunch of garbage. I would never do anything to harm this band. My book...our book...will give them the legacy they deserve."

"Even Johnnie?" Phil Chase glared. "He's a mess who killed his best friend. Now he's left rehab and abandoned you. You think he deserves an untarnished legacy?"

"He deserves to have his truth told once and for all." She marched away with her plate and returned to her table.

"Is Phil Chase still bothering you?" Kurt asked.

"Nothing I can't handle."

Melanie sniffed the air.

"It wasn't me." Mr. Blue laughed.

Melanie laughed lightly. "I smell Caesar's vanilla oil."

Mr. Blue lifted Melanie's arm to his nose and inhaled. "Dear, it's you. I noticed it as soon as I met you. You live in his house so of course you're going to smell like him."

Maybe that's it. *Not Caesar.*

Kurt checked his watch. "Almost time for the press conference."

Melanie's attention turned toward the stage where a table sat. There were four chairs waiting. One for each of them. Including Johnnie. She scanned the crowd. Maybe he hadn't heard about the party. Maybe he hadn't read her email. Or maybe he just didn't want to be there.

Rhett rubbed her back gently. "We'll handle it. It's not a problem."

"And we won't call on Phil Chase," Kurt added.

She nodded, forcing a smile. But her heart ached, and her stomach hurt. *Why Johnnie? Why haven't you come home?*

"It's plain to see that there are four chairs at the table," a reporter began. "Johnnie Vega was scheduled to be here. Can you explain his absence? Is he still in rehab?"

Kurt spoke, "He's still in recovery. As you know, he's been an addict for a long time. He's fighting hard to get sober, and he wasn't ready to be with us tonight."

Another reporter raised their hand. "Ms. Davis...are you and Johnnie still in a relationship?"

Melanie winced. *Of all the things they could ask.* "As far as I know we are."

"That doesn't sound very convincing." A deep voice came from the back of the room.

"It's all I can give you," she replied.

"Is that because you haven't seen him or heard from him in months?"

Melanie knew it was Phil Chase disguising his voice. Rhett motioned for a security guard to escort him out.

But another reporter wanted an answer to the question. "Is what Mr. Chase said true? You don't know where Johnnie Vega is?"

She bit her lip. "Well...you have to understand..."

Someone screamed. Cheers erupted among the crowd. Applause. Melanie saw that someone was pushing their way through the crowd and wondered if Phil Chase was going to cause a scene.

But it was Johnnie who bounded up the steps to the stage, sat down in the chair reserved for him, tapped the microphone, and said, "Sorry I'm late, folks. You know how this L.A. traffic is."

Melanie sat dazed, staring wide-eyed, in disbelief. Rhett and Kurt both smiled and nodded at Johnnie. Then, Johnnie winked at her. That's when she knew. He'd planned to be here. And they were all in on it.

"It appears that my lovely girlfriend is at a loss for words for once in her life, so I'll answer that question. Phil Chase is a lying asshole, and no one should believe a fucking word he says."

The crowd roared with laughter. The Johnnie Vega they knew and loved was back. He flashed her a dazzling smile, mouthed *I love you*, then started answering questions.

"I can't believe everyone managed to keep such a big secret from me." Melanie snuggled closer to Johnnie in the back of the limousine.

Smiling, Johnnie rubbed her arm. "It was actually Mom's idea."

"I thought it would be romantic." Mrs. Smith clasped her hands together. "And it was perfect."

Johnnie kissed his mom's cheek. "Mom's a sucker for those romantic movies, too."

"Caesar would be proud." Mr. Blue patted Johnnie's knee.

Johnnie clutched the older man's hand and squeezed it. "Yes, he would."

"I'm sorry we lied to you," Rhett told her. "I hated to see you hurting."

Johnnie wrapped an arm around her shoulder and pulled her closer. "Rhett and Kurt had a hard time with it. But they understood I needed more time. To be alone...to work at being sober."

She stared in awe at him. "You're here now. That's all that matters."

The limousine came to a stop in front of the hotel where everyone was staying except Melanie and Mrs. Smith. The chauffeur came around and opened the door. Melanie and Johnnie exited so they could say goodbye.

After bidding everyone goodnight, Johnnie motioned for his mother to reenter the vehicle. "You first, Mom."

She kissed his cheek. "Honey, I'm getting a room here so the two of you can be alone."

"Let me pay for it." Johnnie reached for his wallet.

Mr. Blue put a hand on Johnnie's arm. "It's on me."

Johnnie eyed him suspiciously.

"Don't worry. I'll take good care of her. I'll return her safe and sound tomorrow."

Mrs. Smith smiled. "After some site seeing."

Melanie smiled at the older couple. They seemed to have hit it off even more than she'd imagined. But the two of them did have history. They'd known one another for years.

"Why do I get the feeling that my mom is getting laid tonight?" Johnnie asked as the limousine pulled back into traffic.

Melanie laughed. "Because she's with Caesar Blue, Sr."

"He was always a ladies' man."

"Like father...like son."

"I feel like I'm supposed to be the gallant son and stop it from happening."

"Why didn't you?"

"Because Blue Sr. is a cool guy. When Caesar and I became friends, I spent so much time at their house and even moved in for a while. I always wished I had a father like Mr. Blue. One who understood me and accepted me."

Melanie stretched out on the back seat, placing her feet in Johnnie's lap. He pulled off her shoes and began massaging them. She unpinned her hair, letting it down.

"Baby, I'm sorry I didn't contact you sooner. Rhett told me you were upset, but you know me. I like grandiose gestures, and I thought it would be a cool way to surprise you."

"It was an amazing public relations tactic."

"Exactly what Kurt said."

"He's right." Melanie pulled her phone from her purse and opened *Twitter*. She then passed the phone to Johnnie. "Lush is trending."

He stared at the screen and shrugged. "No idea what that means. But if you think it's good, then I'm happy."

"Mind if I take a little nap? I'm exhausted."

He grinned. "Yes, that will refresh you for what's happening later."

"Do we have plans?"

He ran a finger over her lip. "What do you think?"

"I think there's a least one big plan." She rubbed her foot against his cock which was hard.

"Make some room for me." He lay beside her. "I need a nap, too."

Melanie's insides warmed as he cuddled close. The night had gone perfectly. And to have Johnnie reappear in such a surprising manner, topped it off. After leaving rehab, he'd gone into a sober living facility in Arizona. But after two weeks and a discussion with Kurt, he'd moved to another one in California near Kurt's ranch. He'd worked on a neighboring ranch for three months while attending counseling and meetings. Given his time in rehab and the month that they'd lived together with Caesar, Johnnie had been sober for ten months. She knew his sobriety would be an ongoing process, but she had faith in him. More importantly, he now had faith in himself.

Johnnie punched the gate security code to let them into the yard. They walked hand in hand to the front door.

"The one thing I worried most about was you finding a man to replace me."

Melanie stopped in her tracks, turned to him, and put her hand to her mouth. "I forgot to tell you."

"Tell me what?" His eyes widened, then he shook his head. "No don't tell me."

"The other man..." She unlocked the front door.

"Damn it!" He slid his hand through his hair and rubbed his head. "It's alright. I understand. And I did cheat on you."

"I'm glad you understand." She stepped inside the house. "Come on, you can meet him."

"You have a new man living in *my* house, and you're telling me *now*?" Johnnie's voice rose as he followed her in, closing the door behind him. "You know what, Melanie? I do mind. I should go."

CJ zoomed into the room at full speed, attached himself to Johnnie's pants leg and began climbing.

"What the hell is this? Some crazed wild animal?"

"Meet my new man." Melanie detached the kitten and stroked his fur. "This is CJ."

Laughing, Johnnie shook a finger at her. "Oh, you're going to pay for that. You had me ready to fight someone."

Melanie kissed him, and CJ swatted his chin.

"Looks like he's ready to fight over you, too." Johnnie scratched the kitten's head. "CJ huh? Caesar and Johnnie. Why couldn't his name be JC?"

"CJ had a better ring to it." She set the kitten down and headed into the kitchen. CJ followed, and so did Johnnie. "You're not jealous, are you?"

Johnnie gathered her into his arms. "Always."

And then his lips were on hers. Soft, sensual kisses that set her body on fire. He pulled away, stared into her eyes, then kissed her harder.

CJ meowed loudly.

"Someone else is jealous, too," Johnnie noted.

"I'll feed him and turn on the television. He likes to watch it, and he has a bunch of toys to play with in there. That should keep him busy."

"Good. I don't need him scratching any other body parts." Johnnie smiled and kissed her again. "I'll meet you upstairs."

"I want to take a shower."

"With me?"

"If you'd like to join me."

"Of course." As he hugged her, he sniffed her neck.

"I know."

"That reminds me." He opened his jacket and pulled something out of the inside pocket. A gift. "For you. Not that you need it. You still smell like him."

Melanie unwrapped it. It was a glass jar of perfumed oil. She unscrewed the top. "Is this the real thing?"

"Did I mention I flew to Thailand for a few days?"

"And you found it?"

"You should know by now I have special skills."

"It's been awhile." She kissed him. "You'll have to remind me."

"Meet me in the shower in five minutes."

"Deal."

When Melanie stepped into the shower, Johnnie was standing under the showerhead, letting the hot water blast him. She ran her hands over his chest and up to his head. She dug them into his hair which was much longer now.

"I've been growing it out," he explained. "You can play with my curls."

"I like it." She smiled as she stretched one of the curls almost to his shoulder. "Mr. Poodle head."

He took the soap he had in his hands and rubbed it over her breasts, creating a bubbly lather. Her nipples hardened. She turned around and allowed him to wash her back and butt. He reached around and rubbed the soap between her legs as well. His cock pressed into her butt as his hands moved back to her breasts. He moved her hair aside and kissed her neck.

"I've missed you," he whispered hotly against her skin. He put the soap down and moved away from the spray of water.

"I missed you so much." She ducked under the water to rinse.

He stepped out of the shower, grabbed a large, fluffy towel and dried himself off. When she exited, he had a towel waiting for her. He ran the plush softness over her skin, drying her slowly and very sensually.

She sighed. "That feels so wonderful."

"How wonderful?"

"Come see." She guided his hand between her legs. A small gasp escaped her mouth as he touched her. He inserted two fingers.

"Is this all for me?" He kissed her again.

"You make me so wet."

He placed her hand on his cock. "And you make me rock hard."

She kissed him. "Make love to me, Johnnie."

"I plan to."

Melanie lay down on the bed, and he slipped in beside her. His mouth was on hers again, kissing her over and over. Their tongues danced together as he moved his body over her. She parted her legs inviting him in.

"Melanie, babe...I love you." Gazing into her eyes, he pushed inside her.

She held his face in her hands. "I love you, Johnnie."

As he moved, a tear escaped his eye and plopped onto her face. Immediately her own tears began sliding down the sides of her face.

"Why are you crying?" he asked.

"Why are you?"

"Because I'm so happy to be with you again. To be inside you again. You feel so good."

"Magic pussy." She smiled.

He kissed away each tear. "Magic pussy, indeed."

Chapter Twenty-nine

Melanie and Johnnie

Melanie and CJ slipped out of the house early. Johnnie wasn't up yet. They'd made love so many times, he was probably exhausted. She smiled thinking he'd want to play his drums at some point today.

Leaning against the deck railing, she inhaled the wonderful scent of the sea. In a few days, it would be the one-year anniversary of Caesar's sudden appearance in her life. So much had changed since then. She was a successful documentary writer and producer as well as a best-selling author. She'd already checked the *Amazon* book ratings this morning, and the autobiography was sitting at number one in sales.

A strong cool wind whipped through her hair. It sent CJ scampering back into the house. She tightened her robe around her. And then she heard a familiar sound. Children laughing. Her children. She could see Caesar watching over the girls as they strolled along the beach toward the house. The morning sunshine danced in his curls and projected a warm glow on his face. He was beautiful.

But something inside her had changed. She felt no need to rush to her babies. There was no desire to run to Caesar and hold him. They were a part of her past. Johnnie was her future. And he was everything.

As Caesar and the girls walked closer, he glanced her way.

I understand. His voice inside her head.

"Thank you," she whispered.

He nodded, smiled, and blew her a kiss. She blew one back.

"What are you doing up so early?" Johnnie's arms encircled her waist and his lips pressed against her neck. "Never mind. I already know. Damn, I've missed this beautiful view."

She watched Johnnie scan the endless horizon. *He doesn't see Caesar.*

He doesn't need to. Caesar's voice again.

Her heart ached for Johnnie.

"After I left, did Caesar stay long?"

Does he sense his presence?

"Two days."

He hugged her tight. "He hasn't been back?"

Melanie looked again at Caesar running in circles with Leila and Lily. The three of them stopped for a moment and waved. In her heart, she felt this was the last time she'd see them. Yet, somehow there was no pain in that knowledge.

The three of them were laughing loudly as they ran toward the water.

"Melanie?" Johnnie kissed her neck once more.

Melanie turned. "No. He hasn't."

"I'm sorry." He caressed her cheek. "I'm sure you miss him."

She smiled. "I was lucky to have known him. You were lucky to spend time with him again. But he's gone. It's time for us to move on, don't you think?"

"I loved him most of my life, but I love him even more for bringing you to me."

Melanie pressed her lips against his and then hugged him.

Johnnie pulled away and grinned. "But you're right. It's you and me now. How about we make a life together?"

"I'd love that."

"Oh wow! Check it out...you were right. There are dolphins. Look! Three of them!"

Melanie didn't need to see. Instead, she stared at Johnnie, loving his smile and his stormy blue eyes that were filled with excitement.

Johnnie looked at her. "You don't want to watch them?"

"I'd rather watch you."

He glanced at the ocean and then back to her. "You're right. We can watch them later."

She squealed in delight as he picked her up and carried her back into the house.

About the Author

A Florida native and graduate of the University of North Florida, Cherié Summers has spent the last two decades teaching reading and writing. Her previous publications include a short story in *Children's Digest* and newsletters for nonprofit organizations. *Eternally Wild* is Ms. Summers fifth book. All have been inspired by her favorite musical icons. She wrote the first draft of her first book when she was eighteen, but it wasn't until she turned fifty that she began getting serious about pursuing a career in writing.

Writing is only one of Ms. Summers' creative passions. She is also an avid photographer, specializing in portrait photography of animals, nature, and people. Another creative outlet she revels in is belly dancing. She teaches the art of Middle Eastern dance through her local community education program. She also enjoys traveling to music concerts and pop culture conventions with her daughter, Kayla. Atlanta is a favorite destination, and Ms. Summers' dream is to move there when she retires from her day job.